BIG SWISS

Big Swiss is Jen Beagin's third novel. *Pretend I'm Dead* and *Vacuum in the Dark* (shortlisted for the Bollinger Everyman Wodehouse Prize) were published by Scribner US and Oneworld in the UK to wide critical acclaim. Jen holds an MFA in creative writing from the University of California, Irvine. In 2017, she was awarded a prestigious Whiting Award for her debut novel *Pretend I'm Dead*. She lives in New York.

Further praise for *Big Swiss*:

'Hilarious and consistently surprising about trauma, sex and friendship, I took it with me on a solo holiday and finished it before leaving the house on the first day.' Megan Nolan, *Observer*

'A strange and seductive book that will stick with me for some time. *Big Swiss* is a visceral and confronting reading experience that made me laugh and think too much (the right amount?) about sex and death and honesty, and why we're all so bloody obsessed with trauma.' Monica Heisey

'The word-of-mouth, cult read of the summer, *Big Swiss* is a startlingly unique novel . . . Smart and unusual, this is modern romance of the highest and most imaginative order.' *Harper's Bazaar*

'An offbeat, unhinged and brilliant tale . . . This is a funny, sex-filled, entertaining read celebrating women in ways you can't miss.' *Stylist*

'*Big Swiss* is about the extent to which love takes place in our own heads, and the way in which desire can warp the reality of another person . . . It was also a delight to read about the unfettered desire of an older female protagonist.' *AnOther Magazine*

'What begins as a jokey, almost cynical critique, one that might sound right in the mouth of Eleanor Shellstrop from *The Good Place*, veers for a while into thriller terrain, and winds up a kind of delayed coming-of-age story about a woman who has relied on her wits and her tragic upbringing to deflect real feeling. That Greta begins healing in a town full of alleged healers is part of the book's irony – and its charm.' *Washington Post*

'Beagin presents her two heroines as opposite models for coping with formative wounds . . . The book is wry, fresh, and absorbing, without flashbacks, maudlin confessions, or self-seriousness.' *The Cut*

'In *Big Swiss*, trauma and sexual obsession intertwine to create a sprawling and delightful mess . . . Beagin's witty and tender rendering of Greta keeps the reader rooting for her, even when Greta begs to be abandoned.' *LA Review of Books*

'[Beagin's] prose has the acerbic warmth of the first friend you'd tell you're sober.' *Chicago Review of Books*

JEN BEAGIN

BIG SWISS

faber

First published in the UK in 2023
by Faber & Faber Limited
The Bindery, 51 Hatton Garden
London EC1N 8HN

This paperback edition published in 2024

First published in the USA in 2023
by Scribner, an imprint of Simon & Schuster, Inc.
1230 Avenue of the Americas, New York, NY 10020

Interior design by Laura Levatino
Printed and bound in the UK by CPI Group (UK) Ltd, Croydon, CR0 4YY

A CIP record for this book
is available from the British Library

ISBN 978–0–571–37857–9

2 4 6 8 10 9 7 5 3 1

For Stefan

1

Greta called her Big Swiss because she was tall and from Switzerland, and often dressed from top to toe in white, the color of surrender. Her blond hair was as fine as dandelion dander and looked like it might fly off her head in a stiff breeze. She had a gap between her two front teeth, but none of the easy charm that usually came with it, and her pale blue eyes were of the penetrating, cult-leader variety. She turned heads wherever she went, including the heads of infants and dogs. Her beauty was like Switzerland itself—stunning, but sterile—and her Teutonic stoicism made the people around her seem like emotional libertines or, to use a more psychiatric term, total fucking basket cases.

But most of this was pure speculation on Greta's part—she'd never actually met Big Swiss in person and probably never would. Nor had she ever traveled to Switzerland. She'd seen pictures, though, and it didn't look like a real place. Big Swiss, however, was very real. Greta knew her by her initials (FEW), her date of birth (5-23-90), her client ID (233), and her voice, which was low and loud and a little sad. Perhaps because Big Swiss was so deadpan, and because Greta couldn't see her face, her voice conjured a bunch of random crap. Such as a dog's nipples. Such as wet pine needles. Such as Greta herself, hiding in a closet, surrounded by mink coats. Otherwise, it had a distinct tactile quality Greta approved of. It was a voice you could snag your sweater on, or perhaps chip one of your teeth, but it was also sweet enough to suck on, to sleep with in your mouth.

Currently, Big Swiss was talking about her aura, which would've been unbearable in any other voice. Apparently, according to Big Swiss, auras varied not only in color but also in size, and hers was "the size of a barge." It entered rooms before she did and you either got out of the way or were mowed down—your choice. Big Swiss suffered, as well. Her aura prevented her from spending more than twenty minutes in a room with low ceilings, and she could never in a million years live in a basement. She felt uncomfortable with anything near her face, including other people's faces. She slept without a pillow. She disliked umbrellas. On a separate note, she couldn't eat anything unless it was drowning in hot sauce, or some other intense condiment, such as Gentleman's Relish, which contained anchovy paste. She put salt on everything, even oranges. She had trouble being in her body in general, which was why she liked to be roughed up by the elements and was always either sunburned, windblown, or damp from the rain.

"Your aura is giving me a head injury," Greta would've said, had they been in the same room. "I'm clinging to the side of the barge, bleeding from the scalp."

But Greta and Big Swiss were not in the same room, or even the same building. Greta was miles away, sitting at a desk in her own house, wearing only headphones, fingerless gloves, a kimono, and legwarmers. Her job was to transcribe this disembodied voice, to tap out its exact words, along with those of the person Big Swiss was talking to, a sex and relationship coach who called himself, without a hint of irony, Om. His real (and perfectly good) name was Bruce, and Big Swiss was one of his many clients. Nearly everyone in Hudson, New York, where Greta lived, had spilled their guts on this man's couch. He was writing a book, of course, and had hired Greta to transcribe his sessions. So far, she'd produced perhaps three dozen transcripts, for which he paid her twenty-five dollars an hour.

At Greta's previous job, she'd sorted and counted pills, and then she put the pills in bottles, and when the patient picked up the Rx, they talked to Greta about their turds. "I'm a pharm tech," Greta would say gently. "Not a nurse." They'd switch gears. Before she could stop them, something like this came out: "My husband beat me for thirty years. I've had multiple concussions, and I don't have children to take care of me. Could you fill this prescription for Soma right now and give me a discount?" In cases like these, Greta had often turned to the pharmacist, a bitter alcoholic named Hopper. "I'm a pharm tech, not a shrink," she'd whisper. "And this lady's Rx has zero refills. *You* deal with her." Hopper was relatively young (fifty-two), suffered from hypertension and kidney problems, and had chemical compounds tattooed on his forearms. Not the usual corny crap, such as the chemical structure of love, and not dopamine or serotonin, either. He preferred drug molecule tattoos—caffeine, nicotine, THC—and was completely useless if all three weren't in his bloodstream at the same time, plus alcohol.

Greta liked knowing people's secrets. That wasn't the problem. The problem was being glared at by dope fiends under fluorescent lights while "I'd Really Love to See You Tonight" or "Touch Me in the Morning" played over the speakers. The pharmacy was hot, bright, and stagelike, and Greta found herself exaggerating her body language and facial expressions, as if acting in a silent film. At the end of the day, the dope fiends just wanted their dope, and Greta just wanted to sit down. Her legs and feet throbbed. For the first time in her life, she'd taken to wearing pantyhose, and not just one pair but two, along with black compression socks. It wasn't a great look, but she felt the need to be held. Squeezed.

And then one day a man handed her a prescription for oxy 30s and a pair of trousers, demanding she fill the Rx *and* mend his pants. "I'm a pharm tech, not a tailor," she'd explained, "and this scrip is fake, sir." He'd given her a disgusted look and pulled out a gun. It was Christmas Eve. Hopper immediately forked over 260 oxy 80s and the dope fiend skipped away, laughing. He died of an overdose two days later. A week after that, Hopper committed suicide in the pharmacy, after hours. It made the evening news and all the papers.

And Greta? Unflappable, as always, so long as her socks were tight, tight, tight. When she removed the socks: remote sadness, nothing serious. This upset people (her fiancé), who expected visible signs of distress (inconsolable sobbing), especially given her mother's suicide when Greta was thirteen, after which Greta had lived with various aunts in California, Arizona, and eventually New Hampshire, where she went to high school. Her fiancé kept patting her down, checking her pockets for pills, worried she was planning to take her own life. "You're watching too much TV," Greta had said. "That's not how this works. It's not one-for-one." Besides, Greta's attempts were like root canals—painful, humbling, and almost always followed by a lengthy grace period. Her current grace period was good for another five years.

Although she had not been the one to find her mother's body, she'd discovered Hopper's. He'd shot himself in the heart, not the head, but he'd missed and had died of a heart attack. Her mother had shot herself in the head, not the heart, and had not missed. They'd both left notes, as well as what Greta considered to be unintentional postscripts. Hopper's PS was that he'd died on his side next to Dyazide, which, if he'd used it as directed, might have prevented his death. Her mother's PS was a long strand of hair attached to a small piece of scalp, a postscript that had tormented Greta for years.

"Aren't you just a tiny bit triggered?" her fiancé asked, bewildered.

"My triggers are covered in wet sand," she'd said, "because my head is a giant cement mixer."

"So, you *do* have feelings," her fiancé said. "They're just buried. In cement. Maybe it's time you start breaking up the cement."

"With what, a jackhammer?"

"How about a psychologist?"

So, Greta had taken another stab at therapy. After hearing her whole story, which had taken ten weeks to tell, the shrink diagnosed her with emotional detachment disorder, which seemed like a stretch to Greta, who preferred to think of it as "poise" on a bad day, "grace" on a good one, and, when she was feeling full of herself, "serenity." He'd made several over-the-top recommendations: hot yoga, hypnosis, primal screaming, eye movement desensitization and reprocessing (EMDR), acupuncture, and swing-dancing lessons. He also recommended she quit caffeine and nicotine.

Instead, Greta quit therapy. Then she quit her job, ended her relationship, moved across the country, and switched careers. Years ago, she'd worked for a "document preparation company." The job had entailed transcribing audio for high-tech businesses, scientists doing qualitative research, journalists, professors, and psychologists. She'd held on to the equipment all these years because she'd genuinely enjoyed the eavesdropping aspect, the isolation of working from home, the not speaking for many hours at a time. She'd been a listener all her life and tended to surround herself with people in love with their own voices. It didn't bother her that the work required very little skill and could be easily performed by robots or software. When she'd landed in Hudson, she emailed the six shrinks in town and offered her transcription services. Only Om responded.

Now secrets were fed directly into her ears, without any of the piped-in music or body pain. In fact, Greta barely moved these days. Only her fingers moved, and not very fast. Although by no means an excellent typist, she was semidiscreet, and because Hudson was so one-horse and gossipy, discretion was everything. She'd signed what looked like a pretty official confidentiality agreement, so she was forbidden to talk shit about Om's clients. Not that she wanted to—she'd always been less of a shit-talker and more of a shit-thinker, and she barely left the house. She typically waited until midafternoon to get started and then worked until bedtime. They talked, she typed, nighty-night.

So far, Big Swiss was unlike Om's other clients. She lacked their habit of tacking a question mark to the end of every sentence, even when asking an actual question. She never exclaimed. When she sneezed, she said "achoo" in the same way she said "hello" and "thank you." She spoke slowly, enunciating every word, at the exact speed Greta typed, so it felt as though they were performing a piece of music together, something improvy and out-there, at a concert with no audience. Greta rarely had to rewind for another listen, or give up altogether and type [INDISCERNIBLE], which she hated doing. There had been some [SIGHING], [SNEEZ-ING], and [THROAT-CLEARING] on the part of Big Swiss, but Om didn't want any of that in the transcripts. Nor was Greta allowed to include a [WEIGHTY SILENCE] or any of the many [PAUSES], and no [WHIMPERING]. For some reason, Om's style sheet permitted [WHISTLING], [SINGING], and [APPLAUSE], even though no one did those things in therapy, along with [LAUGHING] and [CRYING]. Oh, and [FIRE-BREATHING], which he sometimes did with clients who were open to kundalini, one of his passions.

Om's first session with a client tended to run at least five to seven minutes longer than usual, but his first session with Big Swiss was a full fifteen minutes *shorter*. This was how Greta knew Big Swiss was beautiful—Om had forgotten to hit the record button. Either that, or he'd erased the first fifteen minutes, which wasn't like him. Also, his voice had dropped an octave, and he kept fidgeting with his pen.

OM: While you were talking about your aura, I thought I detected a faint accent. Where are you from originally?

FEW: Where do you imagine I'm from?

OM: Hang on, let me think. You're from . . . the Midwest somewhere. Not Illinois. Not Ohio. No, not Nebraska—

FEW: Don't hurt yourself. I'll just tell you. I was born in—

OM: Wait, I got it. Michigan!

FEW: No.

OM: You're originally from Wisconsin.

FEW: Wrong.

OM: Minnesota?

FEW: I'm from S—

OM: South Dakota.

FEW: *Switzerland.*

OM: That's why you're so tall and blond!

FEW: Switzerland. Not Sweden.

OM: It's funny, I grew up listening to ABBA on cassette—

FEW: Swiss, I repeat. Not Swedish. *Swiss.* Like the cheese.

OM: Aren't there a lot of tall, blue-eyed blondes in Switzerland?

FEW: There are many. But most Swiss people are brunettes of average height, and my eyes are gray.

OM: So they are. Remind me what else Switzerland is famous for.

FEW: Cheese, chocolate. Suicide, I guess.

OM: Is everyone killing themselves in Switzerland?

FEW: Well, it's legal. Suicide tourism is big there right now.

OM: Are you, or have you ever been, suicidal?

FEW: No.

OM: How long have you lived in Hudson?

FEW: I don't live in Hudson. I live on the other side of the river. I moved to the US for college.

OM: Your voice is very unusual—and interesting—and I'm wondering, do you sing? Are you a singer?

FEW: I'm told my voice is like a blade. When I pick out pastries at the bakery, it sounds like I'm ordering someone's execution.

OM: Says who?

FEW: Various people. My mother says my voice loosens the teeth in her head.

OM: Wow. What a curious thing to tell your daughter.

FEW: She's been saying that to me for years.

OM: I'm wondering if you see your trauma as being part of your . . . *aura*.

FEW: No.

OM: The word "aura" is present in the word "trauma," I just realized.

FEW: If anything, something in my aura may have caused the trauma. Or in any case, my aura made the trauma worse.

"What trauma?" Greta said out loud.

OM: Don't you think you might be uncomfortable with people near your face because of what happened?

"What?" Greta said.

FEW: You want me to say yes. You seem to want cause and effect.

OM: Well, it is a real thing. You must have been affected in some way. Can we talk a little bit about how your trauma has affected your relationships?

FEW: Can we stop using the word "trauma"?

OM: Why?

FEW: I don't use what happened to me as an excuse.

OM: An excuse for what?

FEW: Laziness or inertia. I don't use it to explain my own rage or aggression. I'm not attached to my suffering. I'm not attached to what happened to me. I don't believe it explains everything about me, because I haven't made it part of my identity. I'm a worker, not a wallower. I would never call myself a "survivor." I'm just—I'm not one of these trauma people.

OM: What's a trauma person?

FEW: Someone who can't stop saying the word "trauma." Trauma people are almost as unbearable to me as Trump people. If you try suggesting that they let go of their suffering, their victimhood, they act retraumatized. It's like, yes, what happened to you is shitty, I'm not denying that, but why do you keep rolling around in your own shit? If they stopped doing that for two seconds and got over themselves, even a little, they might actually become who they were meant to be.

"Whoa," Greta said. "Hello."

OM: So, suppose someone has been gang-raped at gunpoint and can't seem to pull themselves together, stop drinking, return to work, or find meaning in their lives, would you tell them to just "get over themselves"?

FEW: Well, there is a hierarchy, isn't there?

OM: I don't think so.

FEW: If you didn't think there was, you wouldn't have used that example. You would have said, "Suppose someone has been molested by a neighbor" or "neglected by their mother" or "bullied all their lives." But there is a hierarchy. Trauma people don't like to hear that. To them, all trauma matters.

OM: Where would you place your trauma on the hierarchy?

FEW: All I'm saying is that trauma doesn't get you a lifelong get-out-of-jail-free card. It also doesn't necessarily confer wisdom, or the right to pontificate, which I realize I'm doing right now.

OM: Well. I'm willing to concede that life handles some people more roughly than it does others, and that you do have a choice in how you deal with it. You can decide what you want to do with it, but not until after you address it, which—I'm sorry to say—involves talking about it, for as long as it takes, identifying fears and triggers—

FEW: Triggers. God. This is why I'm not crazy about therapy. I really hate the language.

OM: Do you have nightmares?

FEW: What?

OM: Do you have night terrors or trouble sleeping?

FEW: I have bad dreams occasionally, like any other human being.

OM: Do you consider yourself an addict?

FEW: No.

OM: Do you drink or use drugs?

FEW: I'm not an addict, Om, and it's not because I'm in denial. Nice try.

OM: If "trauma" isn't a word you use, what do you call what happened to you?

FEW: I call it what it is—a beating.

"Yikes," Greta said.

OM: You were assaulted.

FEW: I took a beating, yes.

OM: How has the . . . beating affected your relationships?

FEW: It hasn't. I'm here because I don't have orgasms.

"Oh?" Greta said.

OM: Did that start after the beating, or before?

FEW: I've never had an orgasm in my life, even by myself.

"Come again?" Greta said.

FEW: Here's the funny part: I'm twenty-eight.
 OM: Age is just a number.
FEW: I'm married. I've been married for six years.
 OM: Marriage doesn't necessarily guarantee satisfying—
FEW: I'm also a gynecologist.

"Is this a joke?" Greta said.

 OM: Are you married to a man?
FEW: Yes.
 OM: Does he know you're here?
FEW: This was his idea.
 OM: Would you describe your marriage as low-sex or sexless?
FEW: I would describe it as mostly hand jobs and blow jobs.
 OM: How does that feel to you?
FEW: It feels like a chore, but I also feel better afterward. It's sort of
      like walking the dog and drinking wheatgrass at the same time.
 OM: You have a dog?

"You have a *dog*?" Greta repeated. "Really, Om?"

Greta glanced at her own dog, Piñon, a black-and-white Jack Russell. Piñon was licking the door—again. She paused the audio, noted the time, and removed her headphones. She was due for a break anyway.

"Piñon," Greta said. "No licking, goddammit."

He ignored her. His eyelids fluttered. He seemed to be in a trance. Greta threw a slipper at him, but it fell short.

The door, along with all the walls in Greta's room, as well as the ceiling, was covered in many layers of ancient lead paint. The paint had been chipping for a hundred years. Whenever a truck rattled by outside, flecks of paint would fall onto the floor or the furniture or in many cases Greta's pillow as she lay sleeping. The cheerful blue and yellow flecks showed up easily in her long hair and on her bright white sheets. Sometimes she wondered if she was suffering from lead poisoning, hence her decreased IQ and increasingly dumb dreams, but supposedly the paint would have to be falling directly into her mouth, which it wasn't. It was falling directly into Piñon's mouth, however, and he only weighed nineteen pounds.

"Show me your tongue," said Greta.

He paused, tongue still on the door, and looked the other way. He liked to pretend not to know if she was speaking to him or some other dog, but he was the only dog here. He thought he could wear the door down by licking it to death, which was what he did to tennis balls, licking the woolly nap for forty-five minutes before skinning it with his nubby jujube teeth and then licking the hollow rubber core until all the air went out of it and the ball was officially dead. Rats were easier and less time-consuming than tennis balls. He'd killed over a dozen so far—big, fat country rats—along with mice, woodchucks, baby rabbits.

She let him out of the house and listened for her other housemates. Only a faint buzzing came from the basement. She descended the stairs carefully in her socks, watching where she stepped. Her housemates had started dying soon after she moved in. Sometimes they were only half-dead and twitching on the floor, and she'd step on them by accident, which was of course upsetting. She'd never thought of them as individuals, but now that they were dying, she made sure to look at each one. Such hairy bodies! Such oddly shaped eyes! Sometimes they died in pairs and seemed to be holding hands. She found them everywhere, on windowsills and countertops, in cups and drawers. Last week she'd found one in her hairbrush.

Her housemates were sixty thousand honeybees. And one human named Sabine, who was still alive and smoking a cigarette. No, she wasn't French. She loved smoking, however, and butter. She also knew a few things about wine, had superior taste in art and bed linens, worked as little as possible, and would snort a line of cocaine or pop a few pills if you put them in front of her but stayed away from hallucinogens. An empty nester in her midfifties, Sabine was newly divorced and single. Rather than join a dating site, she'd purchased the ancient

Dutch farmhouse in which she and Greta now lived. The house sat on twelve acres and was surrounded by fruit and dairy farms. Although it felt like the edge of nowhere, they were only a one-cigarette drive from town.

Greta had heard the house described as "the *Fight Club* house with comfy furniture," but it was a century and a half older and way more beautiful. Dutch, not Victorian. Built by wealthy fur traders in 1737, the house had been uninhabited for over a hundred years. No, it wasn't haunted. Its only amenities, however, were electricity and running water, and it was completely uninsulated.

From a distance, the brick exterior looked sturdy and no-nonsense. Inside, however, it was all-nonsense—albeit beautiful nonsense: crumbling plaster walls; layers of peeling wallpaper you could count like the rings on a tree; large windows with cracked or missing panes; wide Dutch doors with original hardware; wide pine plank flooring with gaps between the boards, which made for easy eavesdropping; and an enormous fireplace in the kitchen with an iron crane for hearth cooking. Sabine lived on the top floor, Greta lived on the first floor in what used to be the living room, and the bees lived in the kitchen, which was in the basement.

Greta suspected the fur traders had owned slaves, and that the slaves had lived in the little room off the kitchen, where Sabine now grew marijuana and where Greta sometimes double-checked for ghosts. She never saw any, but perhaps Piñon did? The black fur on his face had turned a stark and sudden white about a week after they moved in. Shock, presumably, from seeing the souls of dead slaves, or (more likely) finding himself in the Hudson Valley after living in California all his life. Many more of Greta's hairs had turned white, as well, and Sabine had a white streak on the left side of her head, which she claimed had been given to her by the devil.

"When?" asked Greta. "Recently?"

"At birth, ding-dong," Sabine said.

Otherwise, Sabine's hair was the color of dry tobacco and dense enough to hide things. Such as a pair of earrings. Such as a spare key. Sabine often used her hair rather than a handbag to shoplift, and occasionally a lost or stolen item suddenly resurfaced. The other day, it had been a pair of reading glasses she'd stolen from CVS, along with a woven bracelet from god knows where. She never got caught, however, and Greta suspected it was because she had the scrubbed good looks and general air of unkemptness that people associated with old money, and in fact Sabine had grown up wealthy before her father lost everything in the stock market. She'd been something of a spiv ever since.

Personality-wise, she reminded Greta of one of those exotic vegetables she was drawn to at the farmer's market but didn't know how to cook. Kohlrabi, maybe, or a Jerusalem artichoke. Not very approachable. Not sweet or overly familiar. Not easily boiled down or buttered up. Not corn on the cob. Greta felt an instant kinship with Sabine, since she, too, was kohlrabi.

Bees weren't bothered by kohlrabi, apparently. Neither of them had been stung, not even once. If a bee landed on Greta's arm or face, she calmly brushed it off and carried on with whatever she was doing. If she happened to startle a few bees while they were performing some task, she simply ducked or walked away. They never came after her.

Now she was sweeping up the dead bees around Sabine's feet. She swept gently, as they tended to stick to the broom.

"You want the vacuum?" said Sabine.

"Too noisy," Greta said.

Sabine sat next to the open fireplace, which was big enough to fit a bathtub or a medium-size coffin, and the hive was directly above her head. The hive was massive, estimated to be over thirty years old, and nestled between two exposed joists in the ceiling. Roughly seven feet long and sixteen inches wide, it snaked along the length of the joists in a wavy fashion.

Sabine had discovered the hive shortly after she bought the house. She'd heard buzzing in the ceiling and so she'd knocked it down with a sledgehammer. There she discovered the hive at the height of production. Rather than remove it like a normal person and perhaps transfer it outdoors, Sabine asked a local beekeeper to build an enclosure for it. She liked having bees in the kitchen. The beekeeper, a Christian back-to-the-land type named Gideon, built a hatch, a simple screened-in wooden box with a Plexiglas bottom, which he installed in the ceiling. If you stood directly underneath the hatch and looked up, you could plainly see the hive and all its activity. You could also reach up and open the hatch to expose the hive, but they never did that. The hatch kept the bees out of their hair, as it were, but there were always about a dozen flying around Greta as she made coffee in the mornings.

"These bees seem Japanesey," said Greta. "There's something kamikaze about the way they're crashing into shit. Seems like they might be committing suicide."

"They're deeply altruistic," Sabine said.

"I wonder if that's because all bees are siblings," said Greta.

"My siblings are dicks," Sabine said. "I'd never die for them."

Another bee threw itself against the window, knocking itself unconscious. In a minute or so, it would start buzzing again but would remain on the floor, kicking its legs.

"It's autumn," Sabine said. "Leaves fall. Maybe bees fall, too."

"Or they're sweating to death," Greta said, and emptied the dustpan into the huge fire. She wondered if the still-living bees could smell the burning bodies of their lost siblings.

"Or they're just reducing their staff to a skeleton crew," Sabine said. "For the upcoming winter. For the sake of efficiency."

Greta listened to the fire crackle. The bees used to be louder than the fire. She used to be able to hear them buzzing in her stupid dreams, because the hive was essentially underneath her bed, one floor up.

"Do you happen to know any Swiss people?" Greta asked. "On the other side of the river?"

"Five," Sabine said. "Two of them are artists, two of them are assholes, and the other works in the trades. They're really boring and really intense at the same time, which is a weird combination when you think about it."

"Is one of the assholes a gynecologist?"

Sabine tossed her cigarette into the fire. "No, why?"

"New patient," Greta said.

"Another sex addict?"

"This one's never had an orgasm," Greta said.

"Wow," said Sabine.

Greta was about to say more but changed her mind. She wanted Big Swiss all to herself. But Sabine looked wan and in need of nourishment.

"Something terrible happened to this Swiss person," Greta said.

A little color returned to Sabine's cheeks. Her only sustenance lately was gossip, especially if it involved money and real estate, and most of Om's clients had both. Sabine lit another cigarette.

"It's only been hinted at," Greta said. "But it seems this person took a terrible beating—"

"In the real estate market?"

"Physically," Greta said.

Sabine's face went back to gray. She only seemed to eat actual food on Tuesdays, Thursdays, and Saturdays, and Greta had never seen her drink a glass of water. Granted, their water came from an ancient well and smelled like toe jam.

"Eat one of those donuts I bought at the gas station," Greta said.

"I'd rather eat ice," said Sabine.

Anorexics eat ice, Greta thought. They love ice, can't get enough of it. In fact, they actually crave ice, don't they? Because it contains iron?

"Does ice have iron in it?" Greta asked.

"No," said Sabine. "But a lot of anemics chew ice, I forget why. I think it makes them feel . . . alive, or alert, or something."

Greta suspected Sabine was anorexic—both traditionally and sexually. She hadn't been laid since her divorce. Romantic relationships seemed to utterly repulse her, and sex wasn't worth the trouble of making small talk. She'd lost twenty pounds in three months, though that was just a guess, as the only articles of clothing Sabine wore were a pair of off-white overalls and an oversize moth-eaten sweater. Anorexia was about control, Greta remembered having read somewhere, and Sabine lived in chaos. Perhaps exercising control over what she allowed into her body made her life feel less crazy.

"What day is it?"

"Monday," said Greta.

"I should score us an eighteen-dollar steak," Sabine said.

Mondays were meat. Tuesdays, cheese. Wednesdays, yogurt, milk, and occasional flowers. Thursdays, fruits or veggies. Weekends were nothing—too many tourists, too many witnesses. But Sabine only stole from super-rich farmers who gouged their customers and were dumb enough to rely on a cash box—the so-called honor system— and she didn't really care who knew about it.

"Are you anorexic?" asked Greta. "You can tell me."

"I'm too old for that shit," said Sabine. "I probably have lung cancer. Or some other cancer. I just hope it kills me quickly."

"If it doesn't, I'll put a pillow over your head while you're sleeping," Greta said. "And then sit on it or whatever."

"You're a good friend," said Sabine seriously.

"I don't think it's cancer," Greta said. "I think it's Lyme."

"If I hear that word one more time . . . ," said Sabine.

They didn't have Lyme disease in California, so when Greta first started transcribing for Om, she'd assumed everyone was talking about limes. Were these limes from outer space? They seemed to have abducted everyone in town and taken over their brains.

Greta was itching to get back to Big Swiss. In the recent past, if Greta didn't excuse herself right around now, Sabine would talk both of Greta's arms off, and then both of her legs, until Greta was twitching on the floor like one of the bees. Sometimes it was necessary to back out of the room slowly while Sabine was still talking, and then do an about-face and run to her room. But Sabine's gabbing had tapered off once the bees started dropping dead.

"Do me a favor," Greta said. "Choke down one of those donuts."

"Yeah, yeah," said Sabine.

GRETA STEPPED OUTSIDE TO FETCH PIÑON, as well as three logs from the woodpile. The only source of heat in her room was a woodstove with a busted damper. The damper was stuck and would not close. Yes, she'd tried banging it with a hammer. One, two, three times.

The flue remained wide open. Consequently, the fire in her room was never mellow and romantic, but rather an angry, raging inferno. The inferno demanded to be fed every three hours, and if Greta didn't obey, it burned out completely and she had to start from scratch. This made sleeping through the night impossible. It was also dangerous—a chimney fire seemed imminent. Luckily, their only neighbor was a fire station.

Greta wrestled the logs into the stove and brushed the dirt off her filthy kimono. Piñon jumped onto the bed with his muddy paws. Last week she'd pushed her desk toward the middle of the room, which was a little warmer. Any day now, Sabine would bring down a box of heavy drapes from the attic and nail them over all the windows, and Greta would work in near darkness. Such was the hardscrabble life in the Dutch House in the Big Woods. She liked to think of herself as a Laura Ingalls Wilder type, i.e., feisty and resourceful, but, if anything, she was more like the blind sister.

She donned her headphones and tapped the foot pedal.

OM: You have a dog?
FEW: Yes. His name is Silas, and he's terrifying.
OM: You're frightened of your own dog?
FEW: Me? No. He's terrifying to other dogs—and their owners.
OM: What do you love about him?
FEW: My dog? He likes to hold hands. He dislikes kissing.
OM: Is that also true of you?
FEW: Yes.

There had been a silence before she'd said yes, a silence that seemed important to include. Greta hit the pause button and jotted down "ask Om about pauses." Maybe he wanted to reconsider their inclusion in the transcripts. She was supposed to meet with him in exactly an hour, and he liked it when she showed up with notes.

OM: Let's return to the reason you're here.
FEW: I want to have children, and I want to have an orgasm during

conception. This isn't scientific, obviously, but I feel that having an orgasm will not only help me get pregnant, it will be good for the baby.

OM: And you.

FEW: What?

OM: It would be good for you, too.

FEW: Oh. Right.

OM: So far, I'm getting the sense that you know your body on an intellectual level, and probably on a medical level, but not an emotional one. I'm getting the impression that you're living life entirely in your head. You seem disconnected from your body.

FEW: Are you referring to my blue fingers? I have poor circulation.

OM: I'm referring to what you've told me about your aura, and to the way you carry yourself.

FEW: How do I carry myself?

OM: A little stiffly, honestly.

FEW: Well, my body shows physiological signs of arousal all day and night, with little to no stimulation. In fact, my underwear is damp right now and all I've been doing is sitting. It's as if I have no control, as if I'm foaming at the mouth.

Greta's ears felt suddenly warm and rigid. She paused the audio, slipped off her headphones, and tugged on her lobes. If her ears had erections, she could only imagine what was happening in Om's pants.

OM: Arousal and desire are two different things. Personally, I have the opposite problem. I desire sex but sometimes have trouble becoming aroused.

Okay, so perhaps nothing was happening in Om's pants. Greta pictured his flaccid penis and shuddered.

OM: When you're aroused, do you want to have sex?

FEW: Only if I'm drunk.

OM: Are you drunk right now?

FEW: It's nine fifty a.m.

OM: I know, I was kidding. Do you masturbate on a regular basis?

FEW: I find it boring, and nothing happens.

OM: Masturbation is a skill. It's totally learnable, like cooking. Have you ever made risotto?

FEW: I'm terrible in the kitchen.

OM: I wonder if you would allow me to share my own journey with you.

FEW: Please don't.

OM: May I ask why not?

FEW: Aren't therapists not supposed to talk about themselves?

OM: A little self-disclosure builds rapport, no? I often use my personal journey to treat clients. I've gathered many tools in my journey, tools I'm willing to—

FEW: Can you not use the word "journey" ever again? It makes my skin crawl. I'm not crazy about "tools," either.

Greta smiled.

OM: My point is, I can help you integrate your intellect with your sexual—

FEW: What are you proposing exactly?

OM: A variety of exercises involving breath, touch, and mindfulness.

FEW: Touch?

OM: There's nothing to fear, I promise. I'll never ask you to do anything you're not totally comfortable with. We all have a sexual narrative or anecdote that intrigues us, or that we identify with on some level. Perhaps I can help you discover a narrative that speaks to you. Are you open to that?

FEW: I guess.

OM: I also want to address what happened to you. The beating, as you call it.

FEW: To be honest, I almost never think about it.

OM: Hmm. I wonder why it was the first thing you mentioned?

FEW: I wanted to get it out of the way. As a piece of background

information. Also, don't read into this too much, but the guy is
getting out of prison next month.

OM: How long has he been in prison?

FEW: Eight years.

OM: Wow. Hold on, I think this is a good time to stop—

"No, no, no—" Greta said.

[END OF RECORDING]

"Dammit," Greta said.

OM'S RELATIONSHIP-COACHING STYLE seemed reminiscent of getting hit on at a bar. Not by a yoga teacher, as his name would suggest,
but by an unneutered therapy animal. He was short, furry, and attentive,
with the most soulful brown eyes Greta had seen in years, eyes that put
you instantly at ease, even as he was humping your leg. Greta had experienced this firsthand during their initial interview, which had taken
place at an abandoned-church-turned-expensive-cocktail-bar on the
edge of town. Om had been wearing a felt fedora that afternoon, along
with black eyeliner, a tasteful white linen tunic, and tight denim shorts.
A women's vintage handbag dangled from his arm, and he'd painted his
short fingernails a color Greta recognized as Lincoln Park After Dark.
He was somewhere in his forties and he seemed unable to stop staring at
her face. At forty-five, Greta was aware of the facts, and the fact was that
her attractiveness, especially in broad daylight, tended to have a delayed
effect: it hit you anywhere from two weeks to two months after you met
her, and sometimes not until after you touched her, and then it stayed
with you for years—or so she told herself—but Om had immediately
asked, "You used to model, correct?"

Greta had laughed and devoured the sixteen-dollar hot dog he'd
ordered for her.

"Every bite of food in this town costs at least four bucks," she said.
"Have you noticed?"

"Your cheekbones remind me of the fins on an old Cadillac," he said.

"I'm forty-five," Greta said.

"By 'old' I meant 'classic,'" he said quickly.

"LOL," Greta said.

He gave her a sorrowful look. "You're uncomfortable with compliments about your appearance."

"Me and everyone else," Greta said.

"Actually, people around here love to be told they're beautiful."

Greta thought of that dog she often saw at the dog park, a dopey white boxer who compulsively licked the mouths of other dogs. His name was Popsicle. He followed the other dogs around, lapping at their open mouths with his long pink tongue while they tried to get away from him. Sometimes he got bitten in the face by Greta's dog, but not even that stopped him.

"That's Japanese denim, right?" Om asked, gazing at Greta's pant leg.

"I believe it's just regular denim," she said.

Disappointment. She remembered that this was an interview for a job she needed very much, and that her days of sixteen-dollar hot dogs were nearly over, along with everything else. She glanced at Om's lower half.

"Cute socks," she said.

"Why, thank you kindly," he said. "So. You've done this before, right?"

"What?"

"Transcribing," he said.

"Oh yeah, of course. I type seventy words per minute and I have a really good ear."

"Me too," Om said. "I have perfect pitch, in fact, which is why I play angklung in a gamelan ensemble. What about you?"

"Bass," Greta said.

Forty words per minute, 10 percent hearing loss in her right ear, never played bass in her life. Although she was newly single and happier than she'd been in years, a small part of her was still ready to die, and still enjoyed telling lies.

"Okay, so, this might be a strange question, but . . . what's your relationship to work?"

"How do you mean?"

"Do you like it?" Om asked.

"Do I like work?" Greta said.

"It's just—I feel like I *have* to ask, because a lot of people in this town—I won't name names, because there's too many—seem to be *allergic* to work, and will do literally *anything* to get out of it, including falling off a roof."

"My last name is Work," Greta said.

"Pardon?"

"My name," Greta said, "is Greta Work."

An incomplete sentence. A curse, a command. In the rare case she introduced herself with her full name, she felt like she was interrupting herself. If there were an S at the end, maybe she'd have felt like a whole person.

"What is that—German?"

"It's English. It derives from the ancient word '*geweorc*,' which means 'work that's done or made,' which may explain why, in my dreams, I'm often toiling away in a factory."

"Cool," Om said. "Are you comfortable signing a confidentiality agreement?"

"Of course," Greta lied.

She loathed official documents of any kind, which was why she hadn't filed a tax return in six years and didn't have health insurance. Her own birth certificate made her sick to her stomach. She also hesitated to sign anything, even credit card slips, because she'd never liked her signature. She'd tried changing it over the years, but it was like trying to change her voice. On the other hand, Hudson was overflowing with people who'd successfully reinvented themselves. *I was a corporate lawyer in the city for years, and then I moved to Hudson and became a flower farmer/doll maker/antiques dealer/chef/arborist/ alcoholic, and I never looked back.* "I moved to Hudson to reinvent my handwriting," she imagined telling someone over drinks. "It's been an incredible journey."

Om had gone on, unnecessarily, to explain that everyone knew everything about everyone in Hudson, even people they'd never actually seen or met, because all people talked about were other people and their problems.

"A wise man once said that Hudson is where the horny go to die," Om said. "And I'm the only sex therapist in town." He smiled patiently, waiting for her to connect the dots. "You'll be transcribing some colorful stories. You may be tempted to share these stories after a couple cocktails, if you know what I mean."

In Greta's experience, everyone did not know everything. It was worse than that—everyone knew only one or two extremely intimate and shameful things, and the thing Greta knew about Om was that his orgasms were loud and high-pitched. "He sounds like a woman when he busts," Greta overheard a guy say about him once. This had not been "after a couple cocktails," but rather first thing in the morning, in line at one of the eight new bakeries in town. The guy, visibly stoned, said he'd heard it from the woman he'd taken home the previous evening, who'd heard it from her housemate, who used to date Om's housemate back when he had housemates, before he'd reinvented himself as a therapist.

"Seems to me Hudson is where the deeply deranged go to die," Greta said. "It's as if my abnormal psych textbook from college grew legs and learned to walk. I mean, have you ever seen so many narcissists gathered in one place? Be honest."

"I've lived in Los Angeles," Om said.

"Me too," Greta said.

"Hollywood?" Om asked.

"Inglewood," Greta said.

"You know, I've seen a rise in borderline personalities in Hudson," he said. "It seems they're very attracted to narcissists. How'd you wind up in Hudson?"

"Sabine," Greta said. "Do you know her?"

"Of course," he said.

"Yeah, well, we live together," Greta said. "But . . . we're not lovers."

Greta always added that last part as a joke, since it was patently obvious Sabine didn't have a gay bone in her body. But no one ever laughed, so maybe it wasn't that obvious. Or maybe it just wasn't funny. She wondered how many of Om's bones were gay. One or two, she decided.

"Didn't Sabine move out of town?" he asked.

"As a matter of fact, yes, but we're only a one-cigarette drive away," Greta said, pointing vaguely behind her. "That way."

"What kind of cigarette?" Om said.

"American Spirit," Greta said.

"Nice," he said. "Can you spare one?"

They stepped outside. He held the cigarette between his middle and ring fingers. More than a couple bones, she thought.

"How'd you meet Sabine?" he asked.

"She picked me up hitchhiking," Greta said.

"In Hudson?"

"Martha's Vineyard," Greta said. "It was more like a kidnapping. I was trying to get some pizza, but she took me to a party on the other side of the island, said Quaaludes would be there. 'Is that a band?' I remember asking. I was only eighteen. Her eyes misted over, as if we were about to encounter a herd of unicorns. 'It's the best drug ever made,' she said. I asked if she'd tried MDMA. 'Yuck,' she said. 'I'm not into hugs and backrubs.' Anyway, the party turned out to be in this hippie whorehouse out in the dunes. We took the Quaaludes, laughed for six hours, been friends ever since."

After their Quaalude excursion, Greta ran into Sabine every couple of years, always when she least expected it—in line for an ATM in San Francisco, in the bathroom at Grand Central Terminal, at an Ethiopian restaurant in LA, walking down the street in New Orleans, and most recently, in a parking lot at Huntington Beach, where Sabine had kidnapped Greta (and Piñon) for a second time. She'd been touring the country in a Mercedes Sprinter van, visiting her kids, and convinced Greta, who'd just quit her job, to join her for a few days. It had been Greta's first taste of freedom in a dozen years. She'd essentially never gotten out of the van.

Om said he rarely left Hudson except to travel to India, to a specific place Greta always immediately forgot the instant she heard its name, but it was the oldest and most beautiful city on earth, a place where nothing was hidden, where literally everything was out in the open—birth, disease, death, lots and lots of garbage, etc.—and you had no choice but to observe life in its culmination. Om traveled to this city once or twice a year—to reaffirm his Om-ness, Greta assumed—but then he said, "Plus I have a guru who tugs on my nadi."

Greta coughed. "Pardon?"

"Every winter, my nadi becomes corroded—"

"What's your naughty?"

"My pulse," Om said. "N-A-D-I. Nadis are channels in our bodies that provide energy to our cells, channels that become blocked—"

"May I ask what your real name is?" Greta asked. "Or is that rude?"

"You can ask me anything. My birth name is Bruce."

"You changed your name to Om . . . in India."

"Twenty years ago."

"'Om' is a little . . . on-the-nose," Greta said, and smiled. "Don't you think?"

"Look around," Om said. "Everything in Hudson is a little on-the-nose."

2

As a pharm tech, Greta had spent eighteen months working in the warehouse of a mail-order pharmacy, filling prescriptions by hand. Warfarin, a blood thinner, was the drug she handled most, but there were about a dozen other friable tablets, usually generic versions of popular drugs, and she often ended her shift covered in pharmaceutical dust. It wasn't long before any kind of dust began to resemble pill dust, particularly the pale yellow dust of Norco 10s. She was convinced she could see floating particles in people's personal breathing zones (PBZs). She saw pill dust on carpets, mirrors, screens, people's sweaters. There it was again, sprinkled all over the popcorn at the movies. Long after she quit the warehouse, she continued spotting pill dust wherever she went.

Now Greta saw transcripts. The transcripts belonged to Om's clients, and they came to her whenever she set foot in Cathedral, the most popular coffee shop in town. The place had perfect acoustics and was crawling with Om's clients, because his office was located directly above it. Greta always heard at least one voice she recognized. She couldn't recall the entire transcript, obviously, as they were often quite long, but if she closed her eyes and concentrated, her memory was good for several pages.

Just now, at the table where she sat waiting for Om, she recognized the drowsy voice of the man seated next to her. She didn't know him personally, but a piece of his transcript came to her while she waited for her Americano. His initials were AAG, and he was sleeping with his sister-in-law. They met in hotel rooms in the city, but right now the man was talking to his wife, presumably, and holding her hand. Like most people in Hudson, they were better-looking than average and dressed like boutique farmers.

OM: What's special about Tamara? What does she have that your wife doesn't?

AAG: We hate all the same things.

OM: Such as?

AAG: Board games, truffle oil, magic realism, Harry Potter, politics, toddlers, the elderly, people who get excited about mac and cheese, scatting—

OM: Scatting?

AAG: That thing jazz singers do. It sounds banal, I know, but I've never had so much in common with anyone.

OM: What do you do together?

AAG: Are you familiar with the eating of the ortolan?

OM: No.

AAG: It's an ancient rite of passage among French foodies. Ortolans are rare, tiny birds. The chef captures them, drowns them in Armagnac, and roasts them whole. Then the entire bird is eaten—feet first, bones included—with a linen napkin draped over the person's head, to retain the aromas and, as the story goes, to hide from God.

OM: This is what you do with Tamara?

AAG: No, but that's how I eat her pussy.

OM: By drowning it in Armagnac?

AAG: With a napkin over my head.

Greta inadvertently smiled at the wife, at whom she'd been staring like a creep. The wife returned her smile. Then AAG looked at Greta and smiled at her, too. Greta scowled at him and then stared at her phone, ashamed.

She was picturing herself walking down the sidewalk with a napkin over her head when she heard another familiar voice order a cappuccino. This voice was deeper and belonged to KPM, a guy in his thirties suffering from PTSD. KPM was being stalked by a lunatic who called herself a life coach, and so he often wore a disguise to Om's office. Greta turned slightly, hoping to get a look at his face, half expecting to see Darth Vader in a turtleneck.

OM: Is that really how your penis looks to you?

KPM: Yeah. I think it's a pretty common dick shape. Sometimes I imagine it whispering to me in the voice of James Earl Jones.

OM: What does it say?

KPM: [DEEP VOICE] "You do not yet realize your importance. You have only begun to discover your power."

OM: Do you believe that's true?

KPM: I'm kidding, dingus. My dick doesn't talk to me.

OM: Well, if it makes you feel any better, mine looks like it's wearing a beret!

KPM: Does it have the voice of Gérard Depardieu?

OM: I wish.

KPM: Yesterday I googled "How many bottles of wine does Gérard Depardieu drink per day?" Guess what the answer was.

OM: Three?

KPM: Fourteen.

OM: Why would you google such a thing?

KPM: Because I'm dying for a drink? Because I'm being stalked? Because I've been forced into this hypervigilant state and it's fucking with my prostate?

As it turned out, KPM had the most unusual forehead Greta had ever seen. It looked as though he'd recently shed antlers and they were just beginning to grow back. Somehow this only increased his attractiveness, as though his forehead were a secondary sexual trait. Additionally, he had a full beard and Willie Nelson braids. He was not wearing a turtleneck but rather a neck brace, and she wondered if it was fake, or part of a larger disguise. He was currently being flirted with by yet another client, a man in his fifties with the memorable initials of BTW. Greta had identified his voice weeks ago—not at Cathedral, but in her own living room, because BTW, whose first name was Brandon, bought weed from Sabine.

Still, three clients in one day was unusual—a sign, perhaps. BTW was himself a huge believer in signs and yet never acknowledged the obvious ones, such as the bloody bandages on his fingertips—telltale signs, in Greta's estimation, of onychotillomania, which happened to be Greta's favorite mania and just fun to say out loud. His condition had never been mentioned in therapy. In fact, he seemed to think he'd achieved total enlightenment. He claimed his DNA was so extraordinary that the government was interested in collecting samples and performing a study. In his sessions with Om, he often practiced breathing instead of talking, which was why his transcripts were so short and easy to remember.

BTW: I have two life lines. They meet in the middle, cross, and then wrap around my wrist. I have the conjurer triangle on my palm, which is extremely rare. I can conjure almost anything.

OM: Can you conjure me a croissant? I'm starving and I forgot to bring lunch.

BTW: I'm currently trying to conjure several hundred thousand dollars for myself.

OM: How's that going?

BTW: We'll see.

OM: Let's talk about what's going on with your skin.

BTW: I've told you twenty times. My aging process is reversing.

OM: You're fifty-two, correct?

BTW: On paper, yes. But my wrinkles are disappearing—that's why I have these little scabs on my face—and the rest of my scars are disappearing, including my belly button.

OM: Oh? Where is your belly button off to?

BTW: It's vanishing entirely. That wound is finally healing. And some of my hair is falling out to make room for new hair. You should feel how soft it is. Here, feel.

OM: It's quite soft.

BTW: My penis is also reverting to its original state.

OM: Meaning . . . ?

BTW: My foreskin is growing back.

OM: I'm afraid that's not possible.

BTW: Why?

OM: I hate to be the one to tell you, but it sounds like middle age. The penis shrinks, or become smaller in size and paler in color—

BTW: I know my own body. Here, can I just show you? Do you mind?

OM: [WHISTLES]

BTW: Right? See what I mean?

OM: You're well-endowed, I'll give you that, but the head is rather . . . *red*, isn't it?

Greta had imagined a pig in a blanket left overnight in a chafing dish.

OM: Are you still sleeping with Mr. Lilywhite?

BTW: God, no.

OM: I'm sorry to hear that. I liked how that relationship was developing for you.

BTW: Do you mind if I lie down?

OM: Please do. If you want, close your eyes and we'll have a minute or two of fire breath.

[FIRE-BREATHING]

BTW: How about a quick gong bath before I leave?

OM: It would be my great priv.

[GONG BATH]

Yes, Om had a goddamn gong in his office. Greta had never seen it because she had yet to set foot in there, but apparently, the gong was quite large and shiny. The first time he'd mentioned it to a client, he'd said, "I waxed my gong for you, in case you wanted a sound bath at the end of our session," which Greta had transcribed as "I waxed my dong for you." Om had texted a few days later: "It's gong, honey, not dong," a phrase Greta now repeated to herself at random.

In any case, Om loved to bathe BTW with his gong—and Greta, by extension—but it felt more like being drowned. Not by a rough sea, but by a stranger's hand holding your head underwater. He really went to town on the thing, banging the crap out of it until you couldn't hear yourself think. In this way, your ego was truly eradicated and you realized the present was all you—

"Sorry I'm late," Om said suddenly.

He was a wearing a white fishnet tank top, a chunky cardigan, and white harem pants. Greta watched him give each of his clients a subtle nod. The ortolan-eater gazed at Om with open affection, as if he wanted to give Om a belly rub. KPM simply returned Om's nod, but BTW looked like he might approach and start blabbing.

"Mind if we sit closer to the window?" Om asked quickly.

"Not at all," Greta said.

They relocated to another table. The barista, who used to date Olin Patterson, who used to date Betsy Hanna, the famous chef who was now engaged to Peter Green, who had a kid with Punk Rock Charlotte, a former skank who used to fuck the drummer for the Dead Kennedys but was now an herbalist, finally delivered Greta's Americano, along with Om's usual. Greta had never introduced to the barista or any of the others. She only knew these things because she lived with Sabine.

"So, I want to talk to you about FEW," Om said. "Have you finished her file?"

"I emailed you the transcript before I left my house," Greta said.

"Very good," Om said. "I'm sending you another file, but it contains really sensitive—and possibly triggering—information, so I wanted to check in with you, make sure you're okay with everything."

"You're worried I'll be triggered?"

"Yes," he said.

"Because I'm a woman?"

"No," he said slowly. "Because you're human. Wait—you are human, correct? You're not a bot? Can you prick your finger real quick, so I can see if blood—"

"Dude," Greta said.

She was bleeding right now, as a matter of fact, and imagined removing her tampon and dunking it in Om's steamed milk with turmeric.

He leaned toward her. "She's uncomfortable talking about it," he said, "but she was the victim of a very violent crime, and she discusses certain graphic and upsetting details."

"I've transcribed rape before," Greta said.

"Yes, I know," Om said. "But this crime was extremely violent, and her abuser is being released from prison—*here in Hudson*—and his name is mentioned. I doubt you know him, but who knows, maybe you do. Maybe you'll run into him next week or the week after. Or maybe you'll run into *her*. I just want to make sure you can handle this."

Greta nodded gravely.

"And I hope you continue to honor the agreement you signed."

She'd been dishonoring the agreement for weeks, but only with Sabine.

"I would've transcribed these files myself, but I don't know how to type," said Om, without embarrassment. "How's it been lately? The transcribing?"

"I'm glad you asked," Greta said. "What's often missing in these transcripts—in my opinion—is the person's pain. Because, well, the pain is rarely in the actual words, which nine times out of ten are imprecise, or the wrong words altogether. People are almost never articulate about their pain, as I'm sure you've noticed. Their pain can only really be felt in the pauses, which aren't included in the transcript. So, I'm wondering if you'll allow me to type something like 'LONG, BEREAVED PAUSE DURING WHICH CLIENT STRUGGLES TO SWALLOW,' or something to that effect."

Om blinked at her. "You want to transcribe . . . silence?"

"It'll make the transcript more accurate," Greta said. "Or, in any case, more complete."

"Hm," Om said. "But your job is to transcribe, not describe. So, maybe don't be so descriptive?"

"Fine," Greta said.

"How's your love life?" Om asked. "Are you dating?"

Greta shook her head.

"You'll meet someone next month," Om said.

"Really? Why's that?"

"You know," Om said. "January."

"New Year's Eve?"

"Yes, and the mad rush to pair up before winter," Om said. "You'll see."

GRETA WASN'T READY TO PAIR UP, but she wouldn't have minded getting a piece. Everyone in town seemed to take turns with one another, as if stranded on a private fuck island, and Greta had never seen so many unusual and unlikely couples. Old with young, rich with poor, drunk with sober, beautiful with grotesque. She'd heard Hudson described as a college town without a college, or summer camp for adults, but it seemed more like a small community of expats. Everyone behaved as if they'd been banished from their native country, or had simply withdrawn allegiance, or were on the lam, and now that they were all living abroad, they bonded with people they never would've ended up with back home.

At any rate, Greta would've taken a turn or two, but the only ones who showed interest were either too broken, not broken enough, geriatric, unemployable, or overly dependent on little blue pills, cocaine, their own feelings and biographies, or the words "toxic," "binary," "identity," and "intersectionality."

Several months ago, however, she'd developed an inappropriate crush on someone half her age. They'd met on her very first day in Hudson. She'd arrived on a Friday, along with a hundred other drips and hipsters visiting from the city. An impatient tour of Hudson ensued, with Sabine speeding up rather than slowing down as they approached intersections and pedestrians, and pointing out the prisons—there were three—and where all the saloons and brothels used to be. The brothels were long gone, of course, but Hudson was still crawling with drunks and sluts, and had been since 1785.

"What kind of sluts?" Greta asked.

"All stripes," Sabine said. "Sluts for nature, sluts for antiques, sluts for astrology. River sluts, real estate sluts, regular sluts. In general, I'd say there's not a lot of shame in this town."

"Uh-oh," said Greta.

"I'm not saying people don't *feel* shame—they do," said Sabine. "It's more like people don't shame each other. Unless you do something extremely fucked-up, of course, like rob an old lady or rape somebody. Otherwise, you can get away with a lot. I think that's why people never leave. Although that's changing now."

Sabine drove up alleys with names like Prison and Rope. She preferred Hudson's backside, she said, but toward the end of the hour she coasted down the main drag, Warren Street, so that Greta could get a look at Hudson's face. A formerly fucked-up face, Sabine insisted, once abandoned and forgotten, now carefully made up and lined with shops selling objects nobody needed. In fact, Sabine's car felt like a giant, moving display case, and Greta felt like a rare object pinned to the passenger seat.

"Why are they staring at us?" asked Greta.

"I know these people," Sabine explained, and honked at a lady with a dog. "They're just wondering who you are and why you're in my car."

As they approached the next intersection, an old man stepped into the street and tried hailing them like a taxi. He looked disheveled and near death, but he had a sharp whistle. Sabine ignored him completely and rolled through a stop sign.

"That man seemed desperate for your attention," Greta said. "I think he's waiting for you to pull over."

"That's my father," Sabine said, and stepped on the gas. "He just wants a cigarette."

She sped through a mostly empty parking lot diagonally, only taking her foot off the gas for a series of speed bumps, and then continued to drive as if the cops were chasing them all the way home. In the driveway, she turned off the engine and opened the door but didn't get out.

"If you're expecting Pottery Barn rustic," she'd said, "you might be disappointed. This house was built in 1737. Just to give you some perspective, George Washington was in kindergarten."

"Totally fine," said Greta. "I hate Pottery Barn."

One side of the house was tall and brick. The other side, short and wooden. It looked old, but not 280.

"Are you a horse person?" Sabine asked suddenly.

Greta shrugged. "Of course."

Anyone could see that Greta was not a horse person. Her hair wasn't long enough and neither were her teeth, and as a child, she hadn't been mistreated by other children. She'd been mistreated by horses, though. When she was thirteen, a horse had stepped on her foot, breaking it in several places, ostensibly because she'd tried to mount it on an incline. She hadn't been taken to the doctor, and her foot still looked fucked-up all these years later.

"I don't have horses," Sabine said. "I'm getting donkeys. Mini-donkeys. They come up to your waist."

Greta looked toward the field, expecting to see a herd of mini-donkeys running in circles, bucking, braying, or whatever it was donkeys did, but all she saw was a few dead apple trees. A stiff breeze was blowing leaves around the yard, along with a large, crumpled paper bag.

"How many donkeys?"

"Two," Sabine said. "I only wanted one, but it's necessary to purchase them in pairs. Otherwise, they die of loneliness." She brought a hand to her chest. "They were born yesterday—literally—on a farm up north, and need to be weaned. We'll get them in a few months."

The stairs that should have led to the front door were missing.

They walked around to the back. As they crossed the yard, the crumpled paper bag rolled slowly toward them. Greta stopped and stared as it rolled right up to her feet. It was not a paper bag, she saw now, but a rooster. A uniformly brown rooster.

"That's Walter," Sabine said. "You never know which end is up because he has feathers on his legs."

"Looks like he's wearing UGG boots," Greta said.

"He only shows up on weekends," Sabine said. "He lives across the road, but he doesn't have any hens."

"Does he have eyeballs? He just walked into that wheelbarrow."

"He's a nightmare," Sabine said. "Just ignore him."

At the back of the house, Greta followed Sabine up a rotting staircase. The back door was unusually wide and beautiful and didn't have a doorknob. Instead, you had to turn a huge rusty ring handle in the center.

"This door," was all Greta could say.

"I know," said Sabine. "It's why I bought the house. This brick side is where you'll be living. It was built slightly later, in 1755, after the Dutch got wealthy. You can tell they had money because the ceilings are high and the windows are twelve-over-twelve."

"What?"

"Each window has twenty-four panes," Sabine said. "That's a lot of glass for back then, and it wasn't cheap. The only bummer is, this place is uninsulated. Are you good with a woodstove?"

"Kind of."

She'd never built a fire in her life. Until very recently, she'd assumed seasoned firewood contained actual seasoning, like paprika and chicory. She followed Sabine into the living room. All the furniture was covered in white sheets like you see in the movies. The walls had that distressed look people pay tens of thousands of dollars to reproduce. Although *distressed* was probably the wrong word. These walls were . . . tormented.

"What's that noise?" asked Greta.

"Are you allergic to bees?"

"No," said Greta.

"Good. There's a hive under your feet," said Sabine. "Downstairs, I mean. I'll show you later. You want to know why this room's so beautiful?"

Greta pointed at the ceiling, which was covered in cracks and had been painted with decorative, mostly worn-off designs.

"The ceiling's great," Sabine agreed. "But the main reason this room is beautiful is because it's perfectly square. A perfectly square room is extremely rare. It does something to your brain chemistry."

Sabine closed her eyes suddenly and bowed her head.

"Are you praying?" Greta asked after several seconds.

Her eyes flew open. "I'm fifty-five, Greta. I'm exhausted."

Greta sniffed. "Is something baking?"

"Weed," Sabine said. "I'm making sugar for pixies and gummies. I sell edibles, which you'll find around the house. Help yourself."

"Eating weed makes me cry uncontrollably," Greta said.

"I hear you," Sabine said. "Anyhow, I'll move some of the furniture out of this room so you can put a bed in here."

A figure emerged from what looked like the closet, a young, shirtless man with ropey arms. He seemed sleepy and didn't acknowledge them. In Greta's confusion, she knocked over a standing lamp, which was caught by the couch, luckily, and didn't break. The young man righted the lamp and looked at them.

"This is Mateo," Sabine said proudly. "He's been staying in the little cave we call the Vermeer Room, but now that you're here, he'll move upstairs. Right, Mateo?"

He brushed past them without a word and headed for the door.

"Go mow the field before it gets dark," Sabine called after him. "If the mower runs out of gas, there's a can under the porch!"

"Your gardener lives with you?" Greta whispered.

"That's my son," Sabine said. "The one I adopted from Nicaragua."

Greta had forgotten about him. There were two others: one from Chile, the other from Honduras.

"He's only here for a week, unfortunately," Sabine explained. "He's building a shed for the donkeys and cutting down some trees. I'm heading to the city later today, so you'll be glad to have him around. Trust me, it gets lonely in this house at night."

"Because it's haunted?"

"It's cursed," Sabine said. "Which is slightly different."

"Cool. Does that mean I'll die here?"

"No," Sabine said. "I'm having the curse . . . canceled."

"How?"

"A lot of women around here call themselves witches," Sabine said, and gave Greta a guilty look.

"You're a witch?"

"Afraid so," said Sabine.

"Since when?"

"Jesus," said Sabine, and punched Greta's arm. "You're still really gullible."

WHILE SABINE WAS IN THE CITY, Greta spent a few lazy afternoons in the yard with Mateo, drinking wine and talking. She sat in an old iron chair and he lay on a blanket near her feet. He was twenty, unable to grow a beard—cute, refreshing—had been a virgin until a month ago, and had already had his heart broken twice. As he talked, she thought of all the things he probably didn't know how to do in bed, as he didn't seem like someone with a porn habit. He had a poem habit, however—unfortunately—and had recited his favorite lines by Rilke while she focused on the strip of skin she sometimes glimpsed between his T-shirt and jeans.

"You know any poetry?" he asked.

"'Yes is a pleasant country,'" she said.

It was the first line of the only poem she knew by heart. According to its author, Yes was a country one could travel to if one felt strongly enough, a place where violets appeared, where love was a deeper season than reason. Yes was a place Greta had never visited, though she longed to retire there. She couldn't seem to get out of Maybe.

Mateo waited for her to recite the rest.

"That's all I got," Greta said.

"e. e. cummings," he said.

"Who's a smart guy?"

Her bad habit was to talk to him like a dog. "Come," she'd said, more than once, and "Stay" and "Go lay down and I'll bring you a treat."

"You blush a lot," he said. "I mean—never mind."

"Go ahead," she said.

He shrugged. "I was going to say, 'for someone your age,' but I don't know how old you are. Around my mom's age?"

"Not quite," said Greta. "Subtract seventeen years, add eight, subtract eleven, add nine, subtract three."

"Forty-one?"

"Forty-five," she said.

"Your math was wrong." He lifted his head and pointed at something behind her. "Some weird creature is walking toward us."

Greta looked over her shoulder. "That's a rooster," she said. "His name is Walter. He only comes over on weekends."

Walter was walking completely upright, for some reason, looking like he'd just climbed off a horse.

"Why's he walking like John Wayne?"

"He's practicing his mating dance," Greta said. "For future hens."

When Mateo asked what Greta did, she admitted to being a transcriber with writing aspirations. She wrote flash fiction, she said. On her phone. With one finger. But the truth was she only wrote notes to her mother. Nine hundred eighty-two notes, to be exact, appropriately located in the cloud.

"You should write a story from a donkey's point of view," he advised. "And the donkeys should talk. I mean, they should have dialogue."

"What should they talk about—their birth charts?"

"Their anxiety," he said. "About being the only donkeys around, or about living here with my crazy mom and a million bees."

The bees had been very much alive at that point, swarming the entrance to the hive, a small hole in the house's brick exterior. From where Greta sat, the hole resembled a fuzzy mouth; the bees, a long, tangled Rip Van Winkle beard.

"But the donkeys aren't here yet," Greta said. "And I'm not Orwell. Although, I should probably learn how to police my thoughts."

"Who's that again?" he asked.

"*Animal Farm*," she said.

He yawned and sprawled out suggestively on the blanket. She felt an overwhelming urge to rest her hand on his lower abdomen, but then Walter moved closer and gawked at Greta with one eye. Since his eyes moved independently of one another, it seemed like he could see things Greta could not. *Where do you imagine you are, Greta?* Walter seemed to ask. *The Italian countryside? Who do you think you are, Diane Lane?*

The only creature more disheveled than Walter was Sabine's eighty-six-year-old father, Seymour. His rusty Fiat pulled into the driveway, as it did every afternoon without fail. Since Seymour seemed made of a combination of wax and papier-mâché, it was always unsettling to see him behind the wheel. On a good day, he bore a strong resemblance to Gene Hackman. On an average day, a wax sculpture of Gene Hackman from Madame Tussauds. On a bad day, a ghoulish funeral effigy of Gene Hackman from an underground chamber of horrors.

He stepped out of the tiny car and began ambling toward Greta. Mateo disappeared into the field. Seymour had shaved his chin and slicked his thinning hair with pomade. He was smiling winsomely, as if he were the most eligible bachelor in town.

"Sabine's not around," Greta said, just as she had yesterday, the day before, and the day before that.

"Oh, but I'm here to see *you*," he said.

This was Greta's cue to blush, or perhaps giggle. A series of small strokes had left Seymour permanently palsied but not at all confused, and, even though his teeth were the color of Brach's butterscotch candy, he seemed to expect Greta to be delighted by his presence, maybe even transported.

He lurched toward an empty chair, lowered himself onto the cushion, and looked at Greta expectantly. She offered him a cigarette.

"Oh *yes*," he said. "Thank you *very* much."

Given his resemblance to Gene Hackman, living or dead, Greta wished he sounded like Popeye Doyle from *The French Connection*, but Seymour had grown up wealthy on Long Island and spoke with one of those old-fashioned lockjaw accents—singsongy, with long, quivering vowels. Like a snob, he pronounced the Ts in "but-ter" and "lit-tle." He had a tendency to emphasize at *least* one word *per* sentence, even if the *words* didn't require *emphasis*. Popeye Doyle would've beaten him up and taken his money.

Except Seymour didn't have any money. Greta savored the disparity between his accent and his present circumstances. Scraping by on social security, Seymour lived alone in a studio the size of a saltine box. His rich and famous friends were all dead. He read the same ghastly novel over and over, John O'Hara's *BUtterfield 8*, and subsisted on cocktail onions and oyster crackers. He didn't drink, but only because he couldn't afford proper booze, and his clothes were frayed and full of holes. And yet, Greta detected not a trace of bitterness. All he asked for were cigarettes and a bit of conversation.

Just now he was looking around as if seeing the place for the first time. The bees were still bearding the hive, and she couldn't help but imagine the beard transferring itself onto his face and neck. Why? Because she was a ridiculous person with too much time on her hands, and morally bankrupt. Lusting after her good friend's teenage son: obscene. Disparaging her decrepit father for no reason: also not great.

"Are you *writing*?" Seymour asked.

"Here and there," Greta said.

Seymour himself was the author of an unpublished novel called *In the Mood*. He'd written it during his midlife crisis thirty-five years ago, hadn't read it since, but referred to it often in conversation.

"I've been writing letters to my mom," Greta said.

"*Wonderful*," Seymour said. "She must love hearing from *you*."

"She's dead," Greta said. "She died over thirty years ago."

"*Well*," Seymour said.

Greta waited, but Seymour had nothing to add.

"I guess it's more like a journal," Greta said after a minute.

"What's *that*?" he asked.

He'd suffered some memory loss, yes, but it often seemed like a performance.

"It's a diary," Greta said.

He asked if the diary was "up-to-date."

"How do you mean?" she asked.

He opened and closed his mouth three times. He swallowed, shrugged, and then tried to look sly and knowing. *Groping for Words*, a one-act play she'd seen many times now.

"You're not wondering if *you're* in my diary, are you?" she finally asked.

She hoped that by phrasing it this way he could only say no, which was what she wanted to hear, but he gave her a relieved smile and said yes, as a matter of fact, he *was* wondering, *thank* you.

"No," Greta said. "But I'll tell you an embarrassing secret: I have a small crush on your grandson."

He smiled nervously.

"Absurd, right?" Greta said. "He'd probably be horrified, which is why I'd never tell him in a million years. I'd hate to make him uncomfortable!"

Seymour pursed his lips. "*Well*, while you were falling for *Mateo*, I was falling for *you*. As a matter of *fact*, I was hoping we could have an *affair*."

Dear god in heaven. So that explained the voicemail he'd left the other day, asking her to dinner.

"I'm forty years younger than you," Greta said. "Forty's a big number, Seymour. It's a whole other person."

"I *know*," he said, proud as a peacock. "I never expected to *feel* this way again. I was *certain* you felt the same way."

Yes, people age horribly. They suffer strokes. Their bodies and brains fall apart. But the male ego? Firmly intact until the bitter end.

Greta's phone rang. It was Sabine, thank god, checking in from the city. Greta turned away from Seymour and cupped her hand over the mouthpiece.

"Your father's here," Greta whispered.

"Why?" Sabine asked.

"Bumming smokes," Greta said. "And . . . professing his love."

"For who, Mateo?"

"*Moi.*"

"Oh god," Sabine said. "His dementia."

"He seems pretty self-possessed at the moment," Greta said.

"If I'm alive at his age," Sabine said, "and I hope I'm not, I'll give myself pneumonia. Surely pneumonia will be sold in vials by then. If that doesn't kill me, I'll think of some other way. Put him on."

Greta passed the phone to Seymour.

"Go home, Dad," she heard Sabine say. "You're making a fool of yourself."

Seymour turned bright red and handed back the phone.

"I won't see *you* again," Seymour said, furious.

"Sorry," Greta mumbled.

In her dream that night, Seymour climbed into her bed while she was sleeping and pressed himself against her back. To her horror, he was hung like a donkey. Greta shrieked, ran out of the room, and climbed the stairs in search of Mateo. She found Mateo asleep in Sabine's bed. She pulled back the covers and groped his crotch, expecting another donkey situation, but there was nothing between his legs. It was all perfectly smooth down there. "You're like a Ken doll," she said in the dream. "I don't want any trouble," he replied sleepily.

And he hadn't gotten any. He'd finished building the shed the following day and driven back to wherever he'd come from—Montana, Wyoming, Idaho, one of those—and she never saw him again, not even at Seymour's funeral six weeks later. Poor Seymour had died in his sleep, alone in his saltine box.

Dear Mom,

I was needlessly cruel to an old man. His name is Seymour, and he told me he had feelings for me, and I was too grossed out to be gracious about it. I behaved like a child and ratted him out to his mother. I mean daughter. In other words, I treated him like a pedophile, even though we're both adults. Now he's dead. He died alone, like you, and I feel terrible. There were only four of us at the memorial and we all looked guilty as sin. Anyway, if you see Seymour, don't be unkind. Let him hold your wrist when you light his cigarette, and tell him you'll read his novel.

PS: Take a quick peek into the future, if possible, and let me know if I'm getting some any time soon.

3

Until last year, Greta had been engaged to Stacy. Most engagements last a year, maybe two. Although Greta couldn't imagine herself with anyone else, she'd felt incapable of making plans for the weekend, let alone a wedding, let alone the rest of her life, and so their engagement had lasted *ten years*. In the meantime, she kept catching the bouquet at other people's weddings. The bouquet was never tossed into the air, it seemed to Greta, but rather hurled directly at her head, and she had no choice but to catch it and then quickly pass it like a football to the woman standing next to her, who always dropped it. "Fumble!" Greta yelled each time. The woman would then pick up the bouquet and pass it back to Greta, and Greta would feel like dying.

Stacy was twelve years older than Greta and originally from Cape Cod. No, he wasn't a woman. But, his name being Stacy, he'd obviously been bullied as a kid, especially since he'd worn Coke-bottle glasses and spoken with a slight lisp. This was why you'd never want to fuck with him as an adult, because—well, buried rage, etc. By the time Greta met him, he wore contacts, his lisp was long gone, and he had muscles. Not huge, stupid muscles, but you could tell that he had abs, and not just in his ab region but, like, all over his body.

They'd met in Los Angeles while Greta was waitressing at a restaurant called Sylvette. Named after a portrait of a blond French woman by Picasso, the restaurant did not serve French, or even Spanish, food, but rather rustic Italian. It was family owned, which was nice, but the family was Indian. Until Greta came along, spaghetti was served by an exhausted woman wearing a sari. If you poked your head in the kitchen, you saw half a dozen Indian dudes in dhotis. But the family had lived in Rome for many years, and the food was authentic and delicious, and the restaurant, though tucked away in a strip mall surrounded by rehab centers, had a loyal, if mostly alcoholic, following. In fact, most of their customers were either on their way to one of these facilities or just getting out.

On the night they met, Stacy pulled into the parking lot in a grandma car from the seventies. Greta watched him step out of the car and sling a messenger bag over his shoulder. He was accompanied by a tall guy wearing a Red Sox shirt and hockey hair. The tall guy weaved rather than walked, and his face was shiny and red, but not from the sun. He had what Greta called a drunk tan.

Stacy, on the other hand, had a regular tan. He was thirty, maybe forty, maybe older, and dressed, unforgivably, in fleece. His gray fleece pullover reminded her of a giant lint trap, and his pants had weird cuffs, drawing attention to his long feet, which were stuffed into stiff black dress shoes. He looked like he might tap-dance his way into the restaurant.

They seated themselves, one of her pet peeves, choosing the small table by the window. Greta delivered menus. Drunk Tan, she imagined, was having a last meal before checking into Bridges to Recovery, and Stacy was his chaperone. Sponsor? Second cousin. He asked if she wouldn't mind stashing his bag in the back.

"My cah doesn't lock," he explained.

She dropped the bag at the waitress station and returned to their table. It was her eleventh day without a cigarette, her eleventh month without sex. She'd been smoking her feelings since she was fifteen, and now, at age thirty-three, her real self was beginning to emerge. Unfortunately, her real self was horny, easily enraged, and no longer interested in making money.

With some effort, Stacy pulled the fleece over his head and deposited it on the floor, where it belonged. When she noticed his T-shirt, she immediately forgave him everything, even the Gregory Hines shoes. It was an old concert shirt for her favorite post-punk band, the Birthday Party.

"Nice shirt," she said.

He looked surprised. "You like the Birthday Pahdee?"

An accent. A speech impediment. Which?

"Big fan," she said.

"We just saw Nick Cave in consit," Stacy said.

"Me too."

"You were there?" Stacy said.

Greta nodded. "In the balcony."

"We were up front," he said.

Drunk Tan seemed on the verge of tears. He wasn't drunk, she decided, but rather newly sober. He coughed, and then kept coughing. She thought he was faking at first, but he coughed with his entire body, arms and legs included. His eyes bulged and he turned away, but she caught the helpless look on his face.

"Pahdon me," he said. "God!"

"You all right?" Greta said. "I can bring you hot water with lemon, if that helps."

He looked insulted, as if she'd offered him apple juice in a sippy cup.

"What's your name?" he asked.

"Greta," Greta said.

"I'm Mahk," he said. "That's Stacy. Quick question: how long would you say it takes to get to Yosemite? By cah."

Okay, so they weren't newly sober, but rather newly arrived New Englanders. Transplants, maybe, like her. Although Greta had been born and raised in Los Angeles, she liked to tell people she was from New Hampshire, because that's where she went to high school, and also because she was unable to bring herself to say, "It's all good," one of the more vapid verbal tics of Californians at the time. She could only ever say, "Well, that's *one* good thing, I guess."

"Five or six hours," Greta said.

"Okay, Stace?" Mark said. "Too fah. Your cah won't make it."

"Yeah it will," Stacy said. "It's only got fotty thousand miles on it."

"Lemme ask you," Mark said to Greta. "Would you date a guy who drove that cah?" He pointed out the window. "The awful beige one."

"It's a Plymouth Volare," Stacy said quietly. "Nineteen seventy-nine."

The original owner probably smoked Old Golds or Benson & Hedges 100s. Greta would have killed for an Old Gold. She wondered if her craving felt more ungainly than usual because it was riding on the shoulders of nostalgia. She wasn't nostalgic for the car so much as the *cah*. Somehow her hearing had improved since she'd quit smoking, or at any rate sounds she used to find grating were now euphonious. Helicopters, for example, the wild parrots living in the palm trees behind her apartment, mariachi music, Massachusetts accents.

"See?" Mark said, and coughed. "No ansa."

"Yeah," Greta said finally. "I'd go out with you."

Stacy gave her a startled smile.

"She's just being polite," Mark said. "You'll never get laid with that thing, not out here, not even if your cock was as long as my ahm."

"Sorry," Stacy murmured to Greta.

"Does it have bench seats?" Greta asked.

"Front and back," Stacy said.

"Well, that's *one* good thing," Greta said. "Right?"

"The seats are made of foam," Stacy said, "so you can spill an entire cup of coffee and it just sinks in."

Mark rolled his eyes.

"Are you guys related?" Greta asked. "You're cousins, right?"

"We were naybuhs growing up," Stacy said. "He's visiting from Boston, but I live around the conna."

"At Sober Clarity?" Greta asked.

Stacy shook his head. "Blue house, white trim."

"I was kidding," Greta said.

"Well, just for the reckid, I'm sobah," he said.

"She doesn't care," Mark said.

"Mahk's upset I bought this cah for our road trip," Stacy said. "He was hoping for somethin else."

"He won't even make an effit," Mark said to Greta. "Everyone back home thinks he's a homo."

Stacy cleared his throat.

"What can I bring you to drink?" Greta asked.

Stacy ordered coffee as if it were Sunday morning, but it was Monday night, an hour before closing. Mark asked for a Bud.

"We only have Peroni," Greta said. "The Italian Budweiser."

"Then bring me a bottle of red," Mark said.

"He'll have a glass," Stacy said quickly. "No bottle."

"Chianti," Mark said. "No, wait—rose."

He pronounced it like the flower.

"Unless—is it like a wine coola?" Mark asked.

"It's dry," Greta said. "And chuggable."

He seemed to appreciate that. She started to walk away but stopped.

"One of you guys have a cig, by any chance?" she asked.

"Pahdon?" Stacy said.

"A cigarette," Greta said.

"A cansa stick?" Mark said.

"I prefer 'stick of joy,'" Greta said.

"Well, but I have cansa," Mark said. "In my lungs. Stage three."

"Mahk," Stacy said. "Don't staht."

Mark shrugged. "Just bein honest."

"Sorry," Greta mumbled. "I quit last week. Never mind."

Mortified, she strode past the waitress station and straight into the kitchen, making a beeline for the walk-in. The light had burned out in there, so it was pitch-black and very private. She liked to put her face in front of the fan, which fucked up her bangs, but it was freezing and nearly as restorative as a first drag. Plus, the dessert tray was right there.

Ricardo, the dishwasher, entered the walk-in as she was piping cannoli cream directly into her mouth. He was hungover, as usual, and holding a flashlight. Greta was holding the pastry bag over her face, squeezing it with both hands. Ricardo looked scandalized, as if he'd caught her jacking off a customer.

"*Sacame la leche*," she said with her mouth full.

He scowled. "A woman doesn't say that."

"*Mamarme la verga*," she said.

He shook his head in disgust. Yesterday he'd caught her licking frosting off a donut, which wouldn't have been a big deal if the donut hadn't been in the trash. Granted, it was only a big deal to Ricardo, who hated having his own behavior reflected at him. Instead of saying "Right behind you," he always sang out, "Coming inside you!"

She returned to the dining room and delivered their drinks. Something skittered peripherally. She looked around for the busboy. He was right behind her, wiping down a table.

"Manuel," she said softly. "Lobster, table thirteen."

Mark perked up. "You have lobsta?"

"Lobster" was code for "cockroach." The owners exterminated regularly, but the roaches seemed to mate every five minutes. Last week, as she was delivering food to table 2, a visibly pregnant one had fallen out of a ceiling panel and landed down the front of her shirt. Somehow, she'd walked away from the table without screaming, but she'd been rattled for the rest of the night. The owners had given her three days off to recover, paid, which amounted to $126.

"We did have a lobster special," Greta said. "Earlier. But we sold out."

Mark squinted at her and ordered the gnocchi.

"How about chicken pahm?" Stacy asked her.

"We have chicken," Greta said.

"No pahm?"

"We have Parmesan," Greta said. "But, you know, it's grated. On the side."

"Any chance you can pull up a chair and join us?" Stacy asked.

She laughed. "I can't sit down. There's . . . cameras." She waved her hand around, as if the cameras were everywhere. "But you want the chicken? It comes with pasta."

"Yes, please," he said. "Thank you very much."

At the waitress station, she casually poked through his bag with her foot. It was full of nerdy library books, including *Gödel, Escher, Bach*. Maybe he had Asperger's? But he made a lot of eye contact and his face was full of emotion. Which emotion, she couldn't begin to guess. Maybe she had Asperger's? Why was she bothering with his bag, anyway? You learned everything you needed to know about a person by waiting on them. Manners, preferences, habits. Were they a little too comfortable being waited on or, sometimes just as troubling, not comfortable enough?

She delivered their food and then sat a few tables away, folding napkins and eavesdropping. Stacy went on at length about a tiya fiya that had been burning since Septemba. He talked about naycha, the enviament, sola powa. In the monning, they would drive to Santa Bahbra and do some light laybuh on his friend's apple orchid. There were hosses on the prahpetty, so maybe they could go hossback ridin? The guy, his friend, was an ahtist who made sculpchas out of metal and eyein. Stacy wanted one for his den and anotha to bring home to his mutha. From there, they would visit various state pahks, maybe make it as fah as South Dakoter or Wyoming.

His voice worked on her like a salt bath. It seemed rich in minerals, including iron—or *eyein*—and relaxed her deeply, almost to the point of sleep. All her muscles, including the ones in her face, seemed to slacken. In fact, fuck, was she drooling? She wiped her mouth and sat up straighter. Then Stacy called her over and pointed at the pasta on his plate.

"I'm not sure this is, uh, angel heya," he said.

"What?"

"Angel hair," he said slowly.

Greta leaned over and peered at it. The hair in question was dark and could've belonged to anyone on staff.

"It's just *my* hair," she said.

"It's yaws?" he said.

"Yeah," she said, and smiled.

"Well, then," he said.

"The kitchen is closed now, but your dinner is on the house, obviously."

He laughed and touched her elbow.

A few minutes after she dropped the check, he approached her at the waitress station. She passed him his bag. Can we get on a plane, she wanted to ask, a long flight, so I can sleep on your shoulder?

"Sorry about Mahk," he said. "He's been hittin the bottle pretty hahd."

Stacy's eyes began leaking all over the place, but he didn't seem embarrassed or surprised, and neither was she. He calmly wiped his face with his sleeve.

"You can't tell by lookin' at him, but he's full of toomahs," he said. "And he's never been west of Ohio. Listen, I hope I'm not bein too fohwid, but you feel like hanging out sometime?"

"Yes," Greta said quickly. "I wish we could hang out right this second, but those people just ordered another round." Greta nodded at her other table. "They've been camped out for hours."

He shook his head. "No regahd."

"Sorry?"

"No regard," he said carefully. "People got no regard for service workers. Everyone thinks they're VIPs."

When he pronounced his Rs, he sounded like Richard Pryor impersonating a white guy, but he couldn't maintain it for more than two sentences.

"I used to tend bah," he explained. "Thing to do is, cut the music and staht sweepin."

Greta smiled. "Your accent."

"You hate it," he said.

"It's comforting."

"Tell you what," he said. "I'm gonna leave my numba, and maybe you'll call and allow me to comfit you."

Dear Mom, she wrote later that night. *Finally, a non-flake. A man with a code. Sober but not humorless, outspoken but not obnoxious, well-mannered, unmaterialistic, able to produce tears, won't abandon me if I get cancer, might in fact drive me around the country. A dream.*

A FEW WEEKS LATER, after he'd returned from his road trip, Stacy suggested they take a walk around the tah pits, maybe dip into the aht museum, and then grab a bite at a place called Whisper, during which Greta insisted they whisper as much as possible. She didn't know why she hadn't thought of this sooner, as nearly everything about her sounded like a secret.

"My mother killed herself when I was thirteen," Greta whispered when Stacy asked if her parents still lived in the area. "So, I was fostered by a few of her siblings. She had six sisters and one brother, and they were scattered across the country and very different from one another, but they all had the same exact voice, so they'd always seemed less like eight people and more like one person with multiple personality disorder."

"Where was your fahtha?"

"Jail. He told people it was for embezzlement, but the truth was he'd been busted for impersonating a police officer."

"Was he a bank robbah?"

"Sadly, he was only trying to pick up women. But even if he hadn't been in jail, living with him was never an option. When I was in high school, he married his accountant. She was sweet, Dominican, half his age. No one knew what she saw in him. A week after their honeymoon, she shaved her head and began dressing in long white robes, because, well, it turned out she was a Santeria priestess. She transformed their living room into a massive shrine to her murdered twin boys, and long story short, she ran away with all his money. In his despair, he stabbed himself in the stomach, samurai-style, except he was too weak to pull the knife toward his heart, and so he just lay there on the linoleum, bleeding out. He waited six hours before calling an ambulance."

"What an awful way to die," Stacy said. "My god."

"He lived. He got married again, twice. Now he's drinking himself to death in the Florida Panhandle. I don't even know his address."

Stacy chewed his straw solemnly. He was drinking seltzer with lime; Greta, the same, plus tequila.

"But enough about me," Greta whispered. "Did you have an okay childhood?"

"It's too boring to whispah about," Stacy said. "My parents are saints. Do-goodahs. If anything, I suffid from too much happiness, which might be why I've always been drawn to dahk-sidahs."

"Docksiders," Greta whispered. "The loafers?"

"Dark-siders," Stacy said slowly. "People who live on the dark side. Like my next-door naybuhs. They had eight kids, right, so they raised rabbits. Not to cuddle—they ate them for suppa. Rabbits don't have vocal cords, but they scream when they're dyin, and it was all I could hear from my bedroom window. Still, you couldn't keep me away from that house. I lost my viginity to one of the oldah girls. Her name was Stacy, too. She worked at Cumbahland Fahms. So, you know what that means."

Free candy, Greta thought.

"It was the beginning of a long, very loving relationship," Stacy said.

"With convenience stores?"

"The bottle," Stacy whispered. "Stacy introduced me to alcohol."

"How old were you?"

"Fourteen," Stacy said.

Greta admitted that her mother had been an addict, too. Her drug of choice: terrible news. Nothing gave her mother more pleasure than hearing about the worst thing that ever happened to you, preferably in exhaustive detail, the more visually disturbing the better. The only metric she used to judge someone's worth: had they suffered enough?

Greta's childhood had been dominated by run-of-the-mill rescue fantasies, most of which ended with Greta's being saved by Chief Bromden from *One Flew Over the Cuckoo's Nest*. Her fantasies finally came true after her mother's death, when Greta was rescued by Dusty, her mother's twin. Like Chief Bromden, Dusty was taller than average (six-one), was nearly deaf (but not faking it), and had spent many months in a nuthouse.

"Were they identical?" Stacy asked.

"No," Greta said. "In fact, they didn't even seem related. Imagine Ali MacGraw and Sissy Spacek sharing a womb."

Greta had moved in with Dusty, who lived in a tract housing development in southern Arizona. Dusty's romantic relationships were with incarcerated men and therefore epistolary, so she spent most of her time at the kitchen table, writing long letters in silence. Dusty seemed utterly fulfilled by these correspondences and didn't want or need anything from Greta. Much of what came out of Greta's mouth seemed suddenly unnecessary, or perhaps better written down. Since she'd always been a letter-writer, she continued writing to her mother, whom she pretended was alive and in prison for murder.

"How'd she end her life?" Stacy asked.

"She blew her brains out while I was at horse camp."

"It's unusual for a woman to shoot herself in the head."

"She was raised in Reno," Greta explained. "She was familiar with guns."

"Did she leave a note?"

"I lost it," Greta whispered. "When I try to imagine it, her handwriting is either blurry or blacked out, like a redacted CIA document."

"Maybe you should see a hypnotist," Stacy suggested.

"I'm not sure I want to remember the note," Greta said. "I'll certainly never forget the PS."

"'I love you'?" Stacy whispered.

Greta shook her head.

"'I'm watching over you'?"

"The PS wasn't written. It was . . . a piece of herself."

Stacy leaned closer.

"I really shouldn't be telling you this stuff," Greta whispered. "We just met. I don't want to scare you."

"But I'm not afraid of the dahk," Stacy said. "Rememba?"

She'd found the horrifying postscript clinging to a fold in the curtains. This had been a few days after her mother's body had been taken away, her room scoured by professional cleaners. But the cleaners had somehow missed the PS, which was strange because it was the first thing Greta noticed. If they'd missed that, Greta could only imagine what a soul-haunting mess the place had been before. The PS resembled a swatch of leather with a long brown hair attached, and the follicle was visible on the back side. Although it hadn't been your customary lock of hair and was in fact grotesque, Greta stored it in a film canister, like weed. She just couldn't bring herself to throw it away. But, after she moved to Arizona, she worried that Dusty would discover it, decide Greta was unstable and therefore unlovable, and then drop her off at the nuthouse and never return.

Rather than bury it in the backyard, Greta tried burying it in the trash beneath the sink, even though it obviously didn't belong there, surrounded by coffee grounds, banana peels, and burned toast, and the bathroom trash wasn't much better. She knew the kitchen trash would eventually be mixed with the bathroom trash, and all trash was not the same to Greta. She was deeply unsettled by the thought of dirty Q-tips and tampons sharing a bag with rotten produce, chicken carcasses, and this delicate piece of her mother's body. And so, she'd wandered into Dusty's garage, opened an old shoebox, and placed her mother's remains in the toe of a patent leather shoe.

The itching started that night. She wondered if the change in climate had given her dandruff, but there were no flakes, only a crawling sensation that kept her awake half the night. She figured it was lice, picked up from Dusty's couch cushions. She waited for the lice to die of old age, but they only seemed to multiply.

A week later, Dusty patiently examined Greta's scalp with the metal comb she used on her cats. She didn't find anything. Greta passed her the magnifying glass and reminded her that they were the size of sesame seeds, that their eggs looked like specks of dirt.

Dusty peered at Greta's scalp under the glass. "There's nothing here," Dusty said finally. "You must have . . . phantom lice."

Stacy gasped. "Phantom lice!"

The phantoms seemed to gather in one place near the back of Greta's head. They took turns sucking her scalp as if waiting in line at the drinking fountain, and the sucking was incessant. Greta's instinct was to blast them with heat, so she burned her scalp with a hair dryer for thirty minutes a day, four days in a row, and then emptied a bottle of peroxide on her head and sat in the blazing sun for six straight hours.

"Anyway, long story short, the itch never went away," Greta whispered. "I'm still scratching that same spot, twenty years later."

Greta was supposed to be in eighth grade that year, graduating with the same twenty-four kids she'd known since kindergarten. Now she was enrolled at a school called Wallace, which had the look and feel of a detention center. Her closest friends in California had been Chinese and Korean, so she tried to ingratiate herself with the Asian Arizonans, but they were hesitant to accept her. Looking back, it was probably her hair—the peroxide had turned it orange—and her way of wearing fishnets with gym shorts, not a popular look at the time.

Greta started writing stories and passing them to the girls in English class. The stories were inspired by but much tamer than the ones she'd studied in *Penthouse*, a stack of which she'd found on the sidewalk, in a box labeled "Larry's business papers." Greta hated the word "cum," for example, but the stories still qualified as erotica, with sex between female students and teachers. The girls had sex in various classrooms and closets while Ralph, the janitor, polished the linoleum with an industrial buffer and touched himself. She made sure to include as many sensory details as possible, such as the clicking noise of the slide projector, the smell of Bactine, the last words written on the chalkboard.

The girls were easily seduced, but Greta was more interested in her English teacher, Mr. Galucci. Hopefully, he would intercept one of these missives and see how firmly she'd embraced his lectures on specificity. She'd been flirting with him for weeks, to no avail. When she brought him an African lily, he said, "This is beautiful, but do you know who would really love it? Ms. Garcia, the Spanish teacher." When she brought him a long rope of red licorice, he insisted on cutting it into twenty-three pieces to share with the whole class. When she offered to rub his shoulders one day, he asked if she was feeling all right and sent her to the nurse, and when he finally confiscated her stories, he delivered them straight to the principal, who suspended Greta for five days.

When the school year ended, Greta was returned to Los Angeles and passed off to Uncle Derek, who lived in a modest ranch house in Inglewood. Derek was quiet and conservative. He'd met his wife at church. Her name was Petra.

Petra was a curvy chatterbox from Croatia, only ten years older than Greta and unemployed, so they were alone together in the house all day. After showering, Petra would wander into the den with a hair dryer, stand naked in the harsh sunlight, unashamed of her rolls and folds, and blow-dry her massive bush, which put Greta in hysterics. At fourteen, Greta was sexually precocious but otherwise weirdly naïve. Petra seemed . . . not stupid, exactly, but superstitious. Greta would often walk by the master bedroom and see Petra on the bed, naked from the waist down, her shapely legs resting against the wall.

"You didn't heard us?" Petra would say in her adorable accent. "I took love from your uncle before. It was very special feeling. I wished for more. I wanted baby before one years."

Poor Petra couldn't seem to get pregnant. That's why her legs were elevated, to encourage the sperm to swim in the right direction. At least she had Greta, who was still technically a child even though she felt forty-five. Since almost everything Petra uttered was in the past tense, Greta felt like they'd lived together for years and were constantly reminiscing. Greta's tactic was to play dumb—or young, rather—so that Petra might keep her forever. She asked as many stupid questions as possible and pretended not to know how to use basic appliances.

"What you is doing?" Petra said, shaking her head. "I will learn you to cook coffee, and I have informations for dishwasher." She seemed defeated. "I think I turn on cigarette again."

Cigarettes were something you turned off and on, like television. Over the next few weeks, it became clear that Petra wanted Greta to be older, not younger. She taught Greta interesting Croatian insults like "*pička ti materina*" (your mother's vagina) and "*idi u tri pičke materine*" (go into your mother's vagina three times). She gave Greta adult gifts: miracle bras, thongs, makeup, hair dye.

"Your eyes was brown," Petra explained. "So you wear blue shadow. But my eyes was blue, so I wear brown."

On Saturdays, they visited bridal shops all over Los Angeles. Petra would tell the salespeople that Greta was engaged, which they couldn't have really believed, but she'd browbeat them into bringing out the gowns. With her new burgundy hair and blue eyeshadow,

Greta looked like a mail-order bride from Lithuania. One of the sales-people, an older man wearing a suit, took Greta aside and asked if she wanted him to call the police. He seemed certain that Petra was a trafficker, that Greta was about to be sold into sex slavery.

"She's my *aunt*," Greta said, and laughed. "She's from *Croatia*."

"Listen to your gut," the man said ominously. "If it doesn't feel right, don't be afraid to tell someone. Go to a neighbor's house. Where do you live?"

"Inglewood," Greta said.

"Call 911," he said.

Other than on Sundays, which Petra and Derek spent at the swap meet alone, and Greta's daily walk to the store, she and Petra spent nearly every minute together. They watched soaps, ate ice cream from the same bowl, sometimes held hands.

"You have fourteen years?" Petra asked one day.

Greta nodded.

"You were virgin, right?"

Greta knew what Petra meant but was unsure what Petra wanted to hear. Tentatively, she said yes, she were virgin but had been to third base. Petra seemed intrigued. Were Greta bleeding? Greta nodded. Were she masturbating? Greta said sure. How? Greta described her technique, leaving out the part about imagining Petra naked with the UPS guy.

It was all a setup, unfortunately. Now, instead of bridal shops, Petra was dragging Greta to a megachurch and begging her to "find Lord," as if He were in the crowd somewhere, or hiding under a folding chair. As it turned out, everyone at the church knew who Greta was, because there was this whole other life Petra had been hiding, and they were all waiting for Greta to be saved. Now Petra warned Greta about hell every five minutes. Greta had never thought of hell as a real place, but according to Petra, you showed up as yourself, a human being with thoughts and feelings, and Satan performed elaborate CIA interrogation techniques on you. Noise torture, bone breaking, force-feeding, enemas, and don't forget about the lake of fire, and the river made of molten lava, and the thirst, the horrible, horrible thirst.

It was easy to see now that she was being manipulated, but at the time she felt—well, tortured. At night, she began covering the gap under the door with a blanket, like she had as a child. It didn't seem like enough, though, so she often moved a few pieces of furniture against the door, just as she had back home, in the months leading up to her mother's suicide.

But Petra knew all about Greta's blanket and barricade. "When you accept Jesus for your personal savior, you never need blanket again," Petra promised. "The Lord was your blanket."

By the time Aunt Deb came to visit at the end of July, Greta was attending church twice a week and praying with her hands in the air. Aunt Deb pulled Greta aside and asked what the hell was going on, and why was she so happy?

"I've been saved," Greta whispered. "I'm born again."

"No, you're not," Deb said, and laughed. "Go pack your bags and get in the car. Now."

Greta just stood there, frozen.

"Chop-chop," Deb said.

"Where do you live again?" Greta said.

"The 'Live Free or Die' state," Deb said.

"Hawaii?" Greta asked hopefully.

"New Hampshire!" Deb said. "Hurry up, our flight leaves in five hours."

While she packed, Greta listened to Deb argue with Petra and Derek in the living room.

"I told you two not to pull this shit," Deb said.

"She was lost," Petra said.

"She's just a kid. Her mother's dead. We were all there to clean up the mess. Where were you? You couldn't even pick up the phone."

Petra mumbled something about a miscarriage. Deb said she liked Petra better before, when she rode a motorcycle and smoked weed.

"New Hampsha," Stacy interrupted at last. "I had a feelin you'd lived in New England. Did you fit in or were you a weido?"

"It was an adjustment," Greta said.

In New Hampshire, Deb treated Greta like a refugee from a war-torn state. Greta had fled her homeland with only a suitcase, and now she was straddling two cultures. It seemed important to Deb that Greta completely abandon her old life.

"What the hell are you reading?" Deb asked one day.

"Um, the Bible?"

"That's not the Bible," Deb said, shaking her head.

"It's the Jesus parts," Greta explained. "That's why it's called *The Word*."

Deb threw the book in the garbage. "I've got some words for you: wake up!" She clapped her hands in Greta's face. "You were brainwashed by dipshits, Greta. It wasn't your fault, but you need to wake up now. Are you awake?"

Greta shrugged. "I guess."

One Sunday, when Greta asked Deb to take her to church, Deb dropped her off at the recessed entrance of one of the oldest buildings in town, a giant stone structure with a bunch of stained glass windows and a huge cylindrical tower.

"I'm not Catholic," Greta said.

"Go check it out," Deb said. "I'll be back in two hours."

It was Greta's first time inside a public library. This one had been built in 1860, apparently, and contained four hundred thousand books, which seemed excessive. On the main floor, Greta avoided the reading room and headed for the stacks, located in the tower. She selected three novels and carried them to the front desk, where they asked for her library card. When she admitted that she didn't have one, they gave her a form to fill out. Greta went back to the tower, tossed the books out the window, and watched them land safely in the bushes. Then she descended the stairs, retrieved the books, and waited for Deb on a patch of lawn.

"I continued stealing books for a whole year," Greta told Stacy. "I hid them in my closet, under my bed, and eventually in the attic. My room essentially became another branch of the library. When Deb finally figured out what I was up to, she made me return the books and go to therapy."

"For how long?" Stacy asked.

"Four years," Greta said.

"You seem cured," Stacy said. "In fact, I hope you don't mind me saying, but I'm surprised you're not married."

She told him about her last boyfriend. He'd had money, a new experience for Greta, but zero upper-body strength. He could barely hold himself on top of her, and when he did, she felt like she was being made love to by a large, trembling finger. They were together two years.

"Was he in a nursing home?" Stacy asked.

"He was my age," Greta said.

"Who ended it?"

"I did," Greta said. "He decided he wanted a family."

"Gross," Stacy said.

"I'm guessing you never had children," Greta said.

"No, I have two," Stacy said. "I only see them once a year."

Dad??? Greta thought hysterically.

Stacy laughed. "I'm kidding—no kids for me, not eva, I hope you're okay with that."

Music to her ears.

SIX WEEKS LATER, they were living together in Stacy's blue-and-white house. Since Stacy was the caretaking type, Greta experienced a second childhood. Or, in her case, a first childhood. Stacy fed her compliments and saucy things from the slow cooker. He took care of the bills, put her through two years of college, helped repair her terrible credit. He guided and protected her. He got her out of the restaurant, eventually, and into the pharmacy, but encouraged her creativity above all. She'd never felt so cherished, nourished, pacified, and . . . sleepy. In fact, she felt distinctly as though she were sleepwalking, or in a perpetual state of daydreaming, and yet they managed to do things like have sex and travel abroad. Stacy took cooking classes; Greta attended meditation retreats. Stacy made Korean food; Greta took long, even breaths through her nose. Mouth-breathing was only for emergencies, she'd learned, but there were never any emergencies with Stacy because he took care of everything.

"Ever hear of RealDolls?" Stacy asked over dinner one night. "The realistic sex dolls made of silicone?"

Fuck, Greta thought. He's been lulling me into a trance for a year, and now the terrible truth is about to come out.

"Lemme guess," Greta said. "You want one for your birthday."

"They cost six grand," he said, and laughed. "And no, I'd rather have a Real*Dog*."

Greta pictured a silicone sex doll in her golden years. Wrinkles, flab, sun damage. She could see how there might be a huge market for that, given everyone's obsession with youth and perfection.

"So, like, older sex dolls?"

"*Dogs*, Greta," he said. "Life-size *dogs* made of silicone."

"I don't get it."

"Well, we could take a RealDog on road trips. We could hang out with a RealDog on the couch. We could take naps with a RealDog—"

"But why not get a real dog?"

"Because you'd never look at me again," Stacy said seriously. "And I'm not sure I could handle that."

"I love dogs," Greta said. "But I'm not the dog-mom type. I don't think of dogs as fur babies."

And so, they'd adopted a dog. A real dog named Piñon, whom they found at a no-kill shelter in El Segundo. It was rare to find a purebred Jack Russell at a shelter, especially one so young (he was five), with long legs. His original owner had dropped dead; Piñon had nowhere to go. All he really required was several hours of exercise per day and to be made the center of their universe. They signed the papers.

Everyone liked to believe their dog was superior to every other dog, but in Piñon's case it was undeniable. He jumped rope. He could ride a scooter. He could surf, skateboard, somersault. He could balance a soccer ball on his nose. He caught balls with his front paws. He slept in until nine or ten, never begged or slobbered, and wasn't food-obsessed like other dogs, often fasting for a day—by choice.

"Why do you let him put his tongue in your mouth?" Stacy asked. They were sitting on the couch, and Piñon was standing on Greta's thighs with his paws on her shoulders. In addition to being a highly gifted and trained athlete, he was a very powerful kisser.

"He's just getting cream cheese off my chin."

"Are you putting food on your face on purpose?"

"No," Greta lied.

His kisses were dry, sweet perfection. His breath smelled like licorice. She'd never known such pure and uncomplicated love. Her life, pre-Piñon, seemed like a formless fog. What had gotten her out of bed in the morning? How had she lived?

IT WASN'T UNTIL STACY asked her to marry him for the second time that Greta had forced herself awake. Nine and a half years had somehow drifted by. She'd coasted through her thirties, easy as you please, and had forgotten how to take care of herself. Now that she was awake, she wanted the feeding tube removed. She wanted to walk on her own feet again, to wipe her own ass. A little wine with dinner might be nice. Perhaps most of all, she wanted her own bed. She recalled her favorite part about being single, about being alive, the only thing for which she'd experienced pure and complete gratitude as well as the existence of God and heaven, her greatest, most unfiltered joy: sleeping alone, waking up alone, not speaking before noon.

So, what was she going to do—ask Stacy to sleep in a separate bed? To keep his mouth shut six hours upon waking? To stop being so loving and helpful? Was she a psychopath? He deserved more, and better.

The actual act of leaving, however, of packing and moving to Hudson, had felt like trying to stay conscious under anesthesia. It had taken every bit of her will. She'd even reached out to her aunts in desperation, hoping for a bit of reassurance.

Aunt Dusty, whose brain had been melted by the Hallmark Channel, thought Greta was crazy for leaving Stacy and suggested therapy. Aunt Petra cursed Greta in Croatian, calling her a wild pig and a big smelly monkey. "But maybe you find Lord again," Petra said. "Fingers cross."

Greta said she'd already found Him. On Hinge. They'd been to third base.

"*Jebem ti sunašce*," Petra muttered before hanging up, which Google translated as "Fuck you, sunshine."

Aunt Deb called Greta a dingbat but wanted to reminisce about the little boxes Greta used to draw as a teenager, boxes that were either closed, partly open, or wide open with flowers spilling out.

"Sounds like you read my diary," Greta said.

"It didn't say 'Dear Diary.'"

"Did it say 'Dear Deb'?"

"I could never figure out what any of it meant."

"It doesn't matter now."

"But what was the code? Tell me."

"The position of the lid corresponded to how suicidal I was on a given day."

Greta listened to Deb rinse something in the sink.

"So what's your lid doing now?"

"Flapping around in the wind."

"Call me before you do anything stupid," Deb said. "Okay? Promise?"

"Promise," Greta said.

4

In her room, she found Piñon standing near a window with his nose to the floor, engaged in his new hobby of resuscitating half-dead bees. He did this by blowing hard out of his nose, directly onto their still bodies. Sometimes he succeeded in bringing them back to life for a few wing beats. Then they stopped moving forever.

"Dead and gone, Piñon," Greta said. "Go to bed, baby."

Piñon jumped onto the bed and mounted his girlfriend, a stuffed alligator. Greta threw a log on the fire and settled in at her desk. As promised, the audio file was waiting in her inbox. She opened a new document.

> OM: Before we get started, can you state your initials for the
> transcriber, please?
> FEW: FEW.
> OM: Thank you. How are you feeling today?
> FEW: Yeah, okay, fine. I'll tell you what happened.
> OM: I didn't say anything.
> FEW: His name is Keith. He was—
> OM: I'm not pressuring you. We can talk about anything you want.
> FEW: Perhaps you're not aware of this, but your every thought is
> written on your face. Not the best quality for a therapist.

"Or anyone," Greta said. "Except dogs." Piñon looked at Greta and smirked.

OM: I'm more of a coach. I'm not an analyst, nor do I pretend to be.
FEW: Look, I don't want to drag this out, because I'd rather focus on other, more pressing—
OM: But I'm not dragging anything out of you.

"Christ, Om, shut the fuck up," Greta said.

FEW: I'll give you what you can't seem to admit you want, and maybe you can return the favor by not being mawkish afterward—
OM: I would never mock you.
FEW: "Mawkish" as in "maudlin."
OM: Oh.

"'Gong,' honey, not 'dong,'" Greta said.

FEW: I'm in the perfect mood for talking about this, now that I think about it.
OM: How long has it been since you told someone?
FEW: A few years. I'm twenty-eight now, but I was only twenty when it happened, living in the city and attending college. It was summer. I was working at as a cocktail waitress in Brooklyn, even though hospitality isn't really my thing, because I'm incapable of small—
OM: Where were you going to school?
FEW: The New School.
OM: Cool.
FEW: Anyway, Keith. That's his name. He was a regular at this bar. Attractive, well-dressed, decent tipper. He often asked to sit in my section, but he never talked to me beyond ordering his drink, and he only ever had one drink. He was picky about how the drink was prepared, and would send it back if it wasn't right—

OM: What was his drink?

"Fair question," Greta said.

FEW: A French martini. It's a disgusting pink drink from the eighties. I admired him for not being embarrassed about ordering it, and for drinking it out of a martini glass. Usually men like him request a different glass.

OM: A less gay glass?

FEW: A rocks glass. I waited on him maybe half a dozen times before he mentioned that he was from upstate originally, which is where I'm from—

OM: I thought you were from Switzerland.

FEW: I moved to New York when I was seventeen. Anyway, he said he was trying to sell his house because he wanted to "travel." That was the first red flag.

OM: Why is that a red flag?

FEW: It let me know how out of touch he was. He still seemed to think traveling made you interesting. It was something a teenager might say, and this guy was in his forties or fifties. When I asked him why he wanted to travel so much, he said it was because he'd been in prison for many years, and so he'd missed out on a few things. Like Europe. And then, to my disbelief, he actually said he wanted to "see the *Mona Lisa*."

OM: A much bigger red flag.

FEW: Right? I honestly couldn't think of anything lamer.

OM: I meant prison. Did you believe him?

FEW: Yes. I figured he must have been locked up a long time, because why else would he think the *Mona Lisa* would work on me. Or anyone my age. He was reading from a very old, very poorly written script. But he had my attention. I asked him what he was doing with himself as a free man, and he said he was a well-known furniture designer. He'd been doing it all his life, was in very high demand, and he rattled off a list of powerful clients, a list that was completely lost on me, because I never know

– **68** –

who anybody is, including Martin Scorsese. Apparently, Martin Scorsese wanted to make a miniseries out of his life story.

OM: [WHISTLES]

FEW: I wasn't impressed. I only wanted to know why he'd been to prison, but I didn't have the nerve to ask. So, I asked him about furniture instead, and he listed all his favorite designers, showing me pictures on his phone. It was kind of sweet. I told him that I've always been attracted to people who work with wood. He responded by suddenly asking me out to dinner, which caught me off guard. I said, "Yeah, sure."

"When?" he asked.

"Someday," I said.

"But today is Someday," he said, and smiled. "Didn't you know that? And I have a reservation at my favorite steak house. It's right down the street. You should join me. Are you hungry?"

I was, in fact. He could see that I was finishing up my shift. I'd worked the day shift, and had already had my shift drink, and I hadn't eaten all day. I watched him pull out a business card. On the back, he carefully wrote the name of the restaurant in loopy cursive.

OM: Did the card look legit?

FEW: I guess. He said if I met him at the restaurant in one hour, he would buy me a steak and tell me his story, and I wouldn't be disappointed, he promised.

OM: Were you single at the time?

FEW: Yes. I spent a lot of time alone, but I was rarely lonely because I like my own brain.

[PAUSE]

"Ask her why she likes her brain," Greta said, fascinated.

OM: Was it unusual for you to have dinner with a stranger?

FEW: Not at all. Earlier that summer, an old man in a wheelchair asked me out to dinner, and I accepted. We had a nice meal at

a nice restaurant. He told me about his life and his dead wife
and then I never saw him again. I've always liked those kinds
of encounters.

OM: Which kind?

FEW: Brief, random, spontaneous.

"Meow," Greta said.

FEW: This guy wasn't in a wheelchair, obviously, but it still seemed
pretty low-stakes.

OM: Even though he'd spent years in prison?

FEW: I figured he'd been convicted of a white-collar crime. Like tax
evasion. He didn't seem dangerous to me. He didn't even seem
like an adult man.

OM: Why, was he small?

FEW: No. We were the same height, but he probably outweighed me
by fifty or sixty pounds. He was only childlike in a social sense.

OM: So, you met him at the restaurant for a low-stakes steak.

FEW: I was twenty minutes late. He was already seated and eating
bread. It wasn't a trendy place, but it was upscale and crowded.
Booths, not tables. Good linen. Dim lighting. I'd never eaten
there, but it was clear Keith had been there many times. I
imagined he usually ate alone, or with some other woman,
because the hostess seemed startled by my presence. As she
brought me to his table, I could see her trying to work out
our relationship in her head, and deciding that Keith was my
father. And, as I watched him eat bread, I realized that he did
in fact look like my dad—they had similar noses and the same
huge hands. Their hands were nearly identical. I was easily
distracted by this kind of thing at the time, and I remember
staring at his hands for the rest of the evening and feeling
surprised when they reached for mine across the table.

OM: He tried touching you at the table.

FEW: He wanted to hold hands toward the end of the meal. But he
was mostly so wrapped up in his own bullshit he barely looked

at me, and he didn't ask me a single question about myself. It felt like watching a very long audition. The acting was atrocious, mine included. I'm not good at playing the passive female.

OM: He told you why he went to prison.

FEW: I got his version, yes. He'd been locked up at Dannemora, and was I aware that Dannemora had a beautiful church? No? Well, it was called the Church of St. Dismas, the Good Thief, and had been built by inmates. Keith noticed that the prison needed new furniture and so he took it upon himself to write a letter to the warden—handwritten, of course, and god, how he wished he still had that letter! The warden was so incredibly moved by Keith's letter that he called Keith to his office, and did I realize what a big deal that was? It almost never happened. The warden said Keith's letter was the best he'd ever received. Not only was it beautifully written; he was blown away by Keith's drawings and immediately granted Keith permission to custom-build industrial furniture for the prison. What would Keith need to carry out his vision? So, Keith gave the warden a list of materials and the warden promised he would find the funding somehow, and, long story short, Keith built fifty tables and a hundred desks for Dannemora, and he got to be outdoors while everyone else was inside, and he got to carry a Walkman! And, best of all, he got to wear shorts— shorts! Can you imagine? It was totally unheard-of. And then, after the project was complete, which took years, he became a teacher at the prison, but first he had to take an exam, and he scored higher on this exam than anyone in the entire history of the prison—

"But why were you in prison?" I asked him.

"Stalking," he said, after a silence.

OM: Oh god.

FEW: Yeah. He clearly didn't want to talk about it. There was another long silence. Finally, I asked him who he stalked. Was it a celebrity?

"My ex-wife's new friend," he said. "This cunt named Linda."

It took a second to sink in. "Your wife left you for a woman," I said. "You must have been upset about that."

"Yeah, but I barely touched her."

"So it wasn't just stalking."

"Aggravated assault," he said. "It sounds worse than it is. I just took her for a ride and tried to reason with her."

"About what?"

"I wanted to see my kid," he said. "We were only gone twenty minutes."

"You did eleven years for twenty minutes?"

And he impatiently explained that he'd had a gun in the car because some of his clients were in the Mafia, and it was supposed to be three to six years, but something about a hung jury? And planted evidence? I don't know. It seemed credible to me at the time, but I was very ignorant about the legal system. I asked him how old he was when he went to prison, because that seemed important, and he said he'd been in his twenties, like me.

"I *just* turned twenty," I said. "I'm not 'in my twenties' yet."

"Okay, well, I'm only forty," he said.

I remember looking closely at his face while he smiled at me. He looked at least fifteen to twenty years older than forty, but he didn't have any gray hair and his teeth were very white.

OM: How were you feeling at this point? In your body, I mean.

FEW: A little drunk and uncomfortable—but not because of his story. I became uncomfortable when I realized the waitstaff didn't like him. At one point, our server's veneer cracked for a second and I could see that she despised him. I think she let it crack on purpose, for my benefit. She wanted to let me know what she thought of him. Also, he'd bragged about having a personal relationship with the chef, but when the chef came out of the kitchen to chat with some of the customers, he deliberately avoided our table, even though Keith waved him over.

OM: Okay, so you felt judged by the staff.

FEW: Not especially, but I'm sure they were wondering what I was doing with him. Anyway, he paid the bill and we were on the sidewalk. He kept looking at his watch. I thanked him for dinner and said I'd see him around. "Where?" he said. I said I'd see him at the bar. "I really wish you'd come see my house so you'll know I'm not full of shit," he said. He looked so sad. His elaborate seduction charade had taken a lot out of him. "Please," he begged. "It's a beautiful night. Let's sit in my garden and have a glass of cognac. I only live a mile away, just south of the park, and I have great roommates. They're probably having a party right now."

I said I thought he owned his house, the "giant Victorian mansion" he'd done a lot of hand-waving about over dinner. "I do own it," he said, "but I rent rooms to a few friends, because it felt strange to live alone after being locked up for so long." He looked at his watch again. He seemed anxious to leave— with or without me—and was already walking to his truck, a legitimate work truck full of equipment, and so I climbed into the passenger seat, which was covered in fast-food wrappers.

OM: Were you scared?

FEW: Not really. I hoped the garden existed, and I hoped it was full of beautiful wooden furniture, and if it was, I decided I would be extra nice to him the next time he came into the bar.

OM: And if it wasn't?

FEW: I'd refuse to wait on him again. Or maybe I'd have him banned from the bar.

OM: Okay.

FEW: Let me ask you, do you think there was a garden?

OM: I'm picturing a pathetic lawn and a few shrubs.

FEW: Well, first there was the house—a huge, brightly painted Victorian, like he said. Unfortunately, you had to walk through the house to get to the garden. As I climbed the steps to the porch, I felt a weird pain in my stomach. I figured it was indigestion, but what I was probably feeling was dread. He hurried inside and held the door open for me. I could sense right away that the inside of the house was a dark, scary dump, but he seemed so relieved to be home.

He immediately disappeared into the kitchen. I looked around for someplace to sit, but all the furniture was piled with dirty clothes and garbage, except for the love seat, which had just one thing on it, a large dark lump that turned out to be a dog. The dog looked at me but didn't move.

OM: What kind of dog?

FEW: An obese chocolate Lab with bloodshot eyes. Keith came back into the living room carrying a wineglass and a bottle of cheap pinot grigio. "Whose dog is this?" I asked.

"Mine," he said.

The dog looked like it had given up being a dog a long time ago. It wasn't even going through the motions. I've never seen a more depressed animal in all my life, not even in India—

OM: You've been to India?

"God!" Greta said.

FEW: Yes, I've been to India a few times.

OM: What part?

"Are you fucking kidding me," Greta said.

FEW: The north, mostly.

OM: Me too. [PAUSE] Go on.

FEW: He poured the wine and took me through the kitchen, which was disgusting, and I wondered if his "roommates" were men like him. Ex-cons. I asked where they were, and he said they were probably upstairs. We were standing outside now, and he was fiddling with a light switch. "The lights aren't working, unfortunately, but can you see?" He seemed nervous. I could make out that it was a large, lush garden, about the size of the house, and very beautiful, actually.

He told me the garden looked better from the balcony upstairs. So, I followed him back into the house and up the stairs. [PAUSE] That's on me. I chose to go up there.

OM: You don't look well. Do you want to stop? We can stop whenever you want.

FEW: I just need some water.

[LONG SILENCE DURING WHICH
PATIENT GUZZLES WATER]

OM: You okay?

[MORE WATER GUZZLING]

OM: Take some deep breaths if you need to.

FEW: I'm fine. There were four or five bedrooms upstairs, and all the doors were shut. I couldn't hear any people. When I saw the padlock on his bedroom door, I realized I was in a halfway house of some kind. He didn't own this house. His roommates were not his friends. I didn't say anything while he removed the padlock, because—well, I didn't know what to say. Suddenly, I felt extremely uncomfortable in the hallway—exposed—so I stepped into his room and looked around at the mess. The only thing I really remember is all the boxes of Just for Men. Dark brown. I looked at his hair and realized it had been recently dyed. The room smelled like ammonia and Speed Stick. He was sitting on a saggy twin bed, calmly removing his shoes and socks, and that's when I saw the ankle bracelet.

OM: What?

FEW: An electronic ankle bracelet. I asked him why he was wearing one, because I was under the impression that he'd been out of prison for years, and he said he was on probation. "I got into it with some Latin people," he said, "and they called the cops on me. It just means I have a curfew now."

And I remember thinking, Latin people?

Then he tried to kiss me. He took my face in his huge hands and kissed my mouth. I stepped back. He pulled me toward him by my shirt, and I laughed. "Nope," I said. "Nope!"

"Why not," he said.

"I'm not attracted to you," I said.

"Then why are you here?"

I didn't have an answer. Morbid curiosity? I couldn't say that. Why are you here? I kept repeating to myself. It was a good question. Meanwhile, he was telling me how amazing he was at oral sex, how he's known for it all over town, how women tell him he's the best they've ever had—

"Don't ever say that again," I said, and laughed. "It's like telling someone you're an excellent driver. Or easygoing."

"But it's true," he said, exasperated. "I'm the best!"

He looked dumbfounded when I tried to leave. Then, a flash of anger. He dug his fingers into my arm and grabbed me by the hair. Since there's literally nothing I hate more than having my hair pulled, I snapped at him. I called him a dumb piece of shit.

Then I said, "I hope you're not planning to rape me. That would be a very bad idea."

That's when everything changed. He punched me square in the face two or three times. I was on the floor now, and he was on top of me. Suddenly he was threatening to kill me, and said he'd rather walk the yard for murder than rape. He'd never, ever walk the yard for rape, he kept saying. He kept punching my face. He seemed certain that killing me was his only option now, even though I hadn't mentioned the police or pressing charges or anything like that. I'd only said the word "rape." In his mind, he was already going back to prison—that much was settled—now it was just a matter of how he'd get there.

He choked me, first with his hands and then with the collar of my shirt and finally with the electrical cord of a hair dryer.

I was kicking my legs, trying to buck him off me, but I wasn't getting anywhere, so I stopped and lay perfectly still. I felt myself leave my body. I left the room altogether and traveled back to Geneva. Suddenly I was floating down the Rhône, where I'd learned to swim. The Rhône is cold, muscular, and has this very rich, very specific mineral smell. I was on the verge of surrendering to it, of letting it carry me out to the lake, and that's when he stopped choking me. I think he sensed that I was about to lose consciousness, and he seemed to want me awake. So, he went back to beating my face. He hit me with his fists mostly, but he also beat the sides of my head with a boot and whatever else he could find, and I realized that what I was smelling was not the river but my own blood. He reminded me again that he was going to kill me. He wasn't a *rapist*, he kept saying, disgusted. I began screaming at the top of my lungs, but no one came to the door—not even the dog. The dog didn't even bark.

At some point, I stopped screaming and began babbling. I was trying to convince him that it wasn't too late—he could let me walk out of there and I wouldn't tell anyone, I promised. When I saw the confused look on his face, I could suddenly hear myself. I was speaking Swiss French. It was as if he'd damaged the language center in my brain. English words weren't coming to me at all. He must have thought I was possessed. For the first time, he looked frightened, and he seemed to give in. It had been going on for close to an hour by then, and he was tired and out of breath. He said I could leave if I took off my shirt, because it was ripped and covered in blood. So, I did that, I took off my shirt. I remember looking around the room for my purse. When I saw how much blood there was on the bed and floor, I knew I must have been in bad shape. I grabbed my jacket and stepped into the hallway in just my skirt, which was also covered in blood, and that's when he changed his mind. He pulled me back into the room by my hair and locked the door again.

I'm not sure why he finally let me go. I think he just ran out of steam. I stumbled out of the house and tried to run. I was convinced he was coming after me in his truck, that he was just getting dressed and collecting himself. I didn't have my phone or wallet, so I couldn't call anyone or get a cab. Whenever a car approached, I hid behind a tree or some garbage cans. I did this for a while, many blocks. At this point, I knew my jaw was broken because my teeth had shifted. None of my teeth were in the right place.

Then a FedEx van stopped in the middle of the street. Its windows were rolled down, and the driver saw me. Do you need help? I said I needed to go to the hospital and asked him to bring me back to my neighborhood on the other side of the park. Neither of us spoke the whole way there, and he never turned down the radio. To this day, whenever I hear the song "Just the Way You Are," I feel nauseated. Unfortunately, I hear it about once a week—

OM: The Billy Joel song?

Greta paused the audio and scrolled up. It was, without question, the longest Om had ever gone without speaking, probably in his entire career.

FEW: Bruno Mars.

OM: Oh god, sorry. You must have been in so much *pain*. Honestly, I can't even imagine how horrible—

FEW: The pain was intense, yes. The driver dropped me off at the ER, and I went directly to the bathroom and looked in the mirror. The whites of my eyes were bloodred. My ears looked like they were bleeding, and my neck was already beginning to bruise. My nose was clearly broken, and my left cheekbone. There was blood in my hair. Mostly, there was a lot of swelling. My face was gigantic. I looked like the villain from *The Spy Who Loved Me*. Oddly enough, it was one of the few films I'd seen as a kid.

OM: Is that with Sean Connery or Roger Moore?

"Jesus Christ," Greta sighed.

FEW: I'm not sure. The villain's name is Jaws, though, and when the doctors examined me, they said my jaw was broken in two places. They wired it shut and scheduled me for surgery. I ended up with steel plates on both sides of my jaw, and steel rods in my chin.

Greta hit pause again and stared at the blinking cursor on her screen. Perhaps Big Swiss was not the blond supermodel she'd been imagining, but rather permanently disfigured, and that was why Om behaved so strangely around her. She probably turned heads in the supermarket because her face looked like an Easter ham.

OM: Did they call the police?
FEW: I told them I'd been mugged.
OM: Why?
FEW: He had my purse, so he knew where I lived. I still believed he was going to kill me, or have someone else kill me. Also, I was embarrassed.
OM: Embarrassed?
FEW: For going to his house.
OM: But you were nearly beaten to death. For absolutely no reason.
FEW: I thought I was better than him. Superior.
OM: Honey, you were! You are!
FEW: I ridiculed him in my mind and to his face. I'm not saying I deserved any of it, but I accept some responsibility. Maybe I wouldn't feel this way if he'd snatched me off the street, but he didn't. I wasn't kidnapped. I wasn't drugged or tied up. I went to his house of my own volition. I climbed the stairs, I stepped into his room. I ignored all my instincts. I thought I had the upper hand, and I didn't.

OM: How was he caught?

FEW: I quit my job. I didn't leave my apartment for over a week, except to go to the hospital. When I realized he wasn't coming after me, I went to the police. Luckily, a nurse at the hospital had taken pictures of my face.

OM: Where were your parents?

FEW: Switzerland.

OM: Did you get counseling?

FEW: Yeah, plenty. I had to testify in front of a grand jury, so I had lots of therapy leading up to it.

OM: Have you ever practiced kundalini?

"No," Greta said.

FEW: [PAUSE] I haven't, but I know what it is.

OM: I wonder if you'd be interested in doing some chanting with me.

"Dear god in heaven," Greta said.

FEW: What sort of chanting?

OM: I was thinking we could chant the word "Har," which is another word for God.

FEW: You're joking, right?

"You wish," Greta said.

OM: "Har" is an ancient mantra for prosperity and good health.

FEW: We'll be repeating the word "Har"? As in, "har, har, har"?

OM: You'll be surprised how you feel afterward.

"You'll feel homicidal," Greta said.

OM: I can start us off, and you can join in if the spirit moves you.

FEW: Okay.

OM: I'll put on some music.

[CHANTING MUSIC]

OM: Raise your arms above your head at about sixty degrees, palms facing out. Good. Curl your fingers toward your palms, but leave your thumbs free. That's right, like that.

[HAR HAR HAR HAR HAR]

The chanting went on for three excruciating minutes, during which Greta strained to hear Big Swiss, but of course Om drowned her out, as he was practically shouting.

OM: How do you feel?
FEW: How am I supposed to feel?
OM: Well, I feel totally cleansed of mental chatter. What about you?
FEW: Vaguely angry.

"Told you," Greta said.

OM: Anger can be cleansing, too, just in a different way. Perhaps this is a topic for next time, but I'm wondering if you've ignored your instincts in any significant way since your assault.
FEW: You mean, have I continued doing dumb shit?
OM: I'm just wondering what you do with red flags when you come across them.
FEW: Well, I'm married. I work at a women's clinic. I don't meet many strange men in my daily life.

[ALARM]

OM: My next appointment is here.
FEW: Do you think I could get a copy of this transcript at some point?

OM: Sure, of course.

FEW: I had a transcript of my grand jury testimony, but it was destroyed in a flood.

OM: Was it something you looked at often?

FEW: Never. But I liked having it in a drawer.

[END OF RECORDING]

Greta might have liked having it in a drawer, as well. She switched on the printer. As she watched the pages collect in the tray, her chest swelled with something wholly unfamiliar, something other than dread. She'd heard plenty of extreme stories, but she'd never known anyone who'd taken such a beating, not even a man, without luxuriating in self-pity. Big Swiss didn't possess the impulse to please, to match anyone's needs or desires. Her only need, seemingly, was to satisfy her own curiosity. That's what drove her into the house and up the stairs. Granted, curiosity killed the cat, or, in this case, broke its jaw in two places. Of course, no one should get their face pummeled for climbing the wrong stairs or rejecting the wrong person, but, given the ridiculous number of red flags—the kidnapping, the prison time, the dumpy house, the super-sad dog—Big Swiss had not only courted disaster, she'd practically bought it a boutonnière.

Greta considered her own behavior around red flags. Her habit was not to ignore them so much as to ingest them, a somewhat laborious mental production that involved placing them in a stockpot with butter, herbs, and mirepoix; cooking over low heat without browning; adding red meat, additional red flags, a jug of red wine; and voilà, four hours at a lazy simmer later, an extremely rich red-flag stew that she forked into her mouth every day like a fucking moron, sometimes for years on end.

But what about the business card? Why hadn't she googled the guy's name? People her age refused to do anything without consulting the internet. Has this toothbrush been vetted? This olive oil? This novel? This guy who just got out of prison? It was a mistake Greta would have made even yesterday, but Greta hadn't grown up with the internet. She wasn't on social media and she texted reluctantly, with one finger. Sometimes she tried incorporating her thumbs or some of her other fingers, but she never got the hang of it.

At age twenty, or even thirty, Greta would have followed the guy up the stairs. But the way Big Swiss had rejected him was completely foreign and unthinkable. Whereas Greta had only learned to say no, like, a couple years ago, it seemed clear that Big Swiss had been saying it her whole life, and not only no, but *nope*. Nope! And when the guy hadn't taken nope for an answer, she'd simply said, "I'm not attracted to you." Truth-telling—a bizarre choice. Greta would have sooner told someone she had herpes or hepatitis. Or a long-standing, extremely pungent yeast infection. She'd have mentioned discharge. She'd have mentioned the *color* of the discharge. "I have no doubt you're some kind of genius at eating pussy," she would have said. "But trust me, you don't want this one." Instead, Big Swiss had said, "I hope you're not planning to rape me." As if it were preposterous, as if it didn't happen every fifteen minutes.

If he'd pretended to be fine with a yeasty vag, Greta would've let him go down on her. To cover up her misplaced shame, she would've complimented his technique. "Wow, you really know what you're doing," she'd have marveled. "Jeez." Perhaps, when he tried to fuck her afterward, he'd have felt good enough about himself to take no for an answer. A polite but firm no, followed by something like, "Call me old-fashioned but I'd rather get to know you first. Is that weird? When can we see each other again?" He likely would've raped her, anyway, because he was a psychopath, but, given the choice, Greta would have taken rape over a broken face. Better the devil you know.

She placed the transcript in the bottom drawer of her desk and clomped downstairs to the kitchen. Although the occasion didn't call for bubbles, the only alcohol in the house was a bottle of prosecco. She opened it, spilled roughly half of it into a large canning jar, and decided to do something she'd never done before, something she'd never felt compelled to do, which was to listen to the last fifteen minutes of the session again, sans headphones.

Now that Big Swiss's voice occupied the entire room, the air shifted. Greta noticed a subtle change in pressure. Big Swiss had an undeniably large presence. When she climbed the stairs to her doom, yet another pane fell from Greta's window. It was hard to imagine Big Swiss being overpowered by anything—confusion, desire, alcohol, a homicidal maniac. The beating was even more unsettling the second time around. Greta became hyperaware of her hands. When Big Swiss descended the stairs with a ruined face, Greta found herself wanting to punch herself. In the face. Just to see what it felt like.

5

The following day, Greta transcribed two sessions. In the first, a man said that Om's amethyst geode reminded him of his ex-wife's vagina, which prompted an embarrassing lecture about the healing properties of crystals, during which Om had the gall to proclaim that geodes helped you see the whole picture and make difficult decisions. In the second, a young woman made a startling pass at Om by suddenly sitting on his lap and calling him Papa, which was somehow more disturbing than Daddy. It had happened suddenly—neither Om nor Greta saw it coming. To Greta's surprise and relief, Om did the right thing and talked about transference, and Greta chastised herself for thinking Om was a charlatan, but then she wondered if the woman simply wasn't Om's type. If the session had ended a different way, Greta never would have known, because Om wouldn't have sent her the file, and if there was no transcript, did anything really happen? Then she wondered if Om had hired her not because he was writing a book—a book he refused to discuss, strangely—but rather to keep himself in check, or hold himself accountable, which seemed wise. Perhaps he'd become a sex and relationship coach because he himself was a sex and relationship addict.

During both sessions, Greta could hear Big Swiss's voice in the background, as if she were talking to someone in the next room, but whenever Greta paused the audio, the voice was still there. Apparently, Big Swiss's voice had earwormed itself into Greta's brain. It played for hours and was as difficult to shake as "Come On Eileen" or "Penny Lane."

At the end of the day, Greta smoked a cigarette at the window. The sun was on its way down and the wind was picking up. A squirrel stuffed dead leaves into its mouth like salad, while another watched from a nearby tree branch, straddling it like a pommel horse and panting. Gradually, Greta became aware of humans loitering near the locust tree. Long-haired guy, short-haired girl, both wearing dirty jeans and muddy boots. Together they gazed at the broken chandelier Sabine had hung from a tree branch. The guy smiled and clasped his hands behind his back while the girl took photographs. They seemed a little too open to awe, and Greta suspected they knew they were being watched.

Greta swung open the top half of the Dutch door. "You guys looking to buy weed?"

They nodded. A gust of wind blew the guy's long hair into the girl's face.

"Sabine should be back in a few minutes," Greta said, "but feel free to wait inside where it's warm."

They followed Greta into the clapboard side of the house, also called "the cottage," where Sabine conducted her weed business. The cottage was the oldest and most Dutch-looking part of the house. It had low ceilings with exposed chestnut beams and charmingly small doors, and contained Sabine's best furniture. On the ground floor, a large living room and tiny bathroom. Upstairs, a loft filled with beds. Four double beds, to be exact, neatly made with crisp sheets, the duvets covered with the softest cotton, block-printed by hand in India, and down pillows all over the place. Sabine was a hopeless pillow addict. Wayward women from town, i.e., Sabine's friends, often occupied these beds, sometimes for weeks, though the beds were all empty now.

The girl introduced herself as Nicole. This was her boyfriend, Ryan. They sat on the sofa while Greta crouched in front of the woodstove, stoking the fire. As she listened to them admire Sabine's taste in art—old paintings, mostly, with ripped or torn canvases—she realized who they were. Ryan (REP) spoke as if he had an entire diaper stuffed in his mouth. His last session had taken fucking eight hours to transcribe. He was a baker but called himself a maker. Greta didn't have many makers in her life, but as far as she understood, makers were producers of physical objects, like cabinets. The makers around here, however, acted like that other maker, i.e., the Prime Mover, which may have been why Ryan felt comfortable referring to himself as a "grain scholar." Nicole (NEM) did some sort of bodywork—not Reiki, but something real—and had a slight Rhode Island accent. They'd been dating six months, but they saw Om on an individual basis rather than as a couple and hadn't presented problems typical of people their age (thirty-two). For starters, Ryan didn't drink or do blow. He was good-looking but hadn't slept with the entire town. He'd been raised on hardcore porn but rarely looked at it anymore, and he wasn't on antidepressants or mood stabilizers.

REP: As a small child, I had a weird habit of collecting hardened pancake drippings from the griddle. I stole them from the kitchen on Sundays and arranged them on my bookcase. I always had about a dozen, and I'd talk to them at night. One day my mother found them. She asked me what they were and I said, "They're cornies, Mom. They're my friends." But the truth was, cornies were my children. I've wanted cornies—I mean kids—since I was little. It's why I've gravitated toward families all my life.

OM: Like Alcoholics Anonymous?

REP: Right.

OM: Have you talked to Nicole about kids yet?

REP: I told her my clock was ticking and all she said was, "Ew."

OM: Okay, so she doesn't want kids.

REP: No, she does. She just considers men who want children weak and repulsive.

Nicole did in fact find Ryan weak and repulsive. Not because he wanted children, but because he drooled and baby-talked during sex, and was constantly calling Nicole "Mommy." When she asked if maybe he could stop calling her Mommy, he claimed he was saying "Mami," not "Mommy." He worked closely with a Dominican and two Mexicans, and was thinking about spending the month of March in the Yucatán, alone.

But Nicole had other, more pressing concerns. Her lifelong kleptomania, which had been in remission for years, was back. Now she was stealing from friends and family. Cheap jewelry, coffee mugs, clothing, toiletries. When said friends or family came to visit, she had to remember which items she'd stolen and hide them. It was exhausting and confusing. She also shoplifted small things from boutiques in Hudson, including the one she lived above.

OM: Are you not afraid of getting caught?

NEM: I've never told this to anyone, and I'll probably regret telling you, but when I'm stressed out, Jason Bateman usually comes to my rescue.

OM: The actor? I didn't know he lived in Hudson!

NEM: He doesn't. But if I'm really nervous, his face pops into my head, almost against my will. His face often lets me know I'm anxious in the first place.

OM: Are you seeing his face right now?

NEM: Vaguely. His face appears very briefly, and I just sort of conjure the rest of his presence energetically. But it's also physical. We're both expressive blinkers. We both do that slow-blinking thing. You know, like this.

OM: Uh-huh.

NEM: Anyway, it's something I've been doing for years, long before his career took off.

OM: Do you do it around Ryan?

NEM: Not often. It happened the other day, though, and I'm trying to remember the occasion. Oh yeah—he said my pussy smelled like an aquarium supply store in Chinatown.

OM: That wasn't very nice.

NEM: Yeah, it stung a little. Jason Bateman popped into my head for a split second, and I turned to Ryan and was like, Blink, blink, excuse me? The fuck did you just say?

OM: And how did he respond?

NEM: He apologized. Then he asked if I was feeling vulnies.

OM: Vulnies?

NEM: Vulnerable.

OM: Were you?

NEM: I guess. We were in bed, idly fucking. I'm not sure why, but I wasn't bothered by "aquarium supply store" so much as "in Chinatown."

OM: Perhaps because everything is so cheap in Chinatown.

NEM: Maybe. What bothered me was how specific it was. Seemed like he'd really given it some thought. Anyway, I didn't react well in the moment. I ended up hitting him kind of hard in the face.

In Ryan's version of the story, which Greta had transcribed a day later, they had not been idly fucking but rather having difficult butt sex. According to Ryan, Nicole had a love/hate thing for anal but begged for it every other Sunday. If Ryan claimed he wasn't in the mood, she became morose. If he expressed too much interest or excitement, she lashed out. In any case, the actual event was somewhat arduous and brought up a lot of feelings.

REP: It's too tight, Om. It's not at all elastic. Sometimes only the head will fit, but she orders me to keep pushing, and if I don't, she calls me names.

OM: Like what?

REP: The other day it was, "Fuck my ass, you little faggot."

OM: Huh. How did you respond?

REP: I gave her face a little porny slap.

OM: Then what happened?

REP: She punched me in the jaw. See this bruise? She says my dick activates her, uh—shit, I'm forgetting the term—

OM: Hemorrhoids?

REP: Feminist rage.

OM: Right.

REP: Along with some deep-seated penis envy left over from childhood. She feels both envious and resentful.

OM: And how do *you* feel?

REP: I love it, but I often wake up feeling like my dick got slammed in the trunk of a car.

OM: Hurts so good?

REP: [LAUGHS] Sometimes love don't feel like it should.

OM: Have you considered—I mean, do you think her rage was perhaps . . . misdirected?

REP: How do you mean?

OM: Was there something else she may have been upset about?

REP: Oh man. Did she say something? Never mind, I know you can't answer that. I think she had PMS. Also, I said her pussy smelled a tiny bit like fish sauce, and she completely flipped out. Even though I love fish sauce. I sprinkle that shit on everything.

Had they been strangers, Greta would have left them alone to wait for Sabine, but they were as familiar as characters from a novel, an overwrought five-hundred-pager that went nowhere but which Greta nevertheless looked forward to reading on the toilet. She was more than happy to suffer these fools and felt genuine affection for them. Was Ryan an entitled crybaby with pretend problems? Sure. Especially next to Big Swiss. Greta wondered if Big Swiss, with her refreshing absence of victimhood, along with her real, actual obstacles—not a single orgasm, not even by her own hand—had ruined Greta for anyone else.

She searched Ryan's face for fresh bruises. All she saw were two neck tattoos: the Latin phrase "Ne plus ultra" and a crudely drawn gravestone carved with the words "Died of thirst." Nicole was tall and tan and young and lovely and covered in cute doodle tattoos of couples fucking. Greta recognized her overly texturized hair as the work of Alexis, of Neptune Hair Design, the hairdresser responsible for every mullet, shag, and bowl cut in Hudson. Alexis considered herself an empath as well as a stylist and possessed a paranormal ability to apprehend the true wishes and desires of your hair, and even went so far as to communicate with your hair's inner child, which was bizarre given that she wore a glove with small blades attached to three of the fingers. Greta recalled her own experience in Alexis's chair. Apparently, the inner child of Greta's hair desperately wanted micro bangs, a desire Greta had been totally unaware of but willing to grant her, just for the hell of it, having no idea how radically unlike herself she would end up looking. The actual haircut had felt like waking up during surgery, unable to speak or move, while Freddy Krueger filleted your scalp. Three and a half months later, Greta's bangs were only halfway to her eyebrows.

"Would either of you care for prosecco?" Greta asked warmly.

Ryan declined, of course, because he was in recovery, but Nicole said yeah, sure, she would have a little.

Greta fetched the bottle and a glass from the other side of the house. On the way back, she checked on Piñon. Still in bed, he lifted his head off the pillow and winked at her.

"We have guests," Greta said. "If you feel like flirting."

He seemed to consider it but didn't get up.

"I'll leave the door open," Greta said.

In the living room Greta passed the prosecco to Nicole and took a seat in the armchair. She watched Nicole look around the room with interest. Greta wondered if she'd try to walk out with something, though there wasn't much to lift, as Sabine didn't believe in knick-knacks. The room's only clutter was a giant cobweb in the corner.

"I heard a bunch of bees live in this house," Ryan said. "Is that true?"

"Fifty or sixty thousand," Greta said, "but they're all dying."

"What happened?" Nicole asked.

"We have a few theories, but no real answers."

They nodded, waiting for her to share said theories, but Greta's mind went blank. For someone who transcribed dialogue seven hours at a stretch, day in and day out, she seemed to have no idea how to make or maintain conversation. Or polite conversation, anyway. Sabine, on the other hand, could talk to a hole in the wall, and often did. Where the fuck was she?

"How old is this house?" Ryan asked.

"The room we're sitting in was built in 1737," Greta said.

"Wow," Ryan said. "So, it's closer in age to the Black Plague than it is to, say, AIDS."

"True!" Greta said, with too much enthusiasm.

Nicole smiled, not at Greta but at something behind her. Greta looked over her shoulder, expecting to see Sabine, but it was Piñon, carrying his new rope toy, which he tossed into the air and caught in his mouth a few times before dropping it at Nicole's feet. He looked at the toy, Nicole's face, the toy, Nicole's face, the toy, Nicole's face, Greta's face.

"He wants you to throw it," Greta said.

"Is he a circus dog?" Nicole asked seriously.

"Only in his mind," Greta said. "He has a rich inner life."

Nicole finally picked up the toy but waited too long to throw it. Piñon snatched it out of her hands and did his whirling dervish routine while making a murderous noise at the back of his throat. Then he threw the toy against the wall and left the room.

"Mic drop," Greta said.

"I have a German shepherd," Nicole said.

Greta could take or leave German shepherds, but Piñon despised them with his entire being and often growled at them simply for looking in his direction.

"You go to the dog park?" Greta asked.

"On weekends," Nicole said. "You?"

"Here and there," Greta said.

Jesus, this was exhausting. She'd never realized how difficult it would be to interact with Om's clients, to pretend to be meeting for the first time when she knew nearly everything about them. She and Nicole had much in common. They could've been bonding over any number of things. Greta rarely paid for lip balm or bottled water, and that was just for starters. "I too have conflicting emotions about anal," she could've added. "More significantly, we've both been raped, and both of our mothers are dead."

Instead, Greta excused herself and pretended to pee in the bathroom. Thankfully, Sabine's car pulled into the driveway just as she was pretending to wipe herself. Greta flushed and waited for Sabine to enter the house and start blabbing. Sabine's blabbing put people either at ease or on edge, with very little in between, and it was always entertaining to see which effect she was having. The effect she had on Greta? The feeling of being driven somewhere while sleeping in the back seat. Sabine herself rarely noticed or cared; she simply kept driving. Just now she sat on the hearth and blew cigarette smoke into the open woodstove. Two small twigs were caught in her hair and mulch clung to the arms of her wool sweater. Her eyes looked bluer than usual.

"I don't know if you guys know the psychic seamstress? She has a little shop that she runs out of her house. There are clothes hanging all over the living room, a sewing machine in the corner, but you're not supposed to acknowledge that you're there to get a reading. You just bring her a garment you want altered. If she's feeling something, she might say, 'Your grandmother wants to speak to you.' If you want to hear more, you follow her into her bedroom and she sits you on her bed and tells you whatever the hell Grandma's saying. So today I brought this dress I never wear and asked her to take it in at the waist. I stood there, pretending to be invested in the alteration, and she abruptly asked me if I had a friend who 'died of drugs many years ago.' So, I tell her yeah, my ex-boyfriend Dave overdosed in '93, and his father refused to tell anyone where he was buried, and so I never got to say goodbye. She nods and asks me if I'm having trouble sleeping. I say yes. She holds open a Bible with an expectant look on her face, and I understand I'm supposed to put money in between the pages. So I put fifty bucks in there and she tells me I'm not sleeping because he's under my bed."

"Who?" Greta said.

"Dave," Sabine said, and shrugged.

"But you said this house wasn't haunted," Greta said.

"It's not," Sabine said. "He just wants to hang out and watch movies. He doesn't know he's dead. To get rid of him, I'm supposed to say, 'Dave, go away,' three times."

Ryan laughed.

"Is anyone under your bed, Greta?" Nicole asked.

"Only the smell of honey," Greta said. "Which is its own sort of ghost, I guess."

"Anyway, you guys want edibles?" said Sabine. "I have peppermint patties, peanut butter balls, pixie sticks, gummy worms, and mints."

They wanted a tin of mints and a package of gummies. Sabine made the mistake of asking what Ryan did for work. Well, he was grain-scholar-in-residence at blah blah. His recipe for poppy seed coffee cake was blah blah unheard-of, because something something croissant dough plus frosting, and some hot-shit food critic said his peasant bread had an old, tortured soul, and so basically Ryan was a really big deal.

"You remind me a little of Jason Bateman," Greta blurted to Nicole.

Exhilaration. Immediate, totally unexpected, joyful. Like she'd broken something you weren't supposed to break—a TV screen, a windshield, a geode, the fourth wall.

The confidentiality agreement. Fuck.

"Forget I said that," Greta said quickly.

"Are you high?" Sabine asked. "She looks nothing like Jason Bateman."

"I know," Greta said. "Sorry. I don't know why I said that."

A cloud seemed to pass over Nicole's face. Then she smiled.

"It's okay," Nicole said. "I'm not offended."

"I love Jason Bateman," Sabine said.

"Yeah, me too," Greta said.

"We should probably get going," Ryan said. "Ready, Mami?"

It was only then that Nicole blushed. Even her ears turned red.

"Thanks for the goodies," Ryan said.

"Any time," Sabine said.

"Great meeting you, Greta," Ryan said.

"Likewise," Greta said.

Nicole hesitated at the door and looked at Greta. "Maybe I'll run into you at the dog park?"

"Sure," Greta said. "Yeah."

Sabine waited until they were pulling out of the driveway to comment on Ryan's orange teeth. A shame, she said, as he was otherwise handsome, though not her type, of course. Nicole, on the other hand, seemed entirely good, and like "one of us." Then she asked what was up with that Jason Bateman business.

Greta shrugged. "Something in the way she blinked."

"You should befriend her."

"I can't have more than one friend at a time."

"I hope you don't mean me," Sabine said.

They'd gone to several bars when Greta first arrived, three months ago. After two sips of tequila, Sabine had a habit of suddenly looking around, realizing she was the oldest person there, and leaving.

Sabine counted the cash and pocketed it. "I guess I'll pay my phone bill before they shut it off," she said. "I'm afraid I'm going to have to get a j-j-j—dammit. I'm going to need a j-j-j—hold on, I almost had it—a juhhh—"

"Juicer?" Greta said.

"*Job*," Sabine said.

One of Sabine's favorite gags was to stammer over the word "job," Greta remembered now. Sabine's eyes drooped shut, as they did every day at dusk, and wouldn't open again until the moon had risen. The rest of the evening was easy to predict. For dinner, they would make popcorn with nutritional yeast. For dessert, a Dutch baby with butter, lemon, and sugar. At ten o'clock sharp, they'd say good night and retreat to their separate quarters until morning.

EXCEPT, WELL, it was raining in Greta's quarters. Real, actual rain had been coming in through one of the windows for about an hour, pooling on the wood floor not far from Greta's bed. Piñon danced in the puddle, ecstatic. Greta stared at the window. Most of the water seemed to be coming in through the missing pane in the middle, the one Big Swiss's voice had dislodged the previous evening. The window's other missing panes were on the sides and in the corners. Greta recalled that thing Big Swiss had said about her voice, how it loosened the teeth in people's heads. Now Greta felt like she'd lost a tooth. An important tooth, not one of the throwaways in the back. You lose one, the others shift around, and before you know it, your smile is full of black holes. Greta knew it was only a matter of time before they all fell out, before rain turned to snow, her bed into a sled, her head into a block of ice. Sadly, she couldn't afford to have all (or any) of the windows reglazed, and neither could Sabine, who'd run out of money months ago. What Greta could afford was heavy-duty electrical tape. Tomorrow she would try taping the panes back in place. If that didn't work, she'd replace the panes with thick pieces of cardboard, after which she'd cover the windows in sheets of plastic, and then nail heavy drapes over everything, and—

The fire alarm went off and wailed for two minutes. The alarm belonged to their neighbor, Becraft Pumper Co. 2, and sounded exactly like an air-raid siren from World War II, the sound of slow panic and impending doom. It blared every morning at ten, and then again whenever a barn burned down, which seemed to happen once a day. "That can't be real," she'd said to Sabine the first time she'd heard it. "Oh, it's real all right," Sabine had said. "Better get used to it." The siren drowned out everything—despair, desire, logical thought, Sabine's running monologue—and there was no tuning it out or talking over it.

It occurred to her now that one only lived this way if they were on really good drugs. If Greta had had prescription painkillers, she'd have been willing to wrestle with the woodstove while it rained indoors. But Greta didn't have any pills. She only had pillows. And a duvet, which she dragged into the little room she called the antechamber. The antechamber was connected to Greta's room by a crooked door and was larger than a closet but too small to be a proper bedroom. Along one wall stood a substantial oak cabinet with sliding doors.

When you slid open the cabinet doors, you expected to find bedding, blankets, boxes filled with curiosities and embarrassing love letters. Instead, the cabinet contained a bed. A *bedstede*, the Dutch called it. The cabinet doors were painted with pomegranates and quinces—for fertility, supposedly, though it was hard to imagine anyone fucking in there. Greta covered the mattress, slightly narrower than a twin, with several sheepskins. Piñon curled up in an open suitcase on the floor. The only other furniture in the antechamber was an old cane rocking chair surrounded by short stacks of dreary European novels.

She supposed, if worse came to worst, she could remain in the antechamber for the winter, even though it was windowless, its only light a bare bulb in the ceiling, and nothing on the wooden walls except peeling wallpaper. Someone, not her, had picked at the five layers of wallpaper like a speed freak. Whoever it was had seemed to be making some kind of map, or topography: hills striped in pink and green velvet; forests full of thorny, vaguely Asiatic foliage; valleys made up of flowering English vines; lakes floating with paisleys and lozenges. She wondered whose work it was, and what it meant.

Mom,

Please tell me this wallpaper map leads to buried treasure. There's no key or legend, though, so I'll likely never find it. I've always sucked at reading maps. Other weaknesses: puzzles, riddles, any kind of problem solving. I never tested well! Privately, I suspected I was dumb, but now I recognize it as a will-to-live thing. Death has been a goal like any other, i.e., on my vision board forever, and so I've never bothered to learn anything useful, thanks in part to you—no offense.

Although, to be honest, ending my life holds little interest lately. I mean, whatever, it's winter. Suicide only occurs to me calmly and out of the blue, i.e., never on Christmas, which Sabine and I spent getting drunk at Spring Garden. It's just a jingle that pops into my head. A few months ago, when the leaves turned and the burning bush in the backyard was engulfed in red and pink flames, I couldn't stop myself from taking a few pictures, even though I've never cared about foliage. The stems, I noticed, were made of cork. In other words, cork is not man-made—it is a kind of tree bark, and I don't know, should I kill myself this afternoon?

Sometimes I wish I still had our notes. I understand why you burned yours, but why couldn't you leave mine alone? It's no wonder I barely remember anything. You didn't burn the final one, though—that's on me. You'd think I would've kept that safe. You'd think I would've placed it, along with my other important documents, in a waterproof envelope of some sort, or perhaps a metal box. Birth certificate, social security card, your suicide note. And yet, I still have concert stubs from the nineties, a few of which I took the trouble to laminate. Still have that dumb rock I found while tripping in the woods, along with a hundred other useless souvenirs. Boxes full of carefully folded notes from people I never really cared about follow me whenever I move. But your last words? Gone, and early on.

Let's focus on the present. I wonder what you would make of this house. Something tells me you'd hate it. You always seemed afraid of antiques. Is that why you're not haunting me?

This house is putting me in contact with some of the more elemental aspects of survival: shelter, water, fire. I've never considered myself spoiled, but apparently, I'm habituated to such luxuries as insulation, thermostats, and drinking water from the tap. Here I build and maintain fires all day and all night. I de-gas the water before drinking it. If I had that incessant, insatiable impulse to thrive that I see in others, I would move out immediately, or at least find a way to fill the cracks in the walls so that I don't see my breath at night. Instead, I sleep with a hair dryer. Or I hide in the antechamber. Sometimes I wonder why I left California for this fucked-up frontier house, why I left my comfortable relationship to transcribe other people's relationships.

Om tells his clients that a romantic partner mirrors how you feel about yourself. Stacy was a skinny mirror. He made me look—and feel—better than I actually looked or felt, which is why breaking his heart has probably given me seven years of bad luck. My other relationships: carnival mirrors, a different kind of distortion.

Big Swiss, on the other hand? We don't even know each other, and so she doesn't mirror anything, really, but I wish I saw myself in her. I've always thought of myself as a non-wallower, as someone who isn't particularly prone to self-pity, who's mastered the (mostly lost) art of sucking it up, but then I wouldn't be lying around in the antechamber, writing notes to my dead mother, would I? I'd have my shit together by now. I'd be on a clear path toward—

Greta's phone vibrated. It was Om, texting from a bar, probably.

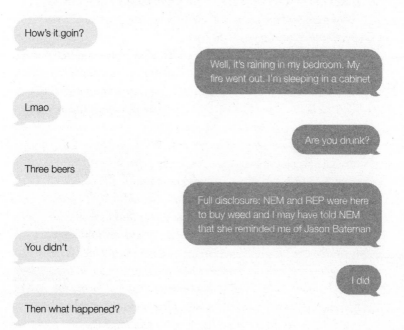

How's it goin?

> Well, it's raining in my bedroom. My fire went out. I'm sleeping in a cabinet

Lmao

> Are you drunk?

Three beers

> Full disclosure: NEM and REP were here to buy weed and I may have told NEM that she reminded me of Jason Bateman

You didn't

> I did

Then what happened?

She invited me to the dog park

Oh ok cool

Is it?

Of course. I want you to have friends.
Just don't tell her you work for me

So, cultivate a friendship
based on a lie?

Yeah

Ok!

Did you listen to FEW?

Twice

Intense, right?

Harrowing

You ok?

Is her face . . . disfigured?

You know I can't tell you

Do you have another file?

Yes

Give it to me immediately

I'm not at home

I'll wait

Go to sleep, Greta

Yeah, okay. She closed her eyes, but her lids didn't feel quite heavy enough. In fact, she felt distinctly that she was being watched. Although there were no windows in the antechamber, quarter-size spiders were embedded in every nook like hidden cameras. One or two looked large enough to jiggle a doorknob. These were called black lace weavers.

"But—have I gone over the stink bug situation?" Sabine had asked weeks ago.

"No," Greta had said.

Sabine removed her glasses. "The stink bugs are out in the field right now, eating all the apple trees, but when the temperature drops, they come inside."

"Where?"

"You'll see," she said. Their favorite place was the Vermeer Room, as Sabine called the antechamber. "I mean, not all of them will be in there. But . . . many."

"Like how many?" Greta asked.

"I mean, not a *million*, but maybe five hundred thousand? Something like that."

"Half a million bugs are coming into the house?" Greta said. "This house?"

"Just to hibernate," Sabine said. "They hide in the closets, mostly, but occasionally you'll find one on your toothbrush or whatever, and you just shake it off, no big deal. Oh, and make sure you shake out your shoes before you put them on, and your coat and so on. They like to hide in sleeves."

But Greta didn't feel watched by stink bugs. They were flying thumbtacks, basically, and she wasn't crazy. More likely it was just the gap under the door, which was too short for its frame. There was a three-inch clearance between the bottom of the door and the floor, a gap that made her feel exposed, though she loved the door itself— primitive, board and batten, painted pale pink.

Moving forward, it might be necessary to cover the gap with a towel. Or a heavy blanket, like old times. Her childhood bedroom had been its own antechamber, but she'd been hiding from a different kind of weather: her mother's gloom, so clingy, oppressive, and noxious it could seep into the tiniest crack. Greta had layered the walls with tapestries, the windows with velvet curtains. The gap under the door she'd covered with a heavy blanket. Only then could she relax and be herself. When forced to emerge from her room, she sometimes covered her mouth when her mother spoke to her, or pinched her nostrils. She didn't like having her skin exposed, or the top of her head, or even her eyeballs, and so she'd worn a hat or hood indoors, even though they lived in Los Angeles. Sunglasses, too, but only at the breakfast table, never at dinner, lest she be accused of drug abuse or insolence. When she was twelve, she asked for a mini-fridge for Christmas. (She didn't get one.) She asked for a microwave, too. (No dice.) What she wanted, basically, was a studio apartment. By then she was pissing in empty orange juice cartons to avoid running into her mother in the hallway, cartons she hid in her closet and carefully dumped out the window at night.

6

G reta listened to the new session without transcribing it, as if it were a podcast or radio interview. Big Swiss's voice tumbled out of the speakers and steadied Greta's nerves as she repaired the windows with Gorilla Tape. The day was warm and bright. Greta felt optimistic for no reason. Perhaps the winter would be mild. Perhaps the windows, which were original to the house, i.e., over two hundred and eighty years old, would keep the weather out. It was a miracle they still opened and closed. The actual panes, made of pioneer glass as potent as Big Swiss's personality, had not shattered or even cracked when they'd fallen, but the timber that held the panes was rotting. Tape, tape, and more tape, that's all. Greta used an entire roll. Since the tape was silver, the windows looked boss in the way that orthodontic braces could sometimes look boss on the right person—

Greta smelled smoke and looked over her shoulder. There stood Sabine, wearing a Victorian nightgown with coffee stains on the chest. Her hair, usually in a loose bun, was tangled around her shoulders.

"Do people say 'boss' anymore?" Greta asked. "You know, as a synonym for 'cool.'"

"Is this NPR?" Sabine asked.

"No," Greta said.

"Whose voice is this?"

"Uh," Greta said. "I don't think you know her."

"Is she serious?"

"As a heart attack," Greta said.

Sabine blew smoke toward the ceiling. Greta was ready to drop everything and unplug the speakers. Luckily, the session abruptly ended.

"Actually, her voice reminds me of . . . metal," Sabine said. "Liquid metal."

"She's Swiss," Greta explained. "Listen, I slept in the antechamber last night, and I may just sleep in there every night, but do you have a chamber pot of some sort?"

"Of course," Sabine said breezily, as if Greta had asked for an extra blanket. "In fact, there's one right there." She pointed at the book-less bookcase, which for some reason always made Greta think of the Headless Horseman. On one shelf sat a broken antique scale. On another, a giant ceramic teacup.

"I can pee in that cup?" Greta asked. "It looks expensive."

"It might be," Sabine said. "It's a legit chamber pot from the nineteenth century."

Sabine supervised Greta's tape work without comment, flicking her cigarette out of the space for the missing pane Greta was aiming to repair.

"We have new neighbors," Sabine said. "South Americans. Come have a look."

"Wait," Greta said. "I'm almost done. Hold this."

Sabine held the final pane in place while Greta applied the tape. Although the tape was very sticky and advertised as all-weather, it had trouble adhering to the wood, which was coated in dirt and chipped paint.

"Like trying to tape a twig to a tree," Greta said. "Or an arm to a dead person . . . covered in sand."

"Jesus. This glass is *very* distorted," Sabine said. "I've never noticed that."

"I feel drunk whenever I look out the window."

"You'll feel drunk when you see who moved in next door."

Greta followed Sabine to the front of the house. They stepped into the yard. Sabine pointed at the empty lot across the road. All Greta saw was a pine grove. No South Americans.

"Look up," Sabine directed. "In that tree."

The tallest pine had been taken over by big black birds. Three or four were perched on every bough, but the tree was huge. Greta lost count at nineteen.

"Thirty-nine," Sabine said. "I counted this morning."

"What the fuck are they?" Greta said. "And why are there so many?"

"Vultures," Sabine said. "Black vultures from South America. They're roosting in these pines here."

"Why?"

"They're confused," Sabine said. "They've been in that same tree for days. I keep waiting for them to move on, but it looks like they're here to stay." She handed Greta a pair of binoculars. "Check out their horrible heads."

A dozen of them stood stock-still, their creepy wings spread wide like capes. They looked like miniature Draculas. Their heads were indeed horrible—featherless, wrinkled as ancient testicles.

"Jesus," Greta said. "What are they doing with their wings?"

"Sunbathing," Sabine said. "They hold their wings out like that to catch a ray. To regulate their body temperature, they shit on their own feet. I read all about them online. A group of vultures is called a committee, which is kind of cute."

"Is this committee stalking Piñon?" Greta asked. "Will they gang up on him and eat him?"

"They only eat carrion," Sabine said.

"I bet they're waiting for Walter to get nailed by a truck. He crosses the road constantly, and he never looks both ways."

"Well, yesterday I saw them feasting on a baby—"

The fire alarm went off next door. The vultures seemed totally unfazed, but Sabine stopped talking and resorted to mime, as usual. She mimed driving and then eating a sandwich and pointed at Greta. Greta shook her head and mimed typing and blowing her brains out. They went inside. The siren subsided as Greta slipped on her headphones.

OM: Can you state your initials for the transcriber, please?

FEW: FEW.

OM: How you feeling today?

FEW: Slightly nervous. This afternoon I'm assisting another doctor in removing endometriosis from a patient's uterus, even though there's a seven-inch tumor attached to her bowel. The tumor is killing her. She will likely die in six months, maybe less. Ordinarily we wouldn't perform this surgery, but she's been bleeding for over a month—

OM: Endometriosis. Remind me what that is again.

FEW: What?

OM: Endometriosis.

FEW: You're a sex therapist and you don't know what that is?

OM: Well, it's not an STD. [PAUSE] Correct?

FEW: Pathetic.

OM: I'm not the gynecologist—you are.

FEW: Many of your female clients find intercourse physically painful. True or false?

OM: Um, I wouldn't say many.

FEW: More than one?

OM: Perhaps.

FEW: And you're probably suggesting that they're not in touch with their bodies, or that that they should try . . . *chanting*.

"Big Swiss, Big Swiss, Big Swiss," Greta chanted.

OM: Are you upset about the kundalini we practiced last time?

FEW: I'm dismayed that you don't know what endometriosis is. Do you know what a uterus even looks like?

OM: Heart shaped, with horns?

"Cock shaped, with balls?" Greta said.

FEW: By "horns" you mean fallopian tubes?

OM: Yeah, those.

FEW: Oddly enough, some women do have heart-shaped uteri, also known as bicornate, which is a congenital anomaly and often a precursor for endometriosis. If endometriosis affected straight men and their penises—never mind. You'd never hear the end of it. I imagine you have male clients who complain of women not being "enthusiastic" enough in bed. Well, chances are the women are in terrible pain. Or just average pain. Most women don't say anything, though, because we're conditioned to suffer, and to make men feel good about themselves.

OM: In bed.

FEW: Pardon?

OM: In bed. I was finishing the sentence for you.

FEW: Don't do that.

OM: Is sex painful for you?

FEW: Only on a psychic level.

OM: When was the last time you had sex?

FEW: A few days ago.

OM: With Luke?

FEW: Yes, Om, with Luke.

OM: It was an innocent question, believe it or not.

FEW: I've never cheated on my husband and don't plan to.

OM: How would you feel about taking me through your experience?

FEW: Do you only want to hear about the sex, or the whole evening?

"Every detail," Greta said.

OM: Whatever you like.

FEW: It was last Saturday. He'd gone on a long hike, alone. He does most things alone or with the dog. He came home and zoned out in the living room. I wanted to go out for a drink, but he wanted to stay in and watch his weird videos. So, I made plans without him. I got dressed up—

OM: What weird videos?

FEW: [PAUSE] He doesn't play video games, but he likes to watch videos of other people playing video games, sometimes for hours.

OM: I'm not following.

FEW: He's obsessed with this video game about an office worker. The office worker wakes up at his desk and discovers that human civilization has ended and the world has been taken over by rabid animals. His new job is to walk through this office park and kill the animals, which are like monsters, really, with machetes. The graphics are very sophisticated and realistic. But he doesn't play the game. He watches professional players who record themselves—who are paid to play, in fact—and they release their videos. His favorite player is some nerd from England. He can't see the player sitting in front of his computer—he's in the game, playing along with him. Except he's not actually playing. He doesn't even own the game.

OM: But why doesn't he buy the game and play it himself?

FEW: Because he's passive.

OM: So, it's sort of like watching sports. Football or whatever.

FEW: Not quite.

"Way off," Greta said.

FEW: Sports are on television. Lots of people watch sports. I don't think lots of people watch these videos. Or maybe they do—I don't know. I don't tell many people about this. I only put up with it because he works sixty hours a week. He's a water engineer.

OM: What else do you put up with?

FEW: His need to drink milk with dinner. His penis. His flat, wide cow tongue. His clicking jaw. His collection of cutlery—

OM: Back up—what was the first thing?

FEW: Milk with dinner. Every single night for as long as I've known him. I don't know why he can't drink beer like an adult. Or wine. Or water.

OM: I meant the second thing.

FEW: Right.

OM: His penis.

FEW: Yeah, I remember.

OM: Were you referring to his actual penis?

FEW: As opposed to what?

OM: His sexual behavior, or his libido.

FEW: [PAUSE] His penis is two different colors.

OM: What colors?

FEW: Dark brown and white.

OM: I see. This is a problem?

FEW: For whatever reason, I wish it were either all brown or all
     white, not both. It's like a saddle shoe.

OM: You're familiar with the term "body shaming"?

FEW: Sorry. It's like a beautiful, well-oiled saddle shoe.

OM: Does he know how you feel?

FEW: It's not a big deal. I shouldn't have mentioned it. Can we talk
     about something else?

OM: [PAUSE] What about milk with cookies—acceptable, or no?

FEW: Om, I thought this was a "safe space" for my "journey."

OM: It is! I'm not judging you, believe me. I'm only trying to
     understand.

FEW: I'm not here to talk about milk. Or penises. [PAUSE] Do you
     mind if we try an experiment?

OM: Absolutely. I love experiments.

FEW: I talk, you listen.

OM: I'm listening.

FEW: No—I talk, you don't talk.

"Fuck yes," Greta said.

FEW: Can you manage it?

OM: Quick question: you said he collects cutlery. Like, silverware?

FEW: [LONG PAUSE] Shivs.

OM: Shivs?

FEW: He collects shivs confiscated from prisoners. He buys them at an antique shop in Hudson. They're surprisingly expensive.

OM: [PAUSE] Where does he keep them?

FEW: In his pockets.

OM: Really?

FEW: Of course not! Can we start the experiment now?

OM: We can try, but—you know, this isn't psychoanalysis. I mean, that's not how this works. What I'd like to help you discover— or *re*cover, rather—is a sexual narrative that you gravitate toward. It doesn't have to be pornographic. In fact, it might be primitive or antiquated. It might be more on the sensual or romantic side. A love scene from a classic film, maybe, or a passage from a novel—

FEW: Are you saying this because I'm a woman?

"Yes," Greta said.

OM: No.

FEW: You've suggested this to men? About novels?

"Never," Greta said.

OM: Of course. I have several male clients whose sexual stories come from books.

"Liar," Greta said.

FEW: Like what?

OM: Well, like *The Fermata*, by Nicholson Baker.

Greta laughed. It was *she* who'd mentioned this novel to Om because, for better or worse, its sexual story spoke to her. Like Greta, the narrator of *The Fermata* was a transcriptionist. Unlike Greta, he had the power to stop time, during which he treated the women around him like dolls. He undressed them, posed them, groped and fondled them, and then he put their clothes back on, restarted time, and no one was the wiser. Well, except him, obviously.

FEW: I don't know what my sexual story is.

 OM: I can tell you mine—

FEW: Please don't.

 OM: It's very short.

FEW: I don't want to hear it.

 OM: Fair enough. Let's go back to your story about last Saturday.

FEW: Fine. I went out for drinks with a friend. We sat in a booth. Two men at the bar bought us a round. My friend waved them over. We chatted with them for a few minutes. I wasn't attracted to either of them, but I flirted a little. When I got home, I initiated sex, which I only do when I've had exactly two point seven glasses of wine, no more, no less.

 OM: How did you initiate?

FEW: I got comfortable on the couch, complained about my period a little, and acted sleepy.

 OM: That's your move?

FEW: He's more attracted to me when I'm drowsy.

 OM: But not unconscious.

FEW: Just tired. And menstruating.

 OM: What does he like about period sex?

FEW: The smell. The way it looks. He seems to want the bedroom to resemble a crime scene. He wants to see blood on the sheets, on his hands. Sometimes he smears it on his chest, or my chest, or he puts his hand around my throat, you know, just before—

 OM: He chokes you.

FEW: Sort of.

 OM: Does he know about your . . . assault?

FEW: It's not violent. He's otherwise very gentle. He lets people walk all over him. It's hard to explain, but his roughness feels like a healthy impulse.

 OM: How's the foreplay?

FEW: Annoying.

OM: Because it's not long enough?

FEW: He's too earnest.

OM: I would think his flat, wide cow tongue might be useful, hint, hint.

FEW: Don't be disgusting.

OM: Do you fake orgasms?

FEW: How can I fake something I've never experienced?

OM: It's called acting? Lots of women—

FEW: It would never occur to me.

OM: How would you describe your sex life to friends?

FEW: Like driving home from work and not remembering the ride.

OM: So, forgettable.

FEW: Yes, but not unpleasant. When the sex is acrobatic, as it sometimes is, I'm observing us from outside the window.

OM: What do you see?

FEW: An attractive couple who looks like they know what they're doing. We look like professionals.

OM: Porn stars.

FEW: I guess.

OM: Do you watch porn?

FEW: No.

OM: Are you anti-porn?

FEW: No.

OM: Does Luke watch porn?

FEW: Probably.

OM: So, you have what sounds like . . . display sex. When you see yourself from outside, are you aroused by what you see?

FEW: My vanity is aroused. I become critical of my body, not always in a bad way.

OM: Does Luke compliment you often?

FEW: I don't respond well to verbal compliments. They seem phony to me.

OM: No verbal compliments. Noted. What about written ones?

FEW: I like letters.

OM: Do you use sex toys?

FEW: No.

OM: Have you ever owned a vibrator?

FEW: No.

OM: Would you be willing to try masturbating with a vibrator?

FEW: I suppose. Not the rabbit, though. A friend of mine has that one, and I don't know, something about the ears.

OM: May I suggest the Magic Wand, which I'm sure you've heard about?

FEW: It looks like a club.

OM: Correct.

FEW: I'll order one online, I guess.

OM: Would you consider ending our session with a breathing exercise?

FEW: I don't think so.

[END OF RECORDING]

Piñon was staring at Greta from under the desk, as he often did while she was working, imploring her to lock eyes with him. In addition to exercise, he enjoyed a lot of sustained and intense eye contact. She let him out of the house and into the yard. He walked directly to the car and took a long piss on the back tire, his way of saying it was a nice day for a drive.

They drove to the unofficial dog park, an open meadow surrounded by woods. People showed up early mornings and late afternoons, but Greta preferred the middle of the day, when the meadow was mostly empty, because Piñon was a loose cannon. His only true interest lay in killing rodents, but anything with four legs was fair game. Not that he was a bully—he was just an alpha born in the wrong body. He had what Greta called trans-breed dysmorphia of the soul and believed himself to be a young wolf trapped in the body of a terrier with worn-down teeth. If a wolf appeared on a television or computer monitor, Piñon dropped whatever he was doing and lovingly licked the screen up, down, and sideways until the wolf disappeared.

Otherwise, he was mellow for a Jack Russell. He'd been unneutered when she'd adopted him and still searched for his balls, which had been comically large, upon waking every morning. He'd mated with multiple bitches back in the day and sired over a dozen pups. He had a definite type: French bulldogs, or anything with hips and a short neck, but was open to all breeds except shepherds and shar-peis. He'd vacationed abroad. His beverage of choice was iced black coffee. Greta thought of him as debonair, a word that meant more to her than simply charming and confident, and applied more to dogs than to men. Piñon took pleasure in most things but wasn't overly attached or committed to any one thing, not even Greta, not even living.

But Greta would never have said any of this shit out loud, not like this corny fool with the pit bull. The guy, late twenties, was all bundled up in a hat, scarf, coat, gloves, and cropped pants, no socks. His bony ankles were fully exposed. The effect was jarring and vaguely obscene. Sort of like the pit bull's long, ruined nipples. The pit had clearly given birth as a puppy, probably more than once. The guy had found her in Mexico, starving in the streets, and said she'd probably have been pregnant again if he hadn't kidnapped her and brought her to New York.

He was blathering to a woman Greta called GILF, because she could never remember her proper name, and because she was attractive, single, and over sixty. Many women in Hudson fit this description, and they all owned small white dogs. GILF's face had been lifted, her cheeks and lips filled, and she had the body of a ballerina. Only her tits had fallen, though not far enough to discourage crop tops, which she wore with high-waisted jeans. Her white hair had tasteful pink and lavender streaks, and her dog's fur had been carefully dyed to match. Sadly, she was known for her grandson fetish. Greta suspected she was there to seduce this clown with ankle cleavage.

"Who knows what her name was before, or if she even had a name, but I call her Jelly Roll because there's something spongy about her," the guy was telling GILF. "And she loves whipped cream."

"She's lucky to have you, hon," GILF said.

"In Mexico, she belonged to no one and everyone. She followed me around this dirty little village for a whole month, growling at any dog that came near me. She was extremely protective of me from the start."

Possessive, *estupido*, Greta wanted to say. You represented food. You were a greasy pork chop to her, and nothing more.

"Now she sleeps on a memory-foam bed," the guy said. "She drinks filtered water. She doesn't have to eat rotting garbage."

"She hit the jackpot," GILF said.

Jelly Roll seemed to want nothing to do with Gringo. She ignored him completely and became fixated on Piñon, who was running around the meadow in zigzags, hunting for ground-dwelling quarry. Jelly Roll chased after Piñon, literally breathing down his neck whenever he stopped moving.

"She wants to play with that dog so bad," Gringo said. "Look at the way she's throwing herself at him."

"Don't act so desperate, girl!" GILF called out.

Jelly Roll was desperate, all right, but only to assert dominance. Piñon was too busy to notice or care, and Greta wasn't worried. As part of his wolf identity, Piñon respected alphas of the opposite sex.

But then Piñon bared his teeth at Jelly Roll, his one psycho move. It made him look deranged, especially when he did it to puppies and children. His canines were looking a little brown from where Greta stood, as if he smoked cigars after dinner every night. She doubted they were having the desired effect. He waited a minute and then bared his teeth again, a little longer this time, but it seemed to only encourage Jelly Roll, as if she thought he was grinning at her. She tried mounting him from the rear. When that failed, she tried humping his head—a mistake. They faced off, lunging and snarling, and then quickly transformed into a roving dog tornado. It was hard to tell who was winning or how bad it was. Luckily, it was over in ten seconds.

Or was it? They'd stopped moving, but Jelly Roll was on top of Piñon, pinning him to the ground with her humongous face. Piñon kicked his legs frantically, trying to get out of the hold, but she had him firmly by the neck.

"Grab your dog," Greta said to Gringo.

"Give it a minute," he said. "They'll work it out."

"No," Greta said. "They won't."

Piñon was wheezing. His eyes kept rolling around, looking for Greta.

"Grab your dog," Greta repeated.

Gringo frowned. "Jelly!" he yelled. "Off! Off!"

Jelly didn't budge. Piñon's paws were twitching like they did when he was dreaming.

"Jelly, drop it!"

"Does she know English?" Greta asked.

Gringo gave her a haughty look, as if she'd said something racist. Jelly was making a disturbing guttural noise.

"Get your dog off my dog," Greta snapped. "Right now."

He whacked the top of Jelly's head with an open hand. "Jelly! Let go! Leave it!"

"Are you joking? Punch her in the nose. Hurry the fuck up."

"She's not a shark," Gringo said, exasperated.

"You want me to do it?" Greta said. "He can't breathe."

A woman appeared, seemingly out of nowhere; grabbed Jelly by her hind legs; and lifted her completely off the ground. Greta had never seen anything like it. Piñon rolled to his feet and coughed. Then they all just stood there, staring at the woman, who continued holding Jelly upside down until Jelly stopped struggling and seemed to relax, which took about three seconds, and then the woman very gingerly placed Jelly's back feet on the ground and gave her a pat on the ass.

"Sit," the woman said.

Jelly sat. The woman removed a treat from her pocket and showed it to Jelly, who immediately lunged for it.

"Wait," the woman said sharply.

Jelly waited, staring directly into the woman's eyes, as if she'd known this woman all her life and was tuned into her every wish. When the woman finally tossed the treat, Jelly swallowed it without chewing and gazed at the woman adoringly.

"Jeez," GILF said. "I wish my dog looked at me that way."

"You guys rehearsed that, right?" Greta said. "You've been coming here for weeks, I bet, and practicing."

The woman shrugged and said nothing. She was long, lean, very pale, and reminded Greta of white asparagus. Except white asparagus is known for its delicate flavor, and there was nothing delicate about this woman. She had a casual, improvised look that had likely taken years to refine, and wore a loose wool dress, a men's hunting cap, and no makeup. On her feet, the exact pair of ankle boots Greta had been coveting for years: soft, slouchy, dark green leather, made in Germany, $600 plus shipping.

Gringo leashed Jelly Roll and reluctantly pulled her away from the woman. "I'm so sorry," he said to everyone. "I swear she's never done that before. She's been to obedience school and everything."

"It might be my dog's fault," Greta confessed. "He can be kind of a dick. He thinks he's a wolf."

"Maybe you should change his name to Dick Wolf," GILF said. "Or Executive Producer."

"Look," Greta said, and pointed. "He's running a victory lap even though he lost."

"What's his name?" Gringo asked.

"Piñon." Greta felt all the heat in her body transfer to her ears. This was pure pleasure at saying Piñon's name, even after all these years.

"He's Mexican, right?" Gringo asked.

"Not at all," Greta said.

Greta felt bad for Jelly Roll. She probably missed her old life, her village, her pups, her real name, which was probably Spanish like Piñon's and had nothing to do with raspberry jam, blues music, or pussy. She probably missed her freedom, too, and fighting, and fucking in the streets.

"You should check your dog's neck," Gringo advised. "Make sure he's all right."

Greta called Piñon, who approached them jauntily, as if he hadn't nearly died a few minutes ago. His breathing was slightly ragged. His neck was bright pink but the skin was unbroken.

"He's fine," Greta said.

"Where did you learn to do that?" Gringo asked White Asparagus. "You were like a loan shark dangling a degenerate gambler off a rooftop. My dog weighs sixty pounds. You must be incredibly strong."

"Yeah," Greta said. "Do you work out?"

"I grew up on a farm," the woman said.

Her eyes were some in-between color, sort of like a newborn's, and kept looking Greta up and down, seemingly in search of something. They landed on Greta's clogs, traveled up and down her legs, blinked twice at her crotch, skipped up to her face, dropped back to her thighs, face again, back and forth between her boobs, and then they left Greta's body entirely. Greta felt strangely abandoned. Rejected.

"I wouldn't recommend that maneuver unless it's an emergency," the woman said. "It could backfire pretty easily."

"Hoist with his own petard," GILF inexplicably said.

"Pardon?" the woman said.

"It's from *Hamlet*," explained GILF. "It means the bomb-maker is blown up by his own bomb. You know, like poetic justice."

"Right, well, if it had been two pit bulls, I wouldn't have done it," the woman said. "The other pit may have attacked me, or—" She turned to the guy. "What's your dog's name again?"

"Big Swiss," Greta blurted.

"Jelly Roll," the guy said, and gave Greta a perplexed look.

Greta felt feverish. Why hadn't she recognized the voice right away? She'd been too distracted by Big Swiss's staring problem. And her face! It was even more beautiful than Greta had initially imagined, before she convinced herself that it was disfigured, except her cheekbones were higher, her nose bonier, her brows darker, her hair longer, wispier, blonder, nearly platinum.

Of course, having listened to Big Swiss's voice for so many hours, Greta felt an immediate intimacy, in the same way her favorite podcast hosts sometimes felt like friends, insofar as she'd gone through divorces with podcasters, the death of parents and beloved pets, and so she couldn't help but feel a little starstruck. Here was Big Swiss, in the flesh! Talking to Greta, a nobody!

"Where's your dog?" Gringo asked. "Or are you here alone?"

"He's wandering those woods over there," Big Swiss said. "He's not really into wide-open spaces. I don't know why I brought him here."

"Dog parks are for people," Greta blurted. "Not dogs."

They all looked at Greta, waiting for her to elaborate. Greta shrugged. Thankfully, GILF's phone rang and she stepped away to answer it, and then Big Swiss began walking toward the woods. Greta resisted the urge to follow her.

"Si!" Big Swiss suddenly yelled at the trees. "Si!"

Gringo made a big show of looking at his vintage pocket watch. "Well, I'm off to work," he said, and took one last long look at Big Swiss. "You ladies should come sit at my bar this weekend. I'll buy you a drink."

By "ladies" he meant Big Swiss, obviously. Greta suspected he tended bar at one of the newer places in town, that he'd moved to Hudson specifically for this job, that the job required a uniform, that waistcoats, suspenders, or vests were part of that uniform, that he made a lot of rye old fashioneds for douchebags visiting from Brooklyn and loved every minute of it.

"Which bar?" Greta asked.

"Farmacy," he said.

Greta nodded. "Right."

"Hope to see you," he said over his shoulder.

Now Big Swiss was circling back toward Greta. Tiptoeing behind her was what looked like a wolf-coyote hybrid. A coy-wolf. A woyote. Sleek, silver, the most beautiful dog Greta had ever seen. She suspected Big Swiss had chosen the dog not for his personality but because he was as stunning as she was.

"Are you two together?" Big Swiss murmured, nodding at GILF.

Greta shook her head. GILF was arguing with someone on the phone. Her dog had not only pink and lavender in its fur, Greta noticed now, but several additional pastels. Dusty peach, honeydew, baby blue.

"Looks like the Easter Bunny paid them a visit," Big Swiss said.

"And jizzed all over their hair."

First thought, best thought, Sabine often said. This wasn't true of Greta.

"Did you just say what I think you said?" Big Swiss asked.

"Yeah," Greta said, and tried to smile.

A wedge of Canadian geese passed overhead, honking.

"Your dog reminds me of the Big Bad Wolf," Greta said. "Is he mean?"

"Not really. He has Akita in him," Big Swiss said. "And a little chow." She took the dog's big head in her pale hands and pried open his mouth, which he didn't seem to mind. "His gums are purple and his tongue has black spots," Big Swiss said, looking directly at Greta.

More arresting were his teeth, which were blindingly white and needle sharp.

"Are those implants?" Greta asked.

Big Swiss let go of the dog's face. "Do I know you from somewhere?"

"You grew up on a farm. In Switzerland?"

"Yeah. Are you Swiss?"

"Me? No." Greta swallowed. "I'm from out west."

Stop acting psychic, asshole. Are you trying to lose your job?

"What's your name?" Big Swiss asked.

Fuck, what's my name? Rebecca.

"Regreta," Greta said. "I mean *Rebecca*."

"Flavia," Big Swiss said, and held out her hand.

Greta had always figured the F stood for Famke, Faye, Freyja. What the hell was *Flavia*? It sounded like the name of a condiment. A dry, savory seasoning you added to broth. An acquired taste, perhaps. Addictive, probably bad for you. Her middle name began with E. Her last name, W. Could Greta really ask for her full name? They'd "just met," but she wanted to be certain Flavia was in fact Big Swiss.

"I've never met anyone named Flavia," Greta said. "What's your middle name, if you don't mind—"

"Eloise," Big Swiss said quickly.

Eloise seemed like a name for someone with warm hands. Big

Swiss's were ice-cold. She wore her wedding ring, a no-frills platinum band, on the wrong finger.

"How did you know I'm Swiss?"

"Just a guess," Greta said. "You seem very European. But classy, not trashy. Your boots were handmade in Germany, right? I've wanted a pair for years."

"You didn't think I was German?"

"Please," Greta said, as if she knew hundreds of Germans personally.

Big Swiss looked toward the trees. Piñon was on the other side of the meadow, nose buried in a hole, ass in the air. He lifted his head suddenly and looked in their direction. Greta watched him notice Silas. Now he raced toward them at top speed.

"Here comes trouble," Greta said nervously.

Silas was submissive, Greta hoped. He seemed calm, but as Piñon got closer, Silas let out a high-pitched shriek.

"My dog doesn't bark," Big Swiss said. "He screams."

The scream startled Piñon, who slowed to a trot. He approached Silas cautiously and examined him from every angle.

"He thinks he's looking in the mirror," said Greta. "He has body dysmorphia."

Piñon clutched Silas's front leg and humped it vigorously. Silas permitted this while gazing at the horizon like a gentleman. Piñon closed his eyes, rested his head against Silas's narrow shoulder, and continued thrusting.

"Well," Big Swiss said.

"He's a leg man," Greta explained.

"Most dogs are afraid of Silas."

"I wish Piñon had a little more fear," Greta said. "Thanks, by the way, for saving his life. What made you pick up a pit bull like a wheelbarrow? I never would've thought of that."

"It was automatic," Big Swiss said. "Your dog was being strangled. A switch gets flipped in me whenever I see someone being overpowered like that. Especially if they're defenseless, you know?"

Oh, I know, honey. I know every goddamn detail.

"Do you work with dogs?" Greta asked. "Like, professionally?"

Big Swiss shook her head. "Not dogs. Pussies."

"Cats?"

"I'm a gynecologist," Big Swiss said, and smiled.

Big Swiss scanned Greta's face without blinking.

"You don't seem surprised," Big Swiss said. "Most people don't believe me."

"That's because they're used to hearing something like, 'I farm sugar beets, and then I make fancy beet juice with my feet, and then I bottle the juice and sell it at the farmer's market for forty dollars an ounce,'" Greta said. "But I figured you were someone with a serious job."

"Well, I'm just finishing my residency."

A minute or so of silence passed.

"You must get this a lot," Greta finally said, "but would you mind taking a quick look at this thing on my labia?"

First thought, worst thought, maybe keep your fucking mouth shut?

"It's most likely a skin tag," Big Swiss said after a moment. "They're very common. If it bothers you, or interferes with your sex life, I can freeze it off with liquid nitrogen, after I make certain it's not genital warts."

"I was kidding," Greta said.

"What do you do?"

"I'm a transcriber. A glorified typist, basically. It's not a real job. I work from home and don't get out much."

"What do you transcribe?"

"Interviews," Greta said. "For journalists. From the city."

She wondered if Big Swiss had gotten her hands on a Magic Wand, the huge, unwieldy vibrator Om recommended to anyone with a vulva, young or old. It was like recommending a cudgel, and, in Greta's opinion, not all clits wanted to be beaten to death. Although, Greta's did. She'd been jackhammering away for over a decade, but only after many years of manual labor. It seemed like the wrong tool entirely for Big Swiss, who acted all hard but probably craved subtlety and nuance.

GILF was off the phone and looked lost. She eyed Silas warily and picked up her dog.

"Did my grandson leave?" GILF asked.

"A few minutes ago," Big Swiss said.

"Damn," GILF said, and hurried to her car.

Her grandson. Her real grandson.

"Her grandson invited us for a drink this weekend," Greta said, and immediately regretted it. "I mean—he offered to buy us a drink at his bar."

"Where?" Big Swiss said.

"Farmacy," Greta said.

"I've been there with my husband," Big Swiss said. "We should go."

Tell her you don't drink, Greta ordered herself. "You free tomorrow?" Greta said instead.

Big Swiss nodded.

"I have work 'til eight," Greta said. Or, rather, I'll be transcribing your next therapy session. "How's eight thirty?"

She felt guilty as she watched Big Swiss create a new contact on her phone.

"R-E-B-E-C-C-A?" Big Swiss asked.

"R-E-B-E-K-A-H," Greta said, just to make things more complicated.

7

The following afternoon, Big Swiss's file landed in Greta's inbox, along with a vague and confusing explanation about why the session had been cut short—or "truncated," as Om said. He claimed he'd felt the need to stop recording when Big Swiss began revealing personal information about Keith, her attacker, such as the exact date and time of his release and where he would be living. Apparently, the thought of Greta's being privy to such information made Om anxious, which of course didn't make logical sense. Wouldn't it be better for Greta to know a violent criminal's exact address, so that she might avoid it?

OM: Will you state your initials for the transcriber, please?
FEW: FEW.
OM: Thank you.
FEW: Who's the transcriber—you?
OM: What? No. It's a robot.
FEW: Really?
OM: I mean, not *literally*, but . . . it's automated. I use software.
FEW: Is it accurate?
OM: More or less.
FEW: Well, I met a transcriber at the dog park today. Her name is Rebekah, with a K and an H.

"Fuck me," Greta said.

OM: How strange. Are you sure she was . . . human?
FEW: Oh yeah. She was around fifty. Attractive. Gay.

"What?" Greta said.

OM: Are you blushing?
FEW: Maybe.
OM: Did she flirt with you?
FEW: Yes. Even after I said I was married.

"I did?" Greta said.

OM: What sort of transcribing does she do?
FEW: She works with journalists. Her clients are in the city.
OM: Did she, uh, make a pass at you?
FEW: Well, no. But she made a joke about Easter Bunny semen.
OM: What joke?
FEW: It won't be funny now.

"It wasn't funny then," Greta said.

FEW: But it was interesting, because as soon as she said it, I found
myself wanting to tell her . . . well, everything. I'm usually
guarded when I meet new people, but it felt like we already
knew each other. She's one of these intuitive types—
OM: Are you an intuitive type?
FEW: Not at all. I'm a thinker, not a feeler.

"Hey, I'm not a feeler, either," Greta said. "Or a thinker."

FEW: Anyway, she intuited a few things.
OM: Such as?

"Nothing," Greta said.

> FEW: Well, I'm certain she knew that I'd experienced the first orgasm of my life that morning.

"Nope," Greta said. "But congrats."

> OM: What! Where!
>
> FEW: At home—where else? I took your recommendation and made a certain . . . purchase, and it came in the mail yesterday.
>
> OM: My goodness, I wish I had some champagne to offer you. I only have gin, and no ice, but I do have tonic—
>
> FEW: Settle down, it wasn't that great.
>
> OM: No?
>
> FEW: I feel like I'm finally in on the joke now, but the joke wasn't as funny as I thought it would be, or it's, like, not my brand of humor.
>
> OM: What kind of humor were you hoping for?
>
> FEW: Something more droll. Or absurd. This was a little too . . . obvious, I guess. And I wasn't crazy about the gadget, to be honest. Felt like I was being electrocuted.

"Hah," Greta said. "Called it."

> OM: Okay. A little too intense, maybe. That might change over time, or you may want to try not putting it directly on your clitoris. If you want, I can demonstrate—
>
> FEW: I'll figure it out, Om.
>
> OM: Were you alone?
>
> FEW: My husband wanted to be there, but I made him wait in the other room. So, I was alone in bed.
>
> OM: Did you fantasize?
>
> FEW: I looked at pictures.
>
> OM: Of your husband?

"C'mon," Greta said.

FEW: Would you ask a man that question?
OM: Of course.
FEW: You'd ask a man if he masturbated to pictures of his wife?

"Not a chance," Greta said.

OM: If he was masturbating for the very first time and happened to be married? Yes.
FEW: My husband wasn't in the pictures.
OM: Were there faces in the pictures, or just bodies? Or were they just faces and no bodies? And were they strangers or did you know them?
FEW: There weren't any people.
OM: Oh. Well, what were they pictures of—animals? Or . . . landscapes?

"Animals? Honest to god," Greta said.

FEW: No, no, nothing like that. Don't overanalyze this, or force any symbolism onto it, but I looked at pictures of flowers.

Greta laughed. "Who's gay now?"

OM: Flower porn. From Japan?
FEW: Not porn, Om, just regular pictures. Are you familiar with jimsonweed?
OM: Is that a singer?
FEW: It's a *plant*. It's growing in my yard, and it often shows up in my dreams. It's also called datura.
OM: Ah, right. I smoked a little of that once. Not a great experience for me. Anyway, your husband must be very excited. Did you celebrate?

FEW: It was the happiest day of his life. Happier than our wedding night. We had breakfast in bed, and he wanted to sniff the gadget, so I let him, and we laughed and cuddled with the dog, blah, blah, and then my phone rang. I was on call, so I thought it was a patient, but it was the New York State Inmate Release Notification System, a service I signed up for seven years ago. I'd registered to be notified of any changes in his custody. He was transferred to another prison at one point, so I knew about that, but they were calling—I mean, I knew he was getting out—I've known that for months—but they gave me the precise time— midnight, isn't that weird?—and I asked if they could send me a recent photo, because I imagine he looks different after eight years, but they said no, they couldn't do that, but they gave me his address—like, his physical address—and that was the surprising part, I guess, because it turns out he'll be living right off 9G, not far from [OVERLAPPING]

[END OF RECORDING]

Jesus! Not far from . . . Greta's house? Maybe they were about to be neighbors, and that's why Om was being so cagey. The only property she could imagine Keith inhabiting seemed to board dogs, along with white supremacists fresh out of prison like himself. There were about a dozen chain-link dog kennels in the yard. The house looked like it had been built in an afternoon, and six or eight men with shaved heads always stood on the porch, smoking. Whenever Greta drove by, the men glowered at her, and her butthole clenched as if she were driving over a high bridge. It seemed she wasn't the only one—the stretch of road in front of the house was covered in loopy skid marks and tire smears, as if the place were cursed and driving past it made you lose control of your vehicle.

Greta's bigger concern, of course, was "Rebekah." How on earth had Om neglected to ask about *her*? He'd been too distracted by Big Swiss's orgasm, obviously, or maybe the whole thing had gone over his head. Problem was, "Rebekah" was having drinks with Big Swiss in less than two hours, and what if they ran into Om?

A mature adult would simply call Om, describe the weird run-in with Big Swiss, along with the subsequent, totally understandable panic at having to introduce herself—never mind, that seemed childish. The thing to do was to roll the dice, meet Big Swiss as planned, have a drink—just one—and then never see her again.

First, Greta climbed into bed and attempted to service herself to images of jimsonweed. Or datura, as it was also called. The flower was highly poisonous, had a dark history with shamans and teenagers. It was capable of killing both humans and livestock. Not even hummingbirds would fuck with it. The blossom itself was large, trumpet shaped, and pendulous. If Greta closed one eye, it might resemble a droopy boob, if she were also very drunk. She decided the flower would only be titillating to a child, say, or a moth. Or Mapplethorpe. Although, it lacked the velvety, asymmetrical, creamy white lips of the calla lily, as well as the schlong-like spadix.

Greta switched to more traditional material, as she did at the end of every workday, and sometimes during, as it was difficult to transcribe sex therapy without touching oneself, even if the sex being described wasn't sexy, and it very rarely was, and the therapist happened to be Om. She chose short videos that she could watch from beginning to end—purely out of respect, like those nerds who refuse to leave the movie theater until they've sat through the credits. If the video was longer than, say, twelve minutes, Greta kept scrolling.

"Knock knock," Sabine announced.

Greta closed the browser on her phone, grateful the volume had been muted. A verbal knocker, Sabine only knocked after she had already entered the room and lit a cigarette, even if Greta was attempting some other form of self-abuse, such as yoga.

Sabine opened Greta's woodstove, which she liked to use as an ashtray, and made a clucking noise. Fixing Greta's fire had become one of her favorite pastimes. She picked up the poker and expertly rearranged the burning logs.

"Are you sleeping?" Sabine asked.

"Wide awake," Greta said.

"Aren't you happy you bought that bedding?"

"Very," Greta said.

Just as one should purchase new underwear in a new relationship, Sabine encouraged new bedding in a new house, even if the house was an ancient, crumbling ruin. Greta's wrought iron bed frame was vintage and worth money, her mattress deep and plush, but her sheets had contained a small amount of polyester. Thirty percent, to be exact. As far as Sabine was concerned, Greta may as well have been sleeping on a stack of newspapers at a bus stop. She'd dragged Greta to the Pine Cone Hill outlet in Pittsfield, where Greta had splurged on a bright white linen duvet cover, matching white sheets and shams, and an ethereal bed skirt with multiple layers of sugar-white tulle. Now her bed resembled an expensive wedding cake, and not just to Greta, but to hundreds of thousands of tiny black ants. Thirty minutes after she'd slipped between the new sheets, a large army had poured out of a crack in the wall, fallen to the floor in clumps, fanned out, and climbed Greta's bedposts. They weren't even marching in a line. It was every ant for himself, and the army was big enough to blanket Greta's entire blanket, and Greta herself, and also Piñon, who couldn't stop sneezing and throwing himself against the door of the antechamber. He hated ants as much as Greta did. They'd spent the following few nights sleeping in the antechamber, even though the ants had only been passing through, evidently, and were gone by morning.

"I was planning to make spaghetti and meatballs for dinner," Sabine said. "But I'm over it."

"I may eat out tonight, anyway. I met this girl at the dog park yesterday, and we're having drinks."

"Drinks!" Sabine gasped. "Finally."

"Maybe I'll put on a skirt."

"What skirt?"

"The long denim one. With the buttons."

"Hold on." She flicked her cigarette into the fire and walked to the door. "Take off your clothes. I'll be right back."

Greta removed her sweatshirt and pajama bottoms. She could

hear Sabine in the closet upstairs, scampering around like a red squirrel, a family of which lived in the attic. Since the house had been uninhabited for an entire century, the squirrels had been wintering in the attic for at least fifty-nine generations, and so it seemed cruel to evict them. Unfortunately, they stayed up late, chattering and shooting marbles, it sounded like, and dragging heavy objects from one side of the attic to the other.

Sabine returned with an armful of garments, including a long, tattered dress that buttoned up the back.

"Don't judge until you put it on," Sabine said.

"My tits will never fit in this."

"Nonsense," Sabine said. "It'll fit you like a glove."

The dress was white and gauzy, with three-quarter sleeves, a built-in slip, and a lot of visual interest—ruffled layers, a raw hem, several dark, splotchy stains.

"Did you use this dress to check the oil?" Greta asked.

"No, it's blood," Sabine said. "Old blood."

"You were stabbed? In the thigh?"

"Not *my* blood. This guy I used to know—" She waved her hand. "Never mind. Turn around."

Greta turned and Sabine buttoned her in.

"I'm against the white," Greta said.

"Ivory," Sabine said, correcting her. "And you shouldn't be. It brings out the olive in your skin."

"Who wants greener skin?"

"Um, lots of people," Sabine said. "You've always dressed like a ghoul, but you need to lighten the fuck up. You live in the country now."

"This seems slightly . . . delicate." She meant shabby, threadbare, raglike.

"It's Japanese voile," Sabine said. "With visible French seams. The underlayer is soft muslin. See how it peeks out under the hem? It's very chic and, if I recall, quite expensive."

"And see-through."

"Well, you can't wear underwear, obviously."

"Can I wear a coat?"

"You don't wear a coat with this," Sabine said. "You wear a cape."

She handed Greta something made of boiled wool. Greta slipped it over her head. It was black, which was nice, and had pockets.

"Did you use this as an ashtray?"

Sabine peered at the fabric. "Fuck," she said. "The moths got to it. They've eaten half my wardrobe."

"It's better with holes. Less formal."

"You look good," Sabine said. "Too bad this isn't a date-date."

"I think she thinks I'm gay, though. Do I seem gay to you?"

"No," Sabine said, after too long a pause. "But you do have bags under your eyes and they're two different sizes. Wait here, I have something."

Above the mantel hung an enormous gilt-framed mirror filled with mysterious black and silver clouds. It made Greta's room feel like a belle-époque brothel, but sometimes Greta wished she could find her face in the thing. Oh, wait. There it was. She did in fact have bags under her eyes, and they were in fact two different sizes. One was a toiletry bag; the other, a weekender.

Sabine came back with two warm, damp tea bags. They were big, about four times the size of regular tea bags.

"I only had family size," Sabine said. "But rest these on your eyes. Models do this after long flights."

THANKFULLY, the lighting at Farmacy was forgiving. In fact, Greta had never seen so many vintage lightbulbs in one place. It was like being in Edison's laboratory. The bar was designed to resemble a nineteenth-century apothecary and was staffed with people who thought they were making vital medicine. Tinctures, bitters, shrubs, and cordials were house-made and kept in amber bottles with antique prescription labels; cocktails were constructed in glass beakers and stirred with foot-long silver spoons. Greta's drink, which she downed in two swallows, had been served in an Erlenmeyer flask. It dawned on her that the entire staff looked related, or like the extended family of Mennonite farmers, minus the straw hats and chin curtains.

Gringo didn't quite fit in, despite his collarless shirt and suspenders, partly because he shook cocktails like a crazy monkey.

"Where's our blond friend?" he asked.

"On her way," Greta assured him.

"Another drink?"

"I better wait," Greta said.

The place had filled up in fifteen minutes, and a large knot of people stood at the door, waiting for tables. Rather than remove the cape, Greta saved the stool next to her by draping her leg over it. Still, someone had the nerve to ask if the stool was taken—a rich, beautiful woman envied by the entire town. Or by Sabine, at least, which was how Greta knew the origin of her wealth (her father invented the pour cap for liquid laundry detergent), her real estate holdings (seven sought-after properties in Hudson proper), and her aesthetic (nonprecious Californian). The woman seemed aloof and unfriendly, and Sabine claimed she was dried up and dead inside, but she'd cried on Om's couch many times, so Greta knew that she was in fact wet (she suffered from restless genital syndrome) and alive (or, at any rate, hooked on methadone), and now here she was, standing less than two feet away, eyeballing Greta without really seeing her. Greta felt invisible but not insignificant. In fact, she felt omnipotent. "I know your greatest fears and desires," she imagined whispering to the woman, "along with many of your fuckups and vain regrets, and what do you know about me? Nothing, my dear, nothing at all."

Om possessed the same knowledge, of course, and way more money than Greta, but not the same power. If he were here and sitting next to her, he could be seen, heard, and spoken to by any number of his clients, and subsequently embraced or ignored, while Greta remained an anonymous, unfathomable mystery, whose name was *Rebekah*. Rebekah, she repeated. And Big Swiss is Flavia. Fla-vee-a. Flavia is a stranger to you, remember, so keep the knowing insights to a goddamn minimum.

At the door, the knot loosened and a figure emerged. Behold, Big

Swiss—*Flavia*—in a white cashmere sweater and silk trousers. She looked windblown but also elated and a little surprised, as if she'd arrived by parachute. She spotted Greta and began walking toward her. People did double and triple takes as she moved through the crowd, but her eyes remained fastened on Greta's face. Greta had been ogled plenty in life, but she'd never been looked at quite like this. She felt like the red balloon in the black-and-white movie: weightless, irresistible, elusive, and out of reach, floating high above all the bullshit and debris. Now that Big Swiss was standing right next to her, the feeling only intensified.

"Did you go tanning?" Big Swiss asked casually.

"Tea-bagging," Greta said, deflated.

"What?"

"I fell asleep with tea bags on my face," Greta said. "Big ones. The kind you use to make iced tea."

Big Swiss arranged herself on the stool with aplomb. Was it Greta's imagination, or did everyone at the bar suddenly sit up straighter?

"The house I live in," Greta went on. "I sleep in the closet sometimes, on an old bed filled with horsehair. Maybe I'm allergic? Although, I was born with bags under my eyes."

Why was she talking like a goober? Her habit of delivering information out of sequence only worsened with alcohol. Nevertheless, she flagged down Gringo and ordered a Sazerac. Big Swiss asked for white wine with a side of ice.

"I didn't catch your names," Gringo said, and held out a hairy hand. "I'm JD."

"Rebekah," Greta said too slowly, as if attempting Flemish.

"Flavia," Big Swiss said.

"This round is on me," he said. "Salut."

He played it cool and wandered away. Big Swiss plopped two cubes into her wine and took a dainty sip. The thing to do now, Greta decided, was to be as off-putting as possible so that Big Swiss never contacted her again.

"Nice sweater meat," Greta said.

"Thanks," Big Swiss said, oblivious.

"I can see your . . . pillow corners," Greta said. "If you know what I mean."

Who was this? A shitty nine-year-old?

"My what?"

"Your Freudian nips," Greta said.

Big Swiss's eyes widened. "Have you been here all afternoon?"

"I beg your pardon," Greta said, "but I've been here twenty minutes. I typed all day. I transcribed a very intense interview with an extremely famous person."

What was more off-putting than name-dropping? Nothing in the world. Her choices, as far as local celebrities: Daniel Day-Lewis, Jessica Lange, Claire Danes, Parker Posey—

"How's the pay?"

"Who?" Greta asked, confused.

"It must pay pretty well," Big Swiss said slowly.

"Oh," Greta said. "Yeah, no, not really. I'm, like, drowning in debt. But I've lived hand-to-mouth my entire life, so I'm used to it. I wouldn't know what to do with money except piss it away as quickly as possible."

A lifelong romance with poverty. Meow, kitty.

"Have you always been a transcriber?"

Greta shook her head. "I've been a pharm tech, waitress, data-entry clerk, barista, ice-cream scooper, pizza slinger."

"I've always wondered if people who work from home bother to get dressed," Big Swiss said.

"I work in my underwear," Greta admitted. "When it's warm enough. Otherwise, pajamas. The house I live in isn't insulated, so it's like camping. Except it's a beautiful house with indoor plumbing, so maybe it's more like glamping."

Glamping—gross. Camping—also not her thing, though she'd done her share with Stacy.

"Anyway, if you know anyone who transcribes interviews from home, chances are they spend most of the day furiously masturbating," Greta said.

Surely, an unsettling visual for someone like Big Swiss, who'd only masturbated once, and not very furiously. So why was Big Swiss smiling? She had not one but several spaces between her teeth. Although the spaces were narrow and uniform, as if placed there on purpose, they made Big Swiss seem mischievous and fun to be around.

"Personally, I'd have to put on a suit in the morning," Big Swiss said. "And shoes. Just to stay awake. Do you have an office?"

Jesus, these were boring questions. But she also seemed to be suggesting that Greta was the boring one, or, at the very least, fighting sleep in her skivvies all day.

"No, I work in my bedroom. My setup isn't very ergonomic. My wrists fucking kill. My hands throb in the middle of the night. Also, I sit on a stool, so I have a lot of back problems."

The luxury of self-pity. Greta wasn't sure how long she could keep grossing herself out, but Big Swiss seemed strangely enthralled.

"I also have a habit of transcribing every conversation I hear," Greta went on. "In my head, I mean."

Like a mental patient.

"Are you transcribing our conversation?" Big Swiss asked.

> G: I am now.
> BS: Must make it hard to be in the moment if you're, like, typing in your head the whole time.
> G: No, I'm taking it all in. Listen, I'm pretty sure JD has a thing for you. He keeps looking over here longingly, but, my god, he should wait until this song is over. Or maybe he selected this song on purpose? I bet he did.
> BS: What song?
> G: You can't hear it?
> BS: I don't know what it is.
> G: The Velvet Underground?

Big Swiss nodded vaguely.

> G: "Linger on your pale blue eyes," hint, hint.

Big Swiss shrugged.

BS: My eyes are gray.
 G: You know, now that I think of it, you remind me of Nico.
BS: I don't know him, either.
 G: Her!
BS: Are you going to make obscure references all night? Because I
    don't know much about American pop culture, and I don't care
    to know.
 G: She's German!
BS: Relax. Drink your drink. Take off your coat.
 G: It's a *cape*.

Greta removed the cape and hung it on a hook under the bar. The
Japanese voile, or whatever the fuck, clung to her back, which seemed
to be covered in sweat.

BS: Gretel.
 G: What?
BS: *Gretel*.

Greta looked around wildly. Obviously, Om was here somewhere,
communicating with Big Swiss via sign language, and had spelled her
name wrong.

BS: Your outfit. It reminds me of Gretel. From "Hansel and
    Gretel"? You keep looking over your shoulder. Are you
    expecting someone?
 G: You're not one of these Disney freaks, are you? How many
    Disney films have you seen in the theater? As an adult. Be
    honest.

More than zero and Greta would feel justified in asking for the
check.

BS: I'm not a movie person.

 G: Not a straight answer.

BS: So, *Gretel*, do you live in a gingerbread house with a cannibalistic witch?

 G: She's not a cannibal. She sells cannabis, though, if you're interested. The house we live in is very old and full of holes. It's like living outside. Which is why the rent's so cheap. I pay $400 a month for the largest room I've ever lived in.

BS: Do you have a brother?

 G: Half brother. His name is Jaime. He's ten years older.

BS: Did your stepmother abandon you in the woods?

 G: My mother died when I was thirteen. I was raised by aunts.

Was this why she hated ants? Should she order another drink?

BS: How many aunts?

 G: My mother was a twin, and she had six sisters and one brother, and they were all under two years apart. My grandmother never wanted kids, but she liked sex, and it turns out the rhythm method doesn't really work.

BS: How did she die?

 G: Old age.

BS: I meant your mother.

 G: Suicide.

BS: Oh. God. Sorry to hear that.

 G: It was my fault.

Big Swiss blinked at her.

 G: I'm kidding.

BS: Did she leave a note?

 G: Wow.

BS: What?

 G: Nosy.

BS: I'm not usually like this. I'm just picking up what you're putting down, as they say.

G: People don't really say that anymore.

Big Swiss smiled again.

G: You're probably aware of this, but you really turn heads when you enter a room. I bet you could turn heads of lettuce.

BS: It's just the hair. If I wear a hat, no one looks twice, believe me.

G: Uh-huh.

BS: Put on a blond wig and walk down the street. See what happens. You'd be shocked. And bitterly disappointed. A lot of dim men are into blondes.

G: Maybe, but it's also your eyes. They have a lot of power. In fact, if this gynecologist thing doesn't work out, you could probably find work as a cult leader.

BS: Well, I grew up in a cult.

G: [COUGHS] Which one?

BS: It was near Geneva, but they ran workshops all over Europe. I spent summers in places like Hungary, Slovenia, and Denmark, attending workshops with my parents.

G: Was it religious?

BS: Their religion was something called radical authenticity.

G: What kind of workshops?

BS: I remember one called Authentic Movement. It was run by a nut named Yara. She made noise on a guitar and you were supposed to close your eyes and "wait to be moved." Some people rocked back and forth like lunatics, while others pitched themselves onto the floor and cried, or pounded the rug with their fists. It was . . . improvisational, I guess. One guy scratched behind his ear like a dog and then violently swung his arms back and forth, while this other guy jumped straight up and down—

G: Sounds like a mosh pit.

BS: What's that?

G: Never mind. What was your authentic movement, or do you remember?

BS: I did some shaking. Like, from rage.

G: So, it wasn't your scene.

BS: I envied the Catholic kids in my neighborhood. I craved structure, rules, discipline, uniforms. You, I can picture in a uniform. Are you Catholic?

G: After my mother died, I stayed with an aunt who convinced me that my mother was burning in hell, in a literal lake of fire, because she'd killed herself. She said I would eventually join my mother because I was a horny nightmare. So, I accepted Jesus Christ as my personal savior.

BS: As a joke?

G: I was fourteen. To my credit, it took two solid months to brainwash me. Then I was born again, praise Jesus, and that was that.

BS: Where?

G: In the bathtub. After thirty-six hours of labor, I emerged from my aunt's vagina. Just kidding. We did it in the living room. She called a preacher on TV, and the preacher prayed for me and said my name on the air, which was thrilling at the time, and I wore a yellow dress, and my aunt kept chanting "Praise Jesus" while the preacher went through his spiel, and then she held me while I wept. And boy, did I weep. It felt—not like a baptism, but like an exorcism in reverse, except it was Jesus who entered my body. I felt totally cleansed and purified, as if I'd fasted for forty days. I still consider it my first real high, and it turned out to be the happiest, most peaceful three months of my life.

BS: Then what?

G: Did you put something in my drink? I don't usually talk about this on a first date.

BS: This is a date?

G: Isn't it?

Big Swiss finished her wine.

BS: Can you be born again and again and again until you actually die?

G: No, it's a one-time deal. There's no reversing it and it doesn't wear off. That's part of the appeal. So, in other words, I can kill someone with my bare hands and still get into heaven.

Big Swiss didn't say anything.

G: I haven't killed anyone—yet—but several attempts have been made on my own life over the years.

BS: Who's trying to kill you?

G: Me.

BS: Have you tried medication?

G: It's just a glitch. Two wires are crossed. It's not a problem with the whole system. I don't need to be rewired.

BS: Can I ask a strange favor? Is there any chance we could . . .

Cut this short? Never see each other again?

BS: Can we be . . . dog friends?

G: What's that?

BS: Dog friends.

G: I don't know what that means.

BS: Like, can we hang out at the dog park together.

Big Swiss looked slightly queasy. Obviously, she didn't want to go to the dog park alone, but did she think Keith would show up there, of all places? His obese chocolate Lab couldn't possibly still be alive, eight years later, and who gets a new dog immediately upon getting out of prison?

Well, Greta might, actually. It might be the first thing she did. But a man? A man would try to get pussy first, followed by . . . revenge?

Big Swiss must have filed a restraining order, but maybe it wasn't in place yet, or maybe she was afraid he'd hire someone to come after her.

> BS: None of my friends are free in the middle of the day, and—I mean, I realize you "work," but it seems like—
> G: Yeah, sure, I'll go to the dog park with you.
> BS: I'll buy you coffee afterward.
> G: Would you be willing to give me a hysterectomy at some point?
> BS: Sorry?
> G: I need my uterus removed.
> BS: Do you have heavy periods, or something more serious?
> G: I have PMS. My periods are like bad jimsonweed trips.

A flicker of recognition crossed Big Swiss's forehead. Greta waited, hoping to hear exactly how jimsonweed had brought her to orgasm.

> BS: My dog ate jimsonweed once and barked at the wall for seven hours. Apparently, the walls melt like butter if you ingest it. [PAUSE] To get rid of PMS, I would have to remove your ovaries.
> G: Fine.
> BS: But I can't do that, Rebekah. Sorry.

Greta didn't like being addressed by her fake name. Why on earth hadn't she chosen a name she'd always wanted? Carmen, Isabelle, Piper—

> BS: What are your symptoms?
> G: Obsessive thoughts. Like, I'm pretty sure one of my feet is significantly bigger than the other, but people tell me they're roughly the same size.
> BS: Do you wear different-size shoes?

G: Well, no, because imagine all the shoes I'd have to buy. Imagine all the leftover shoes, all mismatched. I wouldn't be able to donate them, so they'd all end up in a landfill. I'm also oddly obsessed with my dog's paws.

BS: You seem really in love with your dog. Almost as if he were a human baby.

G: Yes, well, I forgot to have children.

BS: How old are you?

G: Thirty-eight.

Greta was forty-five.

G: I'm not aging well.

BS: Were you focused on your career?

G: I forgot to have a career.

BS: What else did you forget?

G: Tattoos. I forgot to get tattoos.

BS: Are you still transcribing our conversation?

G: Indeed. I'm exhausted.

BS: I bet I know how to keep you from doing that.

Like a boss, Big Swiss didn't utter another word, not even "good-bye" or "good to see you." She simply placed two twenties on the bar, gave Greta's shoulder a gentle squeeze, waved to Gringo, and then slipped out the door.

Greta immediately ordered another Sazerac, just to get ahold of her nerves. Being deliberately obnoxious had been more stressful than she'd realized, but she also hadn't anticipated enjoying herself so much. It had been years since she'd made a new friend, even a dog park friend.

Big Swiss was clearly looking for a bodyguard, though, not a friend, and Greta didn't even work out. Nor did she have any weapons. Perhaps she would start lifting weights, or at least larger logs of wood. She was good enough with a hatchet, but maybe it was time to pick up the axe.

If they walked their dogs together on a regular basis, Big Swiss was bound to bring up Rebekah in therapy again. But what did Om really know about Greta? He didn't even know her dog's name, or his breed. He only knew Greta's age, where and with whom she lived, and that she sometimes slept in the closet.

8

Now that winter was well under way, the fires had to be fed and maintained around the clock. This involved Greta's trudging outside to the woodpile, loading up her arms, trudging back, dumping the wood onto the hearth, stacking it, making sure she had enough kindling. If she went to bed at midnight, it was necessary to set her alarm for three, four at the latest, to pack the stove, and again at six or seven, and then every five hours, all day long. If the fire died, she started from scratch, and the wood was often wet or frozen, or the fire didn't catch. If there was a back draft, her room suddenly filled with thick black smoke, which in turn filled her with rage, and she beat the air with a towel like a demon. She'd nailed drapes over the windows because Sabine didn't own a drill or curtain rods, and it was less drafty, certainly, but staying warm was its own part-time job, and she wasn't getting paid. In fact, she was the one paying. Her only compensation was not freezing to death.

Big Swiss had texted every day for two and a half weeks, which meant they'd walked their dogs together for a total of seventeen hours. Since Greta felt like she was performing a role, she wore the same thing every day: waxed canvas coat and work pants, in monochromatic green. She looked and felt like the groundskeeper at a cemetery. The other day Big Swiss had asked for her last name.

"My last name?" Greta said. "Graves."

Big Swiss watched Greta light a cigarette and take a few puffs.

"What are you, nervous?" she said.

"I'm a smoker," Greta said.

"I know, but your hands are shaking," Big Swiss said.

The shakes were from the night before, which she'd spent in the kitchen with Sabine, drinking Redbreast whiskey in front of the fire. At some point, Greta noticed that Sabine seemed wasted but not drunk, that she was in fact pretending to drink, and telling stories that sounded like historical fan fiction. Although Sabine was terrified of bats, Greta wondered briefly if she'd been bitten. She continued to lose weight, even in her forehead. Greta could literally see her skull. Sabine was keeping something from her, something she seemed on the verge of confessing, but then she'd disappear to the city, sometimes in the dead of night, and was gone for days. Yesterday she'd texted to inform Greta that she was making edibles for a well-known dealer in Jersey, and might be gone for a whole month, and was Greta okay with that? It was a lot of house for one person, Sabine admitted, but she was making good money now and promised to cover the cost of wood.

Back to Big Swiss. Shockingly, despite ample opportunity, Big Swiss had yet to mention being beaten half to death. Not a whisper. Nor had she mentioned, or even hinted at, her attacker's recent release from prison. The restraining order alone would be the first thing out of most people's mouths, and you'd never hear the end of it. Instead, Big Swiss wore a lot of tweed and fixated on her (Rebekah) and was extremely intense (Swiss?) about it. In other words, she reminded Greta of a certain famous psychoanalyst, except she didn't smoke a pipe or cigars. She sucked on something brown and dick-shaped, however: root beer Popsicles, which she brought with her to the dog park, even though it was the dead of winter. Root beer, she said, was her winter flavor. In spring, she would switch to watermelon. Summer was strictly citrus. Additionally, she ate a lot of salty licorice. And apples. Greta herself had never felt compelled to eat an apple. It was certainly never something she'd craved. She disliked fruit in general, but Big Swiss made apples look irresistible. Since Big Swiss's mouth was always full, Greta had gone ahead and told her a few things. A few *hundred* things. Between bites, Big Swiss had peppered Greta with personal questions about her past, which had made Greta uneasy at first, but then Greta remembered that her most basic facts—name, age, birthplace—were outright lies, and the lies made her feel cloaked and anonymous, like a whistleblower in a documentary. After the initial discomfort wore off, Greta talked as blithely as if her face were blurred, her voice digitally scrambled, her exact location obscured.

"Didn't you tell me you were engaged?" Big Swiss had asked, somewhere in the woods.

Greta nodded. "Stacy and I were engaged for a whole decade, but it only felt like a few months."

"Does she live around here?"

"California," Greta said. "And Stacy is a man."

"When did you break up?"

"A year ago," Greta said. "We still talk on the phone, though that's tapering off. His new girlfriend says she doesn't like the look on his face when he talks to me, so I don't call him anymore. But we share custody of Piñon, so they FaceTime."

"He FaceTimes with the dog?" Big Swiss asked.

"Of course," Greta said. "How else are they going to see each other?"

"Why'd you break up?"

"I was ready to live alone," Greta said.

"But you don't," Big Swiss said, and bit into her second apple. "You have a roommate."

"I was ready to *sleep* alone," Greta said. "Stacy was a teddy bear. With a penis. It startled me to cuddle him and then feel an erection. And yet I was extremely attached to him. I relied on him for everything. That's why I'm living the way I am now."

"And here I was convinced you were gay," Big Swiss said. "Are you?"

"Not all the way," Greta said. "I mean, I've had sex with women."

"How many?"

"Oh, I dunno," Greta said. "Five or six?"

"Do you have a type?"

It was hard to say. Apart from her one girlfriend in high school, she'd only ever slept with stone butches, and they were mostly one-night stands, a few long weekends.

"So, like, emotionally distant women?"

"Stone butches prefer to touch rather than be touched. They're not stony, per se. In fact, they're often very doting. The last one told me that I wasn't a bottom, that underneath my girl clothes and makeup, a butch was waiting to emerge. This was news to me. Of course, I never did anything about it except shave my head, which I regretted instantly."

"Why?"

"Turns out I have a criminal head shape."

Speaking of, Greta looked around for Keith. Unless he was wearing camo or hiding behind a tree, she and Big Swiss were alone.

"When did you become aware you liked girls?"

"Puberty."

"Were your parents still married?"

"They split up before I was born."

Greta paused to yell at Piñon, who'd performed an elaborate water dance in the freezing creek and then covered himself with mud, and was now barking in Silas's face. Piñon was a mess, but everything about Silas was immaculate: his feet, his jet-black fur, his calm.

"Are your parents still alive?" Greta asked.

Big Swiss didn't answer. Maybe they were dead.

"What do you miss most about Switzerland?" Greta asked.

Big Swiss shook her head.

"Did you vacation in the Alps?"

No answer.

"I've heard the Swiss are good swimmers. Is that true? And is the chocolate really that much better than—"

"Nice try," Big Swiss interrupted.

"Pardon?"

"You seem to want to change the subject," Big Swiss said.

"What?"

Greta felt Big Swiss studying her profile.

"Your mouth is trembling," Big Swiss said. "Are you suddenly uncomfortable talking about yourself?"

"Wait a minute, were we not having a conversation?"

"I refuse to play into your program," Big Swiss said.

"My program?"

"What's your fear?"

Scientology, Greta thought.

"Are you afraid to reveal too much?" Big Swiss asked. "Tell me your fear, and be honest. Don't compose your answer."

Greta composed several answers. "Ticking clocks," Greta said. "Childbirth. I'm not crazy about confrontation. Marriage, most wood-paneled rooms. *Feet*. In fact, feet might be first. That's partly why childbirth scares me. It's actually a fear of breech."

There, Greta thought. Plenty to investigate.

"You were telling me about your girlfriend in high school," Big Swiss said. "Then you suddenly shifted the focus away from yourself, and it seems habitual, and I'm just wondering what's behind it."

"Maybe I'm just not much of a talker."

"My guess is you adopted this role pretty early on," Big Swiss said. "I imagine it's a role you've been performing your whole life."

"Being polite?"

"Listening," Big Swiss said. "That's your role: listener, confidante, confessor. You sit around all day, not talking, listening to other people talk, writing down what they say, and then you do the same thing in social situations. Are you writing a script right now?"

"Are you always this intense?"

"I'm direct," Big Swiss admitted, "because I don't care if people like me. I distrust people-pleasers. They seem phony to me, and dangerous."

"It's easy to picture you in the schoolyard. Towheaded children tend to look angelic, but they're often little assholes," Greta said, and smiled. "Another fear of mine is seeing old photographs of the person I'm dating. Not baby pictures—I don't mind those—but anything after age five, because a person's essence becomes visible, and I always have trouble reconciling it with who they are now—"

"I protected kids from bullies," Big Swiss interrupted. "That was my role in the schoolyard."

"You bullied other bullies," Greta said.

Big Swiss nodded.

"Well, I hope you'll protect me from . . . yourself."

An uncomfortable silence passed. Maybe it was only uncomfortable for Greta. Big Swiss seemed relaxed and amused, except she wasn't walking so much as skulking. Her steps were measured and cautious, as if she was worried about making too much noise.

"I'm disappointed when someone immediately turns the tables," Big Swiss said. "Seems lazy to me."

"You know, you might want to ease up," Greta said. "We just met."

"Doesn't feel that way. Do you agree?"

Greta shrugged.

"Talk to me about your first girlfriend," Big Swiss commanded, her mouth full of licorice, "and don't hold back."

And so, Greta had told her all about Robin, who'd been a few years older than Greta and, as far as Greta knew, the only other girl in New Hampshire without a perm and waterfall bangs. In fact, her hair had been buzzed all over and bleached platinum, and she dressed like a dude. Everyone called her Rob or Robbie. The first time they'd met, Greta had been at the library, tossing books out of the window. Rob had been on the sidewalk below, doing tricks on a skateboard. Greta watched as the skateboard suddenly flew out from under Rob, and Greta saw—could almost hear—Rob's head smack concrete. She immediately descended the stairs and exited the building. Rob was still on the ground. Greta crouched next to her.

"Were you throwing books out the window?" Rob asked.

"No," Greta said.

"You distracted me. That's why I fell."

"Wasn't me," Greta said.

"You can't steal from the library. It's extremely bad luck."

"I only take books that have more than four copies in circulation," Greta said. "Damaged paperbacks."

Rob gazed at Greta in silence. Greta worried she had a concussion and would die in her sleep that night. The ER was only a block away.

"Fine. I won't do it again. Listen, you should go to the hospital." Greta pulled Rob to her feet. "Can you walk?"

Rob laughed. "I fall every day. I have a hard head. Write your number in one of those books."

Greta chose *My Ántonia*, by Willa Cather. She wasn't sure why she'd stolen it, as it didn't look like it contained swears or sexual situations. Greta figured it would take Rob a month to read it, after which she would call Greta and tell her about it. But Rob called a few hours later.

"Wanna cuddle?" Rob asked.

Greta laughed. "You read that book already?"

"I don't read books!" Rob said. "I want to take you to D'Angelo's. I'll buy you a steak-and-cheese with hots. More importantly, there's a ceiling fan hanging by a thread. We should sit under it and wait for it to fall on our heads. Then we'll live happily ever after."

"Decapitated?" Greta said.

"Rich," Rob said. "We'll sue."

The ceiling fan never fell on their heads or anywhere else, even after ninety minutes, but Greta fell head over heels for Rob, even though Rob drove an unfashionable Trans Am, claimed to be cursed, had terrible stick-and-poke tattoos, and had dropped out of St. Mary's, where Greta would soon become a sophomore. Now Rob worked as a line cook at a diner to support her father, who'd gambled himself into bankruptcy with the French Canadians on the other side of the river. These circumstances were present in Rob's body odor, which worked on Greta like catnip, though Rob claimed to smell earthy because she was half Cherokee.

Later that day, Rob lost her keys, wallet, and dog all within two hours. She broke her arm in four places trying to hunt everything down. A week after that, they went to a party in a tree house that collapsed; Rob landed straight on a nail and got tetanus, which gave her lockjaw. But she made everything she did seem choreographed, including falling down the stairs and running on crutches.

Their relationship lasted six months and was oddly chaste, possibly because Rob still considered Greta a child, but also because Rob played basketball with a few of the nuns from St. Mary's. Rob was probably very Catholic, Greta guessed, even though she claimed luck was her only religion.

"Anyway, it was all hanky and no panky," Greta told Big Swiss. "If you know what I mean."

Big Swiss shook her head.

"Little to no touching below the belt," Greta said. "But we loved making out and humping each other. She ended up dumping me for a waitress at the diner she worked at. I was devastated."

As soon as Greta graduated high school, she bought a plane ticket to California and never saw Rob again. They'd known each other during a much simpler time, when you could move out of state, or even three exits away, and never be seen or heard from again. But then Facebook came along and disrupted the natural order, and suddenly there was a picture of Rob on her screen, her words in a message.

I see you live in LA. I'm here for work. Wanna cuddle?

Greta did in fact wanna cuddle. Just for one night. But did she also wanna chlamydia? Rob was still rough around the edges, no doubt, and cursed. There was also Stacy to consider. They'd been together seven years by that point. But Greta looked forward to not having to explain herself, because Rob already knew most of the beautiful and ugly things about Greta.

A day later, Greta was sitting in a corner booth at a steak house near Rob's hotel, the Farmer's Daughter. Greta was elated to see Rob's face, which looked lived-in but not dilapidated, despite what had probably been twenty years of steady boozing and blackouts.

"Can you still run really fast barefoot?" Greta asked.

"Jolie laide," Rob said.

"What's that?"

"French," Rob said. "It means 'beautiful ugly,' which is how I would describe your face."

"Fuck," Greta said. "Are you negging me?"

"You're uniquely handsome," Rob said, and reached for Greta's hand. "You've been very hard to forget."

"Can you still plunge your hands into scalding water?" Greta asked.

"I'm not a reptile, Greta," Rob said. "I'm a human being. With feelings."

Greta's current feeling was shame. Although she'd had plenty of opportunities, she'd never cheated on Stacy, especially not with her father, because that's precisely who Rob reminded her of—her father, with tits.

"Are you dating anyone?" Greta asked.

Rob shook her head. "My last few girlfriends have been totally deranged. Like, really nuts. I only seem to attract women who are mentally ill."

"College girls," Greta said.

"One or two were in their twenties," Rob admitted. "But you? You, I loved. I still remember our second date. I've thought about it a lot over the years."

They'd gotten high and made out on a slanted rooftop for many hours, during which Greta had injured her back. Later, Greta had eaten Nutella off Rob's boobs.

"It was Cool Whip," Rob said soberly.

"Nutella," Greta said. "I'm not a Cool Whip person."

Rob sniffed. "You must have licked Nutella off someone else."

Greta had fallen hard for Rob that night, had been madly in love with her for months, but it felt dangerous to admit this now, because Rob seemed desperate to hear it.

"I'm just happy we found each other again," Rob said.

Greta cleared her throat. "I'm in a relationship. With a really good guy. We live together. We're engaged."

"Then what are you doing here?"

"My curiosity got the better of me," Greta said.

Rob glanced at her watch. "What do you think? Can we get out of here now?"

"Without paying?"

"Greta," Rob said patiently. "Will you stop treating me like a degenerate?"

"A sexy degenerate," Greta said, correcting her.

They tongued at the table like a couple of losers. Rob smelled more complex than Greta remembered. The top note was the same: the undergrowth of a cedar forest. The middle note varied between almond croissant and armpit musk. When Greta correctly sensed the derision and contempt of the entire waitstaff, she managed to pull away. She decided she couldn't wait to roll around with Rob in her hotel room.

"So, you had an affair," Big Swiss interrupted at last.

"Yes," Greta admitted.

Greta rattled on about how connected Rob had been to old ideas about herself, how strung-out Greta had felt, how her interactions with Rob reminded her of smoking crack—a two-minute high followed by the realization that she'd shit her pants—how ready she was to get off the pipe, to salvage her relationship with Stacy. Instead, she'd ended things with Rob and gone right back to sleep for another two or three years.

"Sometimes I wonder if that's why I never married Stacy, because I knew I was capable of cheating—not just cheating, but developing feelings—and it didn't seem fair."

Big Swiss jiggled the keys in her pocket. Greta realized they were standing next to Big Swiss's car in the parking area. Greta had been so caught up in her story, she had no memory of crossing the meadow.

"How long have we been standing here?" Greta asked.

"Twenty-three minutes," Big Swiss said.

"Jesus," Greta said. "I'm sorry. You must be dying to get home."

"I'm fine," Big Swiss said.

"How's *your* marriage?"

Big Swiss smiled and said nothing.

"I talked your face off," Greta said. "You feel stifled, right, like there's a plastic bag over your head."

"I feel the opposite of stifled," Big Swiss said.

While Greta thought of antonyms—"loose," "released," "persuaded"—Big Swiss kissed Greta's cheek. Then she kissed Greta's other cheek. Then the first cheek again. A Swiss goodbye, Greta assumed, except it happened in slow motion. Greta leaned forward and kissed Big Swiss's barely parted lips. Big Swiss smiled. Kissing Big Swiss's teeth was jarring and humiliating, like kissing a bathroom sink. But maybe that was too unkind. It was like kissing a baptismal font full of holy water.

9

OM: Well, hello. Long time no see. Listen, I had to charge you for last week's session because you canceled last-minute, and I need a full day's notice. Sorry about that.
FEW: It was my fault. I got caught up at the dog park.

"Caught up," Greta said. "Right."

OM: Can you state your initials for the transcriber, please.
FEW: FEW.
OM: I haven't seen you since before Keith got out of prison, correct?
FEW: Yes.
OM: How are you feeling?
FEW: [PAUSE] This may sound slightly paranoid, but I'm being followed.

"What?" Greta said.

OM: Where?
FEW: Here, there, wherever I go.

OM: He's *here*? Hold on [OVERLAPPING] I can't see—wait, move
the [OVERLAPPING] no, other way—*him*? In the ascot? That's
Timmy, honey, he's harmless—

FEW: Not him. *Him*. The guy in the big black [OVERLAPPING]

OM: —understand how he can afford [OVERLAPPING] really kind
of brazen—

FEW: —[OVERLAPPING] over the bridge—

"Fuck," Greta said. "One at a time, please."

FEW: I think he's just monitoring my routine.

OM: It's called *stalking*. Have you called the police?

FEW: No.

OM: Does he ever follow you on foot?

FEW: No, but sometimes a woman does. An older woman with a
harsh face. She follows me at the dog park.

"I hope to hell you don't mean me," Greta said.

OM: You're positive about this?

FEW: She waits for me in the parking area and then trails me,
sometimes for thirty or forty minutes, glaring at me the whole
time.

OM: Does she have a dog?

FEW: Yeah.

OM: Do you feel unsafe? I mean, does she seem dangerous?

FEW: Her presence is slightly menacing, yes, but I'm never alone. I
meet a friend and we walk together.

"Phew," Greta said.

OM: Okay, good.

FEW: It's been quite a distraction, to be honest. She talks incessantly.

OM: Does the woman look familiar?

FEW: I've never seen her before.

OM: Has your friend?

FEW: I haven't mentioned any of this to her.

OM: Why?

FEW: We just met, and it's not a story I'm attached to. I don't consider it part of my identity.

OM: What are you going to do about the stalking?

FEW: Be more vigilant, I guess. I should start keeping track of dates and times. I'm not very good at describing people's faces, but I always remember clothing. The woman wears a felted Nordic wool sweater, gray sweats with a drawstring, tall green rain boots one size too big. The shade of green is called Jasper, and they're made by a French company that sells gardening equipment.

Greta paused the audio and tried to recall a woman fitting this description, but she only remembered dogs. Big Swiss didn't like to linger in the meadow, preferring to walk in the woods, and so the woman would've been following them on the trail. A Rhodesian ridgeback had passed them a few times, but Greta had barely noticed its owner, because she'd been too busy talking. Incessantly.

OM: Is your husband concerned?

FEW: Mildly. He thinks I'm imagining things.

OM: Is that a tendency of yours?

FEW: Lately it is. I don't feel like myself. Or maybe I feel *more* like myself. I haven't been this hyper since high school. It doesn't make sense, but even my blood feels different, like it's increased in volume.

OM: You do seem more . . . energetic than usual.

"It's called lust," Greta said.

FEW: I'm also more absentminded. The other night, when I got home from work, I stood in the yard and stared at the bushes like a crazy person. Luke was inside the house, watching me, and he tapped the window to get my attention. I was so out of it, I didn't even recognize him. I thought a stranger had broken into the house. He said I'd been standing there for twenty minutes. That night I dreamed there were eight Lukes in the house, and I didn't know which one was real. I mean, they were all real, and interacting with me, but I had to figure out which one was authentic, which one was . . . him.

OM: Did you figure it out?

FEW: No.

OM: Are you getting enough sleep?

FEW: I don't know. I daydream most of the day, even at work, and I never remember driving anywhere, unless I'm being followed, and then I'm hyperaware, but of course I never think to look at the license plate.

OM: What are you daydreaming about—revenge?

FEW: Against whom?

OM: Keith!

FEW: He spent eight years behind bars. He did his time.

OM: For all you know, he thrived in prison. Maybe he got to wear shorts again and make furniture.

FEW: You have a good memory.

OM: I glanced at that transcript as I was printing it out for you. Do you still want it?

FEW: Yes, please. Thank you. Anyway, I don't feel animosity toward Keith. My daydreams are about—well, I'd forgotten about this, but I remembered—what do you call it? A sexual story. From my youth.

[PAUSE 01:20]

"Hello?" Greta said.

OM: Well? Are you going to tell me what it is?

FEW: It's not overtly sexual. I mean, I've never thought about it during sex. And I don't think about it while I masturbate, which I'm doing a lot now—

Greta stopped typing and wiped her sweaty palms on her pants.

FEW: But it helped me learn English. It also feels connected to my sexuality because I was a teenager at the time and attracted to one of the characters. Anyway, my dog park friend talks a lot, like I said, and I've been listening closely, in a highly focused way, just as I did back—

OM: But what's the story?

FEW: It's from *Law and Order: SVU*.

"Wow," Greta said. "Bummer."

FEW: Have you watched it?

OM: Uh, once or twice—it's been on for thirty-seven years.

FEW: Nineteen. [PAUSE] Anyway, I used to imagine myself in certain scenarios when I watched it as a teenager.

OM: Were you a special victim in these scenarios?

FEW: Never. I was usually a suspect, or an uncooperative witness brought in for questioning, and I was forced to sit in the little room with the two-way mirror and wonder how I was going to survive in prison.

OM: Were you being observed from behind the mirror?

FEW: Of course. By Olivia Benson.

OM: Oh?

FEW: In one fantasy, my left wrist is handcuffed to the table, and Detective Benson is studying me from behind the mirror, and she watches me eat the snack and sip the coffee like nothing's wrong, like I haven't been arrested for murder, and then she comes in to interrogate me—

OM: Which snack?

"Goddammit," Greta said.

FEW: Hostess Snoballs. The pink ones.

OM: Interesting.

"Is it?" Greta said.

OM: If you had, say, a fetish, what do you think it would be?

FEW: [PAUSE] I'm aroused by fog.

OM: Anything else?

FEW: Being cold. Watching others who are cold.

OM: [SCRIBBLING] Can you be more specific?

FEW: People huddled around a fire, people shivering, stomping their feet, blowing on their hands. I like to see people's breath. What are you writing?

OM: Just making a note.

FEW: Anyway, Olivia Benson interrogates me, but it turns into a conversation. From the outside it seems straightforward, but it's very charged. Olivia has her own agenda, and I have mine.

OM: Is kissing Olivia part of your agenda?

FEW: I wanted to be disciplined by her. Maybe humiliated. But I was young. I think it would be the other way around now.

OM: So, like, spanking?

FEW: The humiliation was *verbal*. I was trying to learn *English*. But now that I think about it, I'm aroused by silky blouses and pantsuits. My new friend doesn't wear pantsuits, of course, but she reminds me a little of Olivia Benson. That might be why I'm thinking of this.

"Aw," Greta said.

OM: Is she a cop?

FEW: No.

OM: How is she like Olivia?

FEW: She has the same complexion, the same way of carrying herself.

OM: Your face is very red, by the way.

FEW: I know, I can feel it. I may have a slight fever. I wouldn't mind hanging my head out the window for a minute. Do these open?

OM: Hold on, I'll turn down the thermostat.

FEW: Like I said, it feels like there's twice as much blood in my body.

OM: Any chance you're pregnant?

FEW: She kissed me.

"Uh-oh," Greta said.

OM: Who?

FEW: My friend. Rebekah.

"Shit," Greta said.

OM: Where?

FEW: On the lips.

OM: At the dog park?

FEW: Yes.

OM: Where was the stalker?

FEW: I don't know—watching us?

"What?" Greta said.

OM: Were you trying to throw her off?

FEW: I wasn't thinking about the stalker.

OM: I see. [PAUSE] Did you kiss back?

FEW: She pushed her tongue into my mouth. I wasn't expecting that, for some reason.

OM: Have you kissed a woman before?

FEW: No.

OM: Well, how do you feel about it now? Would you do it again?

FEW: I don't know.

OM: Does Luke know?

FEW: No.

OM: Have you seen her since?

FEW: No, but I'll see her very soon. She seems to feel the need to tell me everything. She can't talk fast enough. Often she calls and leaves a three-minute voicemail. "I forgot to tell you about such-and-such." Or, "Here are some details I left out of my last story."

OM: Wait a minute, where are you going?

FEW: I have a patient to see.

OM: But we have ten minutes left. Can you be a little late?

FEW: [LAUGHS] No.

OM: Can we talk about this again next time?

FEW: Sure.

OM: All right. I may hold you to it, just so you—

[END OF RECORDING]

MOST WOMEN WOULD LOOK RIDICULOUS in a mink coat and rancher's hat. Big Swiss simply looked like the owner of a mink ranch. She'd shown up on Greta's doorstep unannounced, said she happened to be "in the neighborhood," so she'd decided to "drop by, hope that's okay," which Greta supposed might be true, since Sabine's house was on the way to Catskill, but, as evidenced by Big Swiss's texts ("Meet me at the dog park in 17 min" or "See you at 4:22"), she rarely did anything on a whim.

Greta would've put on a pantsuit if she'd had any notice, if it hadn't been too obvious, if she hadn't thrown out her professional attire months ago. In Hudson, people in office clothes looked like they'd gotten off at the wrong stop. They always seemed to be searching for an address, and the more prim and professional they appeared, the more lost, desperate, and oddly down on their luck. And so, Greta was dressed somewhat like Sabine: four moth-eaten layers, plus extra-long legwarmers that completely covered her feet, calves, and thighs.

Big Swiss requested a tour of the house, of course, because who wouldn't. Sabine wasn't around, so the tour would be succinct and short on context, but okay, here was the kitchen with its low ceilings and stone walls, very European, and these concrete floors should have radiant heat, but, well, it isn't hooked up, because the plumber mysteriously disappeared and left all his tools, and now he won't return Sabine's calls, even though she owes him a bunch of money, and we think he might be dead. Anyway, if you look up at the ceiling here, this is the empty beehive, probably thirty or forty years old, and the enclosure was built by a beekeeper named Gideon, who we've been trying to get over here to assess the situation—oh, that? It's a built-in bread oven, yeah, no, don't stick your head in it, it's probably full of dead animals, but this fireplace is enormous, right, and so the kitchen at least is always warm, and in this little room over here, dry storage— yes, that's weed you're smelling, it's behind that curtain, but follow me up this decrepit staircase to the third floor, because you should see these creepy, closet-size bedrooms, and all the weird layers of wall-paper, and the antique hospital beds, the tiny doors, and then Sabine's lofty bedroom with its exposed beams and lime-plastered walls, blah, blah, so beautiful, so ancient, so . . . untenable, right, I know, but wait until summer.

Big Swiss displayed the usual curiosity about Sabine. No, she's not French, Greta told her. No, not deranged. Not an artist. Not rich, though she owns this place outright, and not exactly a criminal, though she hasn't worked a straight job in years.

"I'm just wondering what kind of woman chooses to buy a house like this," Big Swiss said.

"A heartbroken one," Greta said. "Her ex-husband, whom she adored, had an affair, and I think she bought this place because it encapsulated how she was feeling at the time."

"Old and ruined?"

"Fragile, in need of restoration. She hated how banal and clichéd the end of her marriage was, and so she bought a three-hundred-year-old farmhouse and a pair of mini-donkeys. Pretty much the opposite of getting Botox or a face-lift."

"What donkeys?"

"They're not here yet," Greta said.

Big Swiss nodded at the brick wall near the front door. "Is that what I think it is?"

"You mean is it snowing indoors? I'm afraid so. But only in that one little spot, and it just clings to the bricks, it never . . . accumulates."

"You seem close to her," Big Swiss said. "Why don't you talk about her more?"

"She's away, working in the city, and I feel like she's hiding something from me, but I can't figure out what it is."

"Are you also hiding something from her?"

"Now that you mention it," Greta said, "I never told her that I lusted after her son, who's decades younger than me. Otherwise, we don't keep secrets."

"How many decades?" Big Swiss asked.

"Two," Greta said.

Big Swiss seemed to bristle, and Greta wondered if she was jealous. They were standing in the drawing room, and Big Swiss asked if people drew pictures in drawing rooms, and Greta said no, people withdrew into drawing rooms for more privacy, and was it Greta's imagination, or was Big Swiss blushing?

"So, where do you sleep?"

"Through that door," Greta said. "In what used to be the living room."

Big Swiss took off her hat as if entering a chapel and looked around. Her hair was bright and staticky.

"Wow," she said. "These walls . . . the ceiling . . . it's really . . . something."

"It's difficult to heat this room because the windows are so large, which is why—see that crooked little door? That's the tiny room I call the antechamber. I sleep in there sometimes."

They sat in the armchairs in front of Greta's woodstove, facing each other. Big Swiss cleared her throat. Greta stared at her black fur coat. Christ, was it chinchilla? Chinchillas were cute.

"I have something to tell you," Big Swiss said grimly. "I think about you. When you're not around."

"Don't tell me you talk to me in your head."

"I do," Big Swiss said. "All day, all night."

"Well, we've been spending a lot of time together, so it's only natural. I think about you, too."

"If I don't see you every day, I feel restless and unsettled."

Greta waved her hand. "It'll pass."

"When?" Big Swiss said.

"Is it sexual?"

"It's . . . amorous."

"It's probably a phase," Greta said. "I mean, have you messed with poon before?"

Big Swiss shook her head.

"Imagine my pussy just inches from your face," Greta said. "What're you going to do? Think fast."

Big Swiss blinked.

"Now imagine it hugging your face like the alien in *Alien*."

"Maybe it's me who wants to hug your face," Big Swiss said. "Ever consider that?"

Greta swallowed.

"I'm just letting you know I'm attracted to you," Big Swiss said. "I never told you this, but before we met, I once saw you at a farm stand. I was there to buy tomatoes, but I noticed you in the meat section, pulling venison cubes out of a freezer, and I fell in love with your forearms. I obsessed about them for weeks."

Greta coughed. Forearms?

"I liked to imagine them in different settings," Big Swiss went on. "Hanging out of a car window, resting on furniture, floating underwater."

Sweet Jesus. She recalled a recent transcript in which a new client of Om's had identified as a sex and love addict whose drug of choice was "fantasy and intrigue." The client was married but addicted to fantasizing about and flirting with coworkers, service workers, the kid who bagged her groceries. Maybe Big Swiss had the same problem? Nevertheless, Greta crossed her arms and did some subtle flexing.

Now they were kissing. Or rather, Greta was kissing Big Swiss.

Were her lips soft? Very. But they did not move. It was like kissing a mannequin. Then Big Swiss suddenly opened her mouth too wide.

Greta pulled away. "Is this your first kiss?"

"You kissed me the other day."

"You're straight," Greta said. "Don't worry."

"I just said I'm attracted to you."

"You're confused. Forearms are phallic. It's not like you imagined my boobs hanging out the window."

"I only thought about your forearms because they were pulling meat out of freezers. Boobs can't do that. If you'd been breast-feeding at the farm stand, I may have—"

Greta unbuttoned her shirt.

"Stop," Big Swiss said, and looked away.

Greta laughed. "Gotcha."

"It's not like that—it's just—well, in my fantasies you're fully clothed," Big Swiss said. "*I'm* the one naked."

HER JUTTING HIP BONES reminded Greta of a ship's sails. Otherwise, she was straight, supple, somehow taller without clothes, and covered in tiny blond hairs. So, less like white asparagus, more like white peach. Greta wasn't always a fan—she preferred nectarines and shaved everything, even her forearms—but the fuzz made Big Swiss seem both sturdier and sweeter, and Greta wanted to devour her immediately. So had someone else, it appeared.

"Are those . . . bite marks?" Greta asked.

"Bruises," Big Swiss said.

Greta was reminded of Poland. The country. During high school, she'd accompanied a Polish friend to Kraków to visit relatives. At some point, they'd driven around the countryside in a borrowed car, sharing two-lane highways with horse-drawn carriages and huge semitrucks. There had been many kilometers between villages, and the highways were terrifyingly dark and narrow. One night, Greta noticed a woman walking. Since the highways had no shoulders, the woman walked directly in the road. Her ass cheeks, hanging out the bottom of her micro-mini, had been caught in their headlights, and her bare legs were covered in bruises. "Pull over!" Greta had shouted. "She needs help!"

She'd figured the woman had been raped, but she'd calmly leaned into the car, looked at their pimply teenage faces, scowled, and then kept walking. She'd been the first of many hookers Greta saw that night, trolling for truckers in the middle of nowhere.

"Don't take this the wrong way," Greta said now, "but you remind me of a Polish prostitute."

"I'm a quarter Czech," Big Swiss said. "On my mother's side."

Most women would've focused on the prostitute part.

"Some ground rules: I can penetrate you, but you can't penetrate me."

"Oh? Why's that?" Greta asked.

"I'm married," Big Swiss said. "So, no fingers, just to be clear."

"Oral doesn't count, I take it."

"Ten minutes," Big Swiss said. "No longer, and no kissing."

"Should I pay you now or later?"

"Not funny," Big Swiss said.

HER PUSSY LOOKED like advanced origami. A crisp pink lotus flower folded by a master. Greta briefly rearranged it with her mouth. The flower transformed into an acorn. Then a unicorn. Then back again. Greta dragged her tongue over it diagonally three dozen times. Now it resembled two dragonflies languidly mating on a lily pad. She reached for her phone.

"What do you think you're doing?" Big Swiss said.

"Hold still," Greta said.

Big Swiss lifted her head off the pillow.

"Just a quick pic," Greta said.

"What for?"

"For me," Greta said. "For later."

Big Swiss covered it with her hand. Two fingers, rather. The thing was that pristine and tidy.

"Only if I can photograph yours," Big Swiss said.

"Never mind," Greta said, and dropped her phone.

"I should tell you something," Big Swiss said.

"Now what," Greta said.

"Until a month ago, I'd never had an orgasm, with myself or anyone else."

Greta didn't say anything.

"Did you hear me?" Big Swiss asked.

"Maybe you should turn over," Greta suggested.

"You don't seem surprised," Big Swiss said. "Most people lose their minds when I tell them."

Greta took a breath. "Your area seems very . . . Swiss."

"Meaning what?"

"If it were a person, it might be an uptight perfectionist."

"What's yours?"

"A disorganized enthusiast."

"Let me see," Big Swiss said.

Greta's pussy, still buried under her layers, was a clumsily wrapped Christmas present. Too much wrinkled, recycled paper, not enough tape. At the top, a crooked little bow. In Greta's view, it was the last present anyone would want to open, but, apparently, according to a new study, badly wrapped gifts were better received.

Big Swiss pulled off Greta's legwarmers, followed by her jeans, her fleece leggings, and now her nude pantyhose. She stared at Greta's face.

"Something wrong?" Greta asked.

"Why are you wearing two pairs of pantyhose?"

"I like to be squeezed," Greta said. "Plus, I don't know if you've noticed, but it's kind of chilly in here."

Big Swiss peeled off the second pair, along with Greta's black no-nonsense briefs. Now she looked mildly surprised.

"Merry Christmas," Greta said.

"That's okay."

"Happy Holidays?"

"I don't mind if you don't."

"What are you talking about?" Greta said.

"You have your period," Big Swiss said.

Greta sat up and looked down at herself. Christmas, it appeared, was two weeks early. She lay back down and tried to smile. Big Swiss eyed Greta's nightstand.

"Do you have any lube?"

"Coconut oil," Greta said. "In the drawer."

The coconut oil was cold and clumpy. Big Swiss's fingers, also cold. The fucking felt clinical and slightly painful, not unlike a Pap smear, except the smell of coconut brought the tropics to mind.

"Your cervix might be tilted," Big Swiss actually said. "And your uterus feels ever so slightly . . . enlarged."

"Maybe you should be wearing latex gloves."

Greta focused on a crack in the ceiling. If they were going to do this regularly, she might tack a picture up there. Something calming. The ocean? Although, Big Swiss herself seemed increasingly oceanic: vast, unknowable, capable of swallowing Greta whole. How long had it been since Greta had been with a woman? Years. Men never bothered with fingers, or never for long, and they often didn't know where to put their thumb, what to do with their other hand, where and when to apply pressure, the necessary balance between stillness and movement. It was all coming back to her now. No matter how long a cock, how great its girth, you never felt as thoroughly fucked as you did with a woman. It went on forever, and a dick couldn't do what fingers do. Fingers are flexible. Not to mention the other huge difference: the camaraderie of a female mind.

"What are you thinking about?" Big Swiss asked after a long while.

"What you're doing to my box," Greta said.

"Can you use a different word?"

"Gash," Greta said.

Big Swiss grimaced. She removed her fingers, dug into the coconut again, and now—well, the party moved to the next room. Big Swiss's breathing changed, along with her entire demeanor. Greta felt like she was seeing a photograph of Big Swiss at age seven or eight. She looked both knowing and innocent, more receptive to joy and forgiveness, but there, in the corners of her mouth, the hint of a cruel streak.

At the foot of the bed, Piñon caught Greta's eye and held it. "If you want me to put a stop to this," he seemed to say, "just say the word and I'll bite this bitch's bare bottom."

Greta recalled the time Piñon got a foxtail stuck up his nose while hunting in a wheat field. He'd sneezed about a thousand times before Greta had taken him to the animal hospital, where she'd learned that a dog's nose has many chambers, and that a foxtail required minor surgery to remove. Along with anesthesia. And eight hundred dollars.

Of course, Greta's butthole was not a nostril with many chambers. It was more like an antique keyhole. Big Swiss's middle finger, a bent key. Beyond the extremely tiny doorway, a grand ballroom with a vaulted ceiling. To judge from her face, Big Swiss had finally arrived at the right place and never wanted to leave. Her pupils dilated. Greta could feel her finger looking around the ballroom. Then it swept the floor. Now it rose and fell, slowly and gracefully, in a Viennese waltz.

A few minutes later it emerged, weak and spent. Greta watched to see if Big Swiss might wipe it on the sheets. She did not. Instead, she reached for her sweater dress and slipped it over her head.

"So, it's true what they say," Greta said. "About millennials and ass play."

Big Swiss made a face. "I'm not a millennial."

"You're twenty-eight," Greta said.

"How do you know?"

"You told me," Greta said.

"Did I?"

Hadn't she?

Big Swiss looked toward the window and frowned. She was crashing, it appeared, and the comedown was rough. Greta felt it, too—a doomed sadness. Granted, Greta always felt this way at dusk. Although neither one of them had gotten off, Greta suspected they'd be doing this again, very soon.

"It's getting dark," Big Swiss announced. "I should head home."

To her husband. Luke. Greta had thought of him exactly twice, and both times she'd imagined him standing at his living room window, watching his wife wander their yard in a trance. He'd tapped the window to get her attention and had been met with confusion and bewilderment. Who're you? What are you doing in my house? Then Greta had imagined him tapping her own window. She imagined a pane of glass falling to the floor, his face poking into the room. Who're you? What are you doing to my wife?

But Big Swiss had probably been thinking of him all afternoon. So, although neither of them had gotten off, Greta suspected they would never do this again.

"Next time," Big Swiss said, "you can do whatever you want to me."

Greta exhaled loudly. "Does that include kissing?"

"Yes," Big Swiss said.

"When?"

"Tomorrow, from three forty to five forty-five," Big Swiss said.

"I'll be here," Greta said.

10

There was a house that existed only in Greta's dreams, a house she'd been visiting for years. Sometimes it felt like she'd been dreaming about it her entire life, which was why it seemed as familiar as her own face. And yet, it always disintegrated the second she opened her eyes. She only remembered what it had been consumed by in the dream, and of course that always varied. Water, fire, dirt, dead leaves. If she saw a house in real life that she liked or admired, some aspect of it might later appear in the dream house, and so it was likely a hodgepodge of conflicting styles. At any rate, Greta was usually happy to see it—Here I am again, she often thought, remember this—even though Piñon had died there a dozen times. He was always falling down the stairs or being chased onto the roof, and Greta woke up scream-whispering, or choking on her own despair.

But now, for the first time ever, Greta felt like she was inside the dream house while awake. That's what being inside Big Swiss's pussy felt like, a place she'd been visiting in her dreams for years and forgetting. How exhilarating to finally be awake for this, lucid and somewhat in control. On the other hand, how devastating. She was crushed by the number of years she'd wasted.

"You keep making little gasping noises," Big Swiss said.

"It's so *alive* in here!" Greta said.

As alive and abundant as the universe. If Greta spent time here every day, anything and everything seemed possible. She could pilot a helicopter if she wanted, or act in a play. She could make soap, sweaters, sausage. Maybe dance? She had way more rhythm than she realized, along with more nerve endings in her fingers. It astounded her how satisfying this felt, how natural and innate. No wonder lesbians seemed so smug.

"What's happening to you?" Big Swiss said.

"Nothing," Greta said. "Everything."

"You look like you're . . . mutating," Big Swiss said.

"I might be growing a third eye," Greta said.

Big Swiss sat up. "Whatever it is you think you've discovered—" She shook her head. "Never mind, I'll sound like my mother."

"Go ahead," Greta said. "I'm listening."

"Lie next to me for a minute."

They lay on their sides, facing one another. Big Swiss had given Greta carte blanche, but that was yesterday. Today, just before Greta had entered the dream house, Big Swiss said, "If you want me to come, I'll have to stare long and hard at your face, and you can't stare back." No eye contact, in other words. A tad extreme, but it had worked, twice. Greta had been bowled over by Big Swiss's orgasms. They seemed so guileless, so comprehensive, so stark and new.

But now that Greta had left the dream house, Big Swiss demanded to be looked in the eye.

"You already had it," Big Swiss said.

"What?"

"What you were looking for," Big Swiss said. "It was already there, inside you."

Big Swiss's neck reddened, along with her chest. Her face was almost too beautiful to look at directly. It was like staring at the sun. Greta blinked and rolled onto her back. It dawned on her slowly, a little painfully, that what she'd been looking for inside the dream house, and what she'd found, was her own appetite. She'd been famished all these years without knowing it.

"You seem freaked out," Big Swiss said.

"I guess I'm worried I'll lose my mind or, like, overdose," Greta said. "It's like coming into money and fame and not knowing how to handle it because you've been poor and invisible all your life."

"My vagina isn't made of gold," Big Swiss said.

"Desire," Greta said. "You may not understand this, but I haven't felt real desire in years."

"What else are you feeling?"

"I'm feeling pretty gay, to be honest," Greta said.

"Where are you growing this third eye?" Big Swiss asked.

"On my scalp," Greta said. "You can't see it."

"What else are you hiding?"

My real name, Greta nearly said. "A lot of gray," Greta said instead. "Also, I don't wear reading glasses because they give away my age. That's why I'm always squinting at my phone. I guess I feel pretty old around you."

"Ten years isn't a big deal."

"Seventeen," Greta said. "I'm actually . . . forty-five."

Big Swiss reared back slightly to take in Greta's whole face. "Oh, baby," Greta imagined her saying. "You look incredible for your age. You know that, right?" But Big Swiss said nothing and covered herself with the sheet.

"Has it sunk in?" Greta asked.

"That you can't be trusted?"

"That I'm too old for you," Greta said.

"My last crush was fifty-eight. The one before that, sixty-two."

"It's different with dudes," Greta said.

"They were women."

Greta rolled onto her side once more. "I doubt you were dreaming of having sex with these women. You probably weren't even picturing them naked."

"I watch porn now, thanks to you."

Greta laughed. "Lesbian?"

"Too fake," Big Swiss said.

"Oh, right. MILF."

Big Swiss shook her head. "Those women look like they're in their thirties."

Greta mentally scrolled through the categories, starting with B—babe, BBC, big tits, big ass, big dick, blow jobs, bondage—because nothing under A was coming to mind. Oh, wait a minute.

"Anal?"

"Mature," Big Swiss said.

Greta gulped. Mature—a little too real, even for Greta. Too close to home. Regardless, this was a first. She'd been not skinny enough, not busty enough, not blond enough, not bubbly enough, but Greta had never been not old enough, not even in junior high.

"Has it sunk in?" Big Swiss said.

"That old lady at the dog park," Greta said. "With the pink hair? You'd be okay with, uh—"

"Yes," Big Swiss said.

"Jesus," Greta said. "So, you're saying I'm too *young* for you."

"You can stop worrying about your age," Big Swiss said. "It's not an issue for me."

"What else are you hiding?"

Big Swiss closed her eyes and took a long breath through her nose.

"Have you ever been brought to your knees? And forced to beg?"

"Metaphorically?"

"Have you ever completely prostrated yourself?" Big Swiss said.

"Are you a dominatrix?"

"*Listen*," Big Swiss said. "I'm going to tell you something, but—I'm not sure I have it in me to tell you the whole thing, and I also don't want to ruin your evening." She waved her hand around. "Or this . . . tableau. Our time together here."

Greta braced herself. Obviously, it was about Keith, and it was about time—they'd been baring themselves in so many other ways for weeks now. On the one hand, she'd been anticipating this confession and was slightly offended that it hadn't come sooner. On the other, heavier hand, she dreaded hearing it again. Transcribing it had taken over six hours, so, in a sense, she'd heard this story a hundred times, what with all the rewinding, replaying, tapping it out word for word. In fact, she was probably more familiar with it than almost anyone, and yet, could she really pretend to be hearing it for the first time? She didn't feel capable of arranging her face into the appropriate expression. Of making the right noises. Of saying the right things. She was, in fact, a terrible actress. Friend. Human being. What kind of person pulls a stunt like this? Hadn't Big Swiss suffered enough? Why on earth was Greta putting her through this, and for what? The woman was married. And much too young, though she seemed more mature than Greta. Big Swiss had a savings account, for example, with money in it. She drove a new car. She was a *doctor*. She owned a house. And a carriage house. And land. She took real vacations. On islands. She wanted children. Plural.

Whereas Greta? All her money was in her mouth, which was full of gold crowns. She'd endured at least fifteen root canals. She'd been having orgasms since kindergarten. Her car, almost as old as Big Swiss, was worthless, and her only child was a dog—

"I once had to beg for my life," Big Swiss said. "I'd been beaten up, and my jaw was broken, my nose, the blood vessels in my eyes, and the man beating me kept threatening to kill me. Not threatening—promising. 'I'm going to kill you, I *promise*,' he kept saying. He beat me methodically, tirelessly. I'd never begged for anything in my life, but I begged him to let me jump out the window, even though I knew it meant breaking my leg or ankle. I begged and pleaded."

Jumping out the window? Begging and pleading? Not part of the original transcript. Greta hadn't anticipated hearing a new detail, especially one so disturbing. But why on earth had she expected the same exact story? Stories changed depending on the audience, everyone knew that. Why had Big Swiss withheld this? Because she'd been talking to Om, that's why, and Om was a man, sort of. Obviously, and for good reason, Big Swiss had trouble being vulnerable around men. Or vulnerable, period.

"Anyway, it was a long time ago," Big Swiss said. "But it's still the most difficult thing I've ever done. Even med school was easier."

"Easier than jumping out a window?"

"Begging for my life," Big Swiss said. "Jumping would've been easy. I was desperate to get away from him."

"Oh, okay. So, you didn't jump."

"He wouldn't let me," Big Swiss said. "We were on the third floor, but at that point I didn't care."

"How'd you get away?"

"Miraculously, he let me walk out of there."

"Where?"

"His house. I was a cocktail waitress at the time, and he was a customer. A charming big tipper. He'd done time in prison, he told me, and seemed proud of it, so I figured it was white-collar. He took me to dinner one night and then back to his house. He made a pass, I said no, and he punched me in the face. Then he continued punching my face for ninety minutes, and he spent eight years in prison for it, because he'd beaten up another girl the month before, though not as badly. Anyway, he's a free man now. In fact, I'm worried he knows where you live, because I think he's been following me."

Greta rolled off the bed, went to the nearest window, drew back the drapes. A truck idled in the empty lot across the street, near the pines where the vultures roosted. Greta cupped her hands at the window, but she couldn't make out anything inside the cab. Then the fire alarm started up next door, slowly at first before blaring full blast. Piñon howled, as usual, and the truck suddenly peeled away.

"Does he drive a monster truck?" Greta shouted.

"I'm pretty sure it's a Chevy Silverado," Big Swiss said, after the noise subsided. "Newish, black, tinted windows."

In Hudson, nearly every straight man of a certain age drove the same truck. Greta moved away from the window and threw a log into the woodstove. She lit a cigarette off a burning coal.

"How do you know it's him?"

"I recognize his hand," Big Swiss said. "The way he flicks cigarettes out the window."

"But what does he look like?"

"Weathered," Big Swiss said. "My husband said he looks like a famous actor named Harvey."

"*Keitel?*"

Big Swiss shrugged. "I guess. But that was a long time ago."

"What's his name?"

"Luke," Big Swiss said.

"I know your husband's name," Greta said.

Big Swiss was silent. "Your mouth is trembling again," she said after a minute. "I can see it all the way from here."

"Why aren't *you* trembling?" Greta asked.

"I don't feel like I'm in any real danger," Big Swiss said. "Maybe that's naïve of me."

"He promised to kill you and failed. What if he's spent the last eight years making plans to deliver on his promise?"

"His name is Keith. I don't think he'll risk going back to prison."

Greta tossed her cigarette into the fire. "Is that what you remember most about that night? Begging for your life?"

"It varies," Big Swiss said. "In the ER, there was this really beautiful nurse. Her face was so perfect, I thought I was hallucinating. I was extremely dehydrated and in a lot of pain, and she tried to administer an IV for me, but she couldn't find a vein. She kept trying, though, over and over. My arm, my wrist, my arm again. My hand. My other arm. So, I said, 'Can you look at my face?' She reluctantly looked me in the eye. I could see that I was making her nervous. My face, by the way, looked like a Halloween mask—it was about three times bigger than it is now, and rubbery, and the whites of my eyes were bright red. I said, 'Can you see what kind of night I've had?' She nodded and said nothing. 'Do you think you could do me a favor?' I could tell she thought I was going to ask for water or something, but I said, 'Can you get someone in here who knows what the fuck they're doing?' She ignored me and went back to fumbling with the IV. 'Did you hear me? You suck at this. You're in the wrong profession.' I snatched my arm away from her. Her eyes filled up, which infuriated me, and she started shaking, which made me even angrier. 'Are you stupid? Get someone else in here. I don't want you touching me.'"

Big Swiss draped an arm over her own beautiful face.

"Anyway, I still think about her," Big Swiss said. "Her wet eyes."

"With pleasure?" Greta asked.

"Hey," Big Swiss said.

"Anyone would snap after surviving something like that. It's completely understandable and forgivable. People act out for a lot less, as I'm sure you know. *A lot* less."

"Oh? Are you one of these people?"

"I have the opposite problem—I'm completely shut down. I didn't cry at my mother's funeral. I barely cried as a baby. I've been diagnosed with ED, twice."

"Erectile dysfunction?"

"Emotional detachment."

"You know, they say the eyes are the windows to the soul, but in your case, it's the mouth. You have the most expressive mouth I've ever seen."

"Well, that's weird, because I'm well into my forties and this is the first I'm hearing of it."

"You're not as detached as you think," Big Swiss said. "Anyway, you should know something: the way I treated that nurse wasn't unusual for me. I've always had a low tolerance for weakness. Maybe it's good I was beaten so badly—it took me down a different path. I became kinder. Or more charitable, at least."

"Have you ever been happy?"

Big Swiss scowled. "What kind of question is that?"

"A sincere one."

"Come back to bed," Big Swiss said. "We don't have much time."

As if to demonstrate how charitable she was, Big Swiss put her face between Greta's legs. Greta studied the cracks in the ceiling. She knew them all by heart and she had favorites, but one crack seemed new and out of place. Then it began *moving*. For a moment she thought she was moving it with her mind. Minutes passed. Part of the crack broke off and crawled toward a corner. Because it was a spider. That's when Greta felt something crawling down her own crack. Something hot and wet.

Greta gasped.

"Do you have a towel?" Big Swiss said. "Maybe we should get rubber sheets."

Our first "we," Greta thought.

"Listen," Greta said. "I realize you're a pussy doctor and everything, but where did you learn to do that?"

"I did a little reading last night," Big Swiss said. "The secret is to make contact and then break it, over and over and over, and then kiss it deeply, resting my mouth on it while drawing letters with my tongue. I went through the entire alphabet. What works best on you? The letter I, lowercase, with an extra-long stem and a circled dot. And then, every thirty seconds or so, I let my tongue go slack and still. I wait for all the clouds to pass. I wait for the hard blue sky. It takes about twenty minutes."

"What on earth are you talking about?" Greta said. "What clouds?"

"Your thoughts," Big Swiss said. "I have to wait until all your thoughts pass, until you're not able to think of anything but my tongue, until your entire body feels like it's inside my mouth."

"You studied for this," Greta said. "Like an exam?"

"The books belong to my husband. One is called *She Comes First*."

"Never heard of it," Greta said. "Did he catch you reading it?"

"Yes." Big Swiss smiled at the memory. "He asked me to read a passage aloud."

"And?"

"I did."

"Naked?"

"He kept his clothes on."

"Wasn't he curious about your sudden interest in clam diving?"

"My husband doesn't ask many questions."

"Tell me five things about him."

"Why?"

"So I know he's real," Greta said. "And that you're not mine."

"I'm not his, either," Big Swiss said. "We're not possessive of each other in that way. I've always had my own friends, my own social life. I go to bars and restaurants on weekends, he goes hiking alone. I vacation with my friends every year, sometimes more than once. We give each other a lot of freedom."

Part of Greta wished she'd call Luke by his name. Another part of her was glad she didn't. Both parts were in agreement about one thing, however: no one was getting out of this unscathed. Although, as she watched Big Swiss study her gorgeous reflection in the mirror above the mantel, it was difficult to imagine her being truly wrecked by anything.

"You check yourself out a lot," Greta said. "I probably would, too, if I had your face."

"Maybe I don't see what you see," Big Swiss said. "And you do have my face—our bone structure is similar. Even Luke thinks so."

"How's that?"

"I showed him your picture on my phone," Big Swiss said.

"What picture?"

It was a picture of Greta at the dog park in her groundskeeper getup, lighting a cigarette from another cigarette, looking entirely her age.

"Delete that immediately," Greta said.

"You're the vain one, not me," Big Swiss said. "I'm only checking to see if I exist. I feel like a patch of moving fog most of the time. When I look in the mirror, I'm always startled to see a head and limbs."

"It's your aura," Greta said. "It's as big as one of those tanker ships on the Hudson."

Big Swiss blanched as if she'd seen a ghost.

"Sorry," Greta mumbled.

"You're inside my head. Again."

I'm inside your transcript, Greta thought. It was becoming increasingly difficult to keep track of what Big Swiss had said in therapy and what she'd said in bed. Sometimes, such as right now, Big Swiss seemed on the verge of putting it together. Greta waited and said nothing.

"Will I see you tomorrow?" Big Swiss finally said.

"Yes, please."

To live another day, Greta thought. As Rebekah.

11

Two weeks later, a freak storm dumped two feet of snow. It was late March. What was this shit? What was she doing here? Where was Sabine? She'd been evading Greta for over a month. First, she was "working in the city," then she was in Montreal, Chicago, New Orleans. Her text that morning: "Had to stop in Florida. Home soon, promise." Greta hoped Sabine had acquired a secret lover, or at least some weight in her face.

Speaking of, Big Swiss kept showing up every weekday. She brought Silas with her most days, along with an overnight bag, though she never stayed longer than a few hours. The bag made a clinking noise when she walked. Initially, Greta was worried it contained gynecological tools or torture devices, but it was full of . . . condiments. Big Swiss carried the international food aisle with her wherever she went. She seemed to require food every forty-five minutes. Otherwise, she fell asleep. The condiments in question included banana sauce (Filipino ketchup), *smörgåskaviar* (mayo mixed with fish roe), Aromat *aux herbes* (Swiss seasoning), Maggi Würze (Swiss Worcestershire), Thomy Delikatess-Senf (German mustard), and a variety of hot sauces. The vehicles for these condiments were also in the bag: fresh fruit, walnuts, tuna, sardines, sauerkraut, hard-boiled eggs, something called Fitness Bread, dried meats, various hard cheeses. Not surprisingly, Big Swiss was obsessed with Swiss cheese, though not the kind with holes in it, and dairy in general.

She continued to see Om, and Greta continued to transcribe their sessions, but she didn't talk about Greta in therapy. Not Greta, not Rebekah, not the insane amount of sex the three of them were having. She'd mentioned their first kiss—once. Greta was baffled. Why wouldn't she mention the torrid affair she was having with an older woman, an affair she seemed to be enjoying, to a sex and relationship coach who, by the way, wasn't cheap, who charged, in fact, $186 per session? She wasn't talking about sex at all lately. The last three sessions had been devoted to her *parents*.

Her parents, by the way, were upper-middle-class intellectuals who preferred to live in poverty. Big Swiss grew up thinking they were bankrupt. She was homeschooled, which Greta knew, but her parents were farmers because they were obsessed with manual labor. No sugar or caffeine was allowed in the house, and they were opposed to day-dreaming. Not drugs—daydreaming. As a child, Big Swiss had been constantly jolted out of her daydreaming state. Her parents did this by feeding her intense Turkish food and other Middle Eastern delicacies. They'd forced her to work the land, no matter the weather, and to study deliberately convoluted philosophy. Their only joy and pleasure: "ecstatic and authentic movement," which some people called dancing. All of this explained why Big Swiss craved intensity in relationships, food, work, and the weather, hated being underwhelmed, remained willfully ignorant of popular culture, and refused to dance with Greta or anyone else.

Om was behaving strangely, too. He listened. He seemed to think before speaking. He let Big Swiss steer the conversation. Part of Greta thought they both must have known about her. But Om couldn't have known—he would've fired Greta. Of course, Greta couldn't say anything to either of them, and so she was left to wonder. Was she not important enough to bring up in therapy, or was she too important to bring up to Om? Was Big Swiss keeping their affair from him because she feared his response, his ridiculous opinions and suggestions, or did she suspect something? Was this her way of letting Greta know that she knew, and if so, how could she not say anything?

Her ability to compartmentalize bewildered Greta, who was unable to put Big Swiss's box in a box. In fact, Greta thought about Big Swiss's box every four minutes and was beginning to feel like a dude. Except she also felt more ladylike—or at any rate, Big Swiss treated her like a lady. Big Swiss never showed up empty-handed. She regularly brought wine, flowers, candy, and other gifts. So far, she'd given Greta a pair of cashmere knee socks, real gold earrings, and several robust houseplants. Greta had never felt so wooed.

Now Big Swiss's car pulled into the driveway. She shouted for Greta in the yard. As usual, Greta wanted to go straight to bed, but Big Swiss insisted on taking the dogs for a walk across the field and into the woods. She brought supplies: two pair of snowshoes, two bottles of hard cider, two manuals for identifying trees and birds, and one knife. The knife, called a *karambit*, had been given to her by Luke, ostensibly for protection. The blade was sharp but small and had a crescent curve resembling a claw. Greta could only imagine using it for suicide, but, according to Luke, the *karambit* had been an agricultural tool before it became weaponized, and had been popular among Indonesian women. The women would tie the knife in their hair and use it to rake roots—or rapists, if necessary. Big Swiss seemed entirely comfortable with it, however, and even demonstrated the various striking motions—slashing, hooking, hammering—before using it to gently scrape bark off a tree.

"Smells like cream soda," Big Swiss said, holding the bark to her nose.

"Fascinating," Greta said drily.

Sabine owned some of these woods, but not all of them, and with everything covered in snow, Greta had no idea where her property ended. Clearly, the deer stands belonged to someone else, along with the hunting shack littered with nips and empties, and the abandoned cabin full of charred furniture and weird Christian books.

"Let's free some of these trees," Big Swiss said. "See how the saplings are leaning over? Their limbs are trapped in the snow."

Like an evangelist healing the crippled, Big Swiss went from tree to tree, pulling at limbs, standing back to watch them catapult upward. The trees made a whooshing sound as if sighing with relief, and their bark seemed to weep in gratitude. Big Swiss looked exalted. She began throwing herself at each tree as if on a holy mission.

"Isn't this satisfying?" Big Swiss asked breathlessly. "Don't you feel uplifted?"

Greta looked around. There were still dozens of prostrated saplings, and she suspected they wouldn't be leaving until every single one had been liberated. But Greta was only interested in liberating Big Swiss of her clothing and ordering her to spread out on the bed.

"Can we get out of here now? We're wasting time."

"We have to earn it," Big Swiss said. "Besides, you know I like to get really, really cold."

"Your brain reminds me of Siberia," Greta said. "Which is strange because your down-there is like South America."

"South America is a continent," Big Swiss said. "With fourteen countries. The climate is extremely varied."

"Chile."

"Things are really fucked-up in Chile right now," Big Swiss said. "And it snows there. You should try living in the world or, I don't know, reading a newspaper."

"*Ecuador*," Greta said. "And pardon me, but you couldn't pick David Bowie out of a lineup."

"You couldn't find *Ecuador* on a map if your life depended on it," Big Swiss said. "At least I know where the hell I am and what's happening. Which way is north?"

Greta pointed toward the house.

Big Swiss shook her head and pointed at a random tree. "What's this?"

"West?"

"It's a woodpecker hole," Big Swiss said. "Look, you need to go into the woods with someone who knows things. But the person who knows things also needs you, the person who knows nothing. We need each other."

Why was she obsessed with this person? She was humorless. It was like having an affair with Kierkegaard or B. F. Skinner. The only comedy Big Swiss approved of was anticomedy. Andy Kaufman eating ice cream, et cetera. Greta chugged the rest of her cider and considered sticking her head in the freezing creek. Instead, she dipped her bare hand in the water and brought it to her mouth.

"Don't drink from there," Big Swiss snapped. "Eat snow instead."

"I'm not eating snow! Are you insane?"

Big Swiss pointed at a tall, slim tree with beautiful blond leaves clinging to its branches. The leaves, long dead, had never fallen. Greta approached the tree and shook it vigorously. The leaves didn't budge.

"Why do you hate nature so much?" Big Swiss asked.

"Everything seems so overdetermined," Greta said.

Big Swiss consulted her tree manual. "That's a beech tree you're assaulting."

Greta missed the beach. She missed seeing sand fly as Piñon attempted to dig his way to China. Digging had always been one of his favorite activities. Not anymore. Now he was all caught up in his own torrid homosexual affair. All he seemed to want was to hump Silas's legs, ass, and face. He'd been chasing Silas for thirty minutes, but the snow was too deep. Silas leapt through it like a wolf; Piñon, exasperated, resorted to humiliating bunny hops.

"Poor Piñon," Greta said. "He belongs near the sea."

"He's a *dog*," Big Swiss said. "He's wearing a puffer vest. How much did you spend on that?"

"Do you even like dogs?"

"My first dog was named Ruderboot. He was nine when he disappeared in the middle of winter. We got a lot of snow that year and I couldn't find him anywhere. In spring, I was on the school bus and there was Ruderboot on the side of the road, thawing out, his legs sticking straight in the air. I hadn't seen him in five months. All the kids were pointing at him, but I couldn't speak. I couldn't make a sound for two weeks."

Greta melted. She reached for Big Swiss's hand and held it.

"Sorry you had to go through that," Greta said. "How awful."

"Before we buried him, I asked our neighbor, Lars the butcher, to cut off his head," Big Swiss went on. "I wanted to hang his skull on my bedroom wall. I still have it, all these years later."

Greta stiffened. She was beginning to see a pattern. If she tried to comfort Big Swiss during a rare display of vulnerability, Big Swiss turned to stone.

"What kind of name is Ruderboot?"

"It's German," Big Swiss said. "For 'Rowboat.'"

Row, row, row your boat, gently back to the house. Piñon's sweet little feet were frozen, so Greta carried him on her shoulders, even though she could feel Big Swiss judging her. Once inside, she placed Piñon on his beloved sheepskin in the antechamber, loaded the stove, and waited in bed.

WITH MEN, Greta had always thought of her vagina as a blind driveway. The men drove in and out, but it was largely hidden from Greta, and there was no convex mirror that allowed her to see the entrance, the strange comings and goings. But now that she was behind the wheel, so to speak, and Big Swiss's driveway was so clearly marked, Greta could see every exquisite detail. In fact, she'd become addicted to watching herself go in and out, and resented having been deprived of this view for so long. Of course, the view was overly familiar from porn, but it was altogether different when the POV was your very own.

"I think I get why men are so 'visual,'" Greta said. "It's because they can see their own dicks at all times."

Big Swiss rolled her eyes. "It's sociological. Men are taught to be visual, to objectify. It's not a biological trait."

"I think it might be as simple as see dick, see Jane, see dick go into Jane."

Greta brought her hand to her nose and inhaled. Only one thing rivaled the view, and it lingered longer, affected her like lavender was supposed to, and sometimes got her through the unbearably long weekends, which were off-limits to Greta.

"Nothing gets your smell off my fingers," Greta said.

Big Swiss didn't say anything.

"Yes, I've tried kerosene," Greta said.

"Is this a problem?" Big Swiss said, sitting up. "I mean, is it interfering with your life?"

"Calm down," Greta said. "I was kidding about the kerosene. I stopped washing my hands weeks ago. I relish sniffing my fingers, especially at the grocery store."

"You're different when you're on top," Big Swiss said. "You look different, and your personality changes."

Greta thought about it. "I feel more like myself. My true self, I mean. Not to sound corny, but I feel like I'm accessing—and inhabiting—one of my past lives."

"Which one?" Big Swiss asked.

"I was a guerrilla living in the jungle."

"A big gorilla," Big Swiss said, nodding. "That makes sense. I can see that."

"*Guerrilla*," Greta repeated. "With a U and E. My point is, I feel radicalized, ready to fight."

"We're just having an affair," Big Swiss said.

"Think of all the calls you've missed, the meals you've skipped, how late to work I've made you. Think of all the surprise raids in broad daylight."

Big Swiss shrugged.

"Who have you told about us?" Greta asked.

"Only my therapist," Big Swiss said. "He's local—you might know him. I'm kind of embarrassed to say his name."

"Om," Greta blurted. "He buys weed from Sabine. He's over here all the time and hangs out for hours."

This was a lie. Om knew where Sabine lived, but he didn't know her exact address.

"Your mouth's doing that thing again."

"Can you maybe not be super specific when you talk about me? I don't want him looking at me all knowingly in front of Sabine."

Big Swiss would probably tell him fucking everything now, including all the bad things. She'd already told him Greta's first name, she said, which Greta said was fine, so long as Big Swiss didn't mention where Greta lived, or with whom.

"Who have *you* told?" Big Swiss asked.

"No one," Greta said.

"Not even Sabine?"

"Especially not her," Greta said.

"Why, is she homophobic?"

"Pistanthrophobic."

"What's that?"

"A fear of trusting people, or getting cheated on."

"But you're not in a relationship," Big Swiss said carefully, as if this were news to Greta.

"Yes, but *you* are," Greta said. "I'm sleeping with a married woman almost half my age. She'd say I'd lost the rest of my marbles."

And she would be right. Greta was beginning to feel more than a little unstable.

Big Swiss straddled Greta and pinned her wrists with one hand. She thrust the other hand between Greta's legs. It had been over a week since Big Swiss had touched her down there—or anywhere, really.

"How do you feel now?" Big Swiss asked.

"Like you, maybe. A guarded pillow queen."

"We talked about this," Big Swiss said. "I'm up to my elbows in vaginas all day. Being on top feels like work to me."

Greta sighed. "Pillow queen" wasn't quite right, anyway. When she was on the bottom, Greta felt like one of the Tahitian women in a Gauguin painting. Beneath Big Swiss, Greta felt poor, foreign, and fetishized. She would've said as much, but Big Swiss probably had no idea who Gauguin was, even though a coffee-table book of his paintings lay on the bathroom floor upstairs. The book belonged to Sabine and always seemed to fall open to the painting titled *What! Are You Jealous?*

Outside, Greta heard a vehicle roll into the driveway. Piñon sniffed the air, hackles raised, and gave a low woof. Greta recognized the seductive *thwomp* of a Mercedes door closing. Boots crunched snow. Downstairs, the Dutch door unlatched, creaked open, banged shut. Boots clomped across the concrete floor. An armful of logs fell into the fireplace; newspaper crumpled. Sabine started swearing.

Greta looked at Big Swiss, who was already dressed and leashing Silas. Big Swiss slung her condiment bag over her shoulder.

"Leave the bag," Greta whispered. "Too noisy."

"I can't. I need it."

Greta imagined Big Swiss squeezing Swiss mayonnaise into her mouth as she drove over the Rip Van Winkle Bridge.

"Greta!" Sabine suddenly yelled from the kitchen. "I'm home!"

Piñon whined at the door. He'd missed Sabine as much as Greta had.

"Coming!" Greta yelled.

"Who's Greta?" Big Swiss whispered.

"Greta Garbo," Greta said. "Her nickname for me."

"Who?"

"Forget it," Greta whispered. "I'm going downstairs, you sneak out the front door."

IF LOOKING AT BIG SWISS was like staring at the sun, Sabine was the sun's afterimage, a shimmering red orb with a spectral green halo. Greta switched on a lamp and blinked. The halo turned out to be a hat, and Sabine wasn't shimmering so much as shivering. So were dozens of cobwebs hanging from the ceiling.

"Where the fuck is that draft coming from?"

"Everywhere," Greta said.

They never bothered with pleasantries. Greta thought of the day Sabine kidnapped her in the Sprinter van in California, the beginning of the life Greta was living now. They hadn't seen or spoken to each other in years. Sabine had simply rolled down the window and made a giddyup noise, and Greta had climbed in, no questions asked.

"Whose car was that?" Sabine asked.

"Tinder date," Greta said.

Sabine looked alarmed.

"You've been gone a long time," Greta explained. "I got lonely."

Sabine was mystified by longing of any kind. Well, except longing for warmth—that was allowed. There was a little too much Florida in her face. She looked like she'd been sleeping outside for weeks, but at least she'd put on some weight. She was huggable now.

"I guess I just don't understand how Tinder works in a town this small. Don't you run into these people in person?"

"I only have sex with Airbnb-ers," Greta said.

Sabine sighed and looked around. "Any chance you could have sex with some local tradesmen? We need a lot of work done around here."

"I'm not that good in bed."

"Flirt with some carpenters," Sabine said. "For starters. Also, don't freak out, but we have . . . company."

Greta looked over her shoulder.

"On the roof," Sabine said, and coughed. "There's, uh, one or two vultures up there right now, shitting all over the chimney."

"So that's why you're lighting a fire."

"I threw a few rocks," Sabine said. "They didn't even flinch."

"Why is this happening?"

Sabine shrugged. "Isn't it obvious?"

They were admiring the architecture, Greta imagined. The sunsets or whatever.

"It's an omen," Sabine said, and coughed again. "One of us is about to die."

This may have been Sabine's way of saying she'd finally visited a doctor, a doctor who'd diagnosed her with advanced cancer and told her she had six weeks to live. But there was no way of really knowing, or asking about it directly, because Sabine was a master deflector.

"Is there something you're not telling me?" Greta asked.

Sabine smiled. She looked Greta up and down and then squinted at her face.

"You look real good," Sabine said. "You look more alive than you have in years."

12

OM: Can you state your initials for the transcriber, please?
FEW: FEW.
OM: How have you been?
FEW: [PAUSE] Okay.

"Just okay?" Greta said.

OM: What's happening with the Keith situation?
FEW: I still see his truck in my rearview mirror, but he keeps his distance.
OM: A hundred yards?
FEW: I don't know how far that is.
OM: He should remain out of your line of sight. Like, completely.
FEW: I haven't seen him up close. Other people have, though. He's been spotted at Cousin's. Luke's uncle hangs out there after work and says he sees Keith sitting at the bar alone almost every night.
OM: He's allowed to drink? In bars?
FEW: I don't know. Maybe he only drinks water.
OM: I don't think they serve water at Cousin's.

Greta hadn't been there, but Cousin's was known for its ten-count pours. Its décor: keno, a wall of TVs, and flies. Its patrons: locals, alcoholics, old creeps. And ex-cons, apparently.

OM: Do you worry about running into him?
FEW: I have bigger things to worry about right now.
OM: Such as?
FEW: Are the words "adult" and "adultery" related?

"Oh boy," Greta said.

OM: Good question. I don't think so. [RUSTLING] Let me check. The word "adultery" may derive from "adulterate," which means "to debase or make impure by adding inferior or less desirable elements."
FEW: Okay, well, my marriage has been adulterated by less desirable elements, if you know what I mean.
OM: Cocaine?
FEW: Other adults.
OM: Did something happen?
FEW: It's happening. I mean, it's ongoing. I haven't talked about it because—well, I think I've been in denial. But this morning I was forced to face facts. And now I feel very . . . awake.

"What facts?" Greta said. "Which morning?"

Greta paused the audio and checked the date. They hadn't seen each other on the day it was recorded, a Tuesday, but Big Swiss had uncharacteristically texted, "I miss you. Grievously." Greta saw now that she'd forgotten to text back, even though the word "grievously" had been rather affecting. In fact, Greta had felt what she could only describe as ecstatic exaltation and had been unable to eat, drink, type, or do anything, really, except roll around in bed, moaning.

"So, you realized that you're in love with me," Greta said, and tapped the foot pedal. "Grievously. On Tuesday."

FEW: My brain feels . . . bifurcated. I'm being pulled in two opposite directions. It's been difficult to maintain my composure, to not do anything rash, like confide in my friends or coworkers.

"Honey, I know," Greta said.

OM: Can you start at the beginning?
FEW: Let me think.

"You showed up at my house," Greta said. "In your fur coat. You talked about my forearms."

FEW: I guess the first thing I noticed was the protein shakes.

"The what?" Greta said.

FEW: And the hummus. Hummus on carrots, celery, everything.

"Hmm?" Greta said.

FEW: And then suddenly everything was gluten-free. No more carbs. That whole intermittent fasting thing, keto whatever.

"What's this now?" Greta said.

FEW: And he's working out like crazy. He runs, he jumps rope, he lifts weights. He takes supplements. He drizzles this weird oil all over his salads. He puts the oil in his coffee, too, along with *butter*. He uses an electric milk frother.

"Uh, where's this going," Greta said.

FEW: He signed up for Brazilian jiu-jitsu. Now he goes to the dojo after work and "rolls," as he calls it, for at least three hours, and he doesn't get home until I'm already in bed. He's constantly washing his gi and talking about armlocks, takedowns, gassing out. I couldn't even wrap my head around it at first. It's the last thing I ever imagined him doing, and it's almost impossible to picture him getting breathed on by strangers, let alone *grappling*.

OM: Why?

FEW: He suffers from tactile defensiveness.

OM: What's that?

FEW: You don't know?

OM: You've never mentioned it.

FEW: He has trouble being hugged. He has a hard time wearing shoes, hates tight clothing of any kind, including underwear, and he can't read his own handwriting. He has intense stage fright. He holds his fork wrong. He holds utensils of any kind like they're knives. He has trouble brushing his hair. I mean, he holds the brush strangely. [PAUSE] But overall, it's mild.

OM: Uh, it doesn't sound mild. In fact, it sounds pretty serious.

FEW: Let me ask you something, Om. Am I your only client? Be honest.

OM: Not even close. I have a very long waiting list.

FEW: Well, I'm surprised you haven't encountered people with this condition. They usually have a lot of intimacy problems.

OM: My clients can't *stop* hugging people. They can't stop hugging *themselves*. If they don't wear underwear, it's not because it's too tight, and most of them love reading their own writing, out loud and onstage. Has Luke ever been in therapy?

FEW: Not since high school. He used to not be able to handle noise and strong odors, and so he was constantly walking out of stores, restaurants, parties, meetings. That's how we met—I followed him out of a loud party he was trying to escape.

OM: Is he, uh, on the spectrum?

FEW: Not officially.

OM: He doesn't mind your perfume? What is that scent you're wearing?

"Pussy," Greta said.

FEW: It's called Alien. But I can only put it on in my car. I could never spray it in the house.

OM: It sounds like jiu-jitsu might be good therapy for Luke. Do you agree? It's definitely *immersive*.

FEW: He does seem more integrated, more like a whole person. His own person, I mean, separate from me. He's even made a few friends at the dojo. They have a group chat. Sometimes they go out after. One of them is a woman. He talks about how tough she is, how he enjoys rolling with her. Anyway, this morning I picked up his phone to check the weather—my phone was charging in another room—and his passcode didn't work. It took me a second to realize he'd changed it. He's had the same passcode for *years*. That's when I knew.

OM: Did you ask him about it?

FEW: He was in the shower. [PAUSE] That's another thing: he's been closing the door when he takes a shower, like he doesn't want to be disturbed, and he spends a lot of time grooming himself. He changed his deodorant. He bought seamless underwear. He's growing a *beard*.

OM: Have you stopped making love?

FEW: No. In fact, we're having more sex than we've ever had.

"Pardon?" Greta said.

OM: Has the sex changed? Or has your experience of it changed?

FEW: It's a whole other flavor. Sometimes the orgasms are so intense, I lose my hearing for twenty minutes.

"What?" Greta said. "What?"

OM: So, it's mutually gratifying.

FEW: For the first time, ever.

OM: You're no longer engaging in display sex. You're no longer

going through the motions. You're no longer observing
yourself from outside the window.

FEW: I'm present in a way I've never been before. We keep our eyes
open. We take more time with each other. He even asks me to
wrap my arms and legs around him.

OM: Is he still rough with you? I mean, does he still choke you?

FEW: No. I imagine he's choking other people now. On the mat.
Anyway, there's nothing bottled up about him anymore. And
he doesn't wait for me to initiate sex. He flirts, I flirt back, and
then he picks me up and carries me to bed. He even lights all
the candles.

"Candles!" Greta yelled.

OM: These seem like positive changes.

FEW: Maybe he just needed to have sex with someone else. Someone
other than me. He's had very few partners.

OM: Is it possible you're jumping to conclusions?

FEW: I can tell he's hiding something, some . . . *entanglement*. It's all
in his eyebrows. It's hard to explain.

OM: You sound more intrigued than upset. In fact, you don't seem
bothered at all.

FEW: I'm dying of curiosity. I've even gone through his wallet,
looking for receipts.

OM: Have you thought about confronting him?

FEW: I think about it constantly. But I'm not quite there yet.

OM: Why the hesitation?

FEW: I'm enjoying the mystery for now. Also, if I ask him to confess,
I'll have to do the same. I mean, I'll have to confess my own sin.

OM: Snooping?

FEW: Cheating.

OM: Sorry?

FEW: I'm having my own affair.

"Record scratch," Greta said.

OM: [PAUSE] Since when?

FEW: Few weeks. A month. I've been trying to ease my way into telling you about it.

OM: Why would you do that?

FEW: I'm usually judgmental of people who do this. And now here I am, doing it.

OM: May I ask who it is?

FEW: It's a woman.

OM: Detective Benson?

FEW: Yes.

OM: So maybe it's you who needed to have sex with someone else.

FEW: [PAUSE] My mind is so scattered lately, I'm having trouble remembering how it started.

OM: She put her tongue in your mouth, as I recall, at the dog park.

"Does it get any gayer?" Greta said.

FEW: And then I saw where she lives. Or *how* she lives.

[PAUSE 0:43]

"Hello?" Greta said. "How do I live?"

OM: Does she live in a mansion?

FEW: No, no, she lives in an eighteenth-century farmhouse. It has a lot of character, but it's literally crumbling around her.

Greta laughed. "It's brick, bitch. It's been standing for three hundred years."

FEW: There's no heat. If she doesn't burn wood she'll literally freeze to death. She sleeps with hot stones under the covers like it's 1762, and the tap water is brown and disgusting.

"It's *well* water," Greta said. "It has sulfur in it."

FEW: She has these heavy linen drapes nailed over the windows—they're fully lined, custom-made in Copenhagen or someplace—but when the sunlight hits them in late afternoon, you can see hundreds of dark spots. I always figured it was flecks of paint. Turns out it's a bunch of *stink bugs*. "They're hiding in the lining," Rebekah said casually the other day, "waiting for spring." Can you imagine?

"But what about the windows themselves?" Greta said. "The beautiful panes!"

FEW: I don't know why she doesn't move. She could easily find a place in town, a place with a thermostat. But the only piece of real estate she's interested in is my vagina. She talks about it like it's an apartment she's renting.

"Uh, that's a gross misquote," Greta said. "I compared it to the antechamber, because it's ten degrees warmer in there."

OM: You must be getting something out of it, though. Otherwise, you wouldn't be doing this. Right?

"Right," Greta said.

FEW: She's very demonstrative. Warm, affectionate. Before we met, I felt frozen. Now I'm a puddle on the floor. It's not always . . . comfortable.
OM: How often do you see each other?
FEW: Four days a week, sometimes more, sometimes less. But she refuses to call it an affair.
OM: What does she call it?
FEW: A fuckfest. I'll admit it's very passionate. Our eyes turn completely black almost every time.
OM: How so?
FEW: Your pupils dilate when they see something beautiful. Did you know that?

OM: Oxytocin is a very powerful drug. Women produce more oxytocin than men. So, you're not only high on dopamine, your brains are also flooded with oxy.

FEW: I don't see myself ever identifying as a lesbian.

OM: Do you look alike, by any chance?

FEW: Not really.

OM: Are you sure about that?

FEW: We're not even remotely in doppelgänger territory. [PAUSE] I hope you're not suggesting I'm a narcissist, or that I'm falling in love with myself. As you may recall, I'd never even masturbated until recently.

OM: Are you in love with her?

FEW: It feels that way.

OM: I'm only saying that the risk for love addiction is strong, and you should proceed with caution. Resist the urge to merge. Maintain your separate identities. Do you connect in other ways, other than sexually?

FEW: We're not aligned intellectually—philosophically, I should say. We're not preoccupied by the same things, and we don't share the same interests. I don't read novels or watch movies, and I don't dwell on the past. I'm interested in science, nature, things that take me outside of myself.

OM: Okay, so—not that it's a bad thing, but are you only showing up for the sex?

FEW: Sometimes it feels almost spiritual. Maybe I'm supposed to learn something from her? She acts like she's having a religious experience.

OM: Which religion, if you had to hazard a guess?

"The Church of Euthanasia," Greta said.

FEW: [PAUSE] Hare Krishna.

OM: Interesting.

"Kill me," Greta said.

- 201 -

OM: Is she also married?

FEW: Never married. No kids, no real career, no assets, no retirement, no plans or future goals. She just lives day-to-day like an animal. Sometimes she seems . . . lost.

"You mean free?" Greta said.

FEW: It's kind of difficult for me to relate to her, honestly.

OM: Is she an artist?

FEW: She's a recluse. With a little white dog.

"White and black," Greta said, correcting her.

FEW: Her dog is beyond spoiled. It's probably better that she doesn't have kids. He doesn't come when she calls him. He's small, but he has a big personality.

OM: Does Detective Benson also have a big personality?

FEW: No, but she carries herself like a famous person. If we're outside, she's always looking over her shoulder, as if she's worried about being photographed by paparazzi.

"Or just run over," Greta said. "By Keith."

FEW: Otherwise, there's an air of doom about her. She seems profoundly lonely. It's part of my attraction to her. She reminds me of the church bells of my childhood. In Geneva, all the church bells ring at the same time, every hour on the hour, in every corner of the city, and it's the most melancholic sound I've ever heard, but also beautiful. I think that's why the suicide rate is so high in Switzerland.

"So, I make people want to kill themselves," Greta said. "Wonderful."

OM: Have you told her about Keith yet?

FEW: Yes.

OM: What about Luke?

FEW: Of course. She knows I'm married.

OM: Does Luke know of her existence?

FEW: I've told him little bits. He just thinks of her as my new friend, and he assumes she's emotionally needy.

OM: Is she?

FEW: Very. I tend to attract damaged people like her. Broken toys.

"What the fuck?" Greta said.

FEW: I think she's attracted to me because I'm stable and secure. I have my life together in a way she's probably not used to, and sometimes I feel like I'm helping her.

"Excuse me?" Greta said.

OM: And maybe she's also attracted to your beauty?

FEW: We're about equal in that department.

"Well, well, well," Greta said. "Hare Krishna."

OM: You must make quite a pair, then.

FEW: I love being in public with her, but we don't get out enough. We spend most of our time in bed. Her bed. I've tried dragging her out for drinks—she won't go. But she's agreed to come to my house to meet Luke.

OM: Sounds slightly . . . risky.

FEW: You mean crazy?

"Yes," Greta said.

FEW: It was his idea. He wants to meet the mysterious older woman I'm spending all my time with. I showed him a picture, but he wasn't satisfied. He's insisting on having dinner at the house.

OM: Is it my imagination, or are you not concerned about getting caught?

FEW: When I finally come clean, I think it will be better that he's met her. Who knows, maybe I'll ask him to invite his new "friend" to dinner, as well.

OM: Does the idea of an open marriage hold any interest or appeal?

FEW: I can make ideological space in my mind for it, but in practice it might be . . .

"Suicide?" Greta said.

FEW: Challenging. But it's something I fantasize about trying. I've even read a few books about it.

OM: Which ones?

FEW: *Beyond Monogamy, More Than Two—*

"Millennials," Greta muttered.

[ALARM]

OM: You hear that, my dear? It's my next *client—*

[END OF RECORDING]

Greta had a delayed reaction to most things and often fell asleep in high-stress situations. She'd slept through one car accident, eight or nine root canals, the SATs, prom, pap smears, her twenties and thirties. She'd fought sleep at her mother's funeral—and lost, sadly—and now it appeared she'd passed out at her desk. She woke up drooling and disoriented. Evidently, hearing herself talked about in therapy had been as stressful as dental surgery, but now that it was over, the transcript complete and sent, she needed to make sure it never happened again. It was time to end this, to make a stand, to put her foot down. No one should have such easy access to the private thoughts of their lover—or anyone. It would be one thing if she were eavesdropping in the traditional sense of the word, by hanging from the eaves of Om's office building, straining to hear the conversation within, perhaps catching only snatches, an odd word or phrase, but she was listening from well within, practically from the lapel of Big Swiss's shirt, and catching every goddamn word, every worried swallow, every exasperated sigh. It was snooping times a million, and despicable. Of course, she had no right to be upset by anything Big Swiss said in therapy, but she hadn't realized Big Swiss was demeaning herself with Greta, who'd somehow never thought of herself as a broken toy. She'd never been on this side of things, looking up from the gutter. Was this why Big Swiss had such power over her, why Greta dropped everything the minute she beckoned? Well, never again, goddammit. It was time to end this insanity. Today. Right now.

Her phone vibrated. A text from Big Swiss. "What's your ETA? Dinner will be ready in forty-two minutes."

Greta typed, "Not feeling well. Sorry to cancel last minute. I can't do this anymore."

Her thumb hovered over the send button. Her head felt as heavy as granite and she thought she might pass out again. Instead, she deleted what she'd written and typed: "Coming!!!!!!"

13

Maybe it was the wrong day to try microdosing, but she'd needed *something* to help her get through dinner, and she remembered Sabine's saying that one stem plus one cap equaled a Valium and a cup of coffee, or maybe it was one cap, no stem, two Tylenol PM. In any case, she felt pretty loose as she drove to their house, which she'd always imagined as a Swiss chalet built directly into the side of a mountain. The chalet had very wide eaves, of course, with trim painted dark green, and window boxes full of bright red geraniums, and she kept envisioning Big Swiss on a balcony, dressed in a traditional dirndl, the embroidered bodice laced up tight, her tits spilling out of the low, square neckline, and there was Luke approaching from the rear, lifting her full skirt, letting his lederhosen fall around his ankles. Big Swiss closed her eyes and opened her mouth. Was she singing? She was *yodeling*. She stopped suddenly and started coughing. Luke paused to pat her on the back. Big Swiss pulled a small item from her apron, unwrapped it, popped it into her mouth. "Ricola!" she said, looking right into the camera. There was a close-up of her face. A boom microphone dipped into the frame. "Cut!" the director shouted.

Greta nearly missed the turn and swerved onto their private road. The road meandered over a creek, through a thicket of silver birch, and then under a canopy of budding pear trees. A black wooden carriage house loomed on the right, an undulating meadow on the left, and, straight ahead, the main house, which was not at all chalet-like, but rather entirely modern, low-slung and concise, made of concrete, glass, and steel. They had the Wright style, in other words, were far wealthier than she'd realized, and would probably not be dressed as peasants.

Rather than knock, Greta simply stared at the front door, which appeared to be made of solid chestnut containing many evocative knots. Big Swiss abruptly opened the door and pulled Greta into the foyer. She was flushed, dressed entirely in pink, and seemed to be glowing from within. Greta felt like she was being greeted by a Himalayan salt lamp. Big Swiss kissed the air on either side of Greta's ears: left, right, left.

"Are you good?" Big Swiss said. "Can you handle this?"

"I'm a master of the charade," Greta said, a phrase she'd been repeating to herself for eight hours. "God, it's quiet!"

"We're in the country. What did you expect?"

"Church bells," Greta whispered.

Big Swiss gave her a frightened smile. Stay out of her transcript, Greta ordered herself.

"*Cowbells*," Greta said quickly. "Listen, I may have eaten a tiny amount of mushrooms about an hour ago."

"Fuck," Big Swiss said. "Will you be able to eat fondue?"

"Well, I'm not *hallucinating*," Greta said. "But on the way here, I became completely entranced by a vision of your home life, only to realize that it was a pornographic commercial for Swiss cough drops. And then I wondered why they don't make pornographic commercials in general. Like for potato chips. So, I don't know, I guess I'm a horny mess."

"What else is new," Big Swiss said.

"Here," Greta said, and brought forth two bottles of Grüner Veltliner.

"Perfect," Big Swiss said. "We can't get drunk, though."

You can't, Greta thought. I'm free as a bird. Except I can't fly. Because I'm *broken*.

Greta gazed at the wall of antique mirrors hanging above a vintage settee. The umbrella stand seemed worth six grand. The spiky chandelier, sixteen. Dear god, was that an authentic Cy Twombly scribble painting?

"Where the hell am I?" Greta said. "Who are you?"

Big Swiss shrugged. "Luke's grandfather was an architect. His grandmother was a decorator. Luke always knew he'd inherit this house."

"Which is why he had them killed," Greta said. "Or killed them himself?"

"They died six months apart," Big Swiss said. "Cancer and a broken heart."

Greta exhaled. "You could've warned me."

"Take off your shoes," Big Swiss said.

"I'm not wearing socks."

"The floors are heated," Big Swiss assured her.

They entered what Big Swiss called "the great room." Weeks ago, when Greta had asked Big Swiss what sort of house she lived in, Big Swiss had only described it as "glassy." There hadn't been any mention of twenty-five-foot ceilings, floor-to-ceiling windows, lime-washed walls, or smooth stone slab floors.

For once, Greta could feel her own mouth quivering. Her mouth, and something else. It was like receiving oral from someone with the ability to vary the texture of their tongue. Silk, velvet, leather, chrome, cashmere, sturdy linen—all were present and lapping at her persistently. She'd never seen a double-sided . . . *couch*. Not in person, anyway. Nor had she seen so many small exotic stools, and no two alike, scattered around one room. A huge, freestanding fireplace wrapped in fieldstone separated the living and dining areas. One side of the double-sided couch was oriented toward the fireplace, the other toward the view. Vintage oriental rugs lay at unexpected angles. She loved every lamp immediately, and there were many. A lot of effort had been put into making everything seem unfussy and haphazard—hence, the ancient wicker chaise in the corner—but Greta wasn't buying it. Everything was *just so*, the total opposite of Greta's house, where everything *just was*. And the view—well. The view was highly intentional, clearly the starting point of the whole enterprise. When Greta had first pulled up to the house, she'd sensed something big in the backyard, some grand expanse, and she saw now that it was a clear blue lake. A nearly turquoise lake. On the other side of it, moody purple mountains.

"Is that yours?" Greta asked, and pointed out the window.

"The boat?" Big Swiss said.

"The lake," Greta said.

"Of course not," Big Swiss said. "That's Sleepy Hollow Lake."

Luke wandered in from somewhere, looking a little sleepy and hollow himself, except that he was gripping a hand squeezer. He was both taller and handsomer than she'd imagined, and wore a loose-fitting cashmere sweater with track pants, but Greta immediately pictured him stark naked, gazing out at the lake at dawn, laughing like Howard Roark. He seemed slightly confused by Greta's yellow coveralls.

"Good evening, sir," Greta said. "I'm here to wash your windows."

"You'll be here all week, then," he said softly, and smiled. "Nice to finally meet you, Rebekah."

"Put down the panic gripper, Luke," Big Swiss said.

"Gripmaster," Luke said gently.

He placed it in his pocket and shook Greta's hand. Big Swiss passed him the wine Greta had brought.

"Stick these in the fridge. Bring Rebekah a glass of champagne."

"Anything else, Flav?" he asked.

"The cheese," Big Swiss said. "Check the cheese."

"What am I looking for?"

"Little bubbles," Big Swiss said. "Don't let it burn."

If the whole house hadn't smelled like Gruyère, Greta would've assumed they were speaking in code. She felt unprepared for all the name-calling. Naturally, Luke called Big Swiss by her real name, Flavia, and he called Greta by her fake one, and Greta wasn't used to any of it, because she and Big Swiss only called each other You.

"You want a tour?" Big Swiss said then.

"You just want me to see your bedroom," Greta whispered. "Don't you."

"You *should* see it," Big Swiss said. "You should see our bathroom, too."

"Your call," Greta said. "Actually, can you show me later?"

They wandered over to the dining area, where a long wooden table was set for three at one end. Fresh peonies drooped in bud vases. Three Noguchi pendants floated above the table like pregnant moons. It wasn't quite dark yet, but Big Swiss lit too many candles and directed Greta to sit at the head of the table. Luke approached, carrying the fondue pot. He set it down, lit the burner underneath, and then they settled on either side of Greta.

But where was Silas?

"Sulking," Big Swiss said. "He's upset you didn't bring Piñon."

Thank god she'd left him at home. He would've humped the whole house by now, or at least one or two poufs. And Silas's face, of course, but that was a given. Then again, if he were there, Greta would have been smiling right now. Piñon always brought the party.

"Piñon," Luke said slowly. "Your husband?"

Greta looked sideways at Big Swiss. Did you tell him I'm married? To a man named Piñon?

"Piñon is her child," Big Swiss said. "Except he's a dog."

He's my *inner* child, Greta thought, which is why he growls at you.

"Oh right," Luke said, and shook his head. "Piñon, the Jack Russell. Of course. Flavia tells me they get along great. Which is a relief. Silas doesn't have many friends."

"Oh, they're more than friends," Greta said, and winked.

"How's that?" Luke asked innocently.

"Silas has huge balls," Greta said. "As you know. But he also smells male, which engenders a lot of same-sex aggression and obsession."

Sort of like how your wife's smell affects me.

"What does it engender in the opposite sex?" Luke asked.

"Fear," Greta said.

Luke nodded.

"Have you thought about having him snipped?" Greta asked. "It's not too late. Piñon was neutered at age six."

Luke shifted uncomfortably in his chair. Big Swiss seemed far away, likely lost in a fantasy of having Greta snipped, or doing it herself.

"I prefer to leave him intact," Luke said. "I don't think neutering is really necessary for males."

Blow jobs aren't necessary, either, Greta thought, but I bet you couldn't live without 'em, am I right?

"I imagine he wanders off a lot, though," Greta said. "On the prowl for poon."

"I'm not anthropomorphizing," Luke offered strangely. "I guess I'm just reluctant to do something irreversible when there's little evidence that it does anything good."

"Well, *friends* are good," Greta said, and raised her glass. "To new friends."

"To new friends," Luke repeated, raising his.

"Cheers," Big Swiss said cheerlessly.

They passed around the salad, along with an assortment of dried meats and various breads, including nut and fruit. In the pot, five mountain cheeses, three glasses of wine, two shots of kirsch, some garlic. Greta and Luke dunked lightly, almost playfully, but Big Swiss dragged hers along the bottom, drowning the life out of it before plopping it onto her plate, where it rested briefly before traveling to her beautiful mouth. Rather than devour it in one bite, Big Swiss nibbled off the fork—flirtatiously, it seemed to Greta. Sure enough, Big Swiss and Luke exchanged one or two private smiles.

Where's my private smile? Greta wondered. "You're supposed to flirt with the *other woman*," she imagined lecturing Big Swiss tomorrow, "not your boring husband." But then she remembered that she wasn't in fact the other woman. The other woman would be sleeping with Luke. Greta was the gay lover.

The gay lover was painfully full five minutes later. So was Luke, it appeared, who kept pushing food around on his plate. Like the child of an alcoholic. Greta counted his drinks—five beers, fifty minutes—and thought of various ways to rescue him. But why, when he was clearly very wealthy? She never pitied the rich. And he could easily defend himself. In fact, he looked like he could jiu-jitsu Greta's face off if he wanted. Was he flexing his forearms?

He was *twitching*, she decided. He was tactile defensive! Some texture or other must've been bothering him. He was certainly holding his fork funny. He had trouble brushing his hair, Greta remembered Big Swiss saying, but his hair looked fine, a little unctuous, maybe, and she wondered if the culprit was coconut oil, and whether he spent as much time as Greta slathering it all over himself, slathering it all over his wife, getting it all over the sheets, tracking it to the bathroom, spitting it out in the sink, washing it off in the shower but never quite getting it out of his hair, and whether he could even glance at a coconut without thinking of pussy. But that was Greta's life. Perhaps Luke's life was coconut-free, or, who knows, maybe he was anti-coconut, because of all the monkey labor, those poor pigtailed macaques in Southeast Asia, forced to harvest coconuts on farms for the last four hundred years.

"*¿Habla más de un idioma?*" Luke said in a low voice.

"*Por supuesto no,*" Big Swiss said.

"*Que te pasa, cariño,*" Luke said. "*Estás actuando rara.*"

"*Ninguna cosa,*" Big Swiss said, and shook her head. "*Te diré después.*"

Was she having an auditory hallucination, or were they really speaking Spanish?

"*Hola,*" Greta chimed in. "*Feliz Navidad.*"

Luke looked embarrassed. "Gosh, I'm sorry. We don't mean to be rude. We're just practicing."

"For what?" Greta said.

"Fun," Big Swiss said quickly.

"Ecuador," Luke said.

"Oh?" Greta coughed.

"Did you tell her, Flav?" Luke said.

Big Swiss shook her head without looking at Greta.

"We're going to this fancy eco-resort for our anniversary," Luke said. "We'll be there two weeks—maybe longer. We'll see. But we haven't been to South America in five years, so we're a little rusty."

"Me neither," said Greta, who'd never been south of Tijuana.

"You know any Spanish?" he asked.

Greta cleared her throat. "I only know one phrase."

Don't say it, lady. Not here, not tonight. Just—control yourself. But it was too late—they both looked at her expectantly.

"*Sacame la leche*," Greta said.

Luke blinked. "'Take my milk'?"

"Cum," Greta said. "'Take my cum.'"

Luke blushed deeply. Big Swiss shrugged and looked out the window.

"Well," Luke said slowly. "If all goes according to plan, Flavia will, uh, *sacame la leche* in Ecuador."

"Pardon?" Greta said.

Big Swiss gave Luke a punishing look, which bounced right off him.

"We're trying to get pregnant," Luke said shyly.

Greta immediately stuffed bread into her mouth.

"With twins, Flavia hopes," Luke said. "Twins run in my family."

"Oh wow," Greta said, chewing slowly. "Wow, wow. Cool, very cool."

Now Big Swiss gave Greta the same look she'd given Luke, which affected Greta like kryptonite.

"Twins run in my family, too," Greta said weakly. "My mother was a twin. My grandmother had five kids under the age of five, and then totally lost her mind."

Luke smiled politely.

"Was she institutionalized?" he asked after a moment.

"No," Greta said. "She had three more kids and several miscarriages."

"Oops," Luke said.

Greta smiled and wondered what the fuck she was doing here. They were clearly very married. And very broody. Dinner had been Luke's idea, ostensibly, but why had Big Swiss agreed to this? She watched Luke tear into a fresh baguette. He broke it apart with his handsome hands and passed the heel to Greta, which seemed appropriate.

"Use a knife," Big Swiss snapped. "She doesn't want your fingers all over her food."

Luke sighed. "Do you mind?"

"Not at all," Greta said, and looked at Big Swiss. "You know, I think you might be slightly allergic to alcohol? That's why you get so . . . agitated."

"Ooof," Luke said. "Careful, Rebekah."

Greta carefully scratched her scalp. It had started like any other itch, but it occurred to her now that this was *the* itch, the unbearable crawling sensation at the back of her head, the curse of her adolescence. Phantom lice. Scratching released serotonin, she'd learned long ago, which in turn made the itch worse. Otherwise, she recalled nothing from the few weeks she'd experimented with habit reversal therapy (HRT). Her first impulse was to stab herself with a fondue fork. Instead, she scratched behind her ear like a dog.

"You're being glared at," Luke said to Greta, "by Little Miss Icy Veins."

Greta stopped scratching and sat on her hands.

"Mrs.," Big Swiss corrected him. "And there's nothing little about me. Or icy."

Pedantic seething—not Greta's favorite, but it was Big Swiss's number one hobby.

"Do you think I'm icy?" Big Swiss asked Greta.

"You have cold hands," Greta said quickly, looking past Big Swiss at the lake.

"But do you consider me distant and unfeeling?"

"Nope," Greta said.

"Liar," Big Swiss said.

Greta shrugged.

"The dreaded Swiss stare," Luke said ruefully. "Still raises the hair on the back of my neck. Not always in a bad way." He smiled and tugged at his collar. "Have you been to Switzerland, Rebekah?"

Greta smiled and shook her head. The phantoms whirled like dervishes. She hadn't experienced a flare-up in years, but it was all coming back to her now. Pain was the only way out. Pain interfered with the itch, and if you inflicted enough—on yourself, of course—the itch subsided altogether.

"Can I tell you what goes on there?" Luke said. "I mean, are you curious at all?"

"She already knows," Big Swiss said.

"Go ahead," Greta gasped, digging her nails into her palm. "Please."

"Okay, so, you're on the train, right, minding your own business, and suddenly you feel that you're being *watched*, so you look around. It's the old Swiss woman sitting across from you. She's calm and serious and staring hard at your chest, so you look down at yourself, expecting to find a mustard stain, but there's nothing. Now she's staring at your sleeve, now the buttons on your shirt. Her eyes linger on your collar. You think, Okay, she's moving up to my face. When she sees my face, she'll look away. Nope. Her eyes slip down to your stomach. They travel over your crotch. Your pant legs. You can see her making little judgments and appraisals. Meanwhile, you're just waiting for her to look at your face, because you want her to know that you've caught her staring. Well, the joke's on you, because guess what? She doesn't care. She shamelessly evaluates your face, too, even though you're giving her a look of death. She doesn't even register your expression. She looks you directly in the eyes, but she doesn't see you."

"Yikes," Greta said. "What's her deal? Does she hate tourists?"

"No. Swiss people were never taught that it's rude to stare," Luke said. "They'll stare at anyone. It's like, socially acceptable to stare at a stranger on the train or anywhere else, and they stare at their friends, too." He looked at Big Swiss. "Like how you're staring at Rebekah right now, babe."

"It's called *looking*," Big Swiss said. "If you're Swiss, you simply allow yourself to be looked over. Then it's your turn—you look over the person while they look away. It's a tacit exchange, and totally harmless. It's just a way to pass the time."

"Right," Greta blurted. "I've noticed this about you."

In bed, she wanted to add. It was the very same exchange they performed during sex: I look, you look the other way; now you look while I look away, and if our eyes meet, let's not see each other, okay? Although initially she'd been weirded out, Greta had grown to like this arrangement. Unlike the voyeurism she usually participated in, this brand was open and consensual, and she'd taken it very personally. *I'm irresistible*, Greta often thought during sex. *She's transfixed by my face!* But now that Greta knew it was simply *cultural*, she felt—well, like a nobody, like a stranger on a train. She and Big Swiss were just passing the time, apparently, taking turns looking at each other on their way to somewhere else. Big Swiss was on her way to Ecuador to have the most meaningful sex of her life, and where was Greta headed? Fucking nowhere.

Except we're not on a train, Greta reminded herself. And we're doing a lot more than looking. Much more, for many hours a day, several days a week. Although, it's been a few days, hasn't it? A little skin contact might be helpful right now. Perhaps the phantoms will perish on the spot, and I can stop scratching like a junkie. I'd even settle for footsie.

Greta groped around, located Big Swiss's foot under the table, and realized it was already being caressed. By Luke's foot.

"Oops," Greta murmured. "Sorry."

The phantoms cheered and stomped their feet. They were much rowdier than she remembered. She scratched at them again. And again. And once more. Silas, who'd been pacing in front of the windows, stopped and stared at her.

"We look at each other out of curiosity," Big Swiss was saying. "That's how I would describe it. It's not judgmental, not always. But the Swiss are vigilant—that's true. We like to keep each other in check. Americans could never handle that, because they're such infants, and so easily rattled. They can't ride the train without getting their feelings hurt. They can't walk down the street without being offended."

"We just don't like to be scrutinized," Luke said. "There's nothing childish about that."

"Stop looking at me!" Big Swiss said in a disturbing baby voice.

Luke gave Greta an exasperated smile. "If you throw your trash out the wrong way, the sanitation people will go through it, find your address, and send you a bill. Can you imagine?"

Greta could imagine quite a bit. Such as what sort of sex they'd have later that night, after she was back in her eighteenth-century dump, in bed with her blow-dryer, alternately warming up the sheets and burning her scalp. Maybe they were into something lame, like wax play. It was a little too easy to imagine Luke naked, laid out like a buffet on this very table, to imagine Big Swiss drizzling hot wax onto his hairless chest, to imagine Luke writhing in agony and then whispering his safe word ("Mommy" or maybe just "All right, enough"), after which Big Swiss blew out the candle and picked up the fondue pot, and Luke said, "Oh no, oh god, baby, please, please not that, I'll do anything," but Big Swiss went ahead and poured bubbling hot cheese all over his legs, and now his safe word was a high-pitched scream. Fondue play burns, baby, it burns your skin right off.

"Sorry?" Greta said.

"I was just saying that when you recycle paper, it has to be stacked in symmetrical piles and tied with a string, and the string must be the correct gauge, the piles perfect, or it doesn't get picked up," Luke said.

"Sounds pretty . . . anal," Greta said.

"Very," Luke said.

She wondered if they did butt stuff. Big Swiss was never more tender, more defenseless, more of a mess, than when she was probing Greta's. "Topping from the bottom": a phrase Greta had transcribed more than once but hadn't fully appreciated until just now. If she wanted, Greta could top from the bottom right here at the dinner table. "Luke," she imagined announcing, "your wife likes to freeze coconut oil, insert an icy shard into my back passage, and wait for it to melt. Does she do that to you?"

"The rest of your recycling must be dragged down the block to these bins on the sidewalk," Luke was saying. "Separate bins for brown, green, and clear glass. One bin for tin, another for aluminum.

But there's always at least one Swiss person watching you like a hawk, waiting for you to fuck up, so that they can—"

"Sodomize you?" Greta said.

"I was going to say publicly humiliate," Luke said. "But yeah, it feels . . . invasive."

"It's called the social contract," Big Swiss said.

"Or . . . fascism," Luke said, and smiled.

"If you go to a public restroom in Switzerland, there's rarely urine all over the seat," Big Swiss said. "And if there is, you know whoever did it wasn't Swiss. We're not obsessed with having unlimited personal freedom. We're not careless assholes. We live in a beautiful place and we take responsibility for it. We don't piss all over everything like spoiled children."

"True enough," Luke said. "You're right about that."

"I hate utopias," Greta said. "I'd never feel at home surrounded by majestic beauty and obscene wealth. I wouldn't be able to look out the window without wincing. Plus, is there anything worse than an Alpine hipster?"

"But isn't that just like Hudson?" Luke said.

Greta smiled. "So *that's* why I never leave my house."

"It didn't used to be like this," Luke said.

"That's what I keep hearing," Greta said. "Sooner or later I'll have to . . . move, I guess."

"Where would you go?" Big Swiss asked.

Greta shrugged. "Somewhere cheaper. Trashier."

"The only trash I ever saw in Geneva was the actual word 'trash,'" Luke said. "It was someone's tag, and it was graffitied all over the city in messy black letters."

"Maybe I'll start doing that," Greta said. "In Hudson."

Or here, Greta thought, in this house.

"What's going on?" Big Swiss said, and looked under the table.

Silas was under there, licking Greta's foot with his weird spotted tongue. He'd been at it for a while now, but Greta hadn't said anything. She didn't want to get him in trouble, and besides, his warm, not-too-wet tongue was distracting her from the phantoms.

"He's just hoping I'll drop something. He's probably dying for some cheese." Greta leaned down to pet him. "Aren't you, good doggy? Do you love cheesy bread? You do, don't you. You love it, yes, you do. Don't lie. Are you the best? Yes—"

"Stop using that voice," Big Swiss snapped. "It drives me insane."

"Why? I'm practically *whispering*."

"It's your tone," Big Swiss said.

"Um, have you listened to your own voice?"

"I'm listening to it right now," Big Swiss said.

"Yes, but have you ever heard it recorded?"

Big Swiss tilted her head.

"Like on voicemail." Greta backpedaled.

"I know I don't sound like *you*."

"If your voice was on the radio, people would drive off the road," Greta said. "They'd drive straight into trees!"

"At least I don't mumble," Big Swiss said. "You like to make people work hard to hear you, because you're passive-aggressive."

"Guys?" Luke said.

"Something's actually wrong with you," Big Swiss said, ignoring him. "Silas only licks people when they're really sick."

"That's true," Luke said, nodding. "He wouldn't stop licking my jaw once. Turned out I had an abscess and the infection had spread to my neck. I could've died."

"He's trying to tell you something," Big Swiss said to Greta.

Both Luke and Big Swiss glanced at Silas under the table. Greta covered her right foot—the fucked-up one—with her left. Silas pawed at her leg and whined.

"God," Big Swiss said. "He's really losing it, Luke."

"Silas, go lay down, buddy," Luke said.

Silas didn't move.

"He's just telling me I need a pedicure. Aren't you, good doggy?" Greta turned to Luke. "Sorry about your neck. That must've been really scary."

"Why do you keep scratching?" Big Swiss said, watching Greta's hands. "Please don't tell me you have fleas."

"Dude," Greta said. "You mind taking it down a notch?"

"What?" Big Swiss said.

"Seethe *quietly*," Greta said.

Luke nervously played with the bread on his plate. Then he nervously played with his beard. Greta wished she didn't like him so much.

"I meant to tell you this earlier, but you have gorgeous feet," Greta told him. "They're very rousing. They almost make me want to take up figure drawing. And figure *skating*."

Luke smiled. "Thanks."

"You have a psychotic preoccupation with feet," Big Swiss said.

Greta sniffed. "I know."

"And you always overdo it with compliments. It only draws attention to yourself, not the other person. Are you aware of that?"

"No," Greta said.

"Well, when you lay it on extra thick, it makes it seem like you're desperate for the other person to like you. Like you're only giving in order to get. But what happens when you give and get nothing in return?" Big Swiss made a throat-cutting gesture. "All hell breaks loose."

"Hokay, Big Swiss," Greta said. "Maybe it's time to lay off the chardonnay, honey."

"What'd you call me?"

"Honey," Greta said.

"Big Swiss," Luke said, looking wistful. "I love that. That's perfect."

"It's my secret nickname for her," Greta told him.

"You call me that behind my back?"

"Whenever I'm able," Greta said.

Big Swiss squinted at Greta's forehead.

"You shouldn't provoke me," Greta said. "You might not like what happens."

Big Swiss snorted. "I'm not afraid of you."

"Ladies," Luke said. "If you're going to fight, use your fists, okay? Or wrestle. But please stop bickering like . . . sisters."

"We're more like mother and daughter," Big Swiss said. "In my view."

SHE TRIED PLOTTING HER ESCAPE in the powder room, which was difficult because the powder room was prison themed, or at any rate the walls were institutional green and decorated with Luke's collection of shanks and shivs, all carefully mounted in black shadow boxes. Each box held five or six little weapons, some clearly very old, with a great patina, such as the shiv that was half a scissors, and another with the shank of a screwdriver and a doorknob for a handle, but most looked newish, more crude and brutal, the handles wrapped tightly in electrical tape, plastic bags, and filthy Ace bandages, with little blades scavenged from safety razors. To die, Greta would have to stab herself eighty-six times. So, that was out. But it seemed like the perfect tool for phantom lice removal (PLR).

Forget the shivs, Greta told herself in the mirror. Grow up. Go home. Tell Sabine everything. Confess, unburden yourself, take responsibility. Then what? End this insanity and get on with your life. Try Tinder. Date dudes if you must. Go back to being numb. Dumb. Numb. Mom?

Big Swiss opened the door, shut it behind her, and immediately fastened her mouth onto Greta's neck. Greta felt teeth and pulled away.

"Are you trying to kill me?"

"It's been impossible not to touch you," Big Swiss said. "I thought I would explode. I felt envious watching Silas lick your feet."

"Why are you acting like this?"

"Like what?"

"Cunty," Greta said.

"I'm sorry I lashed out at you," Big Swiss said. "I think Luke's cheating on me, and I'm losing my mind. I've never felt so . . . lost. One minute I'm relieved, the next I'm enraged. Then I feel ashamed—"

"Shame is good. Hold on to that," Greta said. "And it's you who's cheating, not him. Projection!"

"I don't want to go to Ecuador," Big Swiss said. "I was livid when he booked the tickets without asking me."

"You were goading me in there. It seems like you want me to tell your husband we're dating. That's the vibe I'm getting."

"We're not *dating*. Don't be disgusting," Big Swiss said. "I love you."

"Okay," Greta said.

"Okay?"

"I love you, too, but you should ask yourself what you really want," Greta said. "I'm too old for this."

Which was confusing, of course, because Greta had never felt younger. Or more . . . boyish. Maybe she would start playing video games or take up mixed martial arts.

"Can I steal one of these shivs?" Greta asked.

"Don't touch that."

"I'd like to get out of this house now," Greta said. "Okay if I crawl out the back door?"

"I'll tell Luke you're having an allergic reaction."

"To your horrible personality?"

"To the histamines in hard cheese," Big Swiss said. "It's very common. I'll make it up to you tomorrow. For three hours. Would you like that?"

"Maybe," Greta admitted, screaming inwardly.

ON THE WAY HOME, Greta drove with the windows down. Thankfully, the phantoms flew off her head and into the stiff wind. Now that she was clearheaded, she rehearsed her confession. It was long, and she'd have to deliver it right away, possibly with her eyes closed, as soon as she set foot in the house, before Sabine could get a word in edgewise.

In the kitchen, Sabine was hunched over the sink. The sink had a deep basin but no faucet. To do dishes, they filled a dishpan with the hose outside and then carried it back to the kitchen, water sloshing everywhere. If it was warm enough, they simply did the dishes in the yard. Otherwise they collected water from the bathroom. Yes, it was a huge pain in the ass, but the plumber—never mind.

"I have a shameful secret," Greta announced.

"Not as shameful as this," Sabine said, peering at something in the basin. She was holding a magnifying glass. "Yep," Sabine said. "Yep, yep."

The dishpan held a few inches of filthy water and a few pieces of silverware. Floating on the surface, a smelly yellow sponge. Clinging to the sponge like it was a life raft, a poker-chip-size black lace weaver. Greta was accustomed to seeing these spiders in the house, but this one looked crippled and strangely out of focus. It also seemed to be moving, even though it was standing still. Was it having a seizure?

Sabine wordlessly passed Greta the magnifying glass.

Greta peered through the glass and gasped. The giant spider was in fact standing still, but hundreds of baby spiders were crawling all over it in a frenzy.

"She's being devoured," Sabine said. "By her own children."

Greta covered her mouth.

"Pretty much my worst nightmare," Sabine said, and yawned. "I was just about to go to bed, but I suppose we should deal with this now. They're almost done eating."

They smoked a cigarette and discussed options. Five minutes later, they carefully lifted the dishpan out of the sink and carried it out of the house together. The plan was to simply dump it in the woods, but they never made it that far, because Greta dropped her end of the dishpan after a dozen spiderlings ran straight up her arm. She frantically brushed them off while making a Piñon-like noise in the back of her throat.

"Oh god, they're everywhere," Sabine said, looking at the ground.

Greta began jogging toward the house.

"Wait!" Sabine screamed. "Take off your clothes!"

They both removed their coveralls, left them in a pile on the ground, and walked into the house in their underwear. Greta decided to cancel her confession.

IN THE MORNING, she rehearsed again: "Listen, I became infatuated with one of Om's clients, a married woman in her twenties, and I recognized her voice at the dog park, and now we're having an affair, but she doesn't know who I am or what my real name is, and she's being stalked by a psychopath who just got out of prison, and I had dinner at her house with her husband last night, but I think we might be in love? So yeah, I guess I'm fully gay."

It needed work, obviously, but she needed coffee first. She descended the stairs to the kitchen. Sabine was already awake and on her third or fourth cigarette, wearing a baby-doll nightgown with hospital pants, sitting in the Louis XIV chair with the ripped seat.

"I have something to confess," Greta blurted.

"Hold on," Sabine said. "I keep hearing—shit, you hear that?"

It sounded like rain pelting a tarp. Greta went to the window and looked out at the yard. No rain or wind, only flowering weeds. The noise was coming from inside the house, but it sounded different near the window. It had an oozing, vaguely sensual quality. Greta looked at the ceiling.

"Something's in the hive," Greta said.

Sabine slapped her leg. "Thank god. I knew they'd come back. I had a very intense dream about it the other night."

They stood underneath the hatch, squinting up at the hive, but the bees were difficult to see because the Plexiglas was coated with bee debris from the previous generation. Greta idly wondered if bees pooped.

"I don't want to disturb them, but I'm dying to see how many there are, aren't you?" Sabine said. "Fetch me the flashlight."

Sabine swept the light over the length of the hive, all seven feet of it.

"Son of a bitch," Sabine said.

The hive was indeed teeming, but not with bees. Greta groaned and turned away, shielding her eyes like a child. Of course, she thought. Of course it had to be *maggots*. What else?

"Why are they so *enormous*?" Sabine said. "Look at them! There must be hundreds!"

Greta couldn't look. Or listen. She tried to think of something that repulsed her more than maggots. The answer was nothing. Nothing!

"This is a pretty serious infestation," Sabine said. "And they're very large. It's going to be hard to kill these fuckers."

"Kill how?" Greta said.

"Well," Sabine said slowly. "We're going to have to open the hatch."

"Honestly? I'd rather eat shit."

"I mean, we'll have to open it just enough to fit a can of Raid in there. One of us will hold the hatch open while the other sprays. I'm guessing we'll have to empty two full cans. Or maybe we can do some kind of bomb thing."

"In other words, it's going to be raining maggots," Greta said. "In the kitchen. Where we eat."

Sabine shrugged. "What else can we do? We have to kill them before they . . . transform."

Greta felt an overwhelming need for sleep and began climbing the stairs.

"What were you going to tell me?" Sabine said casually. "You said you needed to confess."

"Never mind," Greta said.

14

Now that Sabine was back in the house for good, roaming around like a ghost at all hours, Big Swiss no longer felt comfortable having sex in Greta's room, not even in the antechamber, and neither did Greta, who didn't mention the maggots. Airbnb was too much trouble, not to mention traceable, and so they were forced to meet in bars.

Greta liked to think of herself as having experienced everything except childbirth, enlightenment, prison, one or two other things, but going to bars with Big Swiss was entirely new. It was like having drinks with a Richard Serra sculpture. Big Swiss was commanding enough to alter the space in any room, which in turn affected how people behaved around her. Most became clumsy or visibly self-conscious. One needed to view her from different vantage points to fully understand her—or, as Greta liked to think, to recognize that she wasn't as complex as she seemed—and so even if the bar was mostly empty, Big Swiss was often surrounded by a small cluster of people pretending not to stare at her, or pretending to be annoyed that she was in their way, while others, mainly male tourists of a certain type, approached her brazenly, demanding to know where she was from, what she was made of, their thoughts written plainly on their faces: Is this slab of steel for real? Look at that, she bends. I'm going to fuck this piece as soon as I figure out how to transport it back to my Airbnb. God, this bitch is heavy.

Greta often felt like the little placard next to the sculpture, glanced at out of politeness or mild curiosity, or consulted simply because they wanted more information, but like most gallery text, Greta was usually ignored altogether—that is, until they noticed Big Swiss's wedding band and realized she was married, possibly to Greta, at which point Greta felt like a layer of bumpy rust on Big Swiss's side. To get at Big Swiss, they had to deal with Greta, and not only was she difficult to get rid of; she stained whatever she touched. Most men backed off—too messy, too much work—unless they were German.

Last week, Big Swiss had been approached by a German tourist on the patio while Greta was inside getting drinks. He was a sculptor, he said, and his work was being shown at a gallery down the street, and he wanted Big Swiss to be his special guest at the opening. He lived in Paris and had come all this way just to meet her. "Koo-duh-FOO-druh," he'd said.

"What's that?" Greta asked Big Swiss.

"Love at first sight," Big Swiss said. "He's practicing his French."

Greta sighed. She'd been gone fifteen minutes. She placed their fresh drinks on the table, but the man didn't move, not one inch, and in fact seemed welded to Greta's seat. The patio was crowded, the music loud, and the man was alone.

"What's your name?" Greta said.

"Ree-*schtard*," he said.

"Nice to meet you, Ree-*tard*," Greta said.

"Ree-schtard," he repeated. "Ree-schtard."

"You know, like Richard," Big Swiss said to Greta.

Ah, like Richard Serra himself, only not as old. But just as willful, apparently. He was tall, slender, overdressed in an austere black suit.

"You are the waitress?" he said to Greta.

"Take a walk," Greta said.

"Excuse me?" he said.

"You heard me," Greta said.

"She is your mother?" he asked Big Swiss.

"You're in my seat," Greta said.

He stood and gestured grandly for Greta to sit. "Here, yes, you look *very* tired."

"Go fuck yourself," Greta said.

"Where do I go? Tell me, please." He looked around as if they were locked in a cell together. "You are the police?"

It was as if he'd called her a cunt or a cow. Her right arm felt suddenly spring-loaded and five times more muscular than her left.

"What?" Greta muttered into his ear. "What, motherfucker?"

"What your problem is?" he said. "I am talking to Lahbia."

"It's *Flavia*," Greta said, and laughed.

"But I am not talking to you. I am trying to have private conversation—"

"What!" Greta shouted.

He pointed to his head. "Maybe you need *psychologie*."

"Maybe I do," Greta said and shrugged.

He scowled and walked away. Greta looked around. Everyone was staring, of course, and having a great time, except for Big Swiss, who eyed Greta suspiciously.

"What's happening to you?" Big Swiss asked.

"I'm mutating."

"Again?" Big Swiss asked.

Naturally, the maggots came to mind. The day before, Sabine had brought home a jumbo can of Raid Concentrated Deep Reach Fogger. Greta had held the hatch open—just a crack—while Sabine emptied most of the can into the hive. Of course, about a hundred maggots squirmed out and fell to the floor, wriggling for cover. A few of them had bounced off her shoulders. She'd been under the impression that maggots were blind, but, according to the internet, they had eyes not only in the back of their heads, but all over their disgusting bodies. Not eye*balls*, but primitive eye structures that were sensitive to light, especially bright ultraviolet light, which caused maggot death. Hence their tendency to squirm and wriggle when their bodies weren't buried in fruit or flesh.

Greta squirmed, too, when she wasn't buried in Big Swiss's fruit or flesh. She wished her jealousy were more light-phobic. Why couldn't it die of exposure? It seemed to thrive out in the open, in broad daylight, as well as inside her body. It was parasitic. How long had it lurked in the shadows, waiting for the right moment to take her as its host? Now it was feasting on her red blood cells. Now it was invading her heart. But jealousy didn't kill its host, right? It just felt that way. Eventually, it would pass out of her body completely.

But not yet, apparently, not while Big Swiss crossed and uncrossed her legs in her short black miniskirt. Her crotch shimmered like a mirage. Greta glimpsed actual heat waves, along with red lace. Her vision tunneled. Big Swiss's mouth kept moving, but Greta heard nothing but blood rushing.

"Are you trolling me?" Greta asked.

"Try breathing through your nose."

Big Swiss flashed her again. Greta's heart raced.

"Who's that for?"

"You," Big Swiss said.

"Is it? Because I'm not the only one seeing it."

Had she done the same thing fifteen minutes ago while making direct eye contact with Ree-schtard?

"I'm trying to lighten your mood," Big Swiss said. "Besides, why does it matter? I'm here with you."

"And I'm here with . . . Sharon Stone, folks," Greta said into a fake microphone. "What are you wearing tonight, Sharon?"

"Who?"

"Did you just become unfrozen? How do you not know . . . anything?"

Big Swiss calmly chewed ice. "Internalized misogyny," she said. "That's my guess. You're a self-loathing misogynist, which is one of the worst kinds. You probably inherited it from your mother."

The larger part of her inheritance: morbid jealousy. Her mother had been both pathologically jealous *and* envious, even—or sometimes especially—of her own daughter, and Greta had regularly felt as though she were being poisoned. In the Shakespearean sense. She never drank anything her mother gave her, not even water.

"I need a breather," Greta said, and stood up. "BRB."

"Your mouth is shaking," Big Swiss said. "FYI."

"Try not to flash the entire town while I'm in the bathroom," Greta said.

It was Greta's desire that had mutated, she thought on the toilet. She'd become a vile, greedy nightmare, seemingly overnight. It would be good to go back to the beginning, when all she'd desired was the dream house between Big Swiss's legs, and not, as it were, the entire property. Big Swiss was both too big and too much work, and completely out of Greta's price range. Not that Big Swiss was even on the market.

"She's not a house," Greta reminded herself out loud. "She's a human being *hoping for twins*, and happily married for the most part."

"Who're you talking to?" Big Swiss asked.

Greta looked up. One of the pitfalls of same-sex relationships was that you couldn't break down in public restrooms. At least, not in peace. The bitch followed you in there. You couldn't weep or talk yourself down in the mirror, or even in the stall. She entered the next stall, stood on the toilet, and observed you, as she was doing now.

"Let me in," Big Swiss said.

Greta unlatched the stall door. Big Swiss squeezed inside and straddled Greta. As always, once Greta had her hand inside Big Swiss's underwear, nothing was static, everything was possible, they could do whatever they wanted. And so, they indulged in one of the benefits of same-sex relationships for twenty-five minutes.

When they emerged from the bathroom, the crowd parted to let them pass. Some insect in skinny jeans buzzed around Big Swiss, wanting to know how tall she was and whether she was Swedish or South African.

Greta continued walking through the crowd and then straight out the door. Big Swiss followed. On the sidewalk, Big Swiss pulled a small velvet box from her purse and passed it to Greta.

"I meant to give you this earlier," Big Swiss said.

Inside, a vintage onyx signet ring Greta had lingered over in one of the antique shops on Warren Street weeks ago. They'd been window-shopping that day after having stand-up sex in one of the alleys. When Big Swiss noticed Greta admiring the ring, Greta said she'd totally buy it if money were no object. "It's vain to buy jewelry for oneself," Big Swiss had said. "That's ridiculous," Greta said. "What's vain is using the word 'oneself' in casual conversation." Big Swiss hadn't talked much after that, and then she'd abruptly excused herself and disappeared. At the time, Greta assumed her feelings had been hurt, but they'd never discussed it. And now, lo and behold, the very same ring. Greta felt flattered momentarily, before she remembered that five hundred dollars was chump change to Big Swiss.

AFTER A LONG ABSENCE, they returned to the dog park. The meadow had been landscaped, shrubs planted, ceramic sculptures installed, new paths cut into the woods, benches placed along the paths. The park was crowded with unfamiliar faces and accents. It seemed people came from all over the world now to walk their dogs in Hudson. It was late spring and everything was fragrant and in bloom: the dogwood trees, the dogs themselves, their owners. Big Swiss was a showy white flower in puffed sleeves and linen shorts. Greta, who'd peaked weeks ago, was already wilting and losing her petals.

They walked the dogs in the wooded area and then picnicked on a blanket in the meadow. About fifteen other people had had the same idea. Big Swiss removed her blouse and sunbathed in a halter top. After a while, she unbuttoned her shorts and pulled them down a little. A bunch of blond pubes poked out of her purple panties. Greta stared at them while Big Swiss had her face buried in a tree manual.

"Flowering dogwood trees are bisexual," Big Swiss said. "Like us."

"You're joking, right?"

"Their flowers have both stamens and carpels, or male and female reproductive organs," Big Swiss said. "They're called 'perfect' flowers."

"Listen, letting an older lady fuck you doesn't make you bisexual," Greta said. "Or perfect. You're just . . . bored."

"Most of the trees in this park are male," Big Swiss said, ignoring her. "Which means they don't have seeds or pods. They have pollen, though, which they spew everywhere indiscriminately."

"I knew I smelled semen," Greta said.

"See all the chartreuse dust on the ground? That's why people's allergies are so out of control."

"Have you been inseminated recently?"

Big Swiss closed the manual and looked at Greta.

"Is it leaking out of you right now?"

"Not convincing," Big Swiss said.

"What?" Greta said.

"Your tough-girl routine. It's pretty transparent at this point. Actually, it's been transparent since the beginning."

"Listen, sister," Greta interrupted. "You spent the morning with Luke. Now you're here with me, but—why? What are you doing here?"

"I make it pretty obvious. I'm undeniably attracted to you, I can't stop thinking about you, and I've never said no to you, not once. So, relax. You have more power than you think."

"But you're so stingy with compliments. You won't touch my tits. You won't even hold my hand."

"Maybe you should be with a man," Big Swiss said.

"Oh, because men are so effusive? Why can't you gush a little?"

She sounded as whiny and petulant as some of Om's clients. Quite a few of them behaved like this as a matter of course, and she wondered if transcribing their emotional reactions had somehow influenced her own. Emotional eavesdropping, it was called. She'd read about it online. It was something children did, not adults. But why couldn't she be more like Big Swiss? Because Big Swiss was withholding, that's why, and the more she withheld, the more frantically Greta pursued.

"When I'm fucking you, you get this bored expression on your face. It's confusing, disorienting, and—if I'm being honest—extremely exciting. Then you'll suddenly laugh for no reason, which also excites me. And you're an angelic sleeper. Your face is so serene and at peace, a little smile on your lips—it looks like you're pretending to sleep. I also like that you only speak one language, and when I see your knees in jeans, I get light-headed."

"What else?" Greta said.

"Is that not enough?"

A bright light flashed in the trees just beyond the meadow, about twenty feet away. Greta squinted. The woods were dark, so it was hard to know what was making the flash, but Greta assumed it was a man holding binoculars and that they were trained on Big Swiss's fruity nipples.

"Some dude's hiding behind a tree, spying on you with high-powered binoculars," Greta said. "In case you're interested."

"Don't be paranoid," Big Swiss said.

"It wouldn't be paranoia if I had any control over it."

"Take a breath," Big Swiss said.

Greta stood up and slid into her shoes.

"Sit down," Big Swiss said.

Greta strode toward the trees. Other women were sunbathing, as well, a few of them topless. Greta saw another flash and peered into the woods, her hands cupped around her eyes. A man stood next to a tree ten feet away. He was staring at his phone, his lower half obscured by shrubs and bushes.

"Keith," Greta said. "Pull up your pants and come out of there."

The guy didn't answer.

"Keith!"

He lifted his head and looked in the wrong direction.

"I'm talking to you. Over here."

His head swiveled. "Who?"

"Stop hiding in the woods like a creep, Keith."

"I'm not Keith," the guy said.

He was right. He was much too young to be Keith. Greta turned to address the sunbathers.

"You might want to cover up, ladies," Greta said loudly. "You're being photographed by a sex pest."

"I'm taking *selfies*," the guy insisted. "Not that it's any of your fucking business."

"Frat boy," Greta blurted.

"Gay," the guy said.

"What?"

"I'm *gay*, for heaven's sake." He stepped out from behind the bushes, as if to say, See? Greta *could* see his shapely legs and shiny gold shorts. His bright white socks had green tennis rackets printed all over them. "I don't give a shit about tits. Understand? Go fuck yourself."

Holy hell, it was GMT, whose last session she'd transcribed only yesterday. He'd told Om a story about a guy he'd hooked up with on Grindr, some gorgeous city person he'd invited to his house in the middle of a stressful workday, just to get his mind off things. The city guy's rule was total silence, as in no speaking allowed, as in not one fucking word, which had seemed both arousing and refreshing to GMT. Thirty minutes later, the guy had GMT in his mouth and hands, and then he paused, reached into his pocket for lube, and accidentally dropped it on the floor. GMT saw the lube roll under the bed, but the guy kept crawling around, looking for it. "Under the bed," GMT finally said. The guy's head whipped around. He stared balefully at GMT for ten long seconds. "Sorry," GMT said. The guy stormed out of the house without a word. On his way out the door, he swept everything off GMT's console table.

"Sorry," Greta said now.

GMT said nothing and typed something on his phone.

Her ears burned as she walked back to Big Swiss. She wished they made sunglasses for ears. And mouths. Her mouth was probably trembling so convulsively, it might break loose and fall off her face. At least she had regular sunglasses. Where were they? She must have dropped them in the grass somewhere. She retraced her steps, scanning the ground, and could feel GMT studying her.

"Did you see my sunglasses?" Greta asked him.

"On your head," GMT said.

So they were.

"Sorry," Greta said again.

Just kill yourself, Greta thought. Big Swiss was still watching, waiting, looking pleased with herself. As Greta reached the blanket and was about to sit down, she felt someone coming up behind her.

She spun around and ducked slightly, expecting GMT, perhaps, or flying rocks, food, or trash, but it was one of the sunbathers, a girl wearing a bikini top, bike shorts, and a bunch of doodle tattoos.

"Greta," the girl said. "I thought that was you."

"Hey," Greta said uncertainly.

"It's Nicole," the girl said. "I was at your house recently."

Nicole, a.k.a. NEM, a.k.a. Jason Bateman. Blood rushed to Greta's face.

"Oh, hey. Hi."

"It's Greta, right?"

"Or *Rebekah*," Greta said, and resisted the urge to wink. "Either one."

Nicole was doing very well, Greta knew, having broken up with Ryan and gotten on meds, and was looking for new friends.

"There's a Smithy party tonight," Nicole said. "Wanna come?"

Smithy, whose real name was Billy, was from Baltimore. He was a former record producer and owned an abandoned factory and a French houseboat from the 1930s. Since arriving in Hudson, he'd cultivated a new persona. He freight hopped, whittled wood, collected guns, said "ain't." His parties were usually rustic, ritualistic, and shrouded in secrecy. Invitations were hand-delivered in manila envelopes stamped CONFIDENTIAL and contained ten-page dossiers about what to expect. You might be blindfolded, helped into a canoe, deposited on the shore of a boggy island in the middle of the Hudson, and then expected to participate in a ritual or two.

"Okay if I bring a friend?" Greta asked.

"Sure," Nicole said.

While Greta gave Nicole her number, she watched Nicole notice Big Swiss. Watching women notice Big Swiss had become one of Greta's favorite pastimes. Greta likened it to standing in line at a crowded bakery, focusing intensely on the pastries in the display case, feeling pressured to hurry up and decide because the line was so long, absentmindedly ordering from the faceless counterperson, meeting that person at the register, fumbling with your wallet, dealing with the debit card, and then realizing you're being rung up by Charlize Theron, who's making deliberate eye contact with you.

"Hi," Nicole said shyly.

"This is Big—Flavia," Greta said. "Flavia, this is Nicole."

Nicole slow-blinked à la Jason Bateman, Big Swiss smiled à la Charlize Theron, and Greta felt like the unseemly childhood friend of celebrities.

AFTER MIDNIGHT, alone in the antechamber, Greta broke down and wrote a letter, her first in months:

Dear Mom,

Maybe you remember this: After Robbie dumped me in high school, I went to Florida with your sister Deb. We stayed in a crappy condo somewhere along the Intracoastal Waterway, and I was heartbroken and miserable. On the last night, after Deb went to bed, I swallowed a few of her Ativan, drank most of a bottle of wine, and waded, fully clothed, into the Banana River, which the locals called the Frozen Banana River because it was brown and looked like shit, and which turned out not to be a river at all but a lagoon, and only eight feet deep. I swam toward what I thought was the ocean, but I got turned around. I remember feeling your presence next to me. It was you who pushed me back to shore. I slept on the muddy bank, got mauled by mosquitoes, and was discovered by a geezer fisherman, who returned me to the condo, no questions asked. I was too embarrassed to ever tell anyone, because, well, you were a dolphin.

Anyway, Big Swiss and I went to a party on a houseboat tonight. It was crawling with modern pagans, old ravers, adult Pippi Longstockings, and a bunch of people wearing Victorian evening wear. There was a brass band. Someone played a piano covered in burning candles. Everyone seemed to be carrying a parasol. Big Swiss was getting hit on right and left, but the music was good, the setting romantic, the moon bright and full, and at one point she held my hand and asked what I was thinking, and I told her that you had once been a dolphin in the Banana River, that you had saved me from drowning, that it had felt too Disney to ever say out loud but that I wanted her to know me, I wanted to tell her more, to blow it wide open, and I nearly told her my real name, but I was too startled by her face, her faint smile, the way she nodded her head. I could tell she thought I was crazy, or making shit up, and I suppose I don't blame her. I stared at the deep, dark, dolphin-free Hudson, a real river with a swift current, and thought about trying again.

15

Two days later, Greta received an email from Om:

Greta,
Please transcribe the attached file—your last.
Meet me at my office today @ 5 pm sharp.

"Oh well," Greta said as she opened a new document. She'd been repeating that a lot lately and remembered chanting it to herself as a child. Her first and only mantra. "Oh well, oh well, oh well."

OM: Can you state your initials, please?

FEW: FEW.

OM: You okay? You seem frazzled.

FEW: I realize that affairs are unavoidably messy, but I've been dealing with an alarming amount of jealousy and paranoia. Like, really alarming.

OM: Tell me about the paranoia.

FEW: It's a lot to summarize, but here's a small example: Luke and I own a carriage house that we Airbnb. It's in our yard, basically. I manage the account and always have. Luke's not really involved.

"Uh-oh," Greta said.

> FEW: So, I'm trying to get the place rented while we're in Ecuador, because it'll be good to have someone on the property. Luke's worried that our house is being staked out—
>
> OM: Ecuador?
>
> FEW: Yeah, we're going to Ecuador for our anniversary. We'll be there two weeks.

"Don't remind me," Greta said.

> FEW: Yesterday morning I get a message from a guy on Airbnb, asking if it's available. I write back and say yes, even though it's obvious—it's right there on the calendar, there's no need to ask. He writes back, "What about you? Are you available?" I say, "Sure, I can be there to let you in at 10:00 on Sunday. After that, my husband and I won't be at the property, but we're always reachable by text." He says, "What about dinner?" I explain that meals aren't included, that it's not a hotel, that there's a long list of restaurants in the manual. I figure the guy is older, maybe, and new to Airbnb. He says, "Yes, I understand meals are not included, but what about you—are you included?"

"Fuck me," Greta said.

> FEW: So, now I'm wondering who this person is. "Who are you?" I ask. He says, "My name is Javier, and I'm an actor. I'd love to take you to dinner." I say, "Why? Based on what?" And he says, "Your profile pic, of course. You look like a lot of fun." I'm a little freaked out at this point, but the guy doesn't have my exact address. Mainly, I'm just irritated, because I'm going to have to report him to Airbnb, and I don't have time for this. "What makes you think I'd have dinner with you?" I ask. He says, "Because I'm famous? Perhaps you recognize me?" So, I look at his profile pic. I realize the picture is probably fake,

because the guy is extremely good-looking and dressed up in a suit. So, I'm thinking it's either some twelve-year-old fucking with me, or someone having a mental health crisis—

OM: Or Keith?

FEW: Well, when I told Rebekah about it last night, she asked me if the guy looked familiar, and I said no. She asked me to describe him, and I told her he was conventionally handsome. She asked me if I felt a little tempted, assuming the guy was a real person, and I said no, because he seemed stupid, and anyway, I'm married, and I've never cared about celebrities. Then Rebekah laughed. "It was me," she said. "I was fucking with you."

OM: What?

"Yup," Greta said.

OM: I'm not sure I understand. What was she trying to prove?

FEW: How out of touch I am. Apparently, *I'm* the crazy one, because I have no idea who Javier Bardem is.

OM: Don't you?

FEW: He's a Spanish actor.

OM: I know.

FEW: Anyway, she accused me of suffering from a form of "terminal uniqueness," as she called it. According to her, my ignorance of popular culture is willful. I've never learned the names of celebrities because I'm trying to be unique, to set myself apart from others. Not just apart, but above. She says my persona depends on this, and is constructed around being unconcerned with or unaware of the things most people are obsessed about, because I have a need to feel superior and above it all.

OM: So, you're a snob, basically.

"Yeah," Greta said.

OM: When people try to diagnose you, eight times out of ten they're diagnosing themselves. "Terminal uniqueness" is a term used in twelve-step programs. It's the belief that what you've experienced is utterly unlike anything anyone else has experienced, which makes you an exception to the rule, or exempt from the usual consequences. It can be dangerous. People die of terminal uniqueness all the time. Is she an addict?

FEW: She used to be a pharm tech—maybe she's taking pills? Her mother killed herself thirty years ago. Rebekah has wanted to follow her ever since. I'm concerned she's making plans.

OM: Has she attempted before?

FEW: Yes, but it's been a while. She told me she made suicide pacts with four different people, "just to cover her bases."

OM: So, if she goes first, five people will die?

FEW: She was kidding—I think. Honestly, I don't think she's ever had four friends. Anyway, this thing about terminal uniqueness was just a cover-up. She was trying to bait me, obviously, even though what she did would only work on a child, and she was also trying to get back at me for calling her a misogynist, and for the extremely tense dinner we had at my house with Luke, where I drank too much and became aggressive.

OM: Let's talk about that.

FEW: [PAUSE] I don't feel like it right now.

OM: It sounds to me like she's probably upset about your trip to Ecuador, and upset in general, because she's having an affair with an unavailable woman. She certainly sounds like an addict. With mommy issues.

FEW: Jesus, Om. I hope that's not a phrase you use regularly.

OM: I'd like to discourage you from becoming overly focused on her behavior. It's very easy to fall into the habit of keeping the focus on her misconduct rather than yours, and to blame her for your unhappiness, because she's acting out her emotions. She's made herself an easy target. The more productive thing would be to look at your own part in this, or why you've manifested this person in your life, because she's here for a reason. Your affair with her coincided perfectly with Keith's release from prison and with your desire to become embodied. One experience gave you pain and trauma, and, until recently, the other has been healing and pleasurable. If your relationship with her continues, there's a risk of becoming retraumatized, but you don't seem afraid to take emotional risks. I would proceed with caution, though, because she seems slightly . . . unhinged.

"Maybe I need *psychologie*," Greta said.

FEW: I've never felt such a range of conflicting emotions. On any given day we spend together, I feel lust, disgust, pity, joy, gratitude, and despair.

OM: In that order?

FEW: All at once. The highs and lows are extreme. It feels very love/hate.

OM: I don't believe in love/hate relationships. If it feels love/hate, then it's not love. It's probably not hate, either.

FEW: What is it?

OM: Fear.

FEW: I'm not afraid of her.

OM: You fear engulfment. She fears abandonment. It's not love/hate so much as push/pull, and it's very hard to stop once the cycle starts.

FEW: She seemed embarrassed about the Airbnb thing, but I think part of her found it amusing. She must be ashamed of herself, though, because she asked me never to tell a soul.

OM: Has she done anything else that's made you uncomfortable?

FEW: Too many things to mention. She's made huge displays, both in public and private. We had sex in her room last week while her housemate was running errands. At first it was very rushed and exciting. Then we got rough with each other. Afterward, she was tender, almost tearful.

OM: How rough?

FEW: We wrestled, and she left bruises on my wrists and thighs. I think she likes to leave marks, so that I'm forced to think about her when she's not around.

OM: Would you not think about her otherwise?

FEW: I would and do. Constantly.

OM: How do you explain the bruises to Luke?

FEW: I haven't seen Luke in a few days. He's at some jiu-jitsu conference. Anyway, while we were grappling, she knocked a glass off the bedside table. It shattered, and she stepped on a sliver. It was nothing, a small cut. Well, now there's a hole in her foot, because she's convinced a piece of glass is trapped under the skin, and she keeps cutting her foot open so that the glass can "find its way out." But there's no glass!

"Oh, but there is," Greta said, flexing her foot. "I can feel it."

FEW: I've been getting a weird feeling lately that she's not who she says she is.

"Oh boy," Greta said. "Here we go."

OM: How do you mean?

FEW: Her reactions often don't match what I'm saying. She either underreacts or overreacts, and there's very little in between. When I've told her things about myself, surprising and disturbing things, she acts like she's already heard them. And two people have called her by a completely different name.

"End of recording," Greta said.

OM: What name?

FEW: Greta.

Greta imagined Om's eyes popping out of his head and rolling around on the floor.

FEW: You know her, obviously. I can tell by your face.

Om did some throat-clearing. With any luck, he would spontaneously chant the word "Har" for twenty minutes, and Big Swiss would be forced to leave.

FEW: Is she a client of yours?

"Har, har, har," Greta said.

OM: I can't answer that.
FEW: Who's your transcriber?
OM: It's a service.
FEW: It's done by people, though, correct? Not a robot like you first told me?
OM: Well, yes.
FEW: I only ask because on the last page of the transcript you gave me, it says, "Transcribed by" and the name is crossed out. Actually, it looks violently scribbled out. So, I'm assuming it's a person who lives around here, and I can see by your face that I'm right.
OM: Look, this person signed a confidentiality agreement, which goes both ways. It would be unethical for me to give you this person's name. I won't do it.
FEW: You're in deep shit with me. Very deep. Do you hear me?

"I'm sorry!" Greta said.

FEW: Are you listening?

"Yes," Greta said.

FEW: What else have you lied about? Everything?

"No," Greta said miserably. "Just my name."

OM: You're not talking to me, I hope. Are you?

FEW: Her. Greta.

OM: Don't talk to her. Talk to me, please.

FEW: You better come clean with me. Otherwise, this is over. I'll
      end it and walk away, and you'll wish you never had to see me
      again, but you will, over and over and over, because we live
      in a fishbowl, remember? I'll tell everyone I know about this.
      Everyone. Is that what you want?

"No!" Greta said.

OM: Please don't—

FEW: Are you trying to get me to leave you?

Greta didn't answer.

FEW: It's occurring to me now that she wants me to abandon her.

OM: [PAUSE] Are you talking to me?

FEW: Now I'm wondering if her mother—

OM: I'm going to stop—

[END OF RECORDING]

SINCE SHE'D ALWAYS IMAGINED Om's office as resembling a private yoga studio, with Om himself bouncing around on a yoga ball,
she was startled to find herself surrounded by carefully arranged antiques in what looked like an eighteenth-century boudoir. The walls
had French-inspired panels painted a chalky arsenic green. Suspended from the high ceiling was an enormous gilt-wood chandelier.
There was a working fireplace, along with a Louis XVI marble mantel.
The oak floors were lacquered a weird magenta. The furniture: fringed
slipper chairs, octagonal coffee table, curved couch, cream canopy
bed dressed in blue-and-white chinoiserie.

No wonder people spilled their guts here—they were confused, blindsided by the casual opulence, by its contrast to Om, whose fleshy nipples were visible through his mesh shirt. He'd wrapped his lower half in . . . what on earth was it? A Turkish towel?

"Did you just get out of the shower?" Greta asked. "Or do you consider that business attire?"

"What's wrong with a sarong?" he said irritably.

He looked like he might rip off the sarong and strangle her with it.

"Where'd all of this come from?" Greta asked, looking around.

Om gave her a puzzled look. "Have you not walked down Warren Street?"

"I guess I didn't realize people actually *bought* this stuff," Greta said. "I also didn't realize you *lived* here."

"I don't. I live in Germantown."

"Then what's with the bed?"

"I'm a sex coach, Greta," Om said patiently. "I deal with problems in the bedroom. My parents, on the other hand, deal with antiques, and are extremely established in that world."

"You have sex with your clients? On that bed? Why didn't I know about this?"

"It's not your business, Greta," Om said. "Not anymore."

He led her into a smaller room with a desk, a love seat, and two stuffed chairs. This was more like it, or at least slightly more officelike, though it was still very more-is-more, what with the hand-painted wallpaper. The infamous brass gong stood in a corner, shiny enough to work as a mirror and, to Greta's surprise, as tasteful and expensive looking as an Anish Kapoor sculpture.

"Sit," Om said.

Greta sat on the puffy pink love seat. Om sat across from her without speaking.

"This couch is kind of vag-like," Greta said. "Is that on purpose?"

"Do you feel safe?"

"No," Greta said. "I feel very much in danger. Am I?"

"Well, you're fired, if that's what you mean," Om said. "You probably won't find work in Hudson ever again, unless it's at a restaurant. Did you really expect to get away with this? I'm genuinely curious."

On the coffee table between them sat a box of Kleenex for the wimps and crybabies.

"No," Greta said. "I knew it would blow up eventually—maybe not quite so . . . *flamboyantly*—and I'm sorry about that, Om. I really, truly love this job—"

Her voice cracked. Christ, what was happening?

"Actions have consequences, Greta, like ripples on a pond. Your career as a transcriptionist is over. You'll have to reinvent yourself."

"I'm not sure I have it in me," Greta said. "I'll probably just kill myself."

A strong breeze came in through the window, unsettling the papers on Om's desk. The Kleenex waved frantically at Greta from its box. *Bon voyage.* Greta grabbed one and blotted her eyes.

"I feel a little relieved, to be honest," Greta said. "I couldn't maintain the charade much longer. Believe it or not, I usually avoid conflict."

"Have you told Sabine?"

"No," Greta said.

"Not that I want you to—ever—but I'm curious to hear how you'd narrate this to a third party. Where would you start?"

That was easy. She'd start with the trauma rant in Big Swiss's first session. By that point, Greta had transcribed sixty-eight sessions for Om and was beginning to think that if *everyone* was traumatized, maybe *nobody* was, including her. And then she heard Big Swiss ranting about the trauma people, and comparing them to Trump people, and chastising them for using their trauma as an alibi for whatever, and Greta felt like Big Swiss was speaking directly to her, because Greta had been quietly crutching around on her own shitty history for over thirty years, and maybe it was time to put down the crutches. Maybe Big Swiss had something to teach her about living. About taking responsibility. About eradicating self-pity and perhaps replacing it with something productive.

But how would she narrate this to Om?

"It was a dark and stormy night," Greta began. "At the dog park. My poor dog was being choked by a pit bull, and Big Swiss stepped in and saved his life."

"Big Swiss?"

"Flavia," Greta said.

Om snorted. "Then what?"

"I knew who she was—that voice—and when she asked for my name, I panicked and gave a fake one. Then she wanted to hang out, to be dog park friends, and I was too fascinated by her to say no."

"Well, Greta, you're not alone. Everyone knows who Flavia is. What happened to her—it was a big story around here. People still talk about it. And now they talk about you, too. You and her together." Om coughed. "You've been seen in bars. You've been seen in cars. You've been seen on boats. You've been seen in . . . bathrooms."

You've been seen at Swoon, Greta sang to herself. You've been seen at Half Moon. You've been spotted at Rev, again at Deb's, on the patio at Red Dot, in the Stewart's parking lot, in the bathroom of Spotty Dog—

"You could've been more discreet, at the very least," Om said.

"We were, until recently, and it hasn't been all fun and games, trust me. Do you know how many bathrooms I've cried in? *Thirteen.* I'm coming apart at the seams, Om, acting out like a teenager. I nearly punched a guy for looking at her ankles, and I'm not even the jealous type. I've never felt so . . . *activated.*"

"Well, if you're hysterical, it's historical," Om said, softening. "Your wounds are getting some much-needed air. You've been covering them up for years, probably out of necessity, but wounds need air to heal."

"How long have you known I'm Rebekah?"

"Couple weeks," Om said. "Look, I'm angry and upset, don't get me wrong, but I feel partly to blame. Hiring you was a gamble, I knew that, but you seemed perfect because you were new to town and you didn't know anyone except Sabine. I've known Sabine for years, by the way. If she trusted you enough to live under her roof, I figured you were solid. But I should've known better. This town is too tiny."

"Who'll transcribe your sessions now?"

"I have enough material," Om said cryptically. "But I need to ask: are you really suicidal, Greta? Be honest."

"A little," Greta said.

"Do you have anyone to talk to?"

"Sabine," Greta said. "Piñon."

"I hope I don't regret this, but—well, here's my offer: two or three sessions with me, after which I'll refer you to someone else. Deal?"

"Why?"

"I'd like to help, if I can. I don't trust you right now, but I do care about you."

"Thing is, you were my only client, so . . . I can't afford you."

"I'd like you to transcribe your own sessions, Greta. That's your payment to me."

Dear god in heaven. Talk about eating shit. Was there anything worse than your own recorded voice playing in your ear? In *both* ears? About feelings? Your own feelings? If she were only a little suicidal now, this would probably push her over the edge.

"Fine," Greta said.

16

"**G**reta."
    Her name had never sounded more guttural, more like the wrong note in a musical performance, more like loose gravel, than it did in Big Swiss's mouth.

"Greta."

Greta pulled the comforter over her head and wondered if the stink bugs felt threatened by the voice on the other side of the door. The linens smelled powerfully of their farts. Luckily, cilantro was Greta's favorite herb.

"*Greta*," Big Swiss said again. "Come out of there, please."

Greta held her breath like a coward. Big Swiss had arrived unannounced and let herself into the house, and then into Greta's room, and now she was standing outside the antechamber. Although sleeping in the antechamber was unnecessary at this point—the brick walls had finally absorbed enough sun—Greta had been hiding in there for days, passing out and waking up at odd hours, lost, confused.

"I let Piñon out," Big Swiss said. "He's running around with Silas in the yard. Come out of there now and talk to me."

Greta listened to Big Swiss's heavy footsteps move away from the door. Big Swiss was a heel-striker. Greta's feet, on the other hand, were leaves floating on water. She sometimes envied the nerve of loud walkers. Her mother had been the loudest.

Big Swiss paused at Greta's desk. Her hands shuffled papers, seemingly in search of something. Transcripts, probably.

"Is this your diary?" Big Swiss said.

"What?"

Greta rolled out of the bed, opened the door, and poked her head into the room. Big Swiss sat at Greta's desk with her feet up. Red Swedish clog boots, bare legs, a linen shirtdress the color of unripe olives. They hadn't seen each other in six days, a record.

"There you are," Big Swiss said. "Hello, Greta."

"Are you going to say my name every thirty seconds?"

"Maybe," Big Swiss said. "Do you dislike your name, Greta?"

"I guess you're still mad?"

"Is your last name really Graves?"

Greta felt naked in her nightgown. She was also wearing what she called a blood diaper, having run out of tampons. Nevertheless, she fox-walked across the room and sat in the armchair next to the desk.

"Greta Graves," Big Swiss said gravely. "Sounds fake."

"We were in the cemetery when you asked for my last name," Greta said. "Seemed like a natural choice."

Big Swiss looked alarmed. "We've never been to a cemetery together."

"Haven't we?" Greta asked.

"No," Big Swiss said slowly. "We were at the dog park."

If they remained friends, which seemed unlikely, they'd have to revisit all of Greta's lies. Where and when they were told, how and why. It could take weeks, years, forever. It would be a lot of work.

"My last name is Work," Greta said.

Big Swiss frowned. "Greta Work?"

"Disappointing, right? I've never gotten over it."

Big Swiss freed her hair from its bun. Her red lipstick had been applied very recently, probably in the driveway.

"Did you lose your job?"

"Of course," Greta said. "Did you get my email?"

"I skimmed it," Big Swiss said.

She'd spent six hours writing two paragraphs, roughly the same amount of time she spent on a transcript. It had been nearly impossible to apologize without making excuses. Hence, the dozen times she'd typed and deleted "PMS" and "the wreckage of my past." But she knew that excuses of any kind infuriated Big Swiss, and so in the end she'd simply said she was sorry, which was true, and that the experience had galvanized her into considering therapy again, also true, and that if Big Swiss wanted to see Greta, she had Greta's permission to spank her bare bottom mercilessly, which Greta suspected Big Swiss found appealing, possibly on a very deep level, and then Greta apologized a couple more times.

"I don't accept apologies," Big Swiss said. "Sorry is just something you take off a shelf. It means nothing to me."

"I think I know why you're really here." Greta stood and pulled up her nightgown. "How do you want to do this? With a belt?"

Big Swiss scowled. "I knew you'd look for an easy out. Maybe you should try sitting with your discomfort."

"Maybe you should make sitting more uncomfortable for me," Greta said.

"But then you'd feel like the victim. You see how that works?"

"No belt, then," Greta said. "Just your hand."

"Tell me why you did this. Why you lied to me for six months."

Greta took a breath. "My mother burned everything I gave her in the yard and then killed herself in the house. She didn't think of the mess. When I feel like throwing myself in front of a train, I always think of the poor soul whose job it is to pick up my large intestine and place it in a trash bag. It stops me. But at the end of the day, I'm just as careless and selfish as she was, because I'm acting on my impulses without thinking of the mess, and expecting you to pick up the pieces."

"So, you've been programmed to behave this way. By your past."

Greta nodded. "It's all conditioning."

"You really believe this."

"Yes, but this is new. I was in a stupor before we met. Ask anyone."

"Maybe I'll ask Sabine. Where is she?"

"Picking strawberries at the farm down the road," Greta said.

"She's making galettes for dinner. She's a very good baker, by the way. Sam Shepard once said he loved her scones—"

"Have you told her what you did?"

"Not yet," Greta said.

"Why not?"

"Maybe I'll tell *Sabine* when you tell *Luke*," Greta said. "How's that? Does that seem fair?"

"It's incredible to me that you're still getting mileage out of your mother's suicide. You're still using it as currency, even though it has nothing to do with what you did. In fact, it's kind of psychotic that you're spending that currency on this moment. When will it run out?"

Never, Greta thought. I've been living on it all my life.

Big Swiss went on. "If everything can be explained by your trauma, then nothing is really your fault, right? You always have this convenient out. Your mother killed herself, and so that gives you permission to do whatever you want? To eavesdrop on my therapy sessions? To fuck me?"

"You made the first pass," Greta reminded her.

"Right, which I would never blame on trauma."

"But we see things through a lens, don't we? The lens of our own experience?"

"Why not say that you made a *choice*, that you knew what you were doing was *wrong*, and that you did it anyway? Why continue coasting on your trauma? It's not a good look at your age."

Neither was smoking, but Greta lit a cigarette. Not for the first time, she considered appealing to the gynecologist in Big Swiss. The truth was, Greta only felt "normal" for one week out of every month. The week before her period: rage, lust, and what felt like clarity. The week of: cramping, fatigue, self-pity. The week after: mind-numbing depression. That left one week of feeling "okay" and "like herself," but sometimes she wondered if it was the only week in which she *wasn't* herself, if the other weeks were the real thing, the real her. At any rate, her reactions to events depended on where she was in the cycle, except she never kept track of the cycle, so she never knew where the fuck she was.

"I was curious about you," Greta said. "That's what was driving me at first. I wanted to know more about you. I'd never met anyone who'd been beaten half to death, who'd had to beg for their life, and whether you like it or not, you're inadvertently coasting on your own trauma, because anyone who knows what happened to you—and evidently, everyone knows—is going to treat you a certain way, possibly as someone whose trauma trumps their own. I bet you're put on a pedestal quite a bit. But you're so *accustomed* to this, you're not even aware of it. What you're *not* used to is feeling this stupid and taken advantage of, but keep in mind that this situation only sucks because it's happening to *you*. On paper, eavesdropping and then lying about it isn't that bad. I mean, I'm not suggesting that it's awesome, or ethical, but what you're doing is worse. Much worse."

"Worse than using someone's confidential information to seduce them? To have this false identity, to lie about your own *name*, to act all-knowing, and then to continue *listening* even after we're sleeping together—I mean, you should have recused yourself."

"This isn't a courtroom," Greta said. "And anyway, I'm the stenographer in this scenario, not the judge. In fact, I always typed exactly what you said *without judgment*—"

"I thought you were psychic at one point," Big Swiss said. "I feel totally exploited. I was convinced we had this freakishly deep connection. I mean, I wouldn't even know how to *explain* this—"

"I'm not a con artist. Calm down. What I did was *weirder*, yes, but not *worse*. We're both guilty. I signed a confidentiality agreement, but I'm not *married*. I didn't invite my mistress to dinner with my super-sweet husband. I didn't talk about starting a family in front of her. *You* did that."

Big Swiss held up her hands. "I'm not saying I'm innocent. I'm not playing the victim. I'm fully aware that I've done a terrible thing."

"Yes, but you're suggesting that adultery is somehow more refined—or genteel—than eavesdropping, and it isn't."

But Big Swiss was no longer facing Greta. She'd turned away to peer out the window. The sky was a dusty pink. On the horizon, a ribbon of rust. In the distance, Greta heard high-pitched yipping.

"What is that?" Big Swiss said.

"Coyotes," Greta said. "They're probably in the woods out back. We better get the dogs."

The dogs weren't in the yard, which was large and unfenced. The only reason Piñon ever left the yard was to go on a killing spree. Greta suspected he'd discovered a nest of rabbits in a shallow burrow, that he was systematically killing them one by one. He'd wipe out an entire family, babies included, if he wasn't stopped. She'd have to shout at him, but he never listened once the bloodletting had begun, and so she'd have to physically drag him away. Perhaps it was time she purchased a shock collar. He seemed too old for that now, at age eleven, but maybe one was never too old for a little behavioral modification. Of course, she'd test it on herself before using it on him. Only fair. Maybe they'd both wear one from now on.

The yipping grew louder, rising and falling in pitch, and seemed very near, though there was only the busy road on one side of them and the open field on the other. Either the coyote was hiding in a bush, or its voice was being carried by the wind.

"That's not a coyote," Big Swiss said. "It's Silas."

Greta immediately yelled for Piñon, trying and failing to keep the panic out of her voice.

"He's with Silas," Big Swiss assured her. "Silas must be hurt. He sounds like he's in pain."

They high-stepped across the field, which was swampy in places and covered in tall reeds, waist-high maiden grass, and probably thousands of deer ticks carrying Lyme disease. The frogs chirped fast and loud, and she kept hearing what sounded like zippers being unzipped, as if hundreds of peepers were dropping their pants. Greta was still wearing her nightgown, unfortunately, which was only knee-length, and had neglected to pull on pants or socks. Her blood diaper felt heavy and stiff. She'd also forgotten to bring a leash, so she'd have to carry Piñon all the way home, and he was likely filthy, in some bloodthirsty frenzy, and would try to squirm out of her arms. Sometimes she wished he were some other, dumber breed, or in any case more dependent and lethargic, more responsive to commands and treats. If Greta were dangling a hot dog in front of his face, he'd ignore it entirely and carry on with the slaughter, but hopefully the rabbits were dying of heart attacks before he could snap their necks.

They searched along the tree line where the field ended and the woods began. Perhaps Piñon was hunting chipmunks, his second-favorite target, in which case only his behind would be visible, the rest of him underground. Greta searched for his rigid white tail in the failing light. Please let me see it, she repeated to herself. Please, please, please. And then she did see a flash of white—a doe's tail flicking—and felt despondent.

Finally, they caught sight of Silas, still a good distance away, standing near a locust tree. Big Swiss called him, but he wouldn't come.

"His foot must be caught in something," Big Swiss said, and quickened her pace.

Silas stopped yipping and began howling, and it was as haunting as a wolf's. As they got closer, he began pacing, patrolling the area around the tree. He was either guarding something on the ground, or he had to take a hard shit. He wouldn't shit in front of anyone, not even other dogs, unless he was completely hidden behind a tree or bush. Sometimes he wouldn't shit for days, which was why his shits were so black and evil.

When they reached him at last, Big Swiss grabbed him by the collar and pulled him toward her, and Greta saw the white fur she'd been hoping to see for the last thirty minutes. Silas had been guarding Piñon, who lay motionless in the dirt. His eyes were partly open, whites showing, his tongue hanging cartoonishly out of his mouth, his wiry fur matted with blood. He'd been shot—in the haunch, it appeared—and his back legs were covered in his own feces.

Greta collapsed as if she'd been shoved in the back. His tongue was impossibly long and pale, stretched out like taffy, covered here and there with clumps of dirt, and she didn't see how it would ever fit back into his mouth. Her first instinct was to blow into his nostrils, but she didn't know if that was correct. She wanted to crush him to her chest. He still smelled like himself, like warm Frito pie. She squeezed each of his paws, which he usually never tolerated, and he let her tug at the fur between his toes, so she knew he was either dead or numb with shock. She began chanting his name. Piñon! Piñon! Piñon!

Finally, his tongue retreated into his mouth. His eyes rolled forward and focused on her face. He swallowed and seemed to remember where he was but not what had happened to him. Confused, he tried scrambling to his feet. She held him down and hummed loudly, waiting for his panic to subside. He looked smaller and more exhausted than she'd ever seen him, as if he'd been swimming for sixteen hours, and she saw him in the center of one of the disgusting ponds he loved so much, barking, swimming in circles, mesmerized by sun glitter. It drew a crowd every time, made people mutter to themselves like schizophrenics. What's he doing? Will he come to shore? Why is he barking like that? Is he drowning? She'd have to walk away or hide behind a tree and wait for him to look for her, because he'd only come back if he couldn't see her, and when he finally climbed out of the water, she'd settle a blanket over his shoulders.

If only she had a blanket for him now. He started trembling, and then suddenly he was shaking violently and foaming at the mouth, a seizure she was sure would end his life, and he kept making an awful noise she couldn't quite hear, because there was a louder, even more awful noise drowning it out, and it sounded like a cow dying or giving birth, only much, much worse, and she looked around wildly, trying to locate the source.

But it was herself, wailing. She'd never wailed in her life, but now she was wailing like an old woman from Italy, like a professional, like a woman who'd spent years mourning for money, for movie directors, for Visconti or Fellini. Had it been a performance, it would've been appalling—overwrought, indulgent, way too long—but she really was *shrieking* as if she herself had been shot. She'd never felt such pure and naked anguish. It opened everything within her, every abscess, every abyss, and they were all throbbing and echoing horribly. She could feel her face crumpling and folding in on itself, tears pooling in the pocket above her clavicle, and she would've given anything to feel Piñon's dry tongue licking her face back into place. He'd always been possessive of Greta's tears, lapping at them greedily as if they were some precious, life-lengthening elixir, and she felt the urge to cry directly into his mouth so that he might live. She draped herself over him and sobbed.

"Stop screaming," Big Swiss was saying now. "Listen to me. Stop screaming. Can you hear me?"

Loud and clear. Her voice seemed to loosen something in Greta's stomach, some knot she'd been holding on to for years, and now the knot unraveled and rushed out of her, hot and wet. Mortified, she felt it maneuvering around the blood diaper, soaking the back of her night-gown, rolling down her legs sluggishly, as if it contained dirt or silt. She clutched her stomach. Well, *this* was embarrassing. What *was* this? Piss? Was she really pissing herself right now? She was too flustered to look. Yes, grief can be theatrical, she lectured herself. It can be extrava-gant. It wasn't how she usually operated, but—oh well. Oh well, oh well, oh well. There was nothing wrong with her. Piñon was *fine*. He'd stopped shaking, finally, and was breathing easy. Relief—that's what was leaking out of her. But then the knot tightened again, and the pain was so excruciating, so astonishing, she felt her eyes bulge. Was she being torn in half? It lasted only a few seconds and then she wet herself some more. That same silty water. The silt was shame, she decided. Shame was something you passed like kidney stones, and it was leaving her body at last. Now she could hear herself babbling about freedom. She would feel freer from now on, free from self-consciousness, free from reticence. She would do or say whatever she wanted, she would care less, she would become more . . . Piñonesque.

"Hold still." Big Swiss leaned over Greta and yanked up her night-gown with one hand. The fingers of her other hand dug into Greta's arm. "Stop moving."

Greta was drenched, she knew that, but only on the outside. In-side, she was a janky space heater about to catch fire.

"I think you might be hemorrhaging," Big Swiss said, a little ner-vously. She placed her palm on Greta's forehead. "You have a fever."

Okay, not free. Or not, cough, cancer-free. Obviously, there was some growth inside her, and it had ruptured, and hopefully it was malignant and untreatable, because if Piñon died, how was she going to live? The shadows swimming on the ground made her dizzy, and it finally occurred to her to look up at the sky. It was the vultures. About six of them were circling, their mouths wide open.

"We need to get to the house now," Big Swiss said. "Can you walk?"

Greta picked up Piñon, careful not to touch the bullet wound, and held him like a baby. She'd never held him like this, never once in six years, because he never allowed it. He couldn't stand to be cradled, but his body was limber and slack, and he was wide awake and blinking at her with renewed interest, as if meeting her for the first time. He seemed enchanted by her, and she knew he would be all right if she got him to the hospital.

"*Greta*," Big Swiss said. "Can you stop crying? Can you look at me?"

Greta's hair was curtained around her face. She didn't feel capable of looking at Big Swiss, not without protection of some kind. A blanket would be nice, for old times' sake, but Sabine would be better.

"Sabine!" Greta yelled. "Sabine!"

"Is there any chance you're having a miscarriage?" Big Swiss asked.

Greta spun around and hit her, hard enough to knock her down. She'd done it without thinking, but she wanted to do it again, and she would have if she hadn't been carrying Piñon. Big Swiss stayed on the ground, holding her jaw.

Now four identically dressed men were jogging in their direction. One of them, a kid in his twenties, ran straight up to Big Swiss and helped her to her feet, even though Greta was covered in blood and cradling a limp dog.

"I'm okay," Big Swiss said, brushing herself off. "Thank you."

"'I'm okay'? Yeah? What about 'Her dog has been shot'? Any idea who did this? Was it you? Who are you?" Greta said.

"My name's Rick?" he said. "I'm from next door?"

The firehouse. Of course. They were firefighters. She wondered which one of them manned the air-raid siren, and why wasn't it going off right now, with a killer on the loose?

"Ma'am?" another guy said. "Can you tell me what happened?"

"Someone shot my dog," Greta said, her voice shaking with terror. "He's still out there somewhere."

The guy nodded as if he got this all the time. "A lot of small-game hunting in those woods behind you. Small *and* large game. Deer, bears. We saw a bear just yesterday. But somebody may have mistaken your dog for a hare. He was probably drunk."

A drunk hunter? A bear? A hare? It was *Keith*, obviously. He was probably hiding in one of the deer stands this very minute, covered in camo and face paint, observing them through the scope of his rifle.

"Are you hurt, ma'am? Do you need to go to the hospital?"

"It's my dog's blood," Greta said, though anyone could see that it wasn't.

"I'm texting the vet," Rick, the young one, said. He pulled out his phone and started typing. "He lives just down the road. I'm giving him your address. You live with Sabine, right?"

Greta nodded. Of course, they all knew Sabine. She'd probably thrown darts with them, played pool, shot guns. And then there was that time she'd been burning trash and had accidentally caught the field on fire.

Big Swiss thanked the men, and then she turned to Greta and began talking to her like she was a dog. "Let's go. Come on. Move."

While they walked, Greta tried not to look at Piñon in her arms, lest she start wailing again. She kept her eyes straight ahead and focused on the house. As usual, every single light was on—Sabine never turned off a lamp or lantern, even during the day—and so the house always looked cheerful and welcoming from a distance, and full of people, and like everything worked, and Greta pretended that this was true.

But the house was empty—Sabine wasn't back yet. Greta placed Piñon on his dog bed in the foyer and covered him with his favorite blanket. He was breathing hard through his nose. Big Swiss passed her a bottle of water, and Greta wet Piñon's lips and winced as she poured a little on the wound. She thought about running a bath for him.

"Go get changed," Big Swiss said. "I'll watch him."

In her room, Greta removed her bloody nightgown. She pushed her underwear down to her ankles and stepped out of them. They resembled a twisted mouth, the pad a swollen, mangled tongue. She wasn't bleeding anymore and felt only mild cramping, but she was tempted to jump up and down to see what would happen. Instead, she pulled on a pair of jeans and a long sweater.

A small truck turned into the driveway, the vet. She'd been expecting an ambulance, for some reason, with sirens, and a team of EMTs. Where was the stretcher? The IV? But it was just one guy carrying a canvas tool bag and dressed entirely in spandex, like a professional cyclist. It wasn't a look Greta had ever approved of—she hated it, in fact—but she couldn't take her eyes off him. She was so distracted by his outfit, his shaved calves, his overdeveloped forearms, she didn't catch his name. In one swift motion, he lifted the dog bed and Piñon off the floor and transferred them to the only piece of furniture in the foyer, a large, wooden antique desk, on top of which sat a porcelain lamp and a vase holding a spray of lily of the valley.

"I'll get him stabilized," he said. "What's his name?"

"Piñon," Greta said, and blushed.

He gave Piñon two shots: a painkiller and an antibiotic. He took Piñon's temperature and listened to his heartbeat. He examined the wound, said that dogs got shot all the time around here, usually with pellet guns, but that this was likely a .22, then he shaved the area with an electric razor, carefully cleaned and dressed the wound, and gave Greta a bunch of supplies: more painkillers and antibiotics, a tube of ointment, a plastic cone collar.

"After tomorrow, leave the wound open. Clean it once or twice a day like I showed you, and don't let him lick it. Keep the collar on him."

"Leave it open," Greta repeated. "So the bullet can find its way out?"

He blinked at her kindly. He was so calm and patient. That wasn't how it worked, he said. He kept looking at her bangs as he talked, and Greta wondered what they looked like. Not great, probably.

"The wound needs air," he said. "It'll heal faster."

So I've heard.

"Otherwise, he's in very good shape. His lungs sound clear and he's not overweight."

"Well, he's an athlete," she said, and adjusted her bangs. "Like you."

He smiled. "He'll probably be fine. Just keep an eye on him, and call me if the wound smells bad or doesn't look like it's healing." After a pause he said, "Would you like me to report this to the police?"

God, yes. Thank you, sir. How humiliating for Keith to go back to prison for shooting a dog. He'd probably get shanked on the first day. She wanted to tell the vet about Keith, so that he might mention it to the police, but she didn't know where to start, how to explain, and anyway, it was too late, he was carrying his bag out the door. He hadn't seemed to notice Big Swiss, having only spoken to Greta, and so she was surprised to see Big Swiss follow him to his truck. Greta watched them talk briefly. Big Swiss pulled something out of her pocket. A pen, it looked like, and a pad of paper. She wrote something down and passed it to him, waved at him as he drove away, and then she just stood there in the driveway, hugging herself, obviously reluctant to come back inside.

"He seemed like a real person," Big Swiss announced a minute later. "And good at his job."

Greta said yes, he did seem very competent, but otherwise completely *un*real, and way too attractive to be a vet. He must have been known all over the county for his good looks. What was his name again?

"You're still in shock," Big Swiss said. "His name is Tom and he's completely average looking."

"Then why did you give him your number?"

"You know, you might be perimenopausal," Big Swiss said. "You were having a hot flash out there. And a heavy period. It's common to bleed profusely like that, in spurts. The blood was thin, mostly, and bright pink, but there were a few large clots—so, yes, I'm sorry I suggested it was a miscarriage—it was the first thing that popped into my head, and I wasn't thinking clearly. But I am now." She pulled her phone from her pocket and looked at it. "I have to leave in a minute, but maybe you should let me examine you."

"You didn't answer my question."

"I can still hear you screaming," Big Swiss said. "You know what it sounds like?"

Glenn Close? Greta thought. Meryl Streep?

"Badly played bagpipes," Big Swiss said. "It's giving me a migraine."

"Well, it was my first time screaming. Maybe I'll practice more after you leave."

Piñon whined in his sleep. His brows twitched, and he paddled his front paws. He was distressed. He was reliving his trauma, obviously. If only she could see what he was seeing, she might at least know what Keith *looked* like. But then what?

She thought about moving him to the antechamber. Better to leave him on the table for now. She switched off the lamp. Now she and Big Swiss were standing in the dark. Both halves of the wide Dutch door were open to the yard, which was full of night noise. They listened without speaking for a minute. It was too early for cricket song, but the peepers called in chorus, and it sounded like sleigh bells, and a toad kept belching loudly.

"Do you think it was him?" Greta asked.

"Who?"

"*Keith.*"

"No," Big Swiss said. "You should get that out of your head."

"So—but—did he ask for your number, or did you just give it to him?"

"Who?"

"*Tom.*"

"I wrote him a check, Greta," Big Swiss said. "For twelve hundred dollars."

Greta groaned. Thankfully, Big Swiss couldn't see her face, which she could feel reddening, or her stupid, quivering mouth. But when her mouth trembled, her words did, too.

"You didn't have to do that."

"House calls are expensive, Greta."

"I would've figured it out."

"How? You don't have a job."

"Okay, well, *thank you*," Greta said. "And *you're welcome*."

"What's that supposed to mean?"

"I just gave you another opportunity to feel superior."

"That's not why I did it," Big Swiss said. "You think I'm enjoying this?"

"Luke takes very good care of you. So, I know you're not with me to feel safe and secure. You think you're slumming, right? I've been there—it's exciting at first. Life-affirming. Feels a little dangerous. So, I'm not sure why you're acting all outraged, since you already thought of me as someone beneath you. A broken toy. You don't really care about *privacy*. Or *boundaries*. You're only mad because I had a little power over you, power I didn't deserve, because you hadn't given it to me. But you know what? I'd rather live like an animal than in some fantasy where I have control over everything, where people only have power over me if I *let* them. You millennials and your utopias, honest to god. You're so attached to your vision, to your virtue, to your supposedly good intentions, to being on the right side of everything—"

"You had personal information about me that allowed you some control over my impression of you, which is the definition of power. Of course I care about privacy. I never discussed my therapy sessions with you because they were *private*, because I have *boundaries*."

"Then why are you traipsing around Hudson with me? Having sex with me in bathrooms? Introducing me to your husband?"

"I'm trying to figure that out," Big Swiss said. "Believe me. I'm dying to get to the bottom of it."

Big Swiss raised her arms, laced her fingers, and cradled her head. One of her signature gestures, designed to look casual and innocuous, to make her seem open and unguarded, but Greta knew better. She caught a whiff and felt herself weaken.

"Put those away, please," Greta said.

"What?"

"Your pits," Greta said, and waved her hand. "I'm trying to concentrate."

Big Swiss unlaced her fingers and crossed her arms.

"We can continue arguing about this another time," Big Swiss said. "I'm scheduled for surgery at six a.m. I'll call you after and check up on you."

Silas, who'd been curled up under the desk, loped over to Big Swiss and sat at her feet, ready to be leashed, ready for this nightmare to be over.

"HELLO?" Sabine said from the doorway. "Why's it so dark in here?"

Greta switched on the lamp. Sabine was more disheveled than usual and holding a large basket of strawberries. Greta resisted the urge to embrace her.

"I ran out of gas," Sabine said. "I called and called but you weren't picking up, so I started *walking*. Was almost mowed down, twice, by the same truck."

Sabine automatically moved toward the desk but stopped when she saw Piñon.

"Oh no. What happened? Greta! Him isn't dead, is he? Oh god. Oh god!"

"Him" was Sabine's nickname for Piñon.

"Him was shot," Greta said. "With a twenty-two."

Sabine dropped the basket. Strawberries scattered everywhere.

"He's alive. He's just sleeping."

Sabine smoothed Piñon's forehead. "Poor little Him," she cooed. "Him can have anything he wants when he wakes up, okay? Anything." She looked at Greta. "I'll make biscuits and whipped cream— he loves that. What happened to your face? You look like you've been beaten up. Your eyes are almost swollen shut."

Greta shrugged. "You should've seen me out there. I turned Italian, I turned Chinese, and then I started menopause. I was screaming, sobbing, bleeding all over the place—"

"Listen," Sabine interrupted. "Small confession—her voice stopped me in my tracks. It's like a knife at your throat. I hid in the bushes for a good ten minutes, listening to your conversation. I couldn't bring myself to interrupt. Someone told me they saw you with her the other day, and I didn't believe them. But this is who you've been sleeping with, Greta? Jesus. Why didn't you tell me?"

"I've been trying, believe me," Greta said. "I didn't realize you . . . knew her."

"Well, yeah. She's Swedish. Married. Does something medical."

"Swiss," Greta said.

"She was almost killed years ago, and I met her parents once when they were visiting from Sweden."

"Switzerland," Greta said.

"What's her name again?"

As usual, Greta had to think for a second. It had never been on the tip of her tongue. Not like "Piñon," which felt like one of Greta's first words.

"Flavia," Greta said.

"Right. Her husband comes from money. Great house—I've seen pictures. Anyway, I don't know her personally. But I know her type. She acts all cold and imperious, and she's obviously fastidious about her appearance—that *outfit*, my god—but inside she's a mess."

"What kind of mess?"

"You know—vulnerable."

"Well, if you couldn't tell, I think it's over between us," Greta said. "I lied to her about my name and . . . some other things. There's been a lot of drama. The sex is way too *long*—that's my theory. But even after all this, there's still this *tension*. It makes me feel *insane*. And it feels *mutual*—"

Sabine held up her hand. "Look, if she cheated on her husband with you, her feelings are anything but casual. In fact, I bet she doesn't have a casual bone in her body. Not one." Sabine belched and blew hair out of her face. "Help me with these berries."

They got on their knees and crawled around. Greta picked up each strawberry gingerly and brushed it off with her fingers, but Sabine grabbed three at a time and tossed them into the basket.

"She reminds me of my mother," Sabine went on. "Occasionally, she lets down her guard and you see how delicate she is. Just a glimpse. It's often so subtle you miss it. But your subconscious picks up on it, and it keeps you . . . engaged. Like those commercials with the subliminal messages. You're being shown a picture of someone who seems bulletproof, right, but just below the threshold of conscious awareness, there's an entirely different message."

"Is it . . . satanic?"

"Extremely fragile. That's the message. Handle with care."

Sabine was talking about herself, of course, which was fine and good. Greta thought back to the beginning, when she was just getting to know Big Swiss. Greta once commented on the way Big Swiss sometimes drooled while they were making out, how exciting and endearing it was. The next time they'd seen each other, Greta had caught Big Swiss blotting her tongue with her sleeve when she thought Greta wasn't looking.

"You want a Valium?" Sabine asked suddenly. "Let's both have one."

She plucked two linty pills from the front pocket of her overalls and passed one to Greta. They moved Piñon to Greta's bed. He woke up briefly, and Greta gave him water and comforted him until he passed out again. Greta said she was ready to pass out, too.

"Was Him shot on my property?" Sabine asked.

"We didn't see it happen. We found him on the edge of the field. The firemen said it was probably a hunter, but I think it was Keith." Greta sighed. "It's a long story, but Keith is the man who tried to kill—"

"I know who Keith is, silly," Sabine said. "Get under the covers and I'll sit with you until you fall asleep."

She dragged an armchair to Greta's bedside and lit a cigarette. Greta pulled the comforter to her chin and closed her eyes. Her mind crawled toward the edge of oblivion. Just as she was about to fall off, Sabine started talking.

"Keith comes from a family of twelve called the Hickeys. They've been around forever. They're clannish, high on themselves, high on each other, very us-against-the-world, except they all suck. But Keith—he got away. He grew up refinishing furniture for one of the antique dealers in town and then suddenly he was calling himself a designer and making tables for rich people. Someone married him—

blond, leggy, out of his league—and they moved to the city. He had clients in the Hamptons and on Nantucket. Famous people, supposedly. He'd come back to Hudson every so often to brag and show off. Like all the Hickeys, he's really hard to listen to. You just want to walk away. I'm guessing he was making decent money but at the end of the day, he was still a Hickey, so I wasn't surprised when I heard he beat up his wife. And then, when his wife left him for a woman, he went off the deep end. He's been in and out of prison ever since. You'd think he'd leave, or move out of state, but he's a Hickey, so he's here to stay. And then there's Vera, one of the younger sisters, who was obsessed with Keith, visiting him in prison every week, telling people he'd been framed. I'm always suspicious of people who openly worship their families. Protecting your family—fine. But blatant reverence? Seems like a cover-up, or maybe it's just a sign of stupidity . . ."

Eyes closed, Greta felt like she was eavesdropping on a conversation Sabine was having with herself. It poured out in an unfiltered stream, and she knew that she would miss this aspect of working for Om, the inherent surprise of receiving information she hadn't asked for, or hadn't known she'd been seeking.

She drifted off and immediately started dreaming of feet, an old motif. A man's bare feet climbing over rocks, crossing a creek. The same feet, paler, slightly magnified, floating underwater. Whose feet were these? They were resting in her lap now, cold, heavy, covered in hickeys left by leeches, and she thought they must belong to Keith.

17

Now that she was officially single and unemployed, no longer in thrall to Big Swiss or a confidentiality agreement, she was free to explore, go wherever she wanted, talk to whomever she pleased, and so why was she standing here, of all places, in a narrow alley between two buildings?

To her right stood Cousin's, one of the oldest and least celebrated bars in town. The outside reminded her of the long ash on Grandma's cigarette: gray walls, dirty white trim, red neon sign in the window. She had the feeling she might get burned if she stepped inside, that her presence would be unwelcome, that she would be knocking over the ashtray, so to speak, which, as she could see through the dark glass, was overflowing with crushed butts, or at any rate a bunch of gray geriatrics sitting on stools made of marbled beige pleather. She imagined herself sitting among them, sipping a vodka soda and smoldering, wondering if she should finally extinguish herself.

On the other side of the alley, Cousin's antithesis: Lil' Deb's Oasis, a queer restaurant and destination, welcoming and inclusive, the warmest lap in town but also as wet and alive as a jungle. Their wine descriptions were the best poetry in town, and the place was overflowing with pastels, pineapples, plantains, and performers, and here and there a pop of pink neon. She got the feeling she might drown in gender fluids if she stepped inside, or that her own gender, not all that solid to begin with, might deliquesce like fungi and stain the pink counter stool, but that it might be good for her, just what she needed. She stared at the bright fruit painted on the side of the building and wondered if she should cut her bangs.

Of course, she was more inclined to find friends in the fruit bowl than the ashtray, but would she fit in? She'd never claimed an identity for the same reasons she'd never gotten tattoos: she couldn't imagine settling on anything. In the early nineties, when she'd had the energy for such things, she'd flirted with the idea of getting avocado halves tattooed on her elbows and embracing her bisexuality, but it had all been so rigid back then, so black-and-white, such a commitment, and avocados and bisexuals weren't as cool as they were now, and only seemed to come from California. No one had wanted them on their toast, certainly. It was a consistency thing. They were treated with apprehension at best, or else outright discrimination from both the straight and gay communities. But now that she was oldish, the crowd in there youngish, and it was finally acceptable to be gayish, she might as well sit at the counter and eat some octopus. Right?

She walked into the ashtray instead. The drop ceiling was lit up with strings of colored lights—Christmas in late June—and there were a few small TVs showing harness racing, and a large flat-screen playing a boxing match. Everything was coated in sticky dust. Most of the stools were occupied at the horseshoe-shaped bar, but she found an empty one along the curve.

No one acknowledged her, not even the bartender, the only other woman there. "Caught Up in You" started playing through the speakers, and Greta studied the bartender for nearly the entire song, unnoticed. Her strawberry blonde hair had long white roots, and she wore low-rise jeans and a pink T-shirt with a desert-island cartoon printed on the front—a tiny island with a single palm tree, no castaways— over which ICELAND was printed in frosty blue letters. She was maybe fifty. Greta spent a little too long wondering if her shirt was a meaningless novelty, or if it was about climate change, or if she'd actually traveled to Iceland, and if so, what she'd done there. She had a habit of resting her hands on her hips when she talked to her customers, all of whom resembled old newspapers, and of laughing at her own jokes. Her laugh was manic and grating.

Without looking at Greta, the man sitting next to her said, "What're you having?"

"Vodka soda," Greta said.

"Vera," he called to the bartender. "Get her a vodka soda."

Greta expected a dirty look, but the bartender smiled benignly at her while pouring vodka into a pint glass.

"Lime?" the guy asked.

"Lemon," Greta said, and the guy, her translator, paused before relaying the information, as if she'd asked for passion fruit or lychee. The guy was tan, broad, and muscular, with a creepy little ponytail, and he was watching the boxing match closely, as if he had money on it. He seemed to be drinking seltzer, but since the drinks came in pint glasses, maybe it was gin or vodka.

Vera delivered Greta's drink. "Is my brother bothering you?"

Greta smiled and said no.

"Lemme know if he does," Vera said, and wandered away.

A long minute passed during which Greta could feel individual hairs on her head turning white. She hadn't anticipated sitting next to him. She'd been looking for Harvey Keitel in, say, *The Piano*, minus the face tattoos, because that's who Big Swiss said he resembled, but of course Keith looked nothing like Harvey Keitel. Since his eyes were still glued to the TV, she risked a closer look. He didn't look like anyone. Well, maybe James Caan? Taller, though, younger. And poorer, obviously, but with good posture. He wore a tight white tank top and fitted gray dress pants. Hadn't Harvey Keitel worn something similar in *Taxi Driver*? She could see the resemblance now, though Keith wouldn't have been caught dead in a fedora or pinkie rings. He was more like Mr. White from *Reservoir Dogs*, without the shirt and tie. He had presence, she decided, and seemed aware of every muscle in his body, including the ones in his hands and feet.

His hands. Red, swollen, very wide. Inevitably, she pictured them wrapped around Big Swiss's pale neck, squeezing and releasing, and her own throat tightened. It was easy to imagine his hands doing violence but hard to imagine the look on his face. He had a calm, reasonable face, though she was only seeing his profile. He had yet to look directly at her. And sociopaths can be calm—c'mon. Look at Hannibal and his low heart rate.

She thought of Piñon, hopefully conked out in the antechamber, where she'd left him. They'd spent nearly every minute of the last two weeks together. Tonight was the first time Greta had left his side for more than twenty minutes. He wasn't bouncing back the way he used to, and if the vet had reported the incident to the police, they'd never contacted her.

It occurred to her now that Keith was staring at the TV to avoid looking at her, that he couldn't have cared less about boxing, that he knew exactly who Greta was because he'd been stalking her and Big Swiss for months, that he'd shot Greta's dog in cold blood, and that he was hyperaware of his body because he was a bundle of nerves. But why had he spoken to her at all? To see if she knew who he was. She hadn't known, obviously, but she knew now. Maybe he could sense that she'd recognized him and was praying that she wouldn't call him out in front of his sister and all these newspapers. Of course, she wasn't positive that he'd tried to kill Piñon, but it would be telling to see how he reacted if she said his name.

"Keith," she said.

His face turned toward her slightly but his eyes remained on the screen.

"Huh?"

"That's your name, right? Keith."

"Uh-huh," he said.

"Do you recognize me?"

He reluctantly glanced at her face and then quickly back at the screen.

"You recognize me, right?"

He raised his eyebrows. "Maybe," he said. "Should I?"

"Well, yeah," she said. "I'm Greta."

He gave her a warm look. He thought he was being flirted with. She could mention Big Swiss and watch his face fall, or at least redden, or she could just cut to the chase.

"You shot the wrong dog," Greta said.

"Excuse me?"

"You shot the wrong dog," Greta repeated. "Two weeks ago. You meant to shoot the big silver one, but you shot the little guy instead. My guy."

He laughed as if he'd misheard her. "Slow down. What now?"

"You shot my dog," Greta said slowly. "With a gun. In the leg? Not hers—mine."

Now he swiveled toward her and looked her in the eye. "Where you from, hon?"

"Oh, you know," Greta said. "You know exactly where I live. Next to the firehouse. I've seen your truck across the street. You've probably seen me with her."

"Who?"

"*Her*," Greta said.

He winced and swiveled back to center. "Really not in the mood today, lady."

"Yeah, well, you should know that my dog suffered. This was a really big setback for him. And me."

"I love dogs," he said. "I'd never shoot a dog. Never in a million years."

He finished his drink, and Vera came over.

"One more?" she asked Keith.

"Twist my arm," Keith said.

Vera walked away and poured too much gin into a pint glass.

"I'll put it this way," Keith said in a lowered voice. "I'd shoot *you* before I'd shoot any dog."

Something moved in Greta's stomach. Something sharp. She'd been leaning toward Keith without realizing it. She straightened and gulped down the rest of her drink.

"You heard what I said?" Keith asked, his voice still low.

Vera placed Keith's drink in front of him, but Keith didn't touch it.

"That's how much I love animals," Keith said in a regular voice. "I wouldn't even shoot a deer, and they're everywhere you look. I have six of them living in the bushes in my backyard. But I don't hunt. I don't even own a gun."

"But your dog was obese," Greta said. "And miserable. Remember? So, you don't love dogs *that* much—"

"Lady," he said. "Are you drunk? I don't have a dog."

He exchanged an exasperated look with one of the guys sitting on the other side of him. "Broads," he seemed to say.

"Your *old* dog," Greta said. "The one you had before you—"

"Look, I don't know you, okay?" His voice was louder now. "I don't know you, I don't know your dog, I don't know anything. I'm trying to watch this now."

He shook his head and stared at the screen. The match was over and the ring was crowded with people.

"Great," he said. "Terrific."

"Stop following me," Greta said.

"Get the fuck out of my face," he said loudly. "Dumb city bitch. You don't know where the fuck you're at or who the fuck you're talking to."

Vera came over and cleared Greta's glass. "All set?" she asked sweetly. "Drink's on the house, okay? Don't come back."

Greta's knees nearly buckled as she walked out of the bar, and she could hear Vera laughing.

HER HEART? Still in her mouth as she pulled into the driveway and saw Big Swiss's car. They'd exchanged a few texts but hadn't seen each other since the shooting, and it wasn't like Big Swiss to show up without calling. Had something happened to Silas? Greta rushed inside.

Not only had Big Swiss let herself into the house; she lay diagonally on Greta's bed, legs crossed at the ankle, arms behind her head, gazing at the cracked ceiling as if it were full of constellations, which she supposed it was.

"Where's Silas?"

"Home," Big Swiss said.

"What are you doing here?"

"Just checking up on you and Piñon."

Greta poked her head into the antechamber—Piñon was sound asleep and snoring. Greta decided to sit in an armchair, a safe distance away from the bed and Big Swiss's exposed pits. Her phone vibrated with a text from Sabine, who was halfway to Maine to eat steamers with old friends, as she did every summer, and wouldn't be back for a few days.

"Where were you?" Big Swiss asked.

"Out," Greta said.

"At a bar?"

"Yes," Greta said.

"Did you meet anyone?"

Of course, now would be the time to tell Big Swiss that she'd met Keith, live and in person, along with his enchanting sister, that she'd gotten a good look at his carnie hands, his creepy ponytail, his barely suppressed rage. She was still rattled by the remark he'd made, "I'd shoot *you* before I'd shoot any dog," which she believed to be true. Now that she thought about it, Vera was the one who'd seemed to recognize Greta. Maybe *Vera* was the stalker, the one to worry about. On the other hand, who confronts a violent ex-convict on his own turf and accuses him of attempted murder? Someone stupid, reckless, and insane. And deeply paranoid. *You're* the stalker, Greta told herself. *You're* the one to worry about.

"So?" Big Swiss said.

"I did meet someone," Greta said.

"And?"

"Great guy," Greta said. "Little over-the-hill, maybe."

"You're going back to men?"

"People," Greta said, correcting her. "I'm open."

"Are you open to me?"

"Depends. What do you want?"

"Who're you texting?"

Greta was texting Sabine a bunch of animal emojis. Supposedly "the donks," as Sabine kept referring to them, were arriving around the time Sabine would be back from Maine, but Greta didn't want to share this news with Big Swiss. The donks were none of her business.

"Tell me," Big Swiss said.

"Just making a note in my dream journal."

Big Swiss backed off. For some reason, dreams were sacred to her.

"I'd like to take you up on your offer," Big Swiss said. "The one from your email. You said I could . . . you know."

"If you can't even say it, maybe it's not something you should be doing. Besides, that was before. Wouldn't it feel silly at this point?"

Big Swiss sniffed. "I was thinking it might be . . . cathartic."

For her, sure. For Greta, pure degradation. But maybe this was exactly what Greta deserved for acting on every whim and impulse, for making such a goddamn mess, for not considering the dignity of others—such as Luke, mainly, but also Keith, who was human, after all, and probably hadn't shot her dog, and who had done his time. Had Greta done hers? She'd never been truly disgraced. Maybe this would lead to her deliverance.

Whatever, it was only a spanking. No need to be grandiose about it. She unbuttoned her pants, let them drop to the floor, and then draped herself over the bed's iron footrail, which was more awkward than leaning over the side. An hour ago, she'd been sitting next to the man who'd broken Big Swiss's face, and now she was waiting to be spanked by her. Not quite full circle, but it felt oddly . . . correct. Maybe this would lead to Big Swiss's deliverance. Maybe after this they would *both* be free—

"Is this what they mean by 'closure'?" Greta said.

"You said bare bottom," Big Swiss said.

Greta pulled down her underwear. Big Swiss grabbed Greta's wide wooden hairbrush and tested it on her open palm.

"No mercy," Big Swiss said. "Right?"

"Yeah, yeah, but be quiet about it. Piñon's sleeping."

"What's your safe word?"

"I don't know," Greta said. "'Diarrhea'?"

Big Swiss smacked Greta's right cheek, not once, not twice, but fifteen times—until it was sufficiently red and inflamed, Greta assumed—before moving to the other side. She seemed intent on distributing her blows evenly and with the same amount of force, and she wasn't holding back. Greta hadn't been spanked since kindergarten and never with a brush. It was both louder and more painful than she'd imagined, but Piñon didn't bark. He didn't even wake up.

"Does it hurt?" Big Swiss asked hopefully.

"Like a mother," Greta said.

Big Swiss delivered several more vigorous whacks and then dropped the brush. She was panting. Greta twisted around slightly to gaze at her face. It was as red as Greta's ass, and she'd never looked more . . . embodied.

"I'll miss hearing you process this in therapy," Greta said.

"Yeah, well, I quit," Big Swiss said, still catching her breath. "I need to lie down for a minute."

Big Swiss climbed onto the bed and lay on her side. She raised her arm, indicating that she wanted to be spooned. Greta pressed herself against Big Swiss's back, like old times. She liked to pretend to be stuck to Big Swiss, in the same way dogs were knotted together after mating.

"Why'd you quit?" Greta asked. "I thought he was helping you, in his Om way."

"I'm leaving for Ecuador in a week," Big Swiss said. "I'm sick of talking about myself. But you—I was thinking the other day how difficult it must have been for you not to talk, not to tell me all the things you were transcribing. You must have dirt on everyone in town."

"I do," Greta said.

Big Swiss parted her legs just enough for Greta's hand. Greta paused, but only for three seconds.

"I hope it's as good as you remember," Big Swiss said a few minutes later.

Greta removed her hand. She held it to her face and inhaled.

"Indeed," Greta said.

"I'm not done with you," Big Swiss said. "I'm not sure I'll ever be."

"Me neither, but I'm done sneaking around," Greta said. "You should tell Luke about us before he hears it from someone else. You should tell him immediately. Tonight, as soon as you get home."

18

Four days later, on the day of her first appointment with Om, Greta arrived early to get coffee at Cathedral. She'd already chugged three cups at home, but a little extra would be conducive to taut story-telling, and Om had mentioned that their session would be short. She sat at a table and waited for it to kick in—the sweats, the shakes, hope-fully not the shits—and wondered if all of Om's clients arrived in a similar state, on the verge of a silent heart attack. None of them were there now. The place was full of voices she didn't recognize. At the table to her right, two ladies frowned at fabric swatches. To her left sat two dudes—cooks of some kind, Greta assumed, since they were both wearing checkered chef pants and filthy clogs. The one closest to her smelled like booze and a bag of onions.

"I was outside Lil' Deb's the other night, smoking in the alley, and these two guys stumbled out of the bar next door," Onions said. "That bar nobody goes to."

"Cousin's," the other guy said.

Greta perked up. She'd smoked in the same alley the previous week. From now on, she supposed, she'd have to get gossip the old-fashioned way, by eavesdropping in public like everyone else.

"One of the guys looked like a Patagoniac visiting from the city," Onions said. "The other guy was an older townie—hairy shoulders, tank top tucked into baggy jean shorts. Anyways, they were arguing in the alley about thirty feet away from me, and I figured it was about politics. Trump or whatever. The city guy was all wound up. Not super vocal, but jumpy, ready to throw hands."

"Were they wasted?"

"The townie was, I think. He's one of those dudes who looks drunk no matter what. I bet he gets hammered after two drinks." Onions coughed. "The shampoo effect."

"What's that?"

"It's when your liver is so saturated, it only takes a few drops of alcohol to get lathered."

"That happens to me."

"No, it doesn't," Onions said. "Only serious alcoholics achieve the shampoo effect. It takes years. I'm nearly there myself. Anyways, I don't know what they were arguing about, but the townie tried to walk back into the bar, and that's when the city guy made a big fucking mistake." He coughed again. "He pulled a *knife*. Imagine? He pulled a knife on a drunk townie. In an alley. On a Sunday."

The other guy snorted. "Let me guess—it was an Opinel."

"What?"

"Those fancy French pocket knives."

"No, this was like a hunting knife. I thought it was a cleaver at first, but the blade wasn't broad enough."

"Shit," the other guy said. "Jesus."

"Yeah. And he didn't just brandish the knife—he started thrusting and parrying like he was in *West Side Story*. It was so over-the-top, I almost started laughing."

"Was the townie laughing?"

"Oh no. He was stony as hell. He just watched the kid slice at the air. But then he suddenly came to life—he put up his dukes and started bobbing and weaving. For a minute I thought it was all a performance, and I actually looked around for the film crew, like were they shooting from a rooftop?"

"Yeah, I'm surprised more movies aren't filmed here," the other guy said. "Like at the Basilica—"

"Hold on. The townie—I don't know how he did it, but he moved in really fast and somehow maneuvered the knife away from the city guy. It looked like a magic trick. Now the townie was holding the knife. I thought that'd be the end of it, that he'd just walk away, but—" Onions looked pale and sweaty. Greta watched him mop his forehead with a wrinkled bandana. "He fucking stabbed the kid in the stomach, like eight or nine times."

"What?" the other one said. "He did not!"

Greta's heart fluttered, though she didn't know why—it wasn't the first stabbing she'd heard about in Hudson.

"It happened so fast I thought I was hallucinating. The city guy probably thought he was hallucinating, too. The look on his face? I've never seen such disbelief."

"Holy shit, the poor guy was probably up here for the weekend, staying in an Airbnb, hiking the Catskills—"

"Right, never in a million years thinking he'd get stabbed. I mean, you come here to get *away*."

"Then what?"

"The townie wasn't even winded. It was like he'd just chopped up some chicken for a salad or something."

"What'd you do?" the other one said. "Did you call the cops?"

"I was in shock, dude. People were streaming out of both places, and there was blood fucking *everywhere*. The city guy was completely covered, and there was blood all over the ground in, like, *puddles*."

"It's easy to forget how much blood we have inside us," said the other one.

Greta's stomach gurgled.

"The kid was in the fetal position, clutching his stomach, and blood was still pouring out of him, like a tap had been opened. I'm not ashamed to admit—I started crying. Like, hard. Like a tap had been opened in me, too."

"What was the townie doing?"

"Just standing there. He finally dropped the knife when he heard sirens. All the Deb's people were going berserk, crying, screaming, and a couple of them were comforting the kid, covering him with towels, holding his hand, asking him questions, but the kid just—I mean, he was *weeping*. In the movies, a guy gets stabbed and he's in shock, right, just lying there, blinking at the sky. Not this guy. He was wide awake and, like, fully there. It was fucking *intense*, dude. But I think he lost consciousness before the ambulance arrived."

"What about the Cousin's people? What were they doing?"

"Just standing around, shaking their heads, acting like tourists got stabbed in their alley every day. Then about sixteen cops showed up and arrested the townie, and the poor kid was taken away in the ambulance, but there was still blood everywhere, and some folks were throwing up. Literally vomiting all over the place. I was so traumatized, I couldn't work the next day. I felt like *I'd* been stabbed. I mean, the way he was crying? Like he hadn't cried in years, and it was all coming out, and I remembered reacting like that once when my dad told me he hated my paintings. I was making nude self-portraits at the time and he said that my body—"

"But what do you think they were fighting about?"

Thank you, Greta thought.

"No clue," Onions said.

"I bet it was a turf thing," said the other one. "The city guy probably wandered in there and asked for a mojito, and the townie was like, 'Get the fuck out of here, son'—"

"Yeah, well, the townie seemed like a sociopath. Like my dad—"

"But imagine getting stabbed with *your own knife*, man. I mean, is there anything more humiliating?"

"No," Onions said, and sniffed.

"I wonder if he's even alive," the other one said. "If you lose that much blood, you can't just add it back. It's, like, a whole process. Takes weeks, I think. Not to mention the damage to his organs."

They were quiet for a full minute. Greta noticed she was five minutes late.

"Have you tried the ceviche at Lil' Deb's?" Onions said.

"I usually get the Plato Tropical," the other one said. "With avocado."

UPSTAIRS, Om led her into his office and asked why she was limping. Greta told him she'd stepped on glass and that it was still lodged in her foot. He asked that she take off her shoes, and she reluctantly removed her sandals and sat on the pink love seat. Om sat opposite her, gazing at her bare feet. She thought he might examine her foot, or at least comment on the fact that her feet didn't match. Instead, he got right to it and asked Greta where she'd been on the day her mother killed herself.

Greta cleared her throat. "Some kid got stabbed a bunch of times in the alley next to Cousin's. Did you hear about that?"

Om held up his hand. "This office is a gossip-free zone."

"Since when?"

"Today. We only have thirty minutes," Om said, and looked at his phone. "Let's focus on you. Take me back to that day. Where were you?"

"Don't you want some background about my childhood first? My mother? The years leading up to her death? I've been in therapy before. That's usually how it starts."

He shrugged and reminded Greta that he wasn't that kind of therapist, i.e., the real kind. He seemed adamant that she tell him what she remembered about that day—what she was doing, wearing, thinking, feeling, where she was in her body—and so she told him the truth, that she'd been hundreds of miles away at a horse camp for girls in the Sierra Nevada, even though she'd never ridden a horse in her life.

"She sent you to camp to make sure you weren't home," Om said confidently.

Oh, no, it wasn't like that. Greta had signed up for the camp on her own, had waited until the last possible minute to tell her mother.

"You don't seem like a horse person," Om said.

"I'm not," Greta said.

She'd only gone because she had a crush on a horse girl named Heather. They weren't really friends, but they went to the same school and had known each other for years. The school was tiny, private, Lutheran, located in the South Bay of Los Angeles. Compared with their classmates, both of their families were destitute. Heather and Greta were the only seventh and eighth graders to live in an apartment, for example, and to ride the city bus to school, and to have parents who never showed up for anything, including the Christmas play.

Since Heather's parents were still married, Greta assumed she came from a slightly more stable home, but, as it turned out, Heather simply spent a lot of time in stables. Although she couldn't afford her own horse and probably never would, Heather spent weekends working for equestrians in Rancho Palos Verdes. Her red hair was so long she often sat on it by mistake. Her teeth, also long, poked out of her mouth, and Greta was captivated by her carpet legs, her nerdy passion, the conservative way she dressed and carried herself, her love of nature and muesli, the corny novels she read, how calm, capable, and unselfconscious she seemed. She belonged to another world with its own rules, and it seemed like a good place to disappear. Greta wanted in, but she needed a foot in the door. So, she pretended she wasn't in fact terrified of horses and signed up for this camp. She'd seen Heather's name on the list—the only name—and added her own. The camp was expensive, but she got financial aid through some program, and a month or two later, she was on a bus with Heather and a bunch of other horsey thirteen-year-olds, headed for the Sierras.

Om opened a notebook and began scribbling . . . a bunch of nonsense, Greta imagined. *Shebiscuit. Blinders. Ketamine. My Little ~~Pussy~~ Pony. Sarah Jessica Parker.*

They were on the bus for twelve hours. Besides Heather, Greta didn't know anyone—the other girls were from a different school—and so she and Heather sat together. Heather wore a red bandana around her neck, khaki shorts, hiking boots. Staring at Heather's thigh hair, she kept imagining Heather's bush as resembling a red anthill, something she wanted to gently poke with a stick. They bullshitted about school, the teachers they had in common, but very little bonding occurred because Greta pooped her pants about thirty minutes later. Nothing like that had ever happened to her before, so she was in denial about it for hours, until they made a pit stop and she was

– 284 –

able to see the mess with her own eyes. She was mortified, of course, forced to bury her underwear in the trash, which seemed crazy to her at the time, and she spot-cleaned her jeans in the sink, which took too long. They were all waiting for her to get back on the bus. Everyone knew what had happened by then. They'd known for hours, in fact, and hadn't said anything. The shame Greta felt was so intense it gave her what looked like second-degree burns on her face and chest. In hindsight, she should have enjoyed all of this, because as it turned out, she wouldn't poop again for seven days.

Back on the bus, Greta semi-bonded with a popular horse girl who'd puked into her lunch bag. Puking wasn't as bad as pooping, though, let's face it, so Greta knew she'd never make it into the inner circle. Which was fine. These horse girls, Greta soon realized, were kind of humorless and hard to get to know, and they had zero street smarts. For a while during the long ride, a mustached man in a red convertible drove alongside the bus with his cock out and a big smile on his face.

Old-school pervert, Om scribbled. *Magnum PI vibes.*

Granted, his cock was large, as long and hard as a baton, but you would've thought he'd been beating these girls in the face with it. Greta had never witnessed such outraged screaming and crying. The camp counselors were also in a tizzy, falling all over themselves trying to get the guy's license plate, but Greta barely paid attention. Didn't these dorks know you weren't supposed to react? They were doing exactly what the guy wanted. Greta didn't make any of the girls feel bad about it, however. She wasn't like that. She tried her best to comfort them. Clearly, they came from entirely different worlds. In Greta's world, a creep was exposing himself on every corner, in every Dairy Queen and movie theater, hoping like hell to catch your eye and ruin your day. It was just part of life. So, she tried not to judge these horse girls too harshly. For all she knew, the minute she saw an erect horse penis, she might be the one screaming and crying, and maybe these girls would be the ones consoling her.

8=======D, she imagined Om drawing.

Camping turned out to be a specific kind of hell Greta had never experienced. It was her first time in the woods. They were expected to do physical labor, which Greta wasn't used to, and to sleep on the ground. They'd each been assigned their very own horse. Greta's horse was called Honey. Greta was to spend six days with Honey, riding, feeding, and brushing her, but Honey was no dummy. She took one look at Greta's shoes—Vans high-tops—and knew that Greta was a phony, an interloper. Once Honey was onto Greta, she had trouble taking Greta seriously, and who could blame her? Greta remembered climbing onto Honey's saddle and making the giddyup noise she'd practiced for hours. Honey stubbornly stood still, looking over her shoulder at Greta with bland hatred in her eyes. Sometimes Greta would attempt to lead Honey away from the other horses so that they might bond in private, but Honey wouldn't have it. She seemed to have two moods: quiet, seething rage or extreme sadness. Greta could tell by the way Honey chewed that she was deeply unhappy. For a while, Greta thought maybe Honey had drama with one of the other horses, like maybe she had a crush on one of the males, or maybe it was one of the females, you know, maybe she was gay.

At the time, Greta was just beginning to understand that human relationships were pure folly, because nothing was ever perfectly mutual. One person always liked or loved the other person a little more than they were liked or loved, and sometimes it was a lot more, and sometimes the tables turned and you found yourself on the other side, but it was never, ever equal, and that was pretty much the only thing you could count on in life. This went for relationships between friends, siblings, lovers, spouses, even parents and their children.

"And I'm guessing it went for horses, too," Greta said.

She paused again to watch Om scribble in his notebook. *Gay horses*, she imagined him writing, or maybe just *Gay!!!*

"Go on," Om murmured.

"Yeah, so, Honey broke my heart a little," Greta said. "But she also broke my foot in two places."

Om stopped scribbling and looked at Greta. "Which foot?"

"The right one," Greta said. "With the glass in it."

Ding, ding, ding. Om went back to scribbling. He seemed fully engaged, on the edge of his seat. All this horse and foot imagery, she imagined, was a wet dream for someone writing a book.

"What's your book about?" Greta suddenly asked. "You never talk about it, which isn't like you."

"I'll tell you later," Om mumbled. "Tell me how Honey broke your foot."

They'd been on this grueling five-mile ride. The trail was dusty, full of obstacles and switchbacks. They passed a series of mirrored gems—alpine lakes with inverse images of snowcapped peaks—but apparently the lakes were too cold to swim in. The trail seemed much too advanced for thirteen-year-olds, even those with experience. It was rocky and extremely narrow, and they rode in a long line, eight girls on eight horses, plus the two camp counselors on their horses. Greta and Honey were near the middle of the procession. Greta didn't know how they were going to make it five miles. Honey seemed miserable and exhausted, and Greta was filthy and fed up with horses. She'd stopped taking in the stunning scenery. All she could focus on was the horse's ass ahead of her, the way the poop came out cubed like the ice-cream scoops at Thrifty's.

Bowel obsession syndrome, Om wrote.

At one point, there was a large tree branch growing over the trail. The girls ahead of her ducked under the branch like it was no big deal. They simply hugged their horses' necks and went right under it. But Greta was afraid to hug Honey. So, she grabbed the branch instead and held on, and Honey kept walking without her. Greta dangled, horseless, from the branch, which turned out to be kind of high off the ground. She reluctantly let go of the branch and landed on her feet. The camp counselors told her to stop horsing around and get back on her horse, she was holding up the line, they had a lot of ground to cover. Greta went to mount Honey, but they were on an incline, and Greta was downhill. She should have mounted from the other side, but she didn't. That's when Honey decided to step on Greta's foot. She stepped on Greta's right foot with one of her back feet and then rested her massive weight on it, because she hated Greta's guts, and she wouldn't budge, even though Greta was pounding on her side and screaming.

"That must have been traumatizing," Om said casually.

But it was also a blessing, because now Greta was unable to ride or walk. So, the counselors found this guy with a boat. Greta couldn't remember if the counselors knew him or not. Her guess was no. He seemed to be a random guy who happened to be boating on the lake that day. They asked him to take Greta across the lake and deposit her at the head of the trail, where they would eventually meet her in about, oh, three or four hours, and the guy agreed.

"They left you alone with him? For three hours?" Om asked. "Or someone went with you?"

"It was just me and the guy," Greta said. "And his boat."

Om said nothing and continued scribbling.

The guy's name was Diego, and he had an Italian accent. Greta never knew Italians could have blond hair and blue eyes. He was dressed in white, and his boat, a large skiff, was also white. Greta's clothes were filthy, her unwashed hair full of dust, but he treated her like a princess and helped her onto his boat. He made a bed for her from a pile of blankets, propping her foot on pillows, and they set off. He seemed happy for the company. On the lake, away from the horses, Greta could see that they were surrounded by dramatic granite cliffs, and that Diego was the most visually stunning man she'd ever seen in person. She asked if he was famous, and he said why yes, in fact, he was. She asked which movies he was in and he reached into a basket and pulled out a fancy brass pepper grinder. "I manufacture these," he said. Then he passed Greta a tuna sandwich and a cold root beer. He drank real beer and ate several tangerines, one after the other, tossing the peels into the water. The combination of colors—the bright orange with the turquoise blue of the lake, his white shirt and teeth—opened a door in Greta's mind, a door she usually preferred to keep shut and locked, but now she let herself cross the threshold and roam around. It's not so bad in here, she thought. Maybe she'd spend more time in this room from now on.

"What room?" Om said.

"The future," Greta said.

"Had you started menstruating yet?" Om asked.

"Yeah," Greta said.

Om went back to his notebook. *Period blood. Promised land.*

They took their time crossing the lake. Diego gave Greta binoculars and talked about birds. He seemed obsessed with this mafioso-like female bird called a brown-headed cowbird. The cowbird laid her eggs in the nests of other birds, such as warblers, who don't look anything like cowbirds, making sure there were other eggs in the nest before depositing hers, but anyone could see that they didn't belong. Cowbird eggs are large and spotted. The warbler's eggs are small. The cowbird spied on the nest to ensure that her eggs weren't rejected by the warbler. If they were, she killed the warbler's children by destroying everything, the nest and the nestlings. If the eggs were not rejected, she went on vacation for the winter. Greta asked about the male birds. "They go along with this," Diego said.

Toxic parents.

At one point, Diego examined Greta's throbbing foot. She was able to wiggle her toes slightly, and he said her foot was badly sprained but maybe not broken, and he encouraged her to submerge it in the cold water. He removed his shirt and dove into the lake in one motion, and she watched him sidestroke away from her, his powerful legs making that exaggerated scissor, and then he treaded water about twenty feet away, squinting at her. He must have recognized the look on her face—intense longing—because he took a breath, dove under, and swam straight up to her. Her legs were dangling off the boat, feet submerged, and he grabbed her feet and held them in his hands. She thought he might pull her into the water, but he didn't. He floated on his back, looking directly at her face and blinking, and because his own face was wet it looked like he was blinking back tears, and Greta felt what she could only describe as hysterical rapture.

She'd fallen forward into the water and he was right there to catch her. He kept repeating her name, emphasizing the T each time, which made her feel like someone else but also somehow more like herself, and then he helped her back onto the boat and said she probably had altitude sickness.

A case of the vapors. Sanatorium. Helena Bonham Carter.

Then he held a towel around her while she removed her wet clothes, and, well, you can guess what happened next.

"What?" Om said, startled.

"I'm kidding," Greta said. "Nothing happened. He caressed me, but only with his accent. He read aloud from field guides while my clothes dried, and then it was time for me to go back to horse camp. To stall for more time, I told him it was my birthday."

It had felt greedy and fucked-up even then, but she'd wanted him to fuss over her a little more. On the way to the trailhead, they stopped by his cabin and he gave her a gift—a long rope necklace with a bunch of trinkets hanging off it, including an old horse tooth—and then he stuck a few candles in a brownie and told her to make a wish. She remembered feeling pressured to make the best wish possible, this was her one chance, but she couldn't think of anything specific. She simply wished for a new life, and he sang to her as she blew out the candles.

"Anyway, I worked it out in my head later that it was probably the same moment my mother blew her brains out."

Om grimaced. "Poor you. Were you the one to find her body?"

"No," Greta said.

In fact, she hadn't gotten home until three days later. Her mother's siblings had swooped in by then and packed up the house. They waited for her to get home to tell her what happened.

"But honestly, I don't remember much," Greta said. "Which is odd because I'm known for my memory. I can recite some of your transcripts verbatim."

"Jesus, don't tell me that."

"I only remember seeing everything in boxes, and noticing that they'd forgotten to take the stuff off the fridge. My mother loved decorating the outside of the fridge, and the last thing she'd put up was a *New Yorker* cartoon. We didn't subscribe to the *New Yorker*, so I'm not sure where she'd gotten it, but the cartoon was two women in a store, shopping for lamps, and one of them says, '*It's very me, but I hate myself.*'"

"Did she leave a note?"

Greta nodded. "I don't remember what it said."

"I can help you with that, if you're interested."

"How?"

"I'm a licensed hypnotherapist," Om said.

"Right. Of course you are. Anyway, my wish came true. My life was new, to say the least. I made sure to be very specific with my wishes after that. Now I take ten minutes to blow out candles."

Om closed his notebook. "You realize there probably isn't glass in your foot, right?"

"I'm not claiming to have Morgellons," Greta said. "It's glass, man. See for yourself."

Om sighed and retrieved a pair of reading glasses and tweezers from his desk drawer. He told her to lie back and rest her foot on the arm of the sofa. He talked quietly as he examined the bottom of her foot. He claimed that she'd been living in a straitjacket for decades, a straitjacket that prevented her from fully participating in her own life, from experiencing a full range of emotions. The straitjacket explained her passivity, her inability to defend herself, to take action, to make plans, to dream—

Greta waved her arms. "Are *you* dreaming? What straitjacket?"

"Guilt," Om said. "Your guilt is a straitjacket."

"Then why do I feel so . . . unfettered? I'm flopping around all over the place."

"You're struggling to break free," Om said. "It takes an enormous amount of energy—and *courage*—to free yourself, to follow the path of transformation without abandoning yourself, without fleeing from your pain and all the loss you've experienced. But you need to have more *compassion* for yourself. That's what's missing. It's no accident that this is happening now, after you've transcribed so many sessions for me. In a sense, you've been in therapy with me for many months. Hold on, I see it, Greta, I got it."

He raised his eyebrows and held out his hand. The glass glinted in the light. Sadly, it was only slightly bigger than a grain of sand.

"That's not it," Greta said, and rolled her eyes.

"The rest is in your head, honey. We'll deal with it next time."

Phantom glass, Greta thought. Kill me.

19

She didn't realize how miniature they were until they showed up in a minivan. They bounded out the side door, tails swinging, and began munching grass in the yard. The jack was tan with white spots; the jennet, a moody gray. They were only three feet tall and a little over two hundred pounds, less than half the size of regular donkeys, but their ears were a good five inches long, nearly as long as their faces, and stood straight up. Unlike horses, they had short, spiky manes and no bangs. Their asses were boxy, their knees knobby, and they both had crosses on their backs—a dark stripe running the length of their spines crossed with another over their shoulders—and so it was hard not to think of Jesus when you saw them, *Thy cross I'll carry* and so on, and to remember that they were beasts of burden, though these two didn't look like they could carry more than a bag of groceries.

If she were a different sort of person, she would have said they seemed magical. Like unicorns. But whereas unicorns were symbols of purity and grace and could only be tamed by virgins, these guys devoured gingersnaps straight out of Greta's impure hand while leaning against her bare legs.

She watched them chase each other around a tree, bucking their back legs and farting at the same time. Their farts were loud and endearing, as was the sound of their slow, thoughtful chewing, which made Greta's spine and scalp tingle.

Their ears were extremely mobile. They rotated almost 180 degrees and were moving constantly. It seemed obvious they used them to communicate, though Greta didn't know what they were saying yet. All she knew was that their presence had obvious physiological and psychological benefits, like forest bathing in Japan. When their ears rotated in Greta's direction, she felt a sense of deep well-being, along with the urge to reproduce them in some way. She could render them in pencil, perhaps. Or pastry dough? Donkey Ears: éclair-like pastries filled with chocolate custard and topped with a crunchy *croustillant* made from pistachios, pralines, and . . . holy shit, was she stoned? Why was she thinking like this?

"Ellington," Sabine said, snapping her fingers. "That's the jack's name."

He was an obvious extrovert, as affectionate as a lapdog, and very vocal, though his bray sounded like a deaf man bellowing. The jennet was the opposite: quiet, deerlike, and demure, with lustrous, false-looking eyelashes. She had an Amish quality, seemed both sober and humble, but with an irrepressible glamour.

"What about her?" Greta said.

"Pantaloon," Sabine said.

Ellington and Pantaloon kept stomping their feet as if to test how solid the ground was, or to make sure they weren't dreaming. Compared with the donkey farm, which Greta imagined as bleak and smelly, their new home was heaven. Plenty to browse in the yard and field, all the peonies in bloom, butterflies everywhere, two laughing women feeding them apples and carrots. They were probably pinching themselves.

"Do you deliver donkeys all over New York?" Greta asked the driver, who stood nearby.

"Not around here, usually," he said. "But I have three myself and I live thirty minutes from here, in Tivoli."

"Is it true they can't be alone? I mean, if the jack died, god forbid, would the jennet kill herself?"

"Mini-donkeys need each other," he said. "They prefer to be among their own kind—other mini-donkeys, that is, not just goats or sheep or whatever. If they're alone for too long, they get sick and die."

He seemed reluctant to leave. At first Greta thought he was waiting for a tip, but when Sabine offered him money, he waved it away. He was somewhere in his thirties, and also looked Amish, or maybe it was just his collarless, off-white linen shirt. His shorts were that shade of brown everyone was so hard for—clay, it might have been called, or terra-cotta. He was tall, blue eyed, looked like a Gunter or Hans, and was clearly more than just a donkey chauffeur. It occurred to her that he genuinely cared about the donkeys, wanted to make sure he wasn't leaving them with a couple of rejects.

"What's your name?" Greta asked him.

"Dave," he said.

"Are you a farmer?" Greta asked.

"Farrier," he said.

Greta looked away. What the hell was a farrier?

"So you work with ferrets," Greta said confidently.

Sabine laughed and lit a cigarette.

"I specialize in hoof care," he said. "So when they start standing like ballerinas, with their feet in first position, call me and I'll come trim their hooves."

"With what, hedge clippers?" Greta asked.

"A rasp," he said. "Mini-donkeys were bred for the desert. The earth around here is too soft for them, so their hooves need to be filed down."

Greta wondered what the farrier's feet looked like. She looked down at her own feet. Piñon was currently sitting on her toes. He blinked up at her. Remember me?

Dave wanted to know what the water situation was. They all wandered over to the paddock. Sabine pointed out the faucet, the trough, the salt lick, the haystacks and bags of grain. The shed was clean and cozy and had windows. Sabine had spent hours making it perfect. Greta was surprised she hadn't hung curtains or installed bunk beds with pillows and percale sheets.

"Don't get mad if they shit up the shed," Dave said.

Sabine blinked. "They shit where they sleep?"

"Sure," he said. "Jacks are territorial. He might get upset when you muck out the shed, but you have to do it, anyway, at least once a day."

Sabine nodded. "Oh, I know. I've done my research."

"Hope you don't mind my asking, but why donkeys?" he asked Sabine. "Why not some other pet?"

"Someone told me mini-donkeys could mend a broken heart," Sabine said. "Which—I mean, I realize my heart *seems* like it's in one piece, but, well, it's not. It's all smashed up."

Jesus. Was Sabine on mushrooms? Her eyes were watery, but she seemed more present than usual, and more put together. Her hair was freshly dyed, her overalls freshly bleached, her eyebrows penciled in. Had she snuck something glossy onto her lips?

Dave rubbed the back of his neck. "Will it take thirty years to mend? Because that's how long donkeys live."

"It might," Sabine said, and shrugged.

"I got my donks after my divorce," he said. "They kept me pretty grounded."

They both blushed.

Greta looked at the sky. Why did the light look so honeyed? Why did the word "gauzy" keep popping into her head? Why did her limbs feel bubble-wrapped?

"That granola you made last night," she whispered to Sabine. "Did you bake it on those sheet pans? The ones you use to make edibles?"

Sabine's eyes widened. "No wonder I feel a warm hand on my brain."

Of course she hadn't washed the pans, which had likely been coated with residue. They'd both eaten the granola for breakfast, shoveling it into their mouths by the fistful. Greta felt only half-baked, but Sabine seemed twice-baked and casseroled.

"We accidentally ate weed," Sabine announced to Dave, "but would you care for a blender drink? I have fresh strawberries."

"Sure," Dave said.

"I'll make us a pitcher of daiquiris," Sabine said, giving away her age. "And you can tell me everything you know about donkeys. I want every detail."

They went inside. Greta remained in the yard, where the donks were still munching, ears and tails twitching. It seemed criminal that such adorable creatures would be living in Sabine's backyard for the next thirty years. Greta grew more enamored by the minute, even though she'd always preferred pets you could pick up. She rarely looked twice at anything with hooves, but she felt thoroughly seduced by their various noises and imagined herself recording them, labeling it "Donkey ASMR," putting it on the internet, maybe making a million dollars. Greta would pay money to listen to them chew every day and imagined other people would, too. Piñon, on the other hand, would probably pay to have them kidnapped. She'd never seen him this jealous. He kept yawning and fake sneezing. Presently he was glued to Greta's side, limping dramatically even though his leg had fully healed. When she stopped to pet Pantaloon, he threw himself on the ground and played dead.

In the kitchen, it was daiquiris and donkey talk.

"They're a bunch of different animals rolled into one," Dave was telling Sabine. "Cow, dog, elephant, human."

"How are they like elephants?" Sabine asked.

"Mini-donkeys never forget anything," Dave said. "They're capable of intense grief. They're affectionate, but they also have an intuitive respect for your personal space."

Donkey love was real, apparently, and very deep, because Dave continued gushing for thirty minutes. He said that mini-donks had not been bred down from standard donks. They weren't like teacup poodles. Mini-donks were their own thing, had been around for six thousand years, were first discovered on the Mediterranean island of Sardinia. Some rich guy imported them to the US in the 1920s. Their reputation for obstinacy was really just cautiousness, an interest in self-preservation. When they don't want to do something, it's because they don't think it's safe. You can see it in their eyes, this kind of pulling back.

"They're not dumb," Dave said. "They're deep thinkers."

"Well, I didn't expect them to have such individual personalities," Sabine said. "I'm kind of stunned. And I knew they were cute—the breeder sent pictures once—but I had no idea they were *this* cute. It's like, cute overload."

"Just don't let them get fat. They have a tendency to balloon out. My donks are on a diet right now."

"I'd love to meet them. Where do you live again?"

"Tivoli," Dave said.

"We should have a playdate sometime," Sabine said.

"We should," Dave agreed.

Greta pulled out her phone and texted Sabine right there: "You should eat weed every morning just so I can hear you say shit like 'cute overload' and 'playdate.' He wants to trim your hooves, if you catch my drift. I'm going outside to give you privacy!"

IN THE YARD, the donks stood side by side, swatting flies off each other's faces with their tails. They were geniuses, Greta decided. They trotted up to her, desperate for more gingersnaps. They sniffed her legs, pawed at the ground near her feet.

"I got nothing," Greta said. "My pockets are empty."

They accepted this, stuffing their mouths with grass instead. Greta's phone rang. The same unfamiliar number kept calling and not leaving a message. She answered this time, expected a marketer's recording to start playing, nearly hung up, but then she heard breathing.

"Who is this?" Greta said.

The breathing was heavy and ragged.

"Keith?" Greta said.

Now a loud hiccup, followed by rustling. More pervy breathing.

"Fuck, man, are you drunk?" Greta said. "How'd you get this number?"

Low, brutal keening. Startling, contagious.

"Say something," Greta said, close to tears, "or I'm hanging up."

"It's me," Big Swiss gasped. "I'm calling—I can't—I'm not going to make it tonight."

They'd made plans days ago. Big Swiss and Luke were leaving for Ecuador soon, Big Swiss wanted to say goodbye, Greta had suggested a final roll in the hay in the only private place left to them, the donkey shed.

"Yeah, well, the shed's taken—"

"I won't be there," Big Swiss said. "Everything's different now. I can't see you anymore. All right? I can't see you again."

Greta felt a twinge of vertigo. It had been weeks since she'd had the pleasure—and pain—of hearing Big Swiss's disembodied voice, always sharper without her face to soften it, without her smell to humanize it, but it was even lower-pitched than usual, raspy, and Greta knew that she'd been crying for hours, perhaps days. Now she wept loudly, directly into Greta's ear.

"What happened?"

"Punctured lung," Big Swiss said, wheezing slightly. "Severed spleen."

No wonder she sounded so winded. She'd been *attacked*, her lung *punctured*, her spleen . . . what?

"What'd you say? About your spleen?"

Big Swiss seemed to be talking around something in her mouth. Blood? Broken teeth?

"Where are you? Tell me where you are!"

"The hospital," Big Swiss said, slurring. "Since Sunday. My phone broke. I'm in the ICU."

"I'm getting in the car. I'll be there in ten minutes."

"No," Big Swiss said. "It's *Luke*—Luke's *here*—I'm here with *Luke*."

"Luke attacked you?"

Big Swiss groaned.

"Who did this to you?"

"I *wish* it was me."

Greta collapsed in a lawn chair. The donks stood nearby, munching grass, regarding Greta with their shiny, black, honest eyes.

"I told him everything," Big Swiss said, and blew her nose. "How it started, how it went, how I was desperate for it to continue, and he wasn't angry or upset, just . . . resigned, like he'd made up his mind about something. He wanted to clear his head in the mountains. I told him yes, okay, I understood. He left the house with all his gear, but . . . he forgot the dog. That's when I knew something was off. I called, texted—nothing. Hours later, the hospital called. This was after midnight. His stomach was lacerated, they said, he'd lost a lot of blood. By the time I got here, he was already in surgery."

Greta closed her eyes. Please don't tell me he jumped off the bridge. Let it be something else. Anything.

"Two cops were waiting for me in the lobby," Big Swiss said. "They told me Luke had been *stabbed. Seven times.*"

Greta's throat closed. "With his own knife?"

Big Swiss sobbed again. "Yes, well, he didn't stab him*self*, obviously."

But he may as well have. He'd unwittingly followed in Greta's footsteps and confronted Keith on his own turf. Only a suicidal person would do such a thing. If Greta hadn't been in Keith's face the week before, maybe Keith wouldn't have been so vicious.

"I should've known," Greta said.

"About what?"

"Keith," Greta said.

"So you heard about it," Big Swiss said. "And didn't think to call me?"

Greta's eyes watered. "I heard someone talking about it, but I didn't realize they were talking about Luke. Or Keith," Greta said. "It was just a story I overheard, about a guy pulling a knife on a townie."

"Luke didn't pull anything," Big Swiss said calmly. "He's awake and lucid and remembers everything. He'd gone looking for Keith at Cousin's—to intimidate him. It was something he'd been fantasizing about—training for—but of course it didn't go the way he planned. When he let Keith know who he was married to, Keith said, 'You know your wife's a dyke, right? My sister seen her in the woods, sittin on some lady's face.' A few guys at the bar snickered. Everyone was listening. 'I been there, bro. You don't have to put up with that shit. It's your house, right? Tell her to get the fuck out.' Now everyone turned and stared at Luke. His stage fright kicked in and a bunch of gibberish came out of his mouth. 'You're not makin sense, man,' Keith said, and shook his head. 'You're all mixed up. Seems like you want to let off some steam. I get that, bro. I can help you with that.' He put an arm around Luke and dragged him outside, but Luke twisted away and took Keith out at the knees. They rolled around on the ground. Luke put him in some kind of hold or lock, and Keith looked genuinely frightened, like he might pass out. Luke said he couldn't help but feel bad for him, like he was beating up an old man, so he loosened his grip, and that's when Keith grabbed the knife on Luke's belt and stabbed him in the stomach. Luke rolled away, but Keith kept going, he wouldn't stop. He was like a machine."

Greta's throat felt clogged. It wasn't the story she'd heard, not even close, but of course she couldn't say that. She just sat there, trying to reconcile the two versions, her face wet with tears.

"It took eighty-two stitches to put him back together," Big Swiss said. "He'll never be the same again, and neither will I."

Greta imagined Big Swiss pushing Luke around in a wheelchair, changing Luke's drainage bags, sitting on Luke's paralyzed lap, helping him in and out of a car. She imagined herself in her own car, windows down, blasting Bach's cello suites while accelerating off the bridge.

"I never thought Keith's release would affect him, too," Big Swiss went on, "that he'd have his own private experience of it."

A few feet away, Ellington rested his neck over the crest of Pantaloon. They dozed for a moment. They seemed very much in love. Then Ellington ruined it by attempting to mount Pantaloon, who swung her head around and bit him on the shoulder. He clambered off of her, crestfallen. They wandered away from each other, pulling grass into their mouths and chewing. This was how they processed their feelings, she realized now. By chewing. By ruminating.

Greta considered pulling grass into her own mouth, but it was her turn to say something. It's not your fault? False. It's no one's fault? Also not true. Nothing could be done? Lots of things could have prevented this. What was there to say except sorry?

"I'm sorry," Greta said. "I shouldn't have pressured you to tell him about us. I was just looking for a way to feel better."

"He already knew," Big Swiss said. "He's not stupid. He knew as soon as he met you."

"And I should've told you about my own confrontation with Keith."

"What? Where?"

"Cousin's. The last time I saw you. I accused him of shooting Piñon, and he said he'd shoot *me* before he'd shoot any dog."

"Was this before or after we saw each other?"

"Before."

"So you decided not to tell me, and then you let me spank you . . . like an idiot."

"Seemed like a fitting end to the evening." Greta sniffed. "I didn't realize it would be the last time we'd ever see each other."

When Big Swiss didn't object, Greta felt like walking into traffic. Without Big Swiss in her life, everything would go back to being bland and blurry.

"It should be me in the hospital," Greta finally said.

"You wouldn't have gotten that far," Big Swiss said.

"He called me a dumb city bitch and told me to get the fuck out of his face. It could've turned violent."

"I'm saying you never would have made it to the hospital."

Greta scowled. "Two blocks?"

"You would've died in the alley."

"What makes you say that?"

"You're nothing like Luke. He possesses something you don't, something valuable in situations like these—fuck, never mind."

"I hope you don't mean a dick."

"The will to live," Big Swiss said. "His is strong. So is mine. It saved us both from getting killed."

Greta shrugged. "I've survived a thing or two, same as you."

"Yeah, but you never really fight for anything," Big Swiss said. "Big or small. Remember the time you lost your shoe in the woods? You wouldn't even look for it. You were prepared to hobble out of the forest with one shoe. If you'd been attacked the other night, you wouldn't have fought back. You would've rolled over and . . . perished."

Greta rolled her eyes and said nothing.

"See? You give up too easily, even in arguments."

It's called going with the flow, Greta wanted to say. You might try it. Also, how do you expect me to argue when your husband is essentially a wedge of Swiss cheese, thanks in part to me?

"You barely take care of yourself," Big Swiss went on. "Is there anyone you actually care about?"

"Piñon."

"He'll be dead, probably sooner than you think. Then what? Why are you even alive? Where's your will to—"

"Stop," Greta said. "Stop with the will-to-live shit. It's for the terminally ill, okay? The wrongly convicted, the chronically homeless—people living on the edge. It's meaningless nonsense coming from you. What you and Luke have is confidence, that's all, along with the expectation that things will go your way, because they probably will, because they already have."

Now Big Swiss was quiet. Was she a handful? Yes. But the thought of never handling her again? Unbearable.

"Anyway, suppose by some miracle I did make it to the hospital. Where would you be right now?"

"I chose you," Big Swiss said. "Over and over, for months and months. I even considered ending my marriage for you, which would've been stupid and insane since you're not really interested in living."

"Well, our relationship felt like living," Greta said. "To me, anyway. I've never been more myself with anyone, including myself."

"You're not yourself with yourself?"

"Not really."

"But it's hard to be with someone who simply drifts, who never searches for meaning, who just coasts along, and then wonders why she's so powerless—"

"Suicidal," Greta said, correcting her.

"You're telling me you want to die when my husband was almost stabbed to death by the same man who tried to kill me. Who's the narcissist now?"

"Me, I guess. Me, me, me."

"Besides, I doubt you could summon the will to kill yourself."

Now Ellington brayed. It was hoarse, raw, and very affecting. *This* was the sound she wanted to make. He seemed to be purging himself of something, and Greta wanted to join him. Crying certainly wasn't cutting it. Perhaps in the next life she'd come back as a spotted jackass.

"What *is* that?"

"It's a donkey, braying."

"The imaginary donkeys," Big Swiss said. "Right."

"Oh, they're real. They're right here. They arrived this morning. If you listen to them chew, you'll feel better, I promise. You'll feel brand-new."

Greta held the phone near Pantaloon's mouth for a few seconds.

"You hear that?"

"I should get back to Luke," Big Swiss said. "He's not out of the woods yet. He's still fighting for his life. When you start fighting for yours, maybe we can see each other again."

20

OM: Can you state your initials for the transcriber, please?

GW: I'm the transcriber, Om. I know what my initials are.

OM: Right, of course. Thanks for signing that release form.

GW: You better hope I don't fall into a K-hole. I'll be very upset, and I can't afford to take you to small-claims court.

OM: I only gave you fifty milligrams.

GW: Do you give all your clients ketamine? Is that why they're often sobbing uncontrollably and calling you Dad?

OM: Only those who are experiencing acute suicidal ideation, like you. I also recommend it to people who are unable to experience their bodies as a home they can always return to, or at least an uncluttered, comfortable space they can enjoy spending time in.

GW: So, everyone.

OM: This may surprise you, but a lot of people feel at home in their bodies.

GW: Name one.

OM: In any case, they don't limp around, convinced there's glass in their feet. How do you feel right now?

GW: Strange.

OM: Are you relaxed? Do you feel calm?

GW: I saw Flavia this morning. At a farm stand. I watched her buy a bunch of corn. I didn't recognize her at first because she cut off all her hair. It really rattled me. Not her hair, but seeing her. Without speaking. Without touching. I cried in my car afterward.

OM: What do you miss about her?

GW: Her intensity. Her smell. Her bizarre insights and condiments.

OM: Did she see you?

GW: She pretended not to.

OM: You'll move past it eventually. If you stick around Hudson, you won't be able to enter a room without having weird, sometimes horrifying history with at least four different people.

GW: I may have ruined her life, Om. Her husband's life. They'd be in Ecuador right now, making a baby, if it weren't for me.

OM: I'm all for accepting responsibility for your actions, but blaming yourself for Luke's injuries won't help you get better. Your actions may have hurt him emotionally, but you didn't put him in the hospital—Keith did that. Of course, I'm not suggesting you're blameless. You stalked my client and lied your way into an affair with her. That's yours to carry.

GW: I wouldn't say I *stalked* her—

OM: What would you call it?

GW: [INDISCERNIBLE]

OM: You're not being emotionally honest, Greta. You were stealthy, you were secretive, and I'm pretty sure it's all connected to your mother's death. [PAUSE] What do you think you're doing?

GW: Can you pass the ashtray?

OM: I don't have one.

GW: That thing next to your pencil holder will work.

OM: This? This holds my business cards.

GW: How about that dish with the keys in it?

OM: No. [PAUSE] You can't smoke in here.

GW: Two puffs.

OM: Can we access some of these buried memories?

GW: Be my guest.

OM: First, can you be here more fully? Can you put out the cigarette, close your eyes, and take a deep breath through your nose?

GW: Are we accessing my memories or yours?

OM: Yours.

GW: Then I don't need to breathe, Om. I remember everything. Not to be indelicate, or overly direct, but, well, I killed my mother. That's my big dark secret.

OM: [PAUSE] You murdered your own mother. And made it look like suicide. At age thirteen.

GW: I wanted her out of my life, and I knew one of us would have to die. So, when she threatened suicide for the nine thousandth time, I told her that ending her life was not only a viable option, it was the only sane choice for someone like her, and if it was me who was holding her back, she had my blessing. I'd be better off without her.

OM: Where was your father?

GW: Out of the picture.

OM: So you planned to raise yourself?

GW: We talked about that. How and where she would do it, who would find her, what would happen to me, who I might live with. She assured me that one of her siblings would take me in.

OM: Her siblings were on board with this?

GW: Not in advance, but they were aware of her illness.

OM: Cancer?

GW: Bipolar. She was deeply paranoid at that point. Her only concern was being criticized, disparaged, gossiped about, and so I promised never to bad-mouth her, to always defend her in her absence. Neither of which I've done.

OM: How did this conversation make you feel?

GW: Wild with relief. It was like crawling out of a rain forest and standing in the sunlight for the first time. I could finally stop fake-begging her to live. And she felt better, too. She referenced our heart-to-heart often in her notes to me, how a weight had been lifted, how her brain felt different—

OM: What notes?

GW: We carried on a correspondence for years while living under the same roof, passing notes to each other in tiny, hard-to-read handwriting.

OM: Like prisoners.

GW: Or the Brontë sisters. She had a supreme talent for describing feelings as if they were objects. I loved her on the page, but I always dreaded spending an evening with her—the notes were often so lengthy and detailed, they left little to talk about in person.

OM: What did your notes to her say?

GW: They were mostly dialogue. Snatches of overheard conversations.

OM: Interesting.

GW: Anyway, after our conversation, she cleaned, cooked, and took care of me for once. She stopped coming into my room at night and sleeping next to me like a child. She became less clingy, though I still hated to be touched or looked at by her.

OM: How did she look at you?

GW: Appraisingly. But it was edged with something unsettling. Longing, I guess. Although I hated the sight of her, she couldn't seem to take her eyes off me. It made me want to wear a fat suit around her. I had to barricade myself in my bedroom.

OM: How long did she wait?

GW: Six months. I'd nearly forgotten about it. Then I went to horse camp for two weeks. She was happy to see me go, which should have told me something. Maybe I knew what she was about to do and was in denial. Maybe I signed up for the camp on purpose. I did, after all, want her to die—genuinely, with all my heart—and two weeks was a long time, the longest we'd ever spent apart. I rarely stayed away overnight because I hated coming home. She was great at goodbyes but horrible at hellos, or reunions of any kind. Returning home, even after a day, was extremely fraught. At first she'd seem shocked to see me, like I was returning from the grave, and then she would act all

- 308 -

confused and uncomprehending. It was this whole charade. "You had fun? You rode a roller coaster? With friends? What friends? I didn't know you had friends!" Then she would sulk. But I could always sense a lot going on under the surface, and it was all envy related.

Anyway, I never knew what I was coming home to. But this time felt different. I wasn't dreading seeing her, because I had someone else to think about.

OM: Who?

GW: Diego. The angelic Italian guy with the boat and blond hair. On the long bus ride home, I must have fantasized about him for a solid twelve hours. I kept replaying the scene in the lake—my bare feet in his hands, the way he looked at me—and I felt the same hysterical rapture over and over.

OM: Might that remind you of a certain other blond European?

GW: Good point.

Anyway, I remember trying to write a note, just to ground myself, and being startled when I saw my handwriting. It was chicken scratch. I was delirious, evidently, and dehydrated, and my foot was broken. I don't remember who drove me home after I got off the bus, but I let myself into the house with my key. Her siblings were scattered around the living room, waiting for me, just like we'd discussed months before. They sat me down, told me how sorry they were. She was gone, they said. Everything was in boxes or had been burned in the yard. For a second, I thought she'd simply disappeared. She'd somehow fallen in love, just like me, and had vanished to another country. When her twin sister passed me an envelope, I figured it was just another letter from her. I limped around the house, holding it in my hands. It wasn't until I entered her bedroom that I realized she'd actually gone through with it. I went back to the living room and tried to make myself cry, for appearances. But I just sat there, dry-eyed, and listened to her siblings tell stories about her.

OM: Did you grieve later, in private?

GW: I'd been grieving my whole life. Growing up, I found it impossible to act normal. I'd always felt pressured to hide the exuberance I felt as a child, to stuff it down, to bury it. Everything had to be dampened, tempered, diminished. I could never truly celebrate anything, because I didn't want to arouse her envy or paranoia. I thought all of that would go away after she died, that I would feel free to be myself, but it didn't. I continued hiding. And I never saw a model for my relationship with her. In the movies it was always, "Yeah, I can't stand her, she's horrible, she drinks too much, she beats me—but we're blood, you know, she's my mother, so part of me will always love her." The ties that bind and so on. I never felt any of that.

OM: Was she physically abusive?

GW: No. She showered me with affection, with compliments about my appearance. She liked to pet my hair. When we went to the movies, the only activity she semi-enjoyed, I'd start to feel uncomfortable, like I was being observed, and sure enough, I'd look over to find her staring at my face in the dark. "Why aren't you watching the movie?" I'd whisper. "I'd rather watch you watching the movie," she'd say. It felt like she had a crush on me. She lavished gifts on me, laughed at my jokes, and when I wasn't appreciative enough, she'd lock herself in her room and wouldn't come out for days.

OM: She was sweating you.

GW: Hard.

OM: What do you feel most guilty about?

GW: The malice I felt toward her. When I realized she'd gone through with it, I felt very much like it was me holding the gun.

OM: But she was holding you hostage.

GW: Isn't that what parenting is?

OM: She was holding a pillow over your face. You were suffocating. You were exhausted and trying to stay alive. It's perfectly natural to look for a way out. You didn't pull the trigger—she did. It would be one thing if you gave her your blessing and she killed herself five minutes later, but she waited six months. Do you remember what her note said?

GW: I took it into the bathroom with me to read in private. It was a thank-you note, basically. She told me she loved me and thanked me for releasing her, for giving her permission to end her agony. Since it was written on wedding stationery, I wasn't surprised that she'd included a poem by e. e. cummings.

OM: "I carry your heart with me"? "I carry it in my heart"?

GW: [LAUGHS] No.

OM: "Your slightest look easily will unclose me."

GW: Wrong again.

OM: "Anyone lived in a pretty how town."

GW: "Yes is a pleasant country"—that's the first line. It was something she often said when she wanted to live, which was about twice a year.

OM: What did you do with the note?

GW: I ripped it up into tiny pieces and flushed it down the toilet. I didn't want anyone to find it, to know what I'd done. A few years later, I continued our correspondence—one-sided, of course—and told myself that I loved her in my own way.

OM: Well, I'm beginning to understand what's happening here. You may have wanted her dead, but you nevertheless felt guilty for the pleasure you experienced on the day she died. You associate desire with her death, and with suicide in general, which is why experiencing desire has been dangerous for you.

You've also re-created the conditions of your childhood. The inhospitable house, the gloom and doom, the need to barricade yourself in the antechamber. Perhaps you've put yourself in survival mode again so that you're forced to confront some of this stuff.

You've also unconsciously re-created the attachment patterns you experienced as a child. You're repeating those patterns in your relationships.

GW: Who's my mother supposed to be? Flavia?

OM: It's not fixed or static. Maybe it's you.

GW: I'm my mother?

OM: Yes.

GW: How so?

OM: Are you not suicidal? Are you not seeking permission to live or die?

GW: Who's Greta, then?

OM: It might be Flavia. It might be Sabine. It might be your dog. Maybe they're all different versions of you.

GW: Oh god.

OM: Your consciousness needs to shift, Greta. You need to become aware of yourself as you really are, a human being who can be both aggressive and complaisant, selfish and generous. You've gotten in touch with your desire but maybe not with your hostility. Did you dream of killing her? Poisoning her? Pushing her down the stairs? Smothering her in her sleep? Bludgeoning her to death with a hammer? Stabbing her—

GW: Are you glitching out, Om?

OM: My own mother was an ice queen. I wished her dead all the time, though never to her face. I was absolutely terrified of her. I became a bully. I bullied my classmates, teachers, neighbors—even animals. I used to spit on the kids next door. Two girls, aged three and four. Toddlers. I'd spit on their foreheads and watch it roll down their faces. They weren't old enough to feel humiliated, so it wasn't entirely satisfying. The most disturbing part was that they looked happy. Big smiles! Then I realized they were mirroring my expression, and so I was able to see my own depravity. But it didn't stop me. I'd get them to run and then I would trip them. I liked to watch them fall. I'd laugh and then they'd laugh, too. If they were hurt, if they cried, I urged them to get up and run again, and again I'd trip them. I entertained myself for hours this way.

GW: Alone?

OM: Me and another kid, who I also bullied.

GW: Did you spit on animals?

OM: I sprayed them with Windex. But I threw a cat in a pond once.

GW: Did you gobble a bunch of ketamine while my head was turned?

OM: This is me being real with you, hon. Is any of this resonating?

GW: With what?

OM: Your own experience.

GW: I'm wondering if you're trying to make me feel better or worse, or if you're telling me you're a serial killer, or if you're about to spit on my forehead and then trip me when I try to run out of here.

OM: I was thirteen at the time, the age you were. I hadn't learned to rein it in yet. My point is, we all have an inner shithead, and maybe you need to shake hands with yours.

GW: Oh yeah? Then what?

OM: Stop trying to silence her or pretend she's not there. Remind her that she's not a bad person, that she doesn't need to feel ashamed for having or expressing feelings, positive or negative. You could start by giving her a name.

GW: [SNIFFS]

OM: What are you smelling—gas?

GW: My least favorite kind of therapy: inner-child healing.

OM: I prefer the term "reparenting."

GW: I'm not ready to be a mom.

OM: I just want Big Greta to be nice to Little Greta.

GW: I'm not good with kids, Om. Can we not call her Little Greta?

OM: You have another name in mind?

GW: James.

OM: [PAUSE] Is your inner child a boy?

GW: Rebekah.

OM: That sounds right.

GW: Do you plan to bully my inner child?

OM: Rebekah is already deeply wounded, Greta. She's still

traumatized after all these years because you internalized her wounds without processing or repairing them. Rebekah needs space to heal, and it's up to you to give her that space, to advocate for her. If you heal Rebekah, you heal your mother, too, and everyone else you've hurt, including Flavia and Luke. If everyone did this, the world would be a better place.

GW: Please don't ask me to "journal."

OM: I think transcribing these sessions will be a good first exercise for you. How was your experience transcribing your last session?

GW: Hellish. I hate my voice.

OM: Why?

GW: It's my mother's voice.

OM: When we have three or four transcripts and you're ready to go deeper, I'll give you additional exercises.

GW: You never told me what you're writing. Is it a self-help book?

OM: God, no. It's a novel.

GW: About a relationship coach?

OM: It's a campus novel set in New England. I tend to think of it as *The Secret History* meets *Animal House*.

GW: Who's the transcriptionist?

OM: There isn't one.

GW: A Swiss woman?

OM: Nope.

GW: Maybe you're writing the wrong book, Om.

OM: Maybe you should write your own book, Greta.

GW: Is that the lesson?

OM: I wouldn't wish it on anyone, actually. If you try it, be mindful of our confidentiality agreement. No transcripts. Don't think for a second I won't sue you. I have a very good lawyer—

GW: Settle down.

OM: You know you've been staring at my gong for the past fifteen minutes? Longingly, I might add.

GW: Your dong?

OM: [LAUGHS] Shall I give you a sound bath before you go?

GW: Fine. Make it quick.

[GONG BATH: 10 MINUTES]

[END OF RECORDING]

21

The next morning, Greta woke to the high-pitched whining of insects. Not the scourge of mosquitoes that had visited her room the previous night—something larger, louder. She climbed out of bed and checked the antechamber—nothing. Piñon growled at the floor. The noise vibrated beneath their feet. It was coming from the kitchen.

"Stay here," she ordered Piñon.

Outside her bedroom door, two bees greeted her and slow-danced near her face. They were drunk, bottom-heavy. It was their siblings she was likely hearing downstairs, and it sounded like they had a few, along with their mother, of course. Greta rushed downstairs.

Indeed, the kitchen was filled with bees, more bees than she'd ever seen, a swarm of perhaps a hundred thousand, twice the size of the previous colony. The hatch was hanging open, and so the bees were everywhere she looked. Thousands blanketed the windows from the inside, blocking the weak morning light, making the kitchen darker, but most were in the hive doing major construction of some kind. Others performed separate tasks or rested in various parts of the kitchen. One group seemed to be devouring leftover pork loin on the stove; another lounged on Sabine's collection of chipped French dinnerware.

Greta stood perfectly still, afraid to draw attention to herself. Had they opened the hatch themselves?

"Mother of god," Sabine said from the stairs. She was puffy eyed and dressed in men's pajamas. "They sent scouts the other day, and now it appears the whole clan's moving in. Hi, guys."

Sabine looked happy, as if her kids were visiting for the week.

"Can we maybe close the hatch?" Greta asked. "So I can make coffee without getting killed?"

"They won't attack you," Sabine said, just as a bee landed on her arm. "Ow. Fuck, I just got stung."

"Since when do bees eat meat?" Greta asked, pointing at the stove.

Sabine pulled out her phone and took a picture.

"Maybe they're trying to get the taste of Raid out of their mouths."

Oh god, the Raid. Greta had forgotten about that. They'd bombed the hive weeks ago, but there was probably still a good amount of residue. Was it only a matter of time before they all dropped dead? Would they be sweeping up dead bees until Christmas?

"Get dressed," Sabine said. "We're going to Gideon's house. He'll know what to do."

GIDEON WAS THE BEEKEEPER who'd built the hatch the previous year. He lived with his enormous family on a farm two miles south, the exact address of which Sabine claimed to know, and yet they kept driving around, peering at houses.

"These people are back-to-the-land Christians," Sabine said. "They have about seventeen kids, all homeschooled."

"I can't imagine beekeeping is that lucrative," Greta said. "How do they survive?"

"They're odd-jobber types. They keep bees, they farm, they figure it out. The Lord will provide and so on. Gideon's the eldest." She slammed on the brakes. "There it is."

The property had a postapocalyptic vibe. There were bees everywhere, along with abandoned cars parked in every direction, doors open, flotsam spilling out of the back seats, clothes and shoes scattered all over the brown grass. Littered around the yard, rusted refrigerators and stoves, tractors and lawn mowers.

At the end of the driveway stood a large wooden house. A young man hopped off the sagging porch and approached them shyly. Jesus in a red bathrobe, his dark hair parted down the middle. Trailing behind him were three younger girls wearing prairie dresses. One girl had a squirrel on her shoulder; another petted something in her arms. A tiny kitten, Greta assumed, before noticing the hairless tail.

"Hey, Gideon," Sabine said casually. "I probably owe you money, right?"

"You might," Gideon said kindly.

Sabine pressed several twenties into his palm like he was a bookie or a doorman. He mumbled thank you.

"How's it going with the bees?" he asked.

"Funny you ask," Sabine said. "They all *died*. This was months ago. Long story, I won't go into it. But now there's a giant swarm at my house. They're swarming the hive. We can't even see out the windows, there's so many."

Gideon looked dubious. "Little late in the year for a swarm."

"Problem is, there were maggots in the hive a while back." Sabine shook her head at the memory. "Big ones. Terrifying."

"Wax moths," Gideon said. "I meant to tell you about that."

Sabine coughed. "But here's the thing: we wound up killing them with Raid."

"But they're harmless." Gideon frowned. "Why'd you do that?"

"Because we're assholes," Sabine said, glancing at Greta.

"We panicked," Greta said. "We sprayed Raid into the hive."

"And watched them die," Sabine said.

Sabine had left town shortly after, as Greta recalled. Greta, unable to get her head out of Big Swiss's ass, had stayed put.

"It's probably okay," Gideon said. "But I'll come have a look. I'll swing by on my way to town."

"Okey doke," Sabine said. "Hurry, though. They're taking over the house."

GIDEON SHOWED UP practically naked in a tank top, shorts, and flip-flops. No ventilated suit, no sir. No hat-and-veil combo, either, and no gloves. He carried a stick in one hand and a bee smoker in the other. The smoker was the size of a soda can and emitted less smoke than a cigarette. The stick looked like something he'd picked up off the ground.

Without hesitation, he walked over to the hive, set the smoker on the floor, and began poking around with the stick. The bees didn't seem to mind, though what did Greta know? Maybe they were furious. Greta crouched behind an armchair and watched. He continued digging around, completely at ease, searching for god knows what.

"There's no queen," he said after a moment. "So, this isn't a swarm."

"Oh no?" Sabine said. "Why are they here?"

He looked over his shoulder. "They're robbing the hive."

Sabine snorted. "Of what? Gold?"

"Honey," Gideon said, and smiled.

"Honey," Greta repeated.

"What honey," Sabine said.

"Well, the bottom part's pretty dry. See? You soaked that part with Raid, I guess. Otherwise you got about eighty pounds of unharvested honey in here."

"Get out," Sabine said.

Gideon dropped the stick and stared up at the hive. "I recommend cutting it down. If you don't, these bees will be in your kitchen for weeks, or at least until all the honey's gone."

Sabine looked stung, though not by bees.

"I can cut it down now," Gideon said. "It'll take me about an hour."

Sabine nodded, oddly quiet. Greta was shocked to see tears in her eyes. Gideon went out to his truck and returned with a big knife and some other tools. He asked for a container of some kind. Sabine handed him a large metal bowl she used for salads. They watched him dismantle the hive, hacking at it with his big knife. It took two bowls to catch all the comb. Honey dripped everywhere—all over the concrete floor, all over Gideon's head and shoulders.

By the time he was finished, there were bees stuck to his arms. He didn't seem to notice. He carried the bowls outside and set them on the porch. Most of the bees followed, settling inside the bowls, devouring the honey. Gideon put a finger in his mouth. Then he reached into the grist of bees and pulled out a hunk of comb.

"Here," he said to Sabine. "Don't you want some for yourself?"

"Let the bees have it," Sabine said.

AFTER GIDEON LEFT, they sunbathed and smoked cigarettes in the yard. Sabine still seemed upset about the bees. She was trembling, in fact. Greta assured her that the bees would come back and build a new hive.

"How's therapy going?" Sabine asked.

"Sometimes I feel like we're getting somewhere," Greta said. "Other times I wonder if I'm just not that kind of person."

"Which kind?"

"The kind who gets to the bottom of things."

The donks grazed nearby. When they had to poop, they politely stepped into the bushes. They were visible from the road, Greta realized. Cars kept slowing as they passed. Since anyone with a van could kidnap them, Greta worried they'd be gone by the weekend, whisked away to Canada or someplace.

"Now I have a confession," Sabine said. "You remember how I was gone most of last winter? Well, I didn't travel. I stayed in one place. In a hospital up north."

Finally, Greta thought.

"How bad is it?"

"Was," Sabine said, correcting her. "It's out of my system now."

"You didn't lose your hair?"

Sabine blinked. "Rehab, sweetie. Drugs, not cancer. I was in rehab for drugs."

Now it was Greta's turn to blink. It certainly explained a lot: her extreme weight loss, her lack of interest in food and sex, her increased interest in smoking and sleeping during the day. Her cloudy eyes! Her chronic constipation!

"Oxy?" Greta said.

"I wish," Sabine said. "Oxy would've been more age-appropriate. Instead, I was putting good old-fashioned powder up my nose, the kind you buy on the street."

"What street?"

"Never mind that," Sabine said. "I checked myself into rehab, which, frankly, I didn't think would work. I really suck at group therapy."

"Because you talk too much?"

"I clam up, strangely. Listen, I'm seeing a therapist in town, sifting through the wreckage of my divorce, the death of my parents. I'm trying to figure shit out, but I could really use your help with something."

Sabine reached into her pocket and pulled out a velvet pouch, which she tossed onto Greta's lap. Greta's first thought was that it contained gems, and she hoped they weren't stolen. Was this Sabine's amends? To make Greta rich? So that she might live without working ever again? Greta closed her eyes.

"Are you making a wish?" Sabine asked.

"Maybe," Greta said.

"It's not a gift, ding-dong," Sabine said.

Greta peeked inside. No diamonds. No emeralds or rubies, either, or rocks of any kind, not even dice. Instead, a bundle of little plastic bags containing beige powder. The bags were blue and stamped with the handicap symbol.

"My stash," Sabine explained. "I don't want it anymore. In fact, I feel like puking whenever I think of it. But for whatever reason, I can't bring myself to throw it away. I've tried, and I simply don't have it in me. So I'm asking you to do it. Will you?"

Greta felt both jumpy and poised, the same way she'd felt the few times she'd held a gun.

"If it's too much to ask, I'll figure something out."

Greta examined one of the bags. "How long were you . . . handicapped?"

"Every day for two years," Sabine said. "I was too ashamed to tell you or anyone else. It made me feel less lonely at first, but I grew to really hate it, so I'm not sure why I can't just throw it out."

"Sometimes it's hard to let go of a secret companion, even if they're shitty company."

"I'm sorry I didn't tell you sooner," Sabine said. "I regret keeping it from you."

Greta said she was sorry, too.

Sabine stood and kissed Greta on the cheek. "Thank you for doing this. Next winter I'll take you to Mexico with me, I promise."

Sabine went inside. Greta stared at the bundle in her lap. Enough to end her life with, certainly, or at least save for a rainy day, and wasn't it supposed to rain tomorrow? It would be easy to hide the stuff in the antechamber. On the other hand, why not take Om's advice and do the opposite of her pattern?

She dragged herself to the garbage can at the side of the house, noting the old lethargy in her head and feet. The can was full, of course. Rather than lay the pouch on top, she pulled out all the trash bags—there were four—and dropped the pouch on the very bottom of the can. Then she opened a trash bag and poured it over, burying the pouch in coffee grinds, banana peels, eggshells, leftovers they'd never eaten, plus bathroom trash, which there was a lot of since they couldn't flush toilet paper, because the septic tank was old and—never mind. She opened a second bag and dumped its contents, too, and was reminded of her failed attempt to bury her mother's PS in this precise way, how she wasn't able to do it back then, how she wished someone had taken care of it for her.

She closed the lid and made her way to the donkey pen. She passed the bowl of bees ravaging honey. She passed Walter the rooster, who was walking upright and doing high kicks, some kind of bizarre soldier march. She passed Piñon, lying in the shade of a locust tree.

In the pen, the donks stood face-to-face, blowing into each other's nostrils, their version of kissing. Greta opened the gate and whistled. They trotted toward her and then stopped, stared, and deliberated. They never did anything without considering its necessity, its potential for harm or danger, its goodwill. But they were also timid around Piñon, now sitting at Greta's feet.

"It's all right," she said. "I will never hurt you, and neither will Piñon. Right, Piñon?"

Piñon opened his mouth and smiled.

The donks approached and gently sniffed Greta's bare knees and thighs, inhaling her with their incredibly soft nostrils. It was the same careful way they drank water—not by lapping, but by inhaling.

Now they followed her to the bag of grain. She fed them small handfuls.

"Do that thing," she said.

They knew exactly what she wanted. They leaned against her legs, one on each side, and chewed.

"Ha ha, yes," she said. "Yes!"

THE END

Acknowledgments

Special thanks to Stefan Beck, Sissy Onet, Franny Shaw, Rebecca Goldman, Binky Urban, Ron Bernstein, Kara Watson, Emily Polson, Nan Graham, everyone at Scribner, Helen Manders, Sophie Lambert, Louisa Joyner, Kate Barrett, Piper Olf, Tom DePietro, Andi State, Allison Toombs, Jess Puglisi, Adrian Kudler, Alan Grostephan, Michelle Latiolais, Ron Carlson, Elisa Albert, Raoul Markaban, and the Dutch Foundation for Literature.